TH
WOUL   BE
THE SAME
FOR THEM. . . .

KAY PARKER.   She knew when she married Bill Parker their lives would be far different from her humble farmgirl upbringing. She stood by his side as he became a Navy pilot hero, always wondering why he had married *her*. . . .

FAITH PARKER.   With her dark hair and startling blue eyes, she looked just like her brother Bill. And when news of Pearl Harbor came she refused to stay in college. Instead she followed Kay and Bill to wartime Seattle, and did some fast growing up. . . .

VALERIE ADAIR.   A cool blond beauty, she was determined to reign in high society. And she got her wish when she married the Senator's son Jordan Adair — she just couldn't believe he didn't want the same things. . . .

SYDNEY JACKSON.   Flame-haired and statuesque, she had already lived a lifetime in New Orleans, trying to make a singing career. It was there she had fallen in love with Jordan, never suspecting that he was already taken. . . .

Also by Marion Smith Collins
Published by Ballantine Books:

TRUST YOUR HEART

A
SPARROW
FALLS

Marion Smith Collins

BALLANTINE BOOKS • NEW YORK

Who sees with equal eye, as God of all,
A hero perish, or a sparrow fall,
Atoms or systems into ruin hurled,
And now a bubble burst, and now a world.

Alexander Pope,
An Essay on Man

A Sparrow Falls is dedicated with affection and appreciation to my good friends Rear Adm. Wallace R. Dowd, Jr., USN (Ret.), and his wife, Polly Gresham Dowd, who opened their Washington home to me, shared their memories of wartime Seattle and their military experiences, as well as furnishing me with introductions, a car, and a well-marked map. I would also like to thank:

Carla Rickerson, Pacific Northwest Collection, Suzallo Library, University of Washington, Seattle

Rick Caldwell, Museum of History and Industry, Seattle

Agnes C. Sears, Seattle-King County Chapter, American Red Cross

Lt. Kevin Hostbjor, Sand Point Naval Air Station, Seattle

Linda Harvey, Washington Collection, Tuskegee University, Tuskegee, Alabama

Brian J. Small, Greater Victoria Chamber of Commerce, Victoria, B.C.

Lorne R. Campbell, Chief Purser, British Columbia Steamship Company, Ltd.

Bert Kinzey, author of the Detail and Scale Aviation Publication Series, including a definitive book on the Grumman F4F-3 "Wildcat" aircraft

Don Kennedy, host of syndicated radio show, *Big Band Jump* and

Comdr. G. Vassa Cate, USNR (Ret.), of Calhoun, Georgia, who first mentioned the Communications Center in New Orleans.

These people generously shared their time and knowledge and any mistakes are mine, not theirs.

Author's Note

Though *A Sparrow Falls* is fiction, my goal was to set this story solidly in 1942.

The USS *Shiloh* is a fictitious ship, but I have drawn heavily on the history of two aircraft carriers that saw duty in the Pacific during World War II:

The USS *Saratoga* was torpedoed off the coast of South America early in the war and was returned to Seattle's Puget Sound Navy Yard for repairs.

On September 14, 1942, the USS *Wasp* was sunk in the Coral Sea while escorting a supply convoy bound for Guadalcanal. The loss was not officially announced until October 26th.

I added Seattle to the actual route of the star-studded Victory Caravan, a train that traveled across the country on a war bond–selling tour in the summer of that year.

And the Japanese troops that seized the islands of Attu and Kiska in Alaska remained there until the end of the war.

PART ONE

The historic debate upon the repeal or modification of the Neutrality Act has proved to be a rather listless affair. Fully half of the senators are doing their daily dozing in their own rooms.

"Of All Things," *The New Yorker*, November 8, 1941

Chapter 1

Kay Parker hadn't realized she was dozing until a commotion in the hotel corridor intruded on her drowsiness. It was probably Bill and his pals returning from the game. She stretched her arms over her head and yawned a skin-stretching yawn; the *Newsweek* she'd been reading slid off the bed. She glanced at her watch. Only three o'clock. Her husband had said the football game would be over about five o'clock but not to expect him until six.

Kay was—or had been—enjoying the luxury of a lazy Sunday afternoon all to herself. Magazines and newspapers were strewn on the bed around her; a room service tray was on the floor.

She wished that whoever it was out there would be quiet. As though in answer to her silent wish a door slammed nearby and the noise suddenly stopped. Fully awake now, she sighed her irritation. She sat up, stuffed an extra pillow behind her, and reached for the *Washington Post*.

The headlines were onerous, as usual. The United States was taking control of all Finnish ships in port in this country; civilians were asked to leave Manila as the Far East prepared for war. She had to dig deep inside the second section to find a mention of her husband's testimony before Congress.

Commander William "Wild Bill" Parker had been summoned to Washington to testify before a congressional budget committee. A neighbor in Pensacola, Florida, where Bill was stationed, had offered to take care of the kids so Kay could come along for a few days of R and R. The whole idea of relaxing was a joke, as she'd learned soon after their arrival. She wasn't the type to watch without becoming passionately involved.

3

For four days Kay had seethed as she sat in the hearing room listening to her husband defend the navy's request for additional funds for research and testing. Bill had been chosen as a spokesman not only because he was well known as one of the country's top test pilots, but because he was articulate and knowledgeable. Also, given his firsthand experience, he was personally acquainted with glitches in the equipment.

She had seethed not only against the powerful Bureau of Ordnance, known in military parlance as BuOrd, which claimed that testing was expensive and unnecessary, but also against the outspoken Senator Gerald Nye, who had declared paradoxically that he would fight to the death to keep our country from being involved in another war.

Bill laughed when Kay got heated about the man. He reminded her that the senator was first and foremost a politician. He was committed to speak on behalf of the America Firsters, those isolationists who tended to get hysterical at the drop of a gray fedora, because they had supported him in the last election. While the war in Europe expanded, their number across this country had become frighteningly large and their voice, strong.

But Senator Nye and his constituency didn't have to fly the sluggish 1937 Devastators or the dangerously outdated Brewster's Buffaloes. Bill and men like him, his buddies, did. Moreover the pilots said that the country's defective torpedoes were a real black spot on the reputation of BuOrd. She smiled to herself as she remembered Bill's blunt testimony. Pilots being what pilots are, he didn't quite word it that way.

He thought the country should have declared war on the bastards already. Twice. Right after the sinking of USS *Greer* in September and again after the USS *Kearney* was sunk in October. The United States would be in it all right, he said, full-force and soon. This war would be like none other ever fought, he warned them, the sincerity and honesty ringing in his voice as he spoke. This war would be won or lost on the efficiency of modern technology, most primarily air power. And the outdated condition of our planes was a disgrace to the nation.

As Kay sat in the gallery, watching, her heart swelled with frustration. To her Bill's speech was ominously convincing.

But the senators merely nodded politely. God, they weren't listening!

Politics! Bah! Political expediency wasn't a good enough reason for not upgrading the equipment of the armed forces. Roosevelt wasn't any better. Last year, during his campaign for reelection, he'd declared that the navy was at peak efficiency. Bill almost choked on his donut at that one. Even the former ambassador to Great Britain, Joe Kennedy, was still advising against involvement. And she and Bill didn't even discuss Charlie Lindbergh anymore.

She tore the story out of the paper and laid it aside. The kids would be thrilled to read about their father.

The noise in the hall resumed, louder now. She listened for a minute, wondering what the commotion was all about. Heavy footsteps passed the door in a rush.

Suddenly she had a thought. Dear heaven, was the hotel on fire? She narrowly missed putting her foot into the soup bowl of the room-service tray as she stumbled to the door and opened it a crack. She didn't smell smoke, but there were a number of people milling about in the hallway. Their voices seemed oddly ragged, full of alarm and confusion. She caught two words and her curious frown turned to a look of horror.

Bombs. War.

Kay slammed the door and pressed her body hard against it, as though to put a tangible barrier between her and the words she'd heard, as though she could turn time backward to five minutes ago, erase the knowledge from her brain, still the sudden heavy pounding in her chest. *War . . . my God . . . bombings. My Babies!* Had they bombed Florida?

She flew across the room to the radio, switched it on, twisting the volume button to high. Would the thing *never* warm up? Bombings. Her father, her brothers. Had they bombed Nebraska? Griffith Stadium?

Or New York? Bill's sister, Faith, was in college at Skidmore in Saratoga Springs. Kay shook the damned radio until it rattled. Finally nerve-lacerating static assaulted her ears. The somber voice of H. V. Kaltenborn pierced the quiet in the room, a voice striving for calm but underlaid with sorrow. President Roosevelt . . . Japanese.

Pearl Harbor.

Oh, God.

Bill Parker arrived at the hotel sometime after six. The bar, to the left of the entrance, spilled its clientele into the lobby. He had to elbow his way through the crowds to reach the elevator. Some of the people expressed their belligerence at the underhanded attack on Pearl Harbor in loud voices and broad gestures; others wore a look of stunned confusion. But the majority simply talked in low, worried conversation. It was that way all over the city tonight.

Damn, he should have been here with Kay. For three hours she had been alone with her fear. The stadium announcer, he found out later, had feared the football fans would panic so he didn't inform them of the Japanese attack. They didn't hear the news until they were back in the car.

When he reached the door of their hotel room, however, Bill paused for a moment. War had finally come, and it would be harder on Kay than it would be on him. He would be in the thick of things, too busy to dwell on the day-to-day picture. The wives and mothers, the children, all the people who remained at home—they would have it the worst. And Kay was going through a bad patch just now.

He had been aware for months that, under the threat of war, Kay was drawing in on herself; outwardly she had maintained her usual affability with him and the children, but he often caught a strained look in her eyes, a brooding look that disquieted him. Their intimacy had suffered from the world's rumblings, too, and not only because he was gone so much.

Bill took a long breath and opened the door. He expected tears, maybe even panic but, as usual, his adorable wife surprised him. The sight of her sitting, dry-eyed and quiet, packed and dressed to leave, wearing her red coat, her "earnest" expression, and her hat perched neatly—but backward—on her head, almost overwhelmed him.

Wordlessly, he held out his arms and Kay was in them like a shot. Her slender body was tense and stiff, like a windup toy before you release the mechanism. He took a chance. "Honey," he told her gently, "it's okay to cry." He held her tightly.

She didn't cry but in her husband's arms she felt her fright drain away. She smelled the moisture from his coat, the scent of cigarettes, simple ordinary scents. For a long time they stood like that, silently clinging to each other, while the radio continued to blare out the story.

She finally moved away to the window. Bill stood beside her. A misty three-quarter moon looked down on the darkened city. "What's going to happen next, Bill?" she asked. What she really wanted to ask was, Where will you be?

"Honey, I don't know."

"We have to get home," she said in a voice that was much too high. "The children must be terrified."

"I can't leave, Kay, not now."

Kay turned her head to stare at him for a minute. His thick black hair hadn't a trace of gray though he would soon be forty-two. His sky-blue eyes, lined at the corners from squinting into the sun, were as clear as a baby's. His tanned skin looked healthy in contrast to what she probably looked like right now.

No radical readjustment or expression of her inner turmoil was revealed. She swallowed the grief that was like a creature inside her, wanting to get out, wanting to wail in protest. She would do what she had to do, what she always did. Proud of her calm, she became an extension of him, thinking as he thought. Of course they couldn't leave. The events of the day made Bill's mission for the navy even more crucial. "Of course. I don't know what I was thinking about."

Over the next hour she had to be satisfied with extravagant long-distance phone calls to her children in Florida. Twelve-year-old Millie sounded so brave it made her feel ashamed and Billy, barely six, was quick to inform his father that since the war had started he really needed that cap pistol he'd asked Santa Claus to bring.

Bill called Faith in Saratoga Springs, who capriciously announced she was quitting school immediately to help with the war effort and had to be talked out of it. As if Bill didn't have enough on his mind already, Kay thought. She called her parents in Nebraska to learn that her youngest brother intended to be first in line at the army recruiting office tomorrow morning. Luther was only nineteen, a boy.

After the calls they had a quick supper in the room, and then Bill left. He spent the rest of the night and the next day hurrying back and forth between the Navy Department and Capitol Hill.

He arranged for Kay to be present when President Roosevelt asked Congress for a declaration of war. She entered the gallery of the House of Representatives a few minutes before noon; the president was to arrive around twelve-thirty. The chamber was cold. Or did the fear that ran through it account for the extra chill? For months, years, these representatives had been regaled with stories of our unpreparedness if war should come. Now they were faced with reality. Still, from people seated nearby she heard comments that alarmed her. "Now that we are into this," proclaimed the man behind her, "we can end it quickly." But Kay knew better and not just because Bill told her so.

The United States was a mighty country but the might would now be dispersed over two oceans and who-knew-how-many

new fronts. It was going to be the longest, hardest battle ever
faced by a democracy.

Kay glanced up at the steel girders crisscrossing just under
the ceiling, temporary roof supports for repair work. The roof
was falling, literally. Vice President Wallace and Speaker Ray-
burn sat side by side beneath the vertically draped flag.

There was a sudden hush, a dense texture in the air. The
president entered the chamber, moving slowly and leaning heavily on the arm of his son, James. He greeted the two men on the
rostrum above him.

Kay was shocked. She, like millions of Americans, knew that
the president had been stricken with polio, but she had no idea
how weak he looked in person. The newsreels and magazines
were careful not to show the extent of the affliction or the steel
braces on his legs. His complexion was pasty white as he gripped
the podium to steady his stance. She felt her heart go out to the
crippled man. Could he survive this war?

The president wasted no time; his opening remarks were stark
and brief. "Yesterday, December 7, 1941—a date which will
live in infamy—"

Infamy, thought Kay. How well put. Unlike his appearance,
his voice was strong and confident. She realized it had to be;
his words were going out over the airwaves to the people.

The president went on to describe the diplomatic efforts that
were taking place even as the bombs were falling. He read a
roster of the places in the Pacific that had been attacked in addition to Hawaii; each of his sentences was like a sternly delivered nail in the coffin of the country. Malaya, Hong Kong,
Guam, the Philippine Islands, Wake Island, Midway Island. His
voice rang with outrage against the onslaught.

Kay found the hairs on the back of her neck rising. The president spoke as though this was a terrible tragedy that would
shortly be dealt with. A big push of patriotism should do it. It
was a speech that would "play well in Peoria," but she wasn't
sure that the optimism it projected would serve the country well.
Perhaps the American people should be scared a bit more. Or
perhaps not.

The speech lasted less than ten minutes and, at its end, the
chamber erupted with shouts and applause and with shrill whistles. Congress was on its feet cheering and so was Kay. The
president got his declaration of war.

When she left the Capitol, Kay walked back to the hotel
through the cold mist that seemed to have settled over Washing-

ton like a pall of gloomy prophecy. Her personal thoughts were equally gloomy. She would have to leave soon to return to Pensacola. Alone.

One of the implicit conditions of her marriage, and one that she'd accepted years ago, was that her husband performed a dangerous job. He was a first class flight instructor and one of the navy's top test pilots. But he thought of himself, first and foremost, as a fighter pilot. Period. He would be chomping at the bit to get into the war.

She had never learned to live with the nerve-wracking anxiety that one day he would crash. Sometimes she could put the fear out of her mind for quite a long period and then suddenly something would bring it all back, and the black cavity of dread would open again, reminding her that he would be in danger again, next week, next month.

All Kay wanted was to survive the coming holocaust with: priority one—her family safe; and priority two—her country intact. The order of her preferences might have sounded unpatriotic had she spoken them aloud. She didn't mean it that way. She was very patriotic. You couldn't be a good navy wife unless you were. And she was a first-class navy wife—obediently following Bill around the country to wherever he was stationed next, learning to make a home out of the most decrepit quarters.

But on occasion she still tried to bargain with God. When she was young it had been *I'll sit stone-still, God, and hold my breath until the second hand gets to twelve, and You keep the teacher from calling on me.* Or, on the Nebraska farm where she grew up, *I'll clean up my room and keep it clean for a week—a month—if You keep Daddy from finding out who let the chickens loose.* Or, more seriously, *I'll never tell another lie, God, if You'll please let me get away with this one.*

Sometimes it worked; sometimes it didn't. Possibly God was annoyed by people who tried to bargain with Him but she didn't believe so. With the condition of this world today she thought He was probably happy with what He could get.

Bill called that evening. "Honey, I'll be late. Go ahead and have dinner."

She could tell from his tone of voice that he was deeply affected by the situation, and she knew immediately that it was worse than they'd heard from news reports. She bit back the questions she wanted to ask. "Don't worry about me," she said instead.

When Bill walked into their room later that night, she felt her smile wither around the edges like a dying leaf and prayed that he wouldn't notice. His normally healthy complexion had taken on a dull look, his eyes were dark and discouraged.

"At first we were relieved that none of the carriers were in port," he told her. He'd brought a bottle of Scotch, and he sat slumped in the only chair in the room, nursing a drink and smoking. "The *Shiloh* and the *Lexington* were on their way to Midway Island; the *Saratoga* was on the West Coast; the *Enterprise* was within a hundred miles of Pearl and barely missed the attack. But, as the reports filtered in, we realized that we'd breathed too soon." He stubbed out the cigarette and surged to his feet as though he couldn't bear to sit still.

Kay listened silently as she watched him pace and swear. She hurt for him as he related the stories that had come in through the confusion. The waste and destruction, the lives lost unnecessarily—because there had been warnings, many warnings, that the men in charge chose to ignore. Or just plain missed. Evidently there was some new kind of early warning system called radar—she didn't understand the principle—which, if heeded, could have given them some notice.

She tried to picture the lovely island of Oahu as she and Bill had last seen it, the towering cliffs and romantic beaches, the brilliant colors and scents, the music that seemed to be born from the laughter of the people and scattered by warm Pacific breezes. But the image that intruded on her memories now was of gentle beauty gruesomely distorted, a land devastated by smoke and fire, blood and death.

That night as she lay in her husband's tight embrace, she cried the tears she hadn't allowed herself earlier. She cried because Bill was unaware of the tears that wet his own cheeks. Kay had never seen a man cry before. It alternately frightened and astounded her. She steeled herself, for she felt the worst was yet to come.

Later, looking back on the days that followed, Kay could hardly separate one from another in her mind. Reports continued to arrive through the bewildering disorder and at night Bill would relate the news—what news security concerns allowed—to her. The government's official story was that the fleet had lost one battleship and one destroyer. In reality the backbone of the Pacific Fleet had been concentrated in the narrow waters of Pearl Harbor at the time of the bombings—and now was almost all destroyed.

The *Oklahoma* took seven torpedoes below the water line and capsized. The *Arizona* sank, a tomb for uncounted numbers of men who could be heard tapping on the hull by helpless rescue workers outside. The magazine of the USS *Shaw* exploded. The destroyers, *Downes* and *Cassin*, were sitting ducks in drydock.

Severely damaged were the *West Virginia*, the *Tennessee*; the *California* settled into the mud. The *Pennsylvania*, flagship of the Pacific Fleet, was damaged, as was the *Maryland*. Eighteen ships in all, including eight battleships, were destroyed or seriously crippled.

And the planes. Of the 202 navy planes parked on Ford Island in the center of the harbor, 150 were totally demolished.

"On the ground, by God," grated Bill. "On the ground!" Only a pilot, or a pilot's wife, could understand the frustration in his statement.

"We are so unprepared, Kay, so unaware. The situation is incredibly desperate. The Japanese are ready for war; they've been building toward this for months, years. They won't be turned back quickly. We'll lose the biggest part of the Pacific."

"Hawaii? You mean we'll lose Hawaii?"

"Hell, I don't know why they didn't invade after the bombing. They could have had the island in a minute. Thank God for the mistake they made when they turned around and headed home."

Many times, as she listened to Bill relate the latest report, heard the frustration in his voice, she wished she were back on the family farm in Nebraska, as ignorant of the facts as the rest of the country.

Tuesday passed, and Wednesday. The news was bad. The entire country was thrust into upheaval. People rushed to enlist, but there weren't enough camps to train them. The country was at war now, on both fronts, and it wouldn't be over soon.

During the days, Kay tried to stay busy. She walked the streets, never straying too far from the hotel in case Bill should return. On previous visits to Washington she had always enjoyed buying and reading the newspapers available from all over the United States, such diverse publications as the *Kansas City Star*, the *Chicago Times*, the *Cleveland Press*. This time was no exception, though she was exasperated and disappointed by the content. She wanted details, but the stories were speculative rather than precise.

A rough estimate, as presented by the press, was that between two and three thousand lives were lost at Pearl Harbor. She became angered at the specious count. A thousand, give or take a few! "Those are people out there," she complained heatedly to Bill Wednesday night, "not approximate numbers!"

But she was fascinated by the speedy evolution of the political cartoons. In hopes of generating a smile she saved them to show Bill when he came dragging in each night. The overlying theme of the cartoons was bitter, knife-in-the-back, snake-in-the-grass betrayal. Suddenly the Japanese man, previously depicted as amiable but untrustworthy and more funny than dangerous, had become evil and ominous, sometimes bestial. Uncle Sam, who had been an easygoing guy, became resolute and determined.

Thursday she decided that the subject of her leaving Washington had to be discussed. They couldn't ask their neighbor to care for the children much longer. She mentioned it over dinner that evening. "There's a berth available on the Saturday morning train," she said. "Shall I call for a reservation?"

Bill seemed uncharacteristically averse to the idea of her leaving. "Do you have to go?"

"Honey, yes. The children . . . ."

"Damn it! I wish we'd brought them with us," he said, surprising her.

"The children have school, Bill. We couldn't have taken them out of school." She hesitated. Another question had been churning in her mind since Sunday.

"Do you have any idea where you—where we'll be sent?" she asked, hating the frailty in her voice. She didn't want her stupid insecurities to be a burden to him. She tried to conceal them as best she could, but he could always tell. She was trying very hard to hide her fear from him. Every good navy wife knew that her man shouldn't be distracted by worry about the home front.

Bill was silent for a while, reflecting. Finally he reached for her hand and sighed. "Probably San Diego or San Francisco. Possibly Seattle." He paused again and gave her a compassionate look. "I'm sure to be assigned to a carrier, honey. Long months at sea," he added. Then, with an effort, he smiled, winked. "You'll have to buy yourself a new outfit. Something red."

She laughed and shook her head. Bill often teased her about her secret belief that wearing red made her stronger.

His voice fell to a low tone. "You look especially pretty in red, Kay Parker."

For the umpteenth time, she wondered what Bill Parker,

flight instructor and test pilot extraordinaire, had seen thirteen years ago in a scrawny, mousey-haired, midwestern bookworm. Not that she was unsightly—she'd filled out with the advent of two children and learned the startling effect of a lemon juice rinse on brown hair—but she was still way out of her husband's league.

Deep down Kay marveled that she and Bill had even met. Her life as a Nebraska farm girl was about as far removed from the life of a New England scion as two people could get and still be in the same country. But after she recovered from being drawn into the orbit of glamour that surrounds a navy flying ace, she was very glad they had met. Of course Bill was totally oblivious to the glamour and had no idea—well, maybe just an inkling—that he was handsome. He didn't even know that he was a hero; he thought he was simply a man doing a difficult job fairly well.

She felt about as exciting as yesterday's dishwater. In the back of her mind she wondered when the bubble would burst, when Bill would see her for what she was: a common, garden-variety wife and mother. Oh, she could handle things—as long as they didn't come at her too quickly. Unfortunately this week they were coming one right after the other.

Congress had surprised no one today when it also declared war on Japan's allies, Germany and Italy. Germany and Italy declared war on the United States. Then Rumania, Bulgaria, Finland, and Hungary jumped in, joining the Axis. Great Britain declared war on Japan. Costa Rica and Cuba declared war on Germany. South Africa, China, Egypt, Colombia, New Zealand, Australia, Guatemala—nation after nation—Kay needed a scorecard to keep them all straight.

On Saturday Bill took her to the train station. He settled her in a sleeper, gave her a hearty kiss, then a hungry one. Then he asked, almost casually, "It's been good between us, hasn't it? These last few days?"

Bill Parker? Needing reassurance? The enormity of that hit her like a severe jolt. "Yes, darling. It's been very good," she answered immediately. "Do you think you'll be home by Christmas?"

Bill hesitated, then he gave her a wry grin and said, "Come on, you know the BuOrd. Do you think I'll be home soon?"

Kay retracted the question quickly. "Forget I asked. I know you'll be home when you can."

He smiled. "You're a helluva woman. Give the kids a kiss from me." The whistle screamed and the smile was wiped from his face. "I've got to go."

"Okay." Kay kept her features calm as she walked back through the passageway with him.

When they reached the vestibule of the train he turned to her with a reluctant smile. He pulled the collar of her red coat up to frame her face. "Stay warm," he murmured. Then he touched her cheek. "I love you, Kay."

Her pulse jumped in alarm. "I love you, too." Bill was thoughtful, kind, a good husband, a good father; he was *not* a sentimentalist. Avowals of love were seldom exchanged outside the bedroom. This war would be even worse than he'd revealed to her.

With an athletic grace that was so much a part of him Bill swung himself down to the crowded platform. He stood there looking up at her. She wanted to cry again. Other farewells were being exchanged, some shouted and some whispered. A redcap pushing a handtruck neatly avoided a clinging couple. The train lurched and released a hiss of steam.

Kay grabbed for the handhold to keep her balance. Her throat needed clearing, but she managed a bright smile for Bill. The train started to move. "Hey, I forgot to ask," she called.

"What?" Bill gave her a puzzled look and began to trot alongside the train as it gathered speed.

"Who won the football game last Sunday?"

He threw back his head and laughed, a warm sound that lifted her heart. He stopped, shaking his head in amusement. "You're crazy," he called out.

"Who?" she insisted, griping the handhold, leaning out to hear his answer. They were separated now by a good fifty feet.

"The Redskins did," he shouted. "Twenty to fourteen." He raised his hand in a last good-bye.

So, God, let's bargain, Kay said to the Divine as the train clattered out of the station. I'll be a perfect navy wife, a perfect mother, sister, daughter, and friend. I'll go to church every Sunday. I'll sanitize, organize, systemize, harmonize. I won't complain, grumble, or whine. I won't even ask for things to go back to being the way they were.

Just please take care of Bill and let us outlast, outwear, outlive our enemies. Just let us endure.

Bill watched the train move out of sight. Gradually the smile faded from his face; he turned and walked slowly along the platform toward the station. He could relax his guard now. He didn't have to put on a brave front for Kay; he didn't have to conceal his worry any longer.

Chapter 2

Northfield, Illinois, April 18th, 1942

The things that used to be smart were changing. Sleeping late was no longer smart; nor was an afternoon of bridge and gossip, a day's shopping with lunch in the city, or the purchase of an extravagant hat. Now it was smart to conserve everything—gasoline, food, time, and energy. It was smart to do your daily stint at the British War Relief in downtown Chicago, or the hospital, or the USO Canteen.

Her life was changing, too, thought Valerie Adair. Drastically.

She sighed, thrumming her manicured nails on the mahogany surface of the antique game table, and waited impatiently for the girl across from her to answer a one no-trump bid.

Her partner was the youngest and most inexperienced player at the table. Being rich and well placed made up for the deficiencies. "Two spades," came the tentative reply.

"Four spades," said Valerie quickly, eager to end this last rubber, serve tea to her guests, and send them on their way. She had too much on her mind today to enjoy the weekly bridge game.

"Well," drawled Leonne from her right. "She might at least give me a chance to bid." She laid her cards facedown on the table and reached for a cigarette.

"Sorry, Leonne. Your bid."

"Her mind is on other things, it seems," Leonne remarked to the other two. She inhaled deeply and blew the smoke toward the ceiling. It hung above their heads for a minute, then dispersed.

Valerie hated Leonne's maddening habit of speaking about

rather than to a person, but there was no point in arguing about it now. She managed an apologetic smile.

Carole piped in, a breathless thrill in her voice as she leaned forward. "My mind would be on other things, too. Imagine, your whole life hanging on the contents of one little envelope that you can't even open."

Carole was loyal and sweet, Valerie conceded. One could always depend on her to produce an excuse for the most minor gaffe, even when the excuse wasn't needed or appreciated. She did tend to dramatize things out of proportion, however, and that tendency needed to be squelched.

Valerie frowned, pointedly but not completely unkindly. The fault was her own; she shouldn't have mentioned that Jordan's orders had arrived from the War Department, the orders that would tell him where he was to be stationed.

And she definitely couldn't tell them what was really bothering her. "Nonsense, Carole." She lifted a carefully shaped brow. "My whole life? All of us are involved, aren't we?"

The rebuke was received as sent. Carole subsided in her chair.

Valerie sighed again with a certain amount of empathy though she had been the one to wound. The young woman was so anxious to earn herself a place in their group instead of merely being a fill-in when one of them couldn't play and they needed a fourth. She tried to remember if she had been that overeager when she first stood waiting on the edge of social acceptance. She decided not.

She missed her friend, Peg, the leader, who led them all—the girls of their set—to do volunteer duty at the Red Cross: manning the telephones, rolling bandages—God, would they ever use all those bandages? And they all followed. They had always followed Peggy, not only because she was two years older but because she had that indefinable manner that compelled them to do so. Since Valerie liked her, she rationalized away her own envy of Peg's influence.

Lately Peg's activities had been sharply curtailed. She had taken in the two children of a distant British cousin for the duration. Naturally the others had scrambled to take in refugee children.

Valerie had drawn the line at children. She excused herself to her friends with the fact that Jordan was likely to be reassigned any day and she intended to follow. One couldn't displace a displaced child, could one? she asked righteously.

Truthfully she wasn't ready. She recalled that soon after their wedding Jordan had begun to talk about having a child. Children were important to her, but she pictured them somewhere in the dim future—properly a boy first, tall and strong like his father, then a dainty little girl with her mother's blond hair and blue eyes—perfect children. So she had put him off with the excuse that they should have time together first. And she had continued to put him off. Was that when they had begun to grow apart? she wondered.

Her attention returned to the table to find them all watching her. She dredged up another smile from somewhere. "Jordan will be sent to Washington, of course; I'm simply curious as to when."

"Did you see this morning's paper?" asked Leonne's partner, Betty, the quiet, serious one of the group.

The question sobered them all. The headlines hadn't been encouraging. General Douglas MacArthur had been evacuated from Corregidor, the last U.S. bastion in the Philippines, on order from President Roosevelt.

"Yes." Valerie spoke quietly in unison with the other two. "This whole thing is getting uncomfortably close, isn't it?" she added, surprising herself by her somber attitude. Morale forbade gloom and doom, and she was usually the most resolutely optimistic person in the group.

"I'm sure you will be glad to have Jordan in one place for a while instead of running about all over the country," said Leonne, returning to her subject. "Where is he this week?"

Valerie staunched her annoyance as the other three women exchanged glances. She suddenly remembered why she missed Peg. No one else could pierce Leonne's pompousness quite so effortlessly. With only the inflection in her voice Leonne managed to infer that Jordan was up to God-knows-what when he traveled and having a wonderful time doing it. "Military secret," she said, smiling sweetly. That barb would sink deep. Leonne's husband was 4-F. "But he'll be home tonight. It's your bid, Leonne."

After the bidding was finished, Valerie rose. "I think you'll make four spades, partner. Excuse me; I'll just see to our tea."

On the way to the kitchen she detoured by the library where she paused for a minute on the threshold, then closed the door behind her. With a restless stride she crossed the room, purposely avoiding the desk and the envelope squared in the center of the blotter, to stare through the window at the depressingly gray day. Though April had arrived winter seemed reluctant to release its hold on the suburbs at the edge of Lake Michigan.

Movement caught her eye. The gardener, Toyo, stalked by a tiger-striped cat, was spreading mulch between the rows of the newly planted Victory garden. The roses that had been there before would have been putting out new growth by now. Would she be here to see the vegetables mature and ripen? For that matter, would Toyo? There had been talk of internment for Americans of Jap descent. She shrugged—her father-in-law would take care of Toyo—and looked beyond the garden.

The waters of the lake swelled and ebbed uneasily beyond the brown lawn. Further out a mist, like the inside of a down comforter, blurred the horizon.

As she turned away from the scene she could no longer avoid looking at the envelope. She reached across the desk and shifted it to an angle. It was silly of her to worry. Of course Jordan, with his excellent abilities as a lawyer, would be sent to Washington. Of course he would. Then why, she asked herself, did she feel this unease?

Jordan had a certain amount of leeway in his position. She presumed it was because of his father. Before he'd received his commission in the navy he had done some special work for Senator Truman's defense committee's investigation, and he still received calls and cables that she suspected were from the committee counsel. Getting information out of Jordan, however, was like pulling teeth. He was so close-mouthed. Even now this trip was probably related somehow to the work he had done for Congress.

Surely the navy and the War Department would want to utilize his talents and experience. Surely they would want him in the nation's capital.

And after the war was over Jordan would naturally go into politics. Like his father he would be elected to Congress. Perhaps even to higher office.

As she stood there her unease heightened. A strange, shaky feeling crept through her body, slowly penetrating, settling bone-deep within her, as if ice crystals had formed and frozen there permanently. She chafed her arms to dispel the chill. She was being melodramatic about this. The house was quiet around her, too quiet. Though she knew that others moved beyond the closed door of the library, the silence also made her nervous.

In the living room there would be conversation, subdued except for an occasional murmured groan when a finesse didn't work, or an ace was trumped, but conversation. In the kitchen Mary would be completing preparations for serving tea; in the dining room Curtiss would be setting the table for dinner, checking the silver on the sideboard for the least speck of tarnish. The thought of the servants smoothly going about their tasks restored her, gave her a feeling of continuity and stability that she was surprised to discover she needed in these unstable times. She had always thrived on situations that provoked nervous reactions in others.

Now she found that her nails were digging into the back of the desk chair. She crossed to the mahogany bar and poured herself a small finger of cognac, which she drank quickly. The warming sensation produced by the spirits was pleasant. She felt herself relax.

The luxury of the room soothed her as well—the natural leather upholstery on the chairs and divan, the deep tones in the Oriental carpet, a painting by John Marin that hung over the mantel, the small steel model of a sleek, streamlined train designed by Norman Bel Geddes. All the elegant appointments—the ones that weren't gifts to a powerful senator—had been selected by her mother-in-law before her death. And no one had ever been more qualified to define elegance than the prominent Mrs. Judson Adair.

Valerie was content to be living in Jordan's father's beautiful mansion, among the priceless antiques and works of art. More than content.

When they were first married Jordan had argued that they should have a place of their own. But her father-in-law had insisted they stay. The estate was empty for all but a few months a year; the servants were here; and the place was certainly large enough for them all even when the senator, accompanied by various members of his entourage, was in residence. So she had sided with Jordan's father and here they remained.

Occasionally Jordan would reintroduce the subject but she had become adept at countering his arguments.

Things had changed between them, too. How long had it been since he'd mentioned a house of their own, a child, since he'd argued for anything? At least a year, maybe longer. They no longer talked of plans for the future. It was as if there was nothing important enough between them to argue for. Only a fool would expect marriage to be the same after seven years, but she should have seen trouble coming. Their relationship had lost its warmth, leaving behind a void, a chill that never quite went away. He no longer gazed at her beauty with that old sparkle in his eyes. They had become like two strangers who, meeting for the first time, are exceedingly polite but wholly indifferent.

When they were first married their love had been effervescent, almost giddy. Though she never completely lost sight of who they were, Jordan often did, cutting up on the dance floor, sweeping her off her feet to kiss her passionately in broad daylight in the middle of State Street.

Valerie tried to blame the war, but deep down she was forced to admit that the difficulties between them had begun long before Pearl Harbor. Still, the war was the catalyst for the situation as it now stood between them.

Jordan had dropped his bombshell before he left on this last trip. He wanted her to think seriously about their marriage while he was gone, he'd told her; and when he returned they were going to have an important discussion.

Divorce. The word hadn't been mentioned but it lurked there, behind the polite facade, leaving a burning lump in her throat that she could neither swallow nor dissolve. She didn't want a divorce. Besides the disgrace a divorce would cause, she didn't want to give up everything she had accomplished. She now had what she desired in life, had planned for it all, and she certainly didn't intend to give any of it up.

Now she slid a hand into her pocket and took out a small package of Sen-Sen. She put one of the tiny mints on her tongue. It wouldn't do for the girls to smell brandy on her breath. It wouldn't do at all.

An hour later Valerie thankfully said good-bye to her guests, nodding distractedly when Leonne reminded her that they were playing next week at her house.

A sudden thought, revolutionary as it was, stilled her hand in midair. What if she were not at Leonne's next week? What if she simply dropped out of the group?

The more she thought about the idea, the more she liked it. She might never go to the weekly bridge games again. What an odd notion, in light of the fact that she'd once so needed to be a part of this group. Now it seemed she was willing to give it all up without a qualm. She wasn't sure why, and she would have to think about it very carefully. She was not one to relinquish her options so easily. She liked to keep doors open, in case she changed her mind.

Conditions over which she had no control were causing the changes in her life. Perhaps it made her feel better, more in

command, to think about making one of those decisions herself.
She could find something else to interest her until they moved
to Washington.

One plus would be that she wouldn't have to tolerate any more
of Leonne's snide suggestions about the absence of her husband.
Didn't the foolish woman know there was a war on? One thing
she never had to question was Jordan's faithfulness. His sense
of honor was too finely developed.

Jordan *had* been gone a lot this year, and last. As a lawyer,
a member of the judge advocate general's staff—and the son of
a United States senator—Jordan was often called on to handle
delicate tasks like the ones for Senator Truman's committee.
They were essential assignments, necessary to the country's war
effort.

Half an hour later Valerie was seated at her dressing table
finishing her makeup. She leaned forward to shape her lips into
a provocative bow with the lip brush. She wanted to look perfect
for Jordan tonight.

From the adjoining dressing room she heard a closet door
open and then cringed as it bumped against the wall. Helen
would be brushing the jacket she wore this afternoon, checking
for loose threads or buttons, then hanging the garment on one
of the padded hangers.

An ivory dinner gown had already been placed on the bed
behind her.

The unhurried ritual of dressing for dinner, which she loved,
couldn't distract Valerie completely from her other, more pressing, problem. Jordan. How would he act when he got home?

The sweet coolness of silk rustling over her head, even the
satisfying beauty of the sapphire set sparkling in its velvet-lined
case on the dressing table, failed to calm her misgivings about
facing Jordan tonight. She had to handle this just right.

She was adjusting the dress over her hips when Helen entered
the room. "I'm sorry, Mrs. Adair. Here, let me do that for
you." She hurried to Valerie's side.

"Nonsense, Helen. I'm perfectly capable of zipping my own
dress."

Though the older woman would have liked the title, Helen
wasn't a ladies' maid; those were out of fashion now. Besides
Helen didn't fit the image—she needed to lose quite a lot of
weight. But she did take care of all the little mundane tasks that
would have bored Valerie to tears.

As she fastened the sapphires at her throat, on each wrist,

and at the lobes of her ears, she speculated about taking Helen to Washington with her, then she dismissed the idea. She would find someone more suitable there.

She didn't openly make use of Jordan's father's position; that would have been bad form. But it was a nice bonus, being a senator's daughter-in-law. She enjoyed the power it gave her over her friends.

She had her hopes pinned on becoming Washington's next premier hostess and smiled as she envisioned her debut into Washington society. She pictured herself in the senator's Georgetown home—where else, with the housing shortage?—presiding over intimate little dinners with important people. Her father-in-law would love the idea.

An earring caught in her sleek chignon, necessitating a complete redo. Damn.

All men looked better in uniform, thought Valerie as she watched unobserved from the top of the stairs. And Jordan Adair in his navy dress blues was a magnificent specimen. Fine tailoring emphasized his broad shoulders and lean build; the dark color was an impressive contrast to his gentle gray eyes and sandy hair. His expression, as usual, was a bit too solemn, too unemotional, for her taste. She preferred his rare smiles. But the seriousness didn't detract from his looks at all. Indeed, it added to his authority.

The chandelier reflected light on gold braid and eagle as her husband handed Curtiss his suitcase and hat. He lifted his hand to smooth his hair the way a young boy might on his first or most important date. The comparison pleased her.

"Is Mrs. Adair in, Curtiss?"

"Of course she is, darling," Valerie said from her post. Her voice was light as she hurried down. "Where else would she be when it's time for her husband to come home from his travels?"

Jordan watched her descend the stairs, his expression now guarded. She knew he saw perfection. Perfectly done up, hair, makeup, dress. Moving with perfection, employing graceful and tidy, economical gestures. Perfection of manner, calm loving eyes, perfect smile. That was the way she always wanted him to see her. As perfect.

Perfect, as always, Jordan thought as he advanced to meet her at the foot of the stairs. Perfect and unreachable. Untouchable. Would their marriage ever work again, he wondered. Did he even care anymore?

Valerie went on tiptoe to receive his kiss. She was glad that she barely reached his shoulder; such sizing was in style nowadays. Dainty women, requiring protection, nurturing, went well with big, strong men.

"You look beautiful, Valerie," he offered as he always did. And she was satisfied.

"Drinks in the library, darling," she said, leaning slightly against him, her hand over his heart. She felt a bit of the tension in his body relax.

He wrapped her in the curve of his arm, smiling down at her. "How about a shower and a change of clothes first?"

The affectionate gesture quieted Valerie's misgivings, and her heart swelled. Maybe things were going to be all right. Maybe he'd had time to think while he was away. Maybe he wouldn't even bring up the subject of the state of their marriage.

She looped her own arm around his waist and shook her head. Not a strand of hair fell from its appointed place. "Later, please, darling. I've been an absolute wreck since the morning mail. You have something from the War Department. Never have I been as tempted to open one of your letters."

"The suspense has been killing you, has it?" he quipped easily, but there was something else underlying his tone, something that she couldn't identify.

She tilted her head back to look up at him. As she examined his features more closely, she saw that his face clearly reflected the strain of the trip. The lines at the corners of his mouth were more severe, his dark gray eyes, more shadowed. "You look awfully tired, Jordan," she said softly.

"I am. I'm really beat." He sighed and scraped a hand over his face. "But the report is in the hands of the committee now. My part is finished."

"The thing about synthetic rubber production?" she asked. She kept up with everything Jordan was involved in—everything he would share with her—and she knew that now, since Japan had captured the East Indies, the supply of natural rubber to the United States was almost completely cut off. The threat of gasoline rationing was a pretense to hide the real problem, the critical rubber shortage.

Jordan had spent the last several months—by the navy's leave—interviewing scientists, consulting experts, and preparing a report for Congress concerning the production of synthetic rubber. The synthetic could be made by one of two methods: one using grain alcohol and favored by farm interests, and one using petroleum, favored by oil interests. Jordan would help to make sure whichever way they went they would do it with all the proper authorizations and legitimate sanctions.

Valerie knew how disgusted he'd become over the political wrangling and maneuvering over the issue. "Do you know which process they've decided on?" she asked idly. She had already decided to invest some of the generous allowance, which her father-in-law provided and which Jordan refused to use, in whichever process was approved.

"Haven't a clue, thank God. I don't want to know. It's all up to the president and Congress. Either system will work. The petroleum method is slightly more efficient and the grain alcohol process would be cheaper, so it's a toss-up. They'd better settle their political differences soon, though. The synthetic industry has to be built from scratch, and our rubber situation is growing desperate."

Valerie studied him. "You're really worried, aren't you?" She couldn't keep the surprise completely out of her voice.

He smiled sadly. "Yes, I'm really worried. This is only one of the problems of production we're facing. We have a long way to go. Let's have that drink, shall we? And you can tell me what you've been doing with yourself since I left."

"As a matter of fact, the foursome played bridge here today." Her hip bumped slightly against his thigh as she walked with him into the room where Curtiss had already set out the drinks tray. "I thought I'd scream by the time they left. Sit down, Jordan. I'll fix your Scotch while you open the letter."

He picked up the envelope and the evening paper and relaxed in his favorite wing chair. "God, it's good to be home."

She poured the drinks as he spoke and turned, his highball glass in one hand, her stemmed sherry in the other, to find that he still held the envelope unopened. "You're deliberately torturing me, Jordan," she accused with a pout. "Hurry up. We're meeting Peg and Eric for dinner at the club at eight o'clock."

He took the drink she offered. "Tonight?" That tedious chill crept into his voice; he straightened in his chair. "Valerie, I just got home. I haven't had five hours sleep in the last forty-eight. Damn it, you might have waited until I arrived to make plans."

Valerie caught her breath. Here it was again, the resentment that seemed to be his reaction to everything she did. "I thought you'd be pleased to see Eric again. He's your oldest friend." She hated the defensiveness in her own voice. "Shall I call them and beg off?"

"Please," he answered politely.

She rang for Curtiss and informed him that they would be dining in after all. Then she used the phone on the desk. While she talked to Peg she watched Jordan set down his glass and rip open the envelope, unfold the thick sheets, scan the contents. She might as well have not been in the room.

"Well? Are we going to Washington?" she asked when she'd hung up.

"*A* Washington, darling," he answered. "But not the one on the Potomac, I'm afraid. The JAG office in Seattle," he added, his face unreadable.

Judge advocate general's office in Seattle? This couldn't be right. "Seattle?" Valerie frowned. "How could they have made such a mistake with your orders? We'll have to call your father tonight. He can use his influence—"

"It's no mistake, Valerie," Jordan interrupted quietly. "I requested Seattle. The last thing Washington, D.C., needs is another lawyer. I want to go where I can do the most good, and there's a lot to be done in Seattle."

She could hear the vitality that crept into his voice. She sank into the chair opposite and stared at him, trying to remain composed, to reserve judgment until she heard all his reasons for such an extraordinary request.

Because there was more to come; she could feel that. Like waiting for the other shoe to drop. "You asked for it? Without consulting me?"

He shrugged, tossing the envelope and its contents on the table. "Yes. I'm sorry if you're offended."

"Offended? Certainly I'm offended. It's my life, too, Jordan." Furious is the word, she thought as she rose and began to pace the floor. How dare he do this to her? And to himself? The opportunities, the contacts in the nation's capital, would be invaluable after the war. She attempted to dampen her anger. "Where will we live, Jordan? I've read that Seattle is one of the places suffering an acute housing shortage." She paused meaningfully. "Or maybe you intend to leave me behind?"

Jordan stared into his drink for a minute before he answered. "It won't be the life-style you're used to. I'll be gone a lot. The men and women in the navy need and deserve legal representation, and that's what the JAG office gives them." He didn't add that he had been handed another assignment, one that was off the record. "None of your friends would blame you if you chose to remain in Chicago, Valerie. Neither would I."

"Surely you're not serious?" Her voice quavered.

"Maybe I am." He reached into his jacket pocket for a cigarette and watched her over the flame of a match.

Valerie did wish he would use the gold lighter she'd given him for Christmas last year.

"Maybe it would be best for both of us," he added.

Here was the confrontation she had so dreaded. She fortified herself with a deep breath. "Oh, Jordan," she said finally in a low, controlled tone. "I realize that our relationship hasn't been all that good lately. Things are changing too quickly. It's this damn war. But surely you know that I love you. Surely you know I'd go anywhere to be with you." He said nothing. "Don't you?"

For a long, intense moment she searched his features. Almost panicked now, she slipped to her knees in front of his chair, the ivory gown billowing out around her. "You must believe me. I worship you, Jordan. I always have."

Looking down at his wife in her studied pose of supplication, Jordan Adair felt a sudden, almost ruthless, surge of animosity. With a muttered curse he flung his cigarette into the fireplace, lifted her from her place of entreaty and stood, bringing her to her feet with him. "I don't want to be worshipped, Valerie. I have never done anything to deserve an extreme emotion like that."

The remark, unbidden, unexpectedly brought a rush of vivid memories to his mind. He saw, instead of the eyes in front of him, green eyes, excitement alive in their depths. The smooth blond hair gave way to wild, red hair tumbled by the wind. Instead of his wife's voice, he heard laughter, bright and husky. Dear God, what was wrong with him?

He had made his decision a year ago. And he'd convinced himself it was the right decision. He'd made a vow, to love, to honor, to protect. Divorce was offensive as a option among their set, though he had considered it seriously. But as long as Valerie was willing to try to mend their damaged marriage, he would give her his whole hearted support. He had managed to live with his decision—after a fashion. Whatever it was that had produced these thoughts, he'd better get himself under control, and quickly.

Jordan's hands were hard on Valerie's shoulders. She had the impression that he was about to shake her. She lowered her eyes to hide her surprise. "I can't help how I've always felt," she countered quietly. When she raised her eyes to meet his again, the anger was still there.

"Maybe you'd better try," he bit out. "Worship implies that

you depend solely on me for your happiness and I don't want that responsibility." He exhaled a heavy sigh and dropped his hands. "I can't live up to it anymore."

She returned to her chair. When she was seated he resumed his seat as well and picked up his glass. "What has happened to you, Jordan?" she asked. "Why have you changed so?"

Jordan leaned forward, and when he answered he spoke deliberately. "This war has happened to me, Valerie. It is changing us all and the changes are just beginning. Our country is in desperate trouble; do you understand that? Do you read anything in the paper besides the society section? Hitler has overrun Europe. England is hanging by a thread. And we've been on the defensive in the Pacific for months, retreating. We've lost battle after battle. MacArthur has been ordered to Australia. Corregidor can't hold out much longer—we've lost the Philippines. The next logical step for the Japanese is Midway Island and then it's just a short hop to Hawaii and the West Coast."

She waited silently for the now-familiar outburst to burn itself out. Finally it did. He subsided against the back of the chair with a heavy sigh, rolling his glass between his palms. When he spoke again his voice was thoughtful. "But maybe this war will give us, you and me, a chance to find where our hidden strengths lie. If we have any we'd better find them as soon as possible."

"Jordan, you know I've never shared your bent for philosophy," she told him dryly. "What is it you're trying to tell me?"

He studied her for a long time. Then, raising his glass, he drained its contents before answering. "Valerie, I can't handle my life any longer the way it is. I've struggled with my father for years; I can't—or won't—fight you, too. I need peace and quiet in my home—we'll get precious little of that anywhere else for years to come. And I want a home, not this cold museum. I want to come in at night, maybe have a drink, dinner, read a bit, talk. I realize you're in your element and you're good at the things you do, like your charity work. But I don't need a wife whose one desire is to set the standards for society.

"I'm not happy dining at the club five nights out of seven and having guests here the other two," he went on tersely. "If you were misled into thinking that I would eventually accept this life-style"—he indicated their surroundings with a wave of his hand—"I'm sorry.

"But I've never lied to you, Valerie. You knew long before we married that I wasn't interested in living the way my father does. For the last seven years you seem to have been laboring under the impression that I would change my mind. I can assure you I won't. I applied for duty in Seattle not only because there's important work to be done there but also with the hope that we could escape all this and really start anew.'' He got to his feet, poured himself another drink and took a deep swallow. ''If you want to come with me, it's up to you.''

Valerie stared at Jordan's back. He still wasn't telling her the whole story. But that was something she could think about later. Now her mind was racing in another direction. If she went with him, she would be a long way from home, from her family and friends, from everything that provided her security. Jordan wouldn't be around all the time for her. What would she do? Did he know how much he was asking?

She wasn't sure, but she knew how much she had to lose.

Valerie had decided when she was very young that Jordan Adair and all he represented would make her life completely ideal. He was all she was not.

Her own family, while perfectly respectable, lived on the fringes of real society in suburban Chicago. Nothing was more degrading than living on the fringes of anything. She had made up her mind at an early age—from the moment she'd discovered she was beautiful, as a matter of fact—that someday she would marry Jordan and move right into the center of things.

When Jordan had come home from his last year of law school he found, not a worshipful young girl, but a sleek beauty, one who made it clear she was his for the asking. She had surprised him so, he proposed. She wasn't yet sure what had gone wrong between them but, with plenty of planning and preparation, she was convinced she could make it right again.

The war was playing havoc with standards. Jordan was deluded by the sweet vision of a brave little woman on the home front. A life like that, a woman like that, would bore him in no time. He thought he wanted a settled, quiet, simple existence, but she knew better.

He was a brilliant man. She was convinced that he needed the stimulation of people around him. However, if that was the way he wanted to play it for now, she would go along.

''I'm stronger than you think, Jordan. Of course I'll come with you,'' she said finally when he turned to look at her. ''Perhaps you're right. What time we have together we'll spend it alone. We'll get to know each other again. Maybe our differences won't seem so insurmountable.'' He didn't respond to her smile, so she let it fade. "You shouldn't have made such a decision without consulting me, though. As for the other, I'm sorry if I've forced you into a life-style you don't like." Her last words were delivered stiffly; she knew that but she couldn't control it.

His fingers tightened on his glass. "Let's face it, Valerie; we're mismatched. It's going to take a lot of work to fix things between us."

"Do you want things fixed, Jordan?" she asked bluntly.

His hesitation lasted no longer than it took to blink an eye. Valerie wasn't sure she hadn't imagined it.

"I'm not sure. But I do want the choice to be yours as to whether you go or stay. Don't do it because you think you should or because it will look right to your friends."

One strong point was on her side. Jordan was a traditionalist; he'd made a vow that he would be loath to break. He wouldn't want divorce, either, except as a last resort, and he really had no grounds. Everything she had done was for his own good. For their own good. So she would go where she had to go, do whatever had to be done, including having a child. And when this blasted war was over everything would return to normal. Jordan would return to the private practice of law, eventually move into politics; she would return to her friends, her charity work and social activities, and her secure existence.

"Of course I want to go with you," she repeated. "I love you, Jordan." The stiffness was still in her voice, her body. She sipped from the glass of sherry.

He looked down at her with a strange expression. "Does it bother you that we seem to have lost sight of ourselves?" he asked quietly.

She tried not to sound flippant but she had to be honest. "No, because I haven't lost sight of anything. I know who I am. I'm not a rebel, Jordan. I like the continuity, the security if you like, of being where I know I belong."

His intense regard never wavered. "You may find—"

Tired of this now, wanting it over, she interrupted. "Oh, come on, Jordan. I've said I'll go with you to Seattle; I didn't say I'd like it very much. I'm going because I love you and for no other reason."

Jordan returned to his chair. "But you really think we belong in my father's house, whether here or in Washington," he said heavily.

"Yes, I do. You're a brilliant lawyer, darling. After the war . . . you can't run from your fate or your future. And I want to be there when you find that out.'' She regretted her outburst immediately when he spoke, and she saw that his face was closed to her again.

"Fine," he answered quickly. "We'll give it a try. The military has recently leased one of the downtown hotels in Seattle for the duration.'' He searched his pockets and came up with a scrap of paper from which he read, "The Elysium Hotel. I'll write tonight to put our names on the waiting list."

"A waiting list? Why don't you just tell them who you are?"

He gave her an incredulous look. "Have you understood a word of what I've been saying?" he asked, allowing his anger to show through once again.

Valerie crossed her legs and smoothed the fabric of her gown. "I do understand. This war thing seems to have turned you into some kind of Boy Scout. I just think it's foolish not to take advantage of your connections. Everyone else does."

Jordan sighed. "My father gave me the name of the hotel. That will have to satisfy you, I'm afraid."

"Your father knew that you applied for duty in Seattle?"

"Oh, yes, he knew. He didn't like the idea much more than you do, but for once he didn't fight my decision, either." Actually, thought Jordan wryly, his father hadn't had much choice when the primary, but secret, reason for Jordan's assignment had been explained to him.

Jordan would be coordinating tests for a radical new radio jamming device, one that could shorten the war considerably. This device was the most promising of the several proposals he'd studied while he was at the communications center in New Orleans. He believed in it and in its inventor. But it had to be tested under battle conditions.

After the tests were complete, and he was confident of success, he would have to scout locations for a manufacturing site, negotiate the expenditures, and—most importantly—set up security.

Valerie watched as complicated feelings chased across her husband's face. The senator was aware of the burden of being his son, but he had always made it clear that Jordan was the heir apparent to the Adair political empire whether he liked it or not. There was no one else. If Jordan had had a brother, perhaps, or even a sister who was interested in a political future, he wouldn't have been expected to follow in his father's footsteps.

Valerie had been a willing participant in the senator's strategy sessions during the last election year, sat in on the campaign planning. The senator had encouraged her interest, making it clear that she would be doing the same thing for her husband someday. He felt she should discover as much as possible before that day came. He was a strong believer in a wife's participation, maybe because his own wife had been involved.

Now he would say that her job, her duty, was to support Jordan. She would have thought orders to Washington, D.C., would have been more beneficial to Jordan's eventual career in politics; but if his father approved, who was she to question? She straightened in her chair. "Well, if we have to . . ."

She didn't see the flash of anger in Jordan's eyes as he stood to leave the room. "Tell Curtiss to hold dinner for fifteen minutes, will you?" he said back over his shoulder. "I'm going to clean up."

Jordan returned to the library in less than fifteen minutes. He was still grim-faced but Valerie chose to ignore his expression.

They had just entered the dining room when the telephone rang. "I'll get it," said Jordan.

"Curtiss will get it, darling," Valerie protested.

He stopped the butler's move toward the hall with an upraised palm. "I'll get it myself, Curtiss. It may be important."

Valerie let the butler seat her.

"Shall I serve the soup, Mrs.—"

The man's question was interrupted by a whoop from the hall.

Valerie pushed back her chair and got to her feet just as Jordan came bursting through the door. He grabbed her, lifted her off her feet to kiss her soundly, and whirled her around. Then he released her and slapped Curtiss on the shoulder. Mary and Helen peeped through the door at the commotion.

Jordan laughed and beckoned to them. "Come in. Come in both of you. Curtiss, get a bottle of champagne and glasses. We'll all drink a toast to some wonderful news. We've bombed Tokyo!"

"Bombed? Where?"

"Tokyo, Japan?"

"Who—how?"

"General James Doolittle. Leading a force of bombers off an aircraft carrier! Goddamn! What a feat! Now maybe we can turn this war around!"

Chapter 3

New Orleans, Louisiana, May 26th, 1942

Sydney Jackson opened her eyes to the familiar crack in the ceiling. She sighed. Today was a day for farewells. Tomorrow she was getting married, and in a few days she would be leaving New Orleans, perhaps forever. Anticipation warred with nostalgia at the thought of uprooting her life once again.

Spring wasn't the time to say good-bye to this city. Not spring with its cool nights and warm days, with the scents of *beignets* and chicory-laced coffee drifting out of the French Market in the Quarter, with its citywide explosion of azaleas and flowering cherry trees. She could reconcile herself to leaving the breath-stealing humidity and the steamy streets of summer and fall, or the chilling rain that never seemed to cease in the winter. But the sweetness that crept through her window this morning reminded her cruelly of what she would miss.

The room wasn't much. Even before the war, even before the housing shortage it hadn't been much. But for six years it had been home to her and six years was a big chunk out of her twenty-two.

The boundaries of the room, fourteen by fourteen by fourteen, were as familiar to her as her hand. Now she took a sentimental inventory. Clean but faded chintz at the windows stirred only lightly in the breeze; the room-sized rug, which had once glowed with the jeweled colors of the Orient, was almost worn through in spots; the mattress upon which she lay had a bump that she had learned to accommodate.

As a musician, Sydney also appreciated the sounds of the city; the frequency, the level, the pitch and quality of different tones captivated her. Through the open window she could hear

33

the euphonic peculiarities of the city she loved, as it began to stir and waken. Early morning to late at night, she loved the characteristic flavor of the city as it expressed itself in sound. To a harmonic background of a bird's song, a distant ship's horn mourned the passing of another night; a weary milk truck ground its haggard gears; the paperboy sailed the *Times-Picayune* to the wide veranda beneath her window where it landed with a flat thwack. If the nasty kid hit the spot he had aimed for, the paper would have dropped just between the porch and the privet hedge, making a swishing noise.

Sydney got out of bed and crossed on bare feet to the window. She watched the paperboy's wobbly progress until his bicycle rounded a corner out of sight. Muting a sigh she studied the scene before her.

The old Victorian house sat facing the Esplanade as easily as a heavy dowager settled into familiar surroundings. A narrow strip of lawn and a waist-high wrought-iron fence delineated the square block of the property. At one time the wide boulevard, blessed with the beauty of youth, unblemished and resplendent, had been the sanctuary of the Creole elite. Once the cobblestone streets, lit by gas lamps, rang under the weight of carriage wheels, their passengers intent on business, a day's shopping, or an evening's entertainment. Now only memory or imagination could reproduce the sound.

The house was owned by a proportionately old lady who hadn't asked questions six years ago when a young girl had appeared at her door in response to the advertisement of a room to rent. The woman and the house had long ago given up the illusion of gentility. With the onset of the Depression gentility had become a luxury one in Mrs. Deveraux's position could not afford. Nevertheless, and despite hard times and poverty, the woman, the neighborhood, and the aged house had retained a certain infallible grace and charm.

The screen door beneath her window opened with a refined squeak. She watched Mrs. Deveraux move with early morning stiffness to retrieve the paper.

Sydney knew a moment's misgiving. Through the years they had come to depend on each other in subtle ways. Sydney's was a strong back and a willing hand. Who would look after the older woman when she was gone? The other boarders?

Sydney had learned a lot from the old woman. How fortunate that fate had landed her here. Mrs. Deveraux had seen her through some difficult, rebellious times and had become her confidante, her friend.

The woman lived a life of quiet routine. She rose early and prepared breakfast for her boarders before she started to clean house. A midmorning break for a bottle of Coca-Cola was her only self-indulgence. Sydney was touched by the unchanging ritual. Mrs. Deveraux always uncapped the bottle in the kitchen, wiping the lip carefully in case there was any rust on it or in case the green glass rim had been chipped. Then, rain or shine, she took her drink to the wicker rocking chair on the front porch. She always wrapped the bottle in her handkerchief and she always took exactly fifteen minutes to finish. Not until she was through did she remove the wet linen to check the bottom for the name of the city that was stamped there. That was the fun of it, and she kept a record to which she added any new place. Bottles did travel from the most surprising locales. Mrs. Deveraux was most proud of the entry from Kalamazoo, Michigan.

When Sydney had arrived in New Orleans she'd been overgrown and unpolished. She was still overgrown, but now a few of the rough, dirt farm–bred edges had been smoothed out, thanks to the woman downstairs who had supported her through all stages of the last six years. From the first, as though it were her duty, Mrs. Deveraux had encouraged her to use the library downstairs and read the newspapers every day, had corrected her table manners and her English without hesitation. After a short period of resistance, Sydney had begun to realize the value of the criticism. She knew her handicaps.

New Orleans was a city of eccentrics, exactly what Sydney had expected it to be and not at all what she'd expected. She had arrived on a Friday, dressed in a blue flowered dress made from the prettiest feed sack she could find, her meager savings tucked securely into her bra, and sustained by a heart full of ambition. Ready to tackle the world. It hadn't taken her long to discover that the world tackled back.

Her money and her hopes had dwindled to almost nothing by the time she'd found a job at the Royal Orleans, not the singing job she had dreamed of when she left the farm in Mississippi, but a job as a chambermaid, cleaning fourteen rooms a day, seven days a week.

The work didn't bother Sydney; the loss of her dream did. So over the next months she haunted the clubs in the French Quarter as often as time and her salary allowed.

Trouble was she didn't know jazz, and jazz was New Orleans.

Her voice was husky and rich enough for the style but singing a weekly solo in the Friendship Baptist Church choir back home hadn't prepared her for the intricate phrasing and improvisation. Besides, she wasn't colored. Still she was strangely drawn by the music.

Clyde Cook's, a small club on Toulouse Street, drab and dark even in the daylight, became her favorite haunt. It was a relatively "clean" club, meaning that there was no back room for gambling, dope wasn't sold from behind the bar, and Sydney didn't feel uneasy there even when she went alone.

Clyde was the keyboard man of the group. With his white hair and full beard he looked like a dark brown Santa Claus. The things that man could do with a piano or a xylophone were wonderful. Every now and then she would get a nod of recognition from Clyde and the men in his group when she walked in. Eventually the nod became a smile and conversation. And then one day, four years ago . . .

The thing about jazz, Sydney discovered, is that it clicks. You listen and listen; you know you like the form, you know that it makes feelings boil up inside you but you can't exactly explain why, and then one day it just clicks. She finally talked Clyde into letting her sing. The first time she asked he had stared at her with the oddest expression, almost as though he were afraid of her.

Most people took one look at Sydney and made a judgment. She was tall and full-breasted; her straight shoulders, the angle of her chin, the way she looked at people—right in the eye—created a bold impression. Coupled with her flamboyant red hair and easy smile, her figure suggested a certain kind of woman. The suggestion wasn't flattering.

She couldn't do anything about her height, so she used it to bolster her self-confidence and on occasion to intimidate those prissy enough to earn her disdain. Her hair was another matter. She had once dyed it black. Next to her fair skin the black hair had made her look like a witch. She never tried that again. Sydney Jackson was what she was and anybody who didn't like it could go to hell.

So the colored men took one look at the tall white woman, with hair like the grass on the devil's prairie and a speaking voice like a hangover at dawn, and shrugged. But they let her sing. As her assurance grew and the full-bodied notes rolled over them, their smiles became broader, beaming upon her as though she were their very own accomplished pupil. They stayed on after closing, jamming, as they called it, until the first streaks of daylight leaked through the dusty windows. Clyde even let her play the piano.

Two weeks later the manager of the club offered her a modest contract. She was a sensation, unique, a white woman who sang jazz with affinity and the emotional impact the colored jazzmen thought exclusive to their race. The hole-in-the-wall club had never known such prosperity.

The consensus wasn't unanimous, however. The bass player, Bobby Dick Johnson, who was the only other member of the band under thirty, openly resented her presence. Somehow he discovered that she had lied about her age and threatened to tell the manager, who was very careful to comply with the law of white New Orleans.

"Tell him, then," she declared.

"A white woman don't belong in a colored band."

"White folks come to the club."

"That's different," he argued sullenly.

"I won't beg, Bobby Dick, not you or anybody else."

He studied her for a long time. Despite her bravado she'd been scared as she waited for his judgment.

Finally he shrugged. "Ah, hell. Keep your job. Just stay out of my way."

Sydney was in heaven. Despite Bobby Dick's animosity, being able to do what she loved to do half the night and sleep as late as she wanted the next day seemed like the perfect life. Of course, it wasn't.

Mrs. Deveraux accepted her boarder's new distinction with restraint. Sydney knew the old woman didn't approve of the segment of society that reigned in the French Quarter. But, Sydney told herself, Mrs. Deveraux was from another generation. Times were different, the world was different, more exciting, and she wanted to be a part of it. She tried to be patient with the older woman but sometimes those pointed looks really annoyed her.

Sydney would never have presumed to think of the aristocratic Mrs. Deveraux as a second mother, but that was what she'd become. And her second mother didn't think much of Sydney's impending marriage.

Now Sydney let the curtain drop and left her dreaming at the window. She was getting married tomorrow, and she had a hundred things to do today.

* * *

"You must act as you deem right, of course," Mrs. Deveraux said as they made their way to the club the following afternoon. Her voice was thin with the brittle tones of advancing age, but no less imperious.

Clyde and the boys couldn't come to the wedding tonight because they had to work, so they had insisted on having a little going-away party for her this afternoon.

"You have known this man for only a short time," Mrs. Deveraux reminded her. "Do you love him?"

"Vance is very nice," she countered, brushing aside the question. Love didn't enter into this. "He will make a good husband."

"Did I say he wasn't nice? But why get married now? You thought you were in love last year."

Sydney felt the familiar pain inwardly, but she quickly thrust it away.

She couldn't explain, even to herself, all the complicated reasons for her decision. With the onset of war, the nature of her life had already begun to change. The city was overrun with new faces. Regulars at the club were dropping off, taking jobs in the defense industry, joining up; the new clientele was hurried, impersonal, there for a night's entertainment before moving on.

She was changing, too. The dreams she'd had of a life in the spotlight had dwindled some time ago. With the advent of maturity, a real home, possibly even children, had become pleasant notions. As soon as she met him, she realized that Vance Bingham represented security and comfort. He could give her those things. In the world that was re-forming almost before her eyes, she didn't want to be alone.

"I want to," she said stubbornly.

Mrs. Deveraux snorted.

When they arrived at the club Sydney discovered she wasn't the only one leaving New Orleans in the near future.

The men in the band were waiting with a strange sparkle of anticipation in their eyes. She knew they were happy for her or they wouldn't have planned this good-bye party, but there was something more. Curious, she looked at the others while Clyde and Mrs. Deveraux exchanged guarded greetings.

"Okay, what's going on here?" she asked.

Clyde turned to her, that same sparkle illuminating his eyes. "Bobby Dick is leaving us, too."

"Leaving?" she asked, her curious gaze seeking and finding

the man who had become, despite all his resolve, a friend to a white woman. "Where are you going?"

He smiled, his beautiful white teeth a contrast to his black skin. "I'm going to flight school."

"Flight school? You mean they took you?"

"The army air force is setting up a school at Tuskegee Institute in Alabama. I've been accepted."

Sydney threw her arms around his neck. She felt so happy for him. Bobby Dick's home was on the outskirts of New Orleans near the airport. He had a fascination for airplanes that bordered on the fanatic and, ever since Pearl Harbor, had been trying to get into one of the services that would let him fly.

A colored man hadn't much chance in Louisiana or any other place if he wanted to step out of character. Sad, but a fact of life. The navy wouldn't even consider him for flight school. Until now he'd had no luck with the army, either.

This explained the suppressed excitement in the rest of the band. One of their own had finally gotten something he wanted. "Wonderful! Bobby Dick, I'm so happy for you."

Mrs. Deveraux congratulated him also. "You'll have to study hard now, boy, you hear?"

Sydney held her breath. Her eyes went to him beseechingly. Mrs. Deveraux didn't realize how condescending her words sounded. And if anyone had ever been sensitive to condescension, it was Bobby Dick Johnson.

But he merely smiled. "Yes, ma'am." He turned to Sydney. "Where's Vance?"

"He was going to try to get here, but he wasn't sure. He leaves tomorrow morning and he had a lot to do."

Bobby Dick nodded. "Tough. You won't get to have a proper honeymoon," he commiserated. But no one questioned the activities of a man in uniform anymore.

The champagne flowed; Mrs. Deveraux even had a small glass before she reverted to Coca-Cola. Sydney was impressed and touched by the toasts. Clyde presented her with a present. Tears came to her eyes when she opened it to find a piano charm suspended from a delicate gold chain.

"From all of us. So you won't forget."

"As though I could ever forget. But you shouldn't have done this." Sydney suddenly wished that it wasn't too late to change her mind and call the wedding off.

Sydney and Clyde exchanged a smile. She had known these men for four years. They were good friends. "Thank you, all

of you, for the gift," she said as she clasped the hook at her
nape. "There." She touched the charm. "How does it look?"

"It is a lovely piece," said Mrs. Deveraux.

Sydney had to wipe her eyes again as she said her poignant
farewells. The party was winding down and she and Mrs. Deveraux were about to leave when Vance walked in.

The men greeted him enthusiastically. They were fond of her
fiancé and, once Vance got over his Yankee wariness of colored
people, he liked them, too. Clyde put a beer into his hand,
knowing he would prefer that to champagne, and the others
joined in yet another toast to their marriage.

It was odd but suddenly Sydney felt shy as she looked at her
fiancé. Vance Bingham was eleven years older than she was and
exactly the same height. He was black-haired and hard-featured,
not ugly but certainly not corresponding to the popular definition of handsome. He had a tough, worn look despite the pristine
khaki collar and creased trousers of his uniform. His dark brown
eyes, those eyes that saw so much of her, more than she wanted
to show, were wonderfully kind. He knew her too well; he knew
that she was in love with another man, one whom she could
never have. She had told him that much. Why in the world he
would marry her under those conditions—or she him—was a
mystery she had yet to solve.

Tonight, in the parlor of the Victorian house, she was going
to vow to love, honor, and obey this man for the rest of her life.
She wasn't sure how she felt about that vow. He was almost a
stranger.

Vance had no reservations, however. Beer in hand he came
straight over to her and, wrapping his free arm around her shoulder, gave her a kiss right in front of everyone.

Mrs. Deveraux frowned. "I don't approve of the groom seeing the bride on the day of the wedding," she said.

Vance chuckled. "Blame it on the war, Mrs. D."

"You can't blame everything on the war, young man."

Vance winked at Sydney. "I can try."

Sydney returned his smile. Vance had gotten his orders the
day before yesterday. He was leaving New Orleans tomorrow
on a special flight to Seattle, Washington, to begin work on a
project that he didn't talk about much. Not that she would have
understood what he was talking about anyway. He had something to do with the big communications center downtown, that
was all she knew.

Though Sydney would have to follow him to Washington by

train, he didn't want to wait to get married and she had agreed. It was almost as though he knew she would have second thoughts.

Later she found herself standing next to Bobby Dick. "He's a nice man, Syd," he said. " 'Third time lucky.' You remember that and be good to him."

He was referring to two other men who had made an impact on her life in the last four years. Clyde and his boys knew her better than even Mrs. Deveraux did. They had been her support when each of the two men had taken something precious from her. One, her innocence; the other, her heart.

"I will be," she promised. "And you take care of yourself. As soon as I get to Seattle I'll send my address. Write to me and let me know how your training goes."

Bobby Dick agreed and, when she would have moved away, stopped her with a hand on her arm. "Sydney, thank you."

"For what?" she asked.

"It ain't easy for a colored boy to be friends with a white woman."

"But we are," she said patting his hand.

"I know. I made a mistake about you at first and you never rubbed it in. Thanks for that."

"Oh, Bobby Dick. Don't you make me cry." She blinked against the tears that were in danger of ruining her good intentions and squeezed his arm tightly. "Y'all pulled me back from the blackest moments in my whole life. You're my family."

The bump in the mattress that she had no trouble avoiding when she was alone now dug into her back, reminding her that she was a married woman. As of yesterday, at six P.M., in front of the fireplace downstairs.

Vance stirred. With her head on the pillow beside his, she watched her husband as he fought his last skirmish with sleep. She put out a hand to awaken him; then withdrew it. Husband. *Oh, Christ, have I made a terrible mistake?*

Moving slowly so as not to disturb him, Sydney got out of bed and crossed on bare feet to the window as was her custom, but today she stared at the scene with sightless eyes. For a few minutes she steered her thoughts away from the man in the bed and sent them winging northward, toward the house in Mississippi where she'd lived for the first sixteen years of her life. Later today she would return there, briefly. The prospect filled her with unease.

Vance stirred again and she hurried to join him beneath the patchwork quilt, suddenly needing his warmth. The deed was done. She was married and about to leave everything familiar to go to a place that was so foreign it might as well have been in another country.

She'd left familiar surroundings before, she reminded herself, with less money, less maturity, less self-confidence. There had been problems and she'd made mistakes, terrible mistakes, but she had survived them. Her anxiety faded. She could do it again.

Sydney smiled as she watched him. "Good morning, Chief." She felt warm, relaxed for the first time in months, years. Vance was not an exciting lover, but he was tender and patient.

She made an effort not to compare these feelings with the joy she'd felt in another man's arms. The contrast only added to her guilt. The painful ache inside her chest, born of despair and nourished by perfidy, had never completely dissolved. She was unable to push the memories aside.

But her wedding night had been . . . comfortable. Her life would be like that, comfortable, and she tried to convince herself that she was comforted by the prospect. She reached for his hand, drew it to her cheek. "You're very good."

His rugged features softened into a grin. "I hope that means what I hope it means."

"It means much more than that. I'm so grateful."

There was no overt change in his expression, just a shift in light as though a cloud had passed over his face. The smile that followed seemed forced.

Sydney could have bitten her tongue, but she knew enough not to compound her error by further explanation. Vance knew that she wasn't overwhelmingly in love with him; she had never lied to him about her feelings, but the first morning of their marriage wasn't any time to remind him of that, however unwittingly she had spoken. She would have to watch her tongue more carefully. She threw back the covers and reached for her robe. "Would you like some coffee? I'm dying for a cup."

"Yeah. That'd be fine."

She felt his eyes on her back as she measured water, coffee, and set the dented aluminum pot on the hotplate. Vance had put on a robe, too, and sat propped against the headboard. She pulled down the window shade against the heat of the morning, though today for some reason she would rather have had the sunlight streaming in.

He patted the bed beside him. "Sit here while we wait."

Smiling, she gathered up her robe and sat, curling her legs under her. "I wish you didn't have to leave today."

"So do I. But it won't be for long. You'll soon be with me in Seattle."

Vance didn't miss the shadow of misgiving that passed over her face, though she tried to disguise it. He was learning to understand her so well, her moods, her fears. He had known many women but never one as warm, as generous, or as open and honest as Sydney Jackson Bingham. He loved her from the moment he laid eyes on her.

Clyde Cook's was a favorite nightspot for the guys from the communications center; sometimes they acted like they owned the place. His buddies had been pestering him to go with them and finally he agreed. He'd heard of the gorgeous redhead who sang there a couple of nights a week, but he hadn't expected to be struck by lightning when he walked in the door.

Pride touched his heart like a tender finger at the realization that now he could call this exceptional woman his wife. She didn't love him as much as he loved her, but he was hopeful . . . no, more than hopeful. He was sure, sure that someday she would realize how right they were for each other. He needed her, like the air he breathed, the earth beneath his feet; and she needed him. "You are going to be on that train, aren't you, Sydney?" he asked quietly. "You wouldn't let me down?"

Sydney turned away from the appeal in his eyes. "Of course, I'll be on it," she answered, forcing a light tone that she didn't feel. Then she sighed. Lying wouldn't serve any purpose. "You know me, Vance. I'm a southern cracker who's never been more than five miles west of the river," she added, referring to the broad Mississippi that flowed through the city a short distance away. "It's hard to get used to the idea of going all the way to Washington, but don't worry about me, I'll cope."

She heard the relief in his reserved laughter. "I'm not worried in the least, Red. I'd put you up against the Hun himself when it comes to bravery." He took her hand. "I have something else to talk to you about."

"You make it sound very serious," she accused lightly.

"Not serious, just important." He glanced at the clock. "We have to leave for the airfield soon. Before I go I want to make sure you know some things about our financial situation."

"Oh, Vance—" She didn't want to hear this.

He waved aside her protest. "I went by the legal office yesterday and changed my will."

Sydney was taken by surprise. She had never considered the idea of a will. No one in her family had ever had the need of one. She had a small savings account—very small, she thought, recalling her balance. "Should I have made a will, too?" she asked him with a guilty flush.

Vance laughed. "It isn't necessary unless you want to. I don't have much cash myself, but I've always liked to tinker and I have a couple of inventions that could be worth something someday. The navy has been testing one of them at the communications center here, a radio scrambler that lets ships communicate with each other without the enemy being able to understand what they're saying. You remember Lieutenant Adair who was in town last year from Chicago?" The question was rhetorical and he answered it himself. "Of course you do. He roomed here, didn't he?"

She hoped with all her heart that Vance didn't see a change in her expression. "Yes, he did." The very mention of his name brought the pain back in a flood as unstoppable as the river when it swelled over its banks.

"You probably know more of the guys at the center than I do."

That was true, thought Sydney. As the war heated up the club was always filled with men from all branches of the service, but the predominant number came from the tall building downtown that housed the communications center for this area of the country. The club seemed to be their gathering place; every group had one, she knew. She had met many of Vance's coworkers. They returned faithfully, night after night—until suddenly one or the other didn't come anymore. In fact that was how she had met Vance. Ordinarily she didn't date the customers, but he'd been with a group of men she recognized.

"Anyway," he went on, flipping through some papers he'd taken from the pocket of his robe, "the lieutenant is a lawyer from the judge advocate general's office and was here to see that the military use of my patent was done legally and properly. He'll be in Seattle as well. I'm going to try to modify the scrambler for use in planes." He looked up. "By the way—that's classified information. Not that it matters."

Sydney frowned. "What do you mean—classified? I don't want to know any secrets." She forced herself to laugh lightly, grateful for the fact that the mention of Jordan Adair hadn't provoked a visible qualm.

"It doesn't matter, honey. You've already been cleared."

She stared at him, suspicious. "What do you mean, cleared?"

"I mean that when I told the navy we were getting married, they ran a quick check. You were investigated to be sure you weren't a security risk. It's standard." He looked at her, his dark brows drawn together in a puzzled frown. "Are you angry?"

"I'm not angry," she protested, then conceded, "well, maybe I am." The investigators had done a piss-poor job if she was cleared for classified information.

She climbed off the bed and paced the width of the carpet and back, striving for nonchalance. She paused. She hadn't done anything wrong, had she? Only appearances made it seem so. And maybe the appearances were buried forever. God, she hoped so.

Vance watched her closely. She tried not to flinch under his gaze. Too much. All this information was too much to hit her with all at once. First Jordan Adair. Then an investigation. Hell! She raked her fingers through her hair and faced her husband. "Is all this—" she indicated the papers with a wave of her hand and made an effort to smile, hoping they could drop the subject—"really important?"

Vance was sympathetic to her distress even as he was clearly mystified by it. He tried to explain. "My invention was the reason for the navy's sending me to New Orleans in the first place." He reached up to grab her hand and pulled her back down on the bed. She fell ungracefully into his arms. "Thank God." He gave her a quick kiss, then let go. "And that's why we're going to Seattle—I have to be there to handle the necessary modifications and the testing in the planes." Reaching into the pocket of his robe, he brought out another sheet of paper. "I've made a list for you of my assets and the name of my father and sister and a lawyer in Pittsburgh."

"Another lawyer?"

"The navy insisted I have a civilian lawyer, too, to protect my interests. Copies of all these papers have been sent to him and I've drawn up a power-of-attorney for you."

She stared at him, again uneasy, not liking all this talk about lawyers and attorneys, not liking it at all. "What's a power-of-attorney?"

He leafed through the papers. Selecting one, he scanned it.

She twisted on the bed so she could read it, too, but the words were meaningless to her and all this talk about money added to her guilt. Vance was a good man; he deserved better than her.

"You won't have control over the patents, not as long as there's a war going on, but this gives you permission to act on my behalf if anything happens and I can't take care of business."

To give herself time to think, she stood and walked over to the coffeepot. She used the hem of her robe as a pot holder, filling the two white mugs. "I didn't know you were an inventor," she said as she handed one to him. "Will we be rich?" she asked lightly.

Vance laughed. "We may be, or we may never get a penny out of them. Although the device we've been testing here looks good, there's no guarantee yet that either of them is worth the effort it will take to produce and install them." He handed her a packet. "Now, here are your train tickets and the title to the car, signed over to you and your father."

Her hand wasn't quite steady when she took the last paper he held out. They had already discussed what to do with the car. Vance was sure that tires and gasoline were going to be more and more scarce, so he'd suggested they leave it at her daddy's house in McNeill, Mississippi.

At first she had been against the idea. She hadn't been home since she was sixteen years old. Emotions roiled inside her at the thought of facing her father again, but she didn't want Vance to get the idea she was a coward. He had finally convinced her that they were starting a new life together. They could try to tie up some loose ends of the old life. And her relationship with her only relative was definitely a loose end.

The drive to McNeill would take about an hour and a half. She was leaving directly from the airport after she dropped Vance off. Tomorrow she would take the bus back to New Orleans and in a few days she would begin the long train ride to Seattle. "Vance, I wish you hadn't done all this," she said quietly.

He answered her distractedly, flipping through the remaining papers while he spoke. "We have to be practical, honey. I don't know where I'll be for the next few years. You have to be able to carry on."

"Years?" That surprised her. Sydney hadn't paid a lot of attention to the war. It affected her certainly, what with the shortages and the men in uniform crowding the streets of New Orleans; but it was something that was going on in faraway places. "Everyone says the war will be over at least by this time next year. Especially since we bombed Tokyo."

"Well, 'everyone' doesn't know what the hell he's talking

about.'' She was surprised at the uncharacteristic harshness in his tone. ''The bombing was only impressive propaganda. To make us feel good about ourselves because we're losing the war in the Pacific.''

She'd heard Vance expound on this subject before. She thought he tended to overreact. ''We're bombing Germany, too.''

''We're in for hard times, honey, before we turn things around. Things will be a lot worse before they're better. That's why I want you to be able to take care of our business without having to have my signature on every piece of paper. Ah, here it is. This is the name of the hotel where I'll be staying, the Elysium. Here's a number.''

''A hotel will be expensive. Why don't we look for a small apartment?''

Vance laughed now, a dry sound. ''The area around Seattle and Puget Sound is really crowded. We're lucky to find a place.''

''Are you sure they have room for us?'' she asked wryly.

''I checked before we got married, honey. This hotel has been leased for the duration by the navy. The price for rooms is very reasonable. I believe the wives pitch in and do some of the hotel work to keep the place going.'' He studied her face for a long minute. ''You won't mind helping out, will you?''

''Of course not. You forget, I was a maid in a hotel for two years.''

''Then what's the matter?''

She waved the papers in her hand. ''You trust me with all your business? Everything?''

He looked at her, his brown eyes steady. ''Yes, I trust you. You're my wife.''

Sydney felt overwhelmed for a minute. She dropped the papers on the blanket between them and settled against his chest. ''Oh, Vance, you're so good for me. I promise I'll never let you down. I promise.'' She vowed to herself that she would keep that promise. No matter what.

Vance glanced at the clock and at his suitcase sitting open on a chair. Time enough to repack before he had to catch his plane. He tightened his arms around her.

The sun cast a glare on the windshield. It was almost noon when Sydney drove the black coupe into McNeill, Mississippi, what there was of it.

The music from the radio had lifted her spirits during the

drive, prompting her to hope that maybe the visit would be all right after all.

But as she slowed at the crossroads, her heart gave a sudden lurch and her palms were damp around the steering wheel. She felt like a scared sixteen-year-old again.

A few people were about, but no one looked familiar. As for the town itself there was only one change that she could see since six years ago. A Texaco filling station had been built on the vacant lot across the road from the feed and seed store, which also served as the Greyhound bus station. Next door was the Emporium, which, if it hadn't changed, sold everything from denim overalls to rat cheese, from Blue Horse ring binders to rat-tailed combs. Even the filling station didn't look new, though. The red and green and white sign that swung from an iron post had a rusty slash across the ''aco.''

She sped up, leaving the town behind, and now the radio sounded loud in the quiet countryside, the sights lost on her. When she reached the turn off the highway onto an unpaved side road, she stopped to roll up the windows before continuing.

Dust billowed from out behind the car like a wide ruffled skirt. Four miles beyond the turnoff she came to a gate, if it could be called such—two posts, leaning drunkenly against the dubious constraint of stretched barbed wire and snapdragon vines, a rusted mailbox, weeds gone wild in the ditch. She turned right, the car wheels finding the ruts and settling in without her help.

She saw her daddy in the field, the sling harness connecting his shoulder with that of the mule, Yankee, named that because he was so ornery. One hand dropped from the plow to pull a handkerchief from his pocket. He swiped at the sweat on his brow and squinted at the unfamiliar vehicle.

Setting the brake, Sydney opened the door. She stood on the running board so he could see who it was. She waved. Her daddy nodded and tucked the handkerchief back in the pocket of his overalls. Then he grabbed the plow handle, said something to the mule and continued down the row until he reached the end only a few feet from where she stood.

Sydney felt the sweat prickle around her hairline, over her upper lip, between her breasts. A combative fly buzzed the car behind her. ''Hello, Daddy,'' she said.

He didn't smile; she hadn't expected him to. ''You come home to stay?''

She ignored the accusation in the question and shrugged.

"Just for a day or so. I'm married, Daddy." She thought she saw the faintest flicker of surprise, then anger, then nothing. He hadn't changed at all.

He nodded ponderously. "Got to finish my plowin'." With that he clicked his tongue, snapped the reins against the animal's rump, and headed up the next furrow.

Sydney watched him for a minute through a blur, wondering why she'd been crazy enough to expect he'd be glad to see her. Her daddy only allowed himself one emotion and it certainly would never have been mistaken for gladness. He was an angry man.

She took her small suitcase from the back of the car and walked slowly toward the house. It was in even worse condition than she had expected. The unpainted siding showed signs of age; the corrugated tin roof was rusty. The house had never been underpinned, but now the brick supports looked ready to crumble.

As Sydney mounted the steps she saw that planks from the porch had rotted away, falling to the ground beneath. She tested the strength of the ones remaining before she allowed them to take her weight. The screen door was loose on its hinges and scraped the floor when she opened it.

Without thinking, as though she had never left, as though she had done the same thing each day of the intervening years, Sydney left her case in the front room and went straight to the kitchen. She lifted the iron skillet off the drainboard. With a match she lit the flame of the gas stove. She spooned a bit of lard out of a container on top of the oven and flicked the spoon against the edge of the skillet to loosen the lard. She set it on the lighted eye. While the heat dissolved the fat to liquid, she mixed up a batch of cornbread. Then she stopped to put on the old apron that had belonged to her mother.

By the time her daddy came into the house for his noontime dinner, Sydney had fried ham, reheated some peas she found in the icebox, and made a pitcher of tea to go with the cornbread.

He ate without talking much—a few comments about the weather were not just idle conversation to this man; weather was the god that ruled his life. She asked about a few people in town: some of her classmates, their preacher, the couple who had owned the Emporium. He didn't know what had happened to any of her friends, and, he told her, the preacher had gotten a bigger church in Jackson.

He didn't thank her for the meal, nor did she expect him to, just nodded and went back out into the merciless Mississippi sun. She watched him cross the yard. He had aged a lot in the time she'd been away, but he still walked straight, as though a broom handle were shoved up his back, and his shoulders were still frighteningly wide. He was a strong man.

After she cleaned up the dinner dishes she wandered through the rest of the house. The inside was in as bad a shape as the outside. She had to fight back the tears when she saw the state of her mama's upright piano. The keys were yellow and filthy from what appeared to be six years of dust.

The ghosts of children lingered in the room, the children who had come out to the house on Saturdays for their lessons. Not that there were all that many students; few people had money for piano lessons in the aftermath of the Depression; but there were enough to keep her mother's fantasy alive.

Dorothy Jean Jackson had been a dreamer. Each week she had carefully saved a small portion of money from the lessons. "This is for us, Sydney, you and me," she'd say, laughing as she put the coins away. Sydney loved the sound of her mother's laughter.

Dorothy kept the money in a candy box in the back of her drawer underneath her step-ins. "Someday we're going to take a trip together. We'll go to Jackson or Birmingham or maybe even Atlanta. We'll stay in a real hotel and eat in restaurants. We won't tell your daddy until we're ready to go and then we'll just up and leave."

"Why don't we go to New Orleans, Mama? It's closer, isn't it?"

"Your daddy would never let us go to New Orleans. We went there one time when we were first married, back when money wasn't such a problem, and he said he would never set foot in that town again. He thinks it's a den of iniquity."

Not quite sure what a den of iniquity was, Sydney's eyes rounded nevertheless. From her mother's tone of voice, she concluded that New Orleans must be an interesting place. But if her daddy said they couldn't go there, that was it. They wouldn't go.

"When we take our trip, will we come back, Mama?" Sydney had asked.

Her mother had looked sad then. " 'Course we'll come back." She had tried to explain to Sydney that her daddy hadn't always been like this. When they first married they were so happy. He'd loved the farm, then bad luck and bad weather had taken the laughter out of him. "This will be a vacation, that's all. I figure by the time you finish high school I'll have saved enough.''

The trip was her mother's dream. The anticipation kept her spirits up through whatever hard times befell them. During drought and depression, during the annual tornado season, during the years of creeping poverty and the gradual erosion of her relationship with her husband, the dream preserved a portion of her mother's optimism—and hers, Sydney suddenly realized, gazing down at the keys. From her mother she'd learned to gather her strength, to hold onto her own dreams. Over the past few years, there had been a number of times when Sydney had been ready to give up; but then she would hear her mother's soft voice telling her not to quit.

Sydney had her piano lessons every night during the week, after chores, after homework, after the kitchen was clean; then she and her mother would sit side by side on the hard oak bench, whispering together about the dream.

When Sydney was twelve her mother had come down with the lung disease. Dorothy Jean quit talking about the trip, she quit playing the piano—even for Wednesday night prayer meeting—and she quit laughing. When she died they said it was something to do with a fungus caused by living in the Mississippi Delta; but Sydney knew better. Her mama was bone-deep weary from scratching out a living on an overworked farm and living with a man who had completely lost his sense of humor.

After her mother died, Sydney took over the dream, with some alterations. She would continue with plans for the vacation, but, when the vacation was over, she would never return. She hid the candy box from her daddy and added to the hoard from her part-time jobs. She did some baby-sitting; she swept up in the afternoons at the Emporium; she ran errands after school.

The next four years were hell. While she lived Dorothy had been a buffer between them. Without her mother around any trace of goodwill between father and daughter had been completely wiped away. He had always seemed to take some perverse pleasure in punishing her; after her mother's death, he'd begun to beat her badly.

Two days after her sixteenth birthday, four years since her mother's death, she took the box and an old black leather grip that had belonged to her mother's daddy, and she walked the four miles to town. When the bus pulled out from in front of the feed and seed store, she hadn't looked back. And she'd never regretted leaving.

Now here she was back where she'd started from. Everything was different and everything was the same. She went to the kitchen for a rag and cleaned the piano vigorously. She was trying out the chords, singing softly, a song that Clyde had written, when she heard the screen door bang open. She turned to find her daddy eyeing her with hostility.

"You didn't learn that song singin' in church," he said flatly.

Sydney raised her eyes to meet his hard stare. "No, sir. I've been singing professionally."

He snorted and turned away.

That night after a cold supper of leftovers Sydney washed up quickly, then refilled both their coffee cups and joined him at the kitchen table. She explained that she was moving to Seattle, Washington, to be near her husband. She had to clarify where Seattle was. "I want to leave the car with you."

"Why?" he demanded suspiciously.

"As sort of a present, Daddy." She and Vance had discussed this at length. Aside from the fact that she wasn't keen about driving the car such a distance by herself, the war brought on more shortages every day. Tires were scarce as hen's teeth. There even had been rumors about the government maybe rationing gasoline, and what good was a car if there was no fuel to run it?

As they lingered over their coffee, Sydney tried to explain what rationing meant. When faced with her daddy's ignorance on the topic, she felt a surprising birth of feeling well from within her, pity and something else, a softening in her attitude toward him. The old man didn't understand what was happening in his world. He was confused and afraid to admit it. She started to reach out her hand when he spoke.

"Ain't much of a present if I don't get to use it," he said. His eyes narrowed, the old stubborn anger appeared on his face, and she knew what was coming with a clear realization that quickly wiped away both her pity and her soft feelings.

She should have seen it coming; she should have been prepared. Her mother had said he punished her because she was a girl and he was afraid for her. He wouldn't have been so strict with a son.

Sydney didn't buy that. Still she tried to be a good daughter. The Bible said to honor thy mother and thy father. Oh, God, she'd tried. But the fear that now rose to obstruct her throat was familiar, like a remembered taste.

She talked faster and faster hoping to distract him, but finally he interrupted her with a thump of his fist on the table. "There ain't no call for you to go across the country. You oughta stay here and do for me like your mama woulda wanted. You say this man you married is goin' off on a ship."

Oh, God, thought Sydney. As soon as she refused to stay he was going to hit her. "Yes," she answered slowly. "But his ship is docked in Seattle. He wants me there when it's in port."

"Doin' what? Whorin' around with other sailors? Earnin' a little extra money on the side like you been doin' in New Orleans?"

"Oh, Daddy. I'm not—" She gasped as her words were cut off by a slap.

"Don't sass your daddy! You run away, you sing in one of them honky-tonks, only our Blessed Savior knows what all you do; but you ain't gonna sit here in my house and sass me!"

Sydney, holding her reddened cheek, choked off an hysterical laugh. He made it sound like arguing was the worst of all possible sins. Well, she wasn't a kid anymore, and she wasn't going to cower before him, either.

Despite her dread, she lifted her head, met his eyes defiantly. If she had to, she could take one more beating. He wouldn't find her the vulnerable child she'd been six years ago. She had been through too much to back down in front of a bully, even if he was her daddy. She looked straight at him, waiting for the rest of the attack. To her surprise it didn't come. He stared at her for a moment, then turned his back on her and stomped away. She heard the door to his bedroom slam and, finally, slumped in relief.

The next morning Sydney was up early. A night of fitful sleep had been frequently disturbed by nightmares. Her emotions were in painful turmoil.

Her bag was packed; she was dressed for the trip in a white blouse and dark green skirt and jacket. Breakfast was ready to be dished up when her daddy came out of his room. Wordlessly he sat down at the table. She moved about as unobtrusively as possible. He was drinking his second cup of coffee before she found the courage to speak. "I have to leave soon, Daddy. Will you drive me to the bus stop?"

He looked up, his watery blue eyes full of resentment and self-pity. "I got my plowin' to do," he said.

The four mile walk to town gave her a lot of time to think. By the time she reached the feed and seed store/Greyhound bus stop, she felt better. She was no longer uncertain about her marriage to Vance, or about their future together.

Sydney stood at the edge of the tracks, waiting for the train that would take her to Chicago on the first leg of her trip. The station was cool and shaded. She wore the same green suit she'd worn to Mississippi. Mrs. Deveraux had sponged and pressed it for her, asking no questions about the trip.

Her one large suitcase was at her feet. She'd stored the rest of her things at Mrs. Deveraux's house, intending to send for them later.

"Hello, Sydney."

The sound of Nathaniel Bell's voice jolted her. In an instant she was swept back into a maelstrom of fear, dread, violence. She swung around. "What are you doing here?" she demanded, striving to keep her voice level.

The man sauntered to where she was standing. "I heard you were leaving town. Just thought I'd come down and say good-bye."

She didn't ask how he'd heard; he'd always seemed to know everything. He looked as beautiful as ever. The tailored suit sat precisely on his shoulders. When she was a child her Sunday school teacher had warned that the devil was pretty, too; that was what made him so dangerous. She took a breath and gave him a cold, hard stare. "Well, I didn't know I was going to be sent off in such style," she said, not bothering to hide her sarcasm.

"How are you?" His light hair, his smooth jaw, his tailored white suit reflected his obsession with grooming. But power still exuded from him like sweat from a man hoeing cotton in July.

And the platitudes were a bit incongruous since the last time she'd seen this man she had scratched his face and he had almost broken her arm. She noted that the scratch had left a small scar. If she weren't looking for it, she wouldn't have known it was there. Still, it marred his perfection.

A slight twinge of guilt ran through her at the memory of her last conversation with her husband. She had been investigated and cleared, had she? She wondered.

Should she have, at some time in the past years, mentioned the fact that Nate Bell, her employer for a brief time and a man with significant influence in New Orleans, spoke fluent German and had been an intimate of the notorious Baron Edgar Spiegel von something-or-other, German consul general for the Gulf

Coast, before he was expelled from the United States last year? Who should she have told?

Should she have perhaps told Vance? Oh, by the way, honey, I used to work for this man whom I suspect is a spy for the Germans.

She couldn't tell Clyde and the boys. Oh, they knew about Nate all right but not all of it. What could any of them have done? Gone to the authorities with an accusation that there was a white man in New Orleans, a lofty businessman, who spoke the language of the enemy? And had some strange friends—besides those who ran City Hall, that is?

A lot of people in America were descended from Germans. The government couldn't round them up like they were doing the Japs and put them into a camp somewhere. How would they know? Germans didn't have slant eyes; they looked like anybody else.

The only thing that really bothered her about the whole thing was the threat. Why, if he were an innocent man of German descent, would he have threatened her to keep her mouth shut about his friendship with the baron?

"You're looking glorious, Sydney."

"What are you doing here, Nate?" she repeated.

"Business," he said. One eyelid drooped slightly but his gaze was as intimidating as ever. It was a look she remembered with a sudden chill of forboding.

"Well, good luck to you." She turned away.

He caught her arm. She remembered the surprise she'd felt when she first realized the strength in those hands. And the terror she'd experienced at them. But she had been younger then and easier to intimidate.

"Hey, Syd. Don't go away mad," he said cajolingly. "We were good friends once."

"Is that what you called it? Friendship? You used me, Nate. You took a young inexperienced girl and taught her things she should never have known."

"You were no innocent," he snarled. "You were singing in a second-rate club. I just raised you up to a place with more class, that's all. And you couldn't handle it."

"You're right. I couldn't handle it." She wrenched her arm out of his grasp. "Now get this. I'm leaving this town. I want to forget I ever knew you." She turned to walk rapidly along the side of the tracks.

He made a sound of protest and would have detained her forcibly had they not been in a public place.

"I hear you're married."

The words halted her as force could not have done. Her shock showed plainly on her face. "How on God's green earth did you know that?" But the question was absurd, as she reminded herself.

He shrugged. "I heard it somewhere. You know New Orleans; it's like a small town. Especially the Quarter. What ever happened to that other fellow, the one you were going with last year?" Before she could answer, he went on, "I don't think I've met your new husband. He's a navy man, isn't he? Bingham?"

For some reason Sydney felt another, deeper chill go through her when this man spoke Vance's name. "Yes." Where was the damned train?

"He does something secret, I understand."

She didn't reply but he gave her the explanation anyway.

"I had an interesting conversation with an investigator from the navy the other day."

He was interrupted by the sound of the whistle. He glanced over his shoulder to watch as the train rounded the curve into the station. "He found out you used to work for me."

Sydney watched, too. She held her breath; every muscle in her body was stretched tight; still she didn't say anything. Mentally she urged the huge locomotive forward. Hurry. She just wanted to get away.

"I told him . . ." He let his voice trail off deliberately.

Her gaze flew to him and she knew he could read the dismay in her eyes. The noise increased as the engine passed. She had to lean forward to hear his next words.

"I told him you were a very discreet young lady."

She swallowed. The train hadn't quite come to a stop when the conductor swung himself down. He took out his pocket watch, suspended from a heavy chain that linked one side of his broad belly to the other. Apparently he was satisfied at the time, for he smiled as he met her quick glance and touched the bill of his hat.

Suddenly Nate's voice grew cold, very cold. "You are discreet, aren't you, Sydney?"

She moistened her lips. "Yes," she said softly, fearfully.

"Good. I thought so. We wouldn't want your new husband to find out that singing wasn't the only thing you did when you worked in my club."

She opened her mouth to protest, then closed it again.

He smiled with satisfaction. "Ah, it seems you've learned good judgment since we last met. I'm glad you're not inclined to argue with me. What is this?" He stretched out his hand and caught the tiny charm, tilting it to the light. "A piano. How charming. A gift from your husband?"

She felt the delicate chain bite into the back of her neck but she was afraid to object. He fixed her with his frightening gaze and deliberately tightened his hold.

Suddenly, without warning, he closed his fist around the charm and yanked, breaking the thin chain as though it were a thread.

Sydney's shallow breath had caught somewhere in the back of her throat. He was still smiling. She kept her eyes on his curving lips, his shiny white teeth, with a feeling akin to a nightmare.

The smile faded briefly. "You keep your mouth shut if you don't want something similar to happen to you," he told her in a fierce undertone. Then his facade of geniality returned. "Good-bye, Syd. Have a good trip," he said. He turned his back and walked away, her lovely gift still trapped in his fist.

Sydney scurried up the steps and into the passenger car. She found her compartment and collapsed on the seat, still shaking as a result of the encounter. Maybe when the train was out of the station, on the tracks, and headed for Chicago, maybe then she could breathe normally again, maybe then she would feel safe. Nate Bell and her past would be left behind like forgotten luggage on the platform. She would never see the man again.

Or her little charm. She blinked the moisture from her eyes and tried not to regret her loss. She didn't need the charm, she told herself. She had her memories of her friends.

At last the train began to move, slowly at first, then picking up speed. It moved out of the station and into the sunshine.

Chapter 4

Saratoga Springs, New York, May 26th, 1942

"Deanna Durbin played her last picture entirely without makeup. Doesn't that give you the jitters?"

"M-m-m." Faith Parker was listening with only half an ear to her roommate's chatter as she folded a sweater and laid it neatly in her suitcase.

"Look at this," said Gloria as she tossed one magazine aside and picked up another.

Faith looked over her shoulder at the cover of the latest issue of *Vogue*. "Nice," she said.

"Nice? Is that all you can say?"

Faith shrugged. "I'm not really in the mood to look at clothes."

"But it's *you*, Faith. Black and white with that wild pink jacket. It would look gorgeous with your dark hair. Why don't you try to copy it?"

Faith sighed and sat down on the other twin bed. She reached for the magazine. Her experienced eye studied the model on the cover. "It is a nice suit. The pattern's not too complicated. Probably three yards of black linen would do it. And a yard and a half of the polka dot. It would be hard to find fabric in just that shade of pink, though."

Gloria sighed. "It would in Seattle, that's for certain." To Gloria, anything west of the Hudson River was pioneer country. "I'll look for the fabric when I get to New York and mail it to you."

Faith was surprised by the offer. Glo seldom went out of her way for anyone. "Thanks."

"It'll give me something to do. Mother would have loved it

58

if I'd followed your example and learned to sew. It would have saved her all those Bergdorf's bills.''

Faith laughed. Her roommate's mother didn't worry about the bills, and the woman would have been shocked out of her French lace drawers if Glo had ever shown the slightest desire to learn to sew.

Faith and Glo had been roommates, as close as sisters, for three years. Because her parents were dead and her brother was in the service, often stationed in far places, Faith had spent many of her holidays at Glo's home in New York. Glo's family was more like her own than Bill and Kay Parker would ever be.

Laughing, she dropped the magazine on Glo's lap and returned to her packing. ''Don't rush. I probably won't be wearing anything that fine for a long time,'' she said. She picked up the portfolio that held stationery, stamps, and her address book, and waved it at Glo, who knew exactly what the gesture meant. They both wrote to a number of men in the service. Every girl in the dormitory had at least one man to write to; it was the patriotic thing to do. ''Just because I'm not around to remind you, don't forget to keep up your end of the correspondence.'' She slid the portfolio into a side pocket of the suitcase.

''Okay. I just don't understand you, Faith,'' Glo grumbled. ''You're sure to be Queen of the Ice Carnival next year, not to mention the fact that Miles is ready to pin you as soon as you show him any encouragement at all. All the good men are leaving in droves and here you are throwing away a chance with a four-F who is not only gorgeous but rich.''

''I told you, Gloria, I want to do something to make a contribution to the war effort, something more important than writing letters. I'm not interested in sitting around in a dormitory for another year bemoaning the fact that I don't have a date for Saturday night. Maybe it sounds corny, but I want to get right into the middle of things.''

Plumping the pillows more comfortably behind her shoulders, Gloria eyed her with a bored look. ''You always were too conscientious for your own good. War, war, war! I'm sick of the word.'' She giggled. ''I sound like Miss Scarlett, don't I?'' Her look slid to a family picture on the table between their beds, became speculative. ''Although if I thought I'd meet some man as much like Rhett as Wild Bill is, I might become patriotic, too.''

Wild Bill had made a flying trip to the campus last month to try and convince his younger sister to stay in college long enough to complete her senior year. The resulting row had been the subject for a full week's gossip in the dormitory. "My brother's type is the last I'd go for, and you know it," answered Faith shortly. She reached for another sweater.

"But he's so sexy, my dear," insisted Gloria. "The take-charge sort, devil-may-care, sweep you off your feet, and all that."

"Men who sweep you off your feet usually leave bruises," said Faith dryly. She couldn't argue against Glo's observation, though. She had struggled against her brother's take-charge attitude since she was twelve.

"And how would you know?" Gloria rejoined immediately. She rolled on her stomach to study the picture more carefully. "I must say your sister-in-law doesn't seem his type, either," she mused.

Faith grabbed the picture off the table and slammed it face-down on top of the sweaters. She ignored Glo's comment. She'd never understood the attraction, either, she thought. Despite his shortcomings as a brother, she had to admit Bill was a dynamic man; and, in her opinion, Kay Parker was an insignificant light-weight in comparison.

She hated it, too, when Kay tried to mother her. She'd had a mother, she'd lost her, and she didn't need or want a substitute.

The coming months were going to be an ordeal. She intended to find another place to live as soon as possible. She would be twenty-one soon, the legal age to vote, to live alone, to manage her own affairs. But no matter how temporary, living with them would be a trial except for the kids. She loved the kids.

She had been shocked when Kay wrote to explain about the housing situation in Seattle, and the military taking charge of a private hotel to house the dependents. But she was sure Kay was exaggerating. Surely she'd be able to find a small apartment— or even a single room. She couldn't imagine mealy-mouthed Kay Parker as the military's representative manager of this hotel. The place was probably falling apart.

She closed the suitcase with a snap. "There. That's everything except for my overnight case."

"What time do you leave?"

Faith glanced around at the subdued tone that was so unlike her roomie. Gloria's eyes were aimed at the magazine in her lap. She'd begun to flip through the pages again, too fast for comprehension. She knew what Glo was thinking. Their tears had all been shed when Faith first made the announcement that she was leaving college.

It had been difficult to explain her reasons then and it was no easier now. She had an odd, exhilarating feeling of needing to be in the center of things, of not being left out. Life had to be lived, whether you liked the living or not.

Faith didn't feel as though she *was* living, not in the sense of participating in life. She was only in college at this moment because her brother had forced her to finish out her junior year. She was firmly ensconced in the protective cocoon of dormitory life, of schedules and curfews. She wanted to be a part of the real world. She couldn't face another nine months sitting in college, learning about design and fashion, when the war might be over by the time she graduated. On the other hand, she might never get to use her knowledge if everyone didn't get out there and get busy to help win it.

And if she hadn't been afraid of sounding demented, she would have admitted that she wanted to be in on the excitement.

Before December 7th Faith had taken the rumors of a war mentioned in her sister-in-law's letters to be the natural fears of a military wife. The letters from Kay came regularly, like a duty to be performed. Bill never wrote himself.

The rumors had become reality with the bombing of Pearl Harbor. She had wanted to quit school right then, but Bill had more or less blackmailed her into staying by invoking the memory of their parents, saying this is what they would have wanted.

Now that the time had come to actually pack up and leave, she, too, felt the pain of parting and the wrenching change, the uncertainty and insecurity brought on by war. She felt it deeply; but she was more determined than ever to be a part of it all. There had been a Rhode Island Parker in the service of this country since the Revolution. Her brother had followed the family tradition, and now she would be free to contribute as well.

She brought her thoughts back to Glo's question.

"Eight A.M. Isn't that awful? It was the only train I could take that made all the right connections." She made a face.

"Saratoga to New York to Chicago to Seattle. What an appalling schedule."

"I'll be there in three or four days," Faith protested.

"If you don't get bumped for some poor soldier boy, or a big shot traveling for the war effort, or a pregnant girl trying to make the dock with a preacher before her boyfriend's ship sails." Gloria yawned and glanced at the clock. Suddenly she shot up off the bed, scattering magazines, and raced to her closet. "Ohmigod! We're going to be late for tea at the dean's house. I haven't even decided what to wear."

Faith flung down the skirt she'd been folding and hurried to her own closet. This was what she'd be glad to escape. Tea and crumpets, white gloves and party manners, when the world was going to hell in a handbasket.

PART TWO

The war timetable as seen by Democratic Congress-
men: Victory by spring of 1944. They see some chance
for ending the war by the fall of 1943 but believe the
later date will be closer.

Newsweek, May 25, 1942

Chapter 5

Seattle, Washington, June 2nd, 1942

In the Pacific Northwest a finger of water, known as Elliott Bay, points from the fist of Puget Sound toward the east. Pioneers began to build on its rocky shores in 1851, naming their small settlement for the Indian chief, Seattle, who greeted them with friendship. Nature has generously endowed the area surrounding the city with an endless panorama of beauty, majestic mountains, fresh-water lakes, magnificent trees. In 1942 the stunning vistas remained, but the face of the city was changing.

Seattle was staggering under the weight of people who continued to arrive daily. Even before Pearl Harbor the city was bursting at the seams with the influx of workers from all parts of the country. After war was officially declared the influx turned into a deluge not only due to the military forces stationed at the bases nearby, but also because of aircraft manufacturing out at Boeing. A swarm of people descended upon Bremerton, one of the largest ship-building and repair services in the country. The housing situation was bad all over, but it was acute in Seattle. People were even living in renovated chicken houses on some of the islands in Puget Sound.

Boxes of sand dotted the sidewalks—three per block was the minimum required by city government to fight prospective fires. The boxes constituted just another impediment to be sidestepped by the hundreds, thousands of hurrying pedestrians. Hurrying to work, hurrying home, hurrying to eat, to dance, to a party or a rally. Hurrying to meet, to visit, to gossip, hurrying to make love, to say good-bye.

Fire wardens, store wardens, air-raid wardens, roof watchers added to the congestion. But the crowded streets were nothing compared to the congestion on the waters of the bay and the sound.

This morning Kay Parker was thinking of the hundred and one things she had to do as she wielded the hairbrush for a last twist through her daughter's page-boy haircut. First on the agenda was to collect the new arrivals at the train station, help them settle in, and explain the rather unique policy of the Elysium Hotel.

Sometimes she had to remind herself that it had been less than six months since Pearl Harbor. She felt as though she'd lived a decade, a pain-filled decade but one of growth. She wasn't the same person she'd been six months ago.

She had been seasoned by fear.

Bill had reached Pensacola in time to spend Christmas with them but, as he predicted, before New Year's Day he was aboard an aircraft carrier in the Pacific, the USS *Shiloh*, as commander of a fighter squadron. At the end of February, with the war barely two months old, the carrier was badly damaged in a battle off the coast of South America.

Kay had heard the news from her daughter's sixth grade teacher, who had heard it from another mother, who had heard it from God knows where. Dear heaven, she would never forget that day. She was afraid Millie wouldn't, either.

She had taken Billy to play with a friend and thus had been a few minutes late picking Millie up from school. The teacher had been waiting outside, wearing a somber, sympathetic expression. Kay had gotten out of the car, wondering—without really worrying—if Millie was in some kind of trouble at school.

The teacher had not realized at once that Kay wasn't aware of the battle or the damage to the carrier. She prattled on and on until, at last, Kay had put a hand to her temple and screamed at the woman to be quiet.

There had not been many witnesses to her complete loss of control at the news, but her little girl had been one of them and the child hadn't been herself since.

Kay remembered being unable to stop crying, and she remembered holding onto Millie for dear life while someone else drove them back to their quarters. For two days she didn't recall much of anything else, except being haunted by recurring images of Bill's wonderful cocky smile, his bright blue eyes. On the morning of the third day she awoke clear-eyed, imagining all too explicitly what her husband's reaction would be if he saw her like this. He wouldn't criticize, but his disappointment and concern would be tangible.

Somehow, from somewhere, she resolved, she had to find strength within herself to face what this war would bring. If the strength was hidden inside and untapped, she'd have to uncover and use it; if it wasn't there she'd have to manufacture it. She would have to construct a sense of optimism, and she began by convincing herself that Bill was fine. After all, they only knew that the carrier had been damaged. They had no reports of casualties.

That day something happened to Kay; that day she set aside her silly insecurities—most of them, anyway—and forced herself to carry on. She realized at last that her weaknesses were trivial and petty in the face of war.

Two weeks later her determined optimism was rewarded. She heard from Bill. His letter told her that the carrier had returned to Bremerton, Washington, across Puget Sound from Seattle, for extensive repairs, but his squadron had been sent to New Guinea.

At the end of March, she got the best news of all. Bill was being reassigned to the Naval Air Station in Seattle, commonly called Sand Point. She supposed he had to be near the carrier for some reason, but she didn't quibble over the whys and wherefores. She was simply ecstatic that she would soon be able to join him.

As soon as he was back on American soil, he sent for her. One rainy night in early April she had gotten off the train in Seattle with her two children. She'd been met at the station by her husband and his new commanding officer, Captain Douglas Conway, a confirmed bachelor. If the captain had had a wife the whole story might have read differently.

Navy wives, along with other military wives, knew that when an officer chose the service as a career, they were a part of the package. And the captain had presented her with the offer of an assignment, just as though she was under his command, an assignment that left her somewhat taken aback.

The navy had entered into an agreement with a local hotel, he'd explained, to use their facilities as part of an experiment in alternative military housing. Working with him, of course, she would be the navy's liaison with the civilian manger, and the residents of the hotel would take an active part in its operation.

Kay had no choice but to agree. With her newfound determination intact, she had done what had to be done. It was a formidable task. She had no prior administrative experience beyond a stint as president of the Officers' Wives Club at Naval Air Station, Jacksonville. The last two months had been exhausting, but she was pleased with the results, and she had learned a great deal. She had even been interviewed by the local newspaper. The kids loved that.

Millie turned her head toward the mirror to get the full effect of her new haircut. Through the window the morning sunlight picked up shining glints.

"Hold still, honey. I'm almost through."

"I like it. Do you think Auntie Faith will recognize me with my hair short?"

Kay looked at her daughter with a pretense at speculation. Both of the children had inherited those wonderful Parker genes that revealed themselves in deep blue eyes and hair as black as midnight. In a few years Millie would be as beautiful as her Auntie Faith.

Kay just prayed Millie wouldn't be as rebellious as Faith. She supposed she loved Bill's little sister, but she certainly didn't understand her. Admittedly her own childhood had been very different. Her parents would never have tolerated caustic behavior, not even in a teenager. On a farm there wasn't time for rebelling.

So she was hopeful but also had a lot of misgivings about this reunion.

"Without the pigtails you certainly look older," she answered her daughter, tongue in cheek. "Soon Daddy will have to begin fending off boyfriends."

"Oh, Mama," complained Millie. Her fair complexion flushed slightly. She dipped her head and scratched through the tangle of color in her lap, coming up with a length of blue grosgrain. "I'm not interested in boys." She handed the ribbon to her mother. "Were you, at my age?" she asked too casually.

Kay hid a smile as she slid the ribbon beneath the shoulder length hair and tied it in a bow at the crown. Her little girl was almost thirteen years old, only a few years away from being a woman, at least by today's wartime definition.

She gave herself a moment. "I'm not sure. Probably," she admitted.

"We're going to be late, Mama," said six-year-old Billy, bursting into the room. "Auntie Faith will be lost. She won't know what's happened to us." He had already managed a scuff mark on the knee of his long pants.

Kay glanced at her youngest offspring, the image of his father and inheritor of Bill's impatience with delay. "Tuck your shirt in, Billy. Auntie Faith has been traveling all over the country alone for three years. I doubt she will get lost if we are a bit late meeting her."

"Let's go!" he demanded. He disappeared again through the door and into the hall.

Kay hurried into the other room that made up their small suite. "Go after him, Millie. I just have to put on my hat. If Mrs. Bartlett is waiting in the lobby tell her I'll be right there."

"Mrs. Bartlett?" asked Millie.

"Yes, Diane is going home to Idaho, honey. We're taking her to the station." She didn't have to explain why. Her daughter knew that Ensign Willard Bartlett had been taken prisoner by the Japanese after the fall of Corregidor. The final surrender had been discussed at length by the people in the hotel.

Millie paused at the door to the hall. "If Daddy were a prisoner, where would we be going, Mama?" Millie asked without looking at her mother.

That was a good question, thought Kay, but one for which she had no answer. Bill *was* her home. She had no idea what she would do if he were taken.

"Millie, honey, let's don't borrow trouble. For now Daddy's up on Whidby Island instructing new pilots." Whidby was a hundred miles to the north of the city and was a training base for carrier landings. "Soon he'll come back to Sand Point for a while. We're lucky that he's close and we get to see him occasionally. But when he has to leave again he'll expect us to be strong, won't he?"

"I guess." Millie left the room, closing the door quietly behind her.

Kay watched her daughter go, feeling guilty that she hadn't really dealt with the question. She was worried about Millie. The child was too sad, too serious, and Kay knew she was to blame.

Millie hadn't been herself since she'd witnessed her mother's collapse when the *Shiloh* had been attacked. Though Kay had tried to demonstrate her own optimism, Millie had lost her animation and seldom smiled. The new haircut had been an attempt to rekindle some enthusiasm. For a while Kay had thought it was working.

Maybe Faith's being here would help. Despite the fact that

Bill's sister didn't get along well with her and Bill, she'd always been good with the children.

Bill. Kay paused in the act of putting on her hat and looked at her reflection. She had been lucky to have him relatively close for the past two months, but she knew it wouldn't last much longer. He was chomping at the bit.

The base at Sand Point, five miles away, was used primarily to form and re-form combat squadrons for the Pacific Fleet. Four days after Pearl Harbor the Secretary of the Navy had approved a major expansion of the flight program—from 800 to 2500 students a month. He'd set the flight instructors a goal of 20,000 pilots a year by mid-1943.

Bill didn't argue with the necessity for training new pilots and he knew the navy depended on its instructors. He also realized that he had a knack for spotting the winners. But he was making threats—empty ones Kay knew, if the navy didn't—of quitting the navy and joining the army air force if they didn't let him back into this fight.

Soon he would have his wish. Kay sighed to herself as she thought about it. He'd told her the repairs to the carrier were almost complete. He would probably be leaving next month. The United States, outnumbered in carriers when the war began, desperately needed this one in action, especially since the sinking of the USS *Lexington* during the Battle of the Coral Sea.

She shook off the feeling of dread that sat on her shoulders too consistently nowadays and reached for her purse.

She had her hand on the doorknob when someone on the other side knocked, startling her.

"Valerie," she acknowledged as she stepped back to let the other woman enter. "I was just on my way out."

Valerie Adair glanced back over her shoulder, just now taking in the hat, the purse under Kay's arm. "This won't take but a minute," she said, settling into a chair. "I like that dress." Valerie wouldn't be caught dead in that simple style.

What was up? Kay kept a firm leash on her annoyance and remained standing, though she did close the door. "I really do have to go, Valerie. Bill's sister is coming in on the train, and there are others—"

Valerie waved aside the protest. "That's what I want to see you about—the new girls. I understand you've already assigned the ones who came in yesterday and I didn't get any of them. If we're going to keep the coffee shop open all night, Kay, I have to have more help."

Kay pondered her answer. Valerie had a point. *If* they decided on night hours. There were so many services that had gone to twenty-four hour days—the movie theaters, the canteens, the service organizations like the Red Cross and the Y. People whose nights were as important as their days got hungry, too, and nearby restaurants were always crowded. Those who lived in the hotel deserved a place that stayed open.

"It will mean a lot more work for you."

Valerie shrugged. "I can handle it," she said with an indifference that only fed Kay's annoyance.

Valerie could handle it—it was the *way* she did that was the problem. She tended to bulldoze over other, less assertive girls. She had a way of making them feel as though they had to prove themselves every moment. And Kay wound up drying the tears or pacifying the anger that resulted from such high-handedness. The unpleasant task took a large portion of her own time and energy.

Valerie interrupted her reverie. "How many girls are coming in this morning?"

"Three."

"Isn't your sister-in-law one of them?"

"Yes, Bill's sister will be coming in."

"Is she considered immediate family? I wonder if you're not stretching the rules a bit?" suggested Valerie.

Kay had to bite her lip to keep from responding to the nastiness in her manner rather than the question. "She is immediate family. Their parents died when she was twelve."

"Oh." Valerie gave a careless shrug. "Who are the others?"

"Another girl by the name of Patsy Cabot; I don't know anything about her. And Sydney Bingham, the chief's wife."

"Chief?" Valerie's eyebrows went halfway up her beautiful forehead.

Drat! Kay didn't need this right now. Socializing between officers and enlisted personnel was frowned upon in the service, under the theory that it was difficult to follow orders immediately and unquestioningly if the person giving the order was a friend. As the wife of a naval officer, she was aware of the policy. It wasn't democratic and she didn't particularly agree with it, but it was a fact of military life. However, she didn't intend to explain herself to Valerie.

She decided to apply some high-handedness of her own. She opened the door again, pointedly. "Look, Valerie. I have to go.

If we decide to open around-the-clock, there will have to be some conditions set down. We can go into those later.''

''Conditions?'' The idea obviously didn't set well with the senator's daughter-in-law, but it served to distract her. She rose and came to the door to face Kay. ''What kind of conditions are you talking about?''

She had learned since Valerie's arrival six weeks ago, that the best way to get along with the girl from Chicago was to stay calm and indulge her propensity for command, but Kay was tired of being conciliatory. Her own first meeting had been unpleasant. Val had snubbed her, tried to bulldoze her, and questioned her judgment. Before the *Shiloh*, before the change she had wrought within herself, she would have been easily intimidated, but no more would she allow such feelings the slightest toehold.

''I mean the way you treat the people who already work in the coffee shop. They are not your servants, Valerie. They are volunteers, the wives and children of military officers.''

''They have a duty—''

This time it was Kay who interrupted. ''We all have a duty. Think about yours. You're a highly educated, prominent woman. Think about the kind of example you're setting for the younger girls.'' She helped Valerie across the threshold with a hand under her elbow and closed the door behind them. She turned the key in the lock, removed it, dropped it into her purse. ''See you later.'' She headed for the stairs.

''We'll talk about this after lunch,'' Valerie called after her. She stood thinking for a few moments, until an infant's cry from a nearby room brought her back to the present and sent her hurrying up to the sanctuary of her own floor. Thank God she didn't have to deal with a squalling brat. Or listen to one.

Lord, she was tired of this place. She was tired of living in such close proximity to so many people, sick of the noise and the smells. She was tired of having to clear every move she made with a goody-goody like Kay Parker who thought she knew it all. She bristled every time the woman issued an order.

Most of all she was tired of Jordan's being gone all the time. He'd promised—well, he'd intimated—that they would have a lot of time together. But she had been here for six weeks and he had spent exactly fourteen nights with her. He was constantly leaving for some unknown destination, just as he'd been when they were in Chicago. She knew that he still did work for people in Washington, D.C., in addition to his navy duties.

Jordan was familiar with the framework of the national manufacturing structure as a result of his work with the Truman committee. But the work was more secret now; he didn't share anything with her anymore. Someone had called last week—she thought it was Senator Truman himself—wanting Jordan to look around for a manufacturing facility in the area, one that could be quickly converted to handle something or other. Jordan wouldn't say what. He'd been gone ever since.

The fifth floor was quieter, thank goodness. She fished in her pocket for the key. Jordan would be here in an hour. She needed to change and touch up her makeup before he arrived.

Maybe tonight they could finally spend a nice evening together.

Commander Bill Parker was not, as his wife assumed, at the Whidby Island base; he was 1700 miles from Seattle and 400 miles south-southeast of a little godforsaken island in the Aleutians known as Unalaska.

His plane was big and heavy; he much preferred his little Wildcat. But this temporary duty assignment was to assess an impending situation and report on it to his superiors and that aircraft wasn't really designed for reconnaissance. Regardless of the plane it was good to be flying a mission again. He leaned his head to the left, his gaze traveling a familiar path along the silver fuselage to the nose. Dutch Harbor, Alaska, a lonely outpost on a lonely edge of a country, was shrouded in mist. They called this area the "weather factory of the world" and he believed it. Gray was a color he would always associate with the Aleutians.

He was worried as hell. Dutch Harbor, the only town on the island beneath him, had been a suspected Japanese target from the very beginning of the war.

"Europe First" was the policy of the Roosevelt administration, but that didn't mean they would permit Japan to walk across the Pacific with no opposition. On the 20th of May, American cryptologists had finally broken the Japanese code and suddenly the Allies became aware of enemy plans to invade two places in the Pacific, Midway Island and the Aleutians.

The navy knew that one of the attacks would be a full-scale attack and the other would be a smaller, diversionary tactic. The question was which would be which, and greater minds than Bill's were wondering.

Reinforcements had been sent to both areas, but the lack of

enough ships and aircraft to protect both installations equally had forced a choice on Admiral Nimitz and the Pacific Fleet.

A full-out attack on Alaska, a long curving sweep through the sparsely populated area of western Canada, and the Pacific Northwest would be vulnerable to a Japanese invasion of the mainland of the United States, which was their eventual goal. But, Admiral Nimitz had reasoned, and Bill was inclined to agree, the Japanese way would most likely be straight across the Pacific.

If the Japanese took Midway Island, Hawaii would be their next step. With Hawaii as a launching point the Japanese could hit right in the middle of the West Coast and divide their forces into a north and south flank, heading north to Seattle and south to San Diego at the same time. It would be a faster way to immobilize the ship-building and repair facilities, and the military forces of the Pacific, whose attention was focused on the destruction of the Japanese.

Under such an assault the United States would have to turn its attention to defending its own shores, leaving Russia, Europe, and Africa to fend for themselves. Once Britain had been dealt with, the German forces could move in on the East Coast of America. The country would be fighting on both coasts.

It was a simple plan, and a brilliant one, for the domination of the world. And they key was the United States with its extensive borders to defend.

Now the first step was about to be taken. And would the footprint be left on Midway Island, the tiny atoll in the Pacific, or on the rocky shores of Alaska?

Nimitz had finally made his decision. Bill knew that some of the advisers had argued to the end for Alaska as the primary target, pointing out that it offered another front for Japan's battle against Russia as well. But the admiral had held to his belief and now he had committed the men under him irrevocably. The entire mass of the Pacific Fleet was mobilizing in the waters around one strategic island.

Midway.

But even as a secondary target Alaska was not dismissible. Upon his arrival Bill had been grateful to see the significant buildup of men and equipment. He'd been ordered to help with reconnaissance.

What if we're wrong? he thought again. What if, over the horizon, the entire Japanese fleet is waiting in that fogbank? Ah, hell. He couldn't think like that now. It was too damn late. His eyes swept through an atypical break in the clouds to scan the rugged coastline beneath him. The decision was made, and they would have to live with it.

A down draft caught the plane, and he pulled back on the stick slightly to correct his altitude. Eyes scanning the seas below him, he was listening to a soft rendition of an Old World War I tune broadcast from the base at Dutch Harbor and thinking that this was turning out to be a wild-goose chase, when a word from the navigator interrupted his musings.

"I did a fuel check, Commander. Soon it will be time to turn around and head for home."

Bill glanced at his watch, surprised to find that they'd been gone for as long as they had. He hated to give up just yet. He knew there was *some* force in these waters, and he had to evaluate the strength of that force. What if they missed them; what if they were just out of sight? "How much more time do we have, Cochoran?"

"The limit, sir?"

Bill nodded.

"Maybe fifteen minutes, stretching it, but I don't know what kind of head winds we'll meet going back. If they're severe they could use up a lot of fuel."

"I sure wouldn't want to go down in these waters, Commander," his copilot on this mission put in. The youngster from South Dakota had impressed Bill with his calm acceptance of this dreary duty. He spoke as though instructing a greenhorn. "Even with our protective gear, we'd last only about ninety seconds."

Bill took no umbrage at Thomas's tone. He had flown every type of plane the navy used, under all kinds of conditions, in a lot of places, but this was his first foray over Arctic waters, and he was perfectly willing to listen to the ideas of men more experienced than he in terms of the weather. "Okay, son, let's go in. Give me a heading."

He banked to his left. As he came around, he caught a glimpse of something far off to the south. "Thomas, three o'clock on the horizon! What do you see?"

Thomas peered through his binoculars. "What did it look like, sir?"

Bill couldn't identify what he'd seen in the distance, not specifically; it was more a disturbance on the ocean than anything else. And the ocean was far from calm this far north. Or maybe not. The seas moved in quick undulating rhythm; maybe what he saw was a fixed point, something *not* moving in rhythm, a diversion in the flow. Damn this mist that seemed to hang over everything! "I'm not sure, but I'm going back around for another look."

He continued the bank until he was back to his original heading.

"I see it. Ah, shit! Can we get closer?"

"Not without being spotted ourselves. But we have to take a chance. What do you think it is?"

"It's a carrier, sir," said Thomas quietly lowering the binoculars. "The task force won't be far away."

It wasn't. In a very few minutes they had spotted a cruiser, two destroyers, and two transports. Transports—that meant an attempted landing. If this were the diversion it was going to be a serious one, but not, thank God, the might of the Jap fleet.

Another recon plane was searching to the west of their flight plan and still another to their south-southeast. He was confident now that they wouldn't find much.

This time when he banked, Bill got the hell out of there and headed back to Unalaska as fast as this lumbering giant would take him.

Chapter 6

Friendships grew rapidly in wartime. Like uncultivated wild flowers they often sprang from the most illogical roots to reveal unexpected beauty. Wartime, too, was ever quick to pull those roots out and these days Kay was always saying good-bye to someone she liked.

She descended the stairs into the lobby, a fake smile plastered onto her face. Diane Bartlett had become a very close friend in the relatively short time they'd known each other and despite the eight-year disparity in their ages. Perhaps it was the similarity of their backgrounds that gave them so much to talk about when they first met.

Returning to her parents' farm in Idaho was surely the best thing for Diane. She had changed from a shy girl to a woman, bitter and disillusioned and angry. Her skin had taken on a gray pallor, her steps were clumsier than her pregnancy would account for, and the bright gleam in her eyes had diminished to a dull glimmer. She had been that way ever since she'd gotten the news about her husband's being taken prisoner by the Japanese.

"Ready, everyone?" Kay said. "No, Diane, I'll take your big suitcase. Millie can manage the small one."

"I'd rather he was dead," said Diane, abruptly, unexpectedly.

Kay glanced automatically in the rearview mirror but the kids were engrossed in a squabble. She kept her voice low as she admonished, "Diane, don't say that. As long as he's alive there's hope." Even as she uttered the cliché, she wondered. Three months ago she would have been shocked by the woman's attitude. Now a small part of her agreed. The waiting would be unbearable. Horror stories filtered back, of torture, of mutilation, of mental and physical torment so excruciating that breakdowns were common among Japanese prisoners of war.

The country was teetering on a razor-sharp edge, frantically trying to train the men, to build the ships and planes that would equalize the situation on all fronts. And the only question remaining was: Would they be in time?

Diane went on, "You heard the nurse the other night at the Red Cross group. They bombed the hospital! Marked with a fifty-foot red cross and they bombed it. These people are barbarians, Kay!"

Evacuated by submarine only hours before the surrender of Corregidor, the nurse had painted a vivid picture. The fields next to the tiny hospital lined with rows of cots, the overflow of the wounded. Hundreds of men watching their own death rain down from the sky.

Kay took one hand from the wheel and briefly touched the twisting fingers in her friend's lap. The skin was as cold as death. "I never should have agreed when you insisted on going to hear the nurse's talk."

"It wouldn't have mattered. I'd have gone alone."

"Diane, you're overwrought. Please calm down. This isn't doing you or the baby any good."

A short, harsh grunt of response was all Diane allowed herself but the implication was there, as clear as if she'd spoken aloud—what do you know?

Kay hoped her own sigh hadn't reached Diane's ears. Diane's derision was most likely deserved. How could she offer counsel to her friend, or complain when she was tired or discouraged or worried? Even the two weeks when she hadn't known Bill's fate, she'd not felt the terror of having her husband in enemy hands. How would she react? In spite of all good intentions she would probably fall apart again.

Wild Bill had been in some tricky situations but, so far, he seemed to lead a charmed life. She wished there were some wood to knock on.

"Mama, you missed the turn," said Millie from the backseat.

Damn, what a waste of gasoline.

The King Street Station was a cavernous granite and brick structure that could have been designed in the Middle Ages. Huge arched ceilings amplified the echoing sounds of incoming and departing trains—and the voices and movement of the people they were there for—to a pitch that was almost painful. The people were like ants swarming directionlessly in and out, over and through a particularly big hill.

They pushed through the crowd and skirted a slice of mosaicked floor where a janitor and his mop fought a never-ending battle to keep the floors relatively clean.

Out on the tracks they passed a girl in a Red Cross uniform with a basket on her arm handing free cigarettes through the windows of a troop train that had already begun to move. The boys tossed letters into her empty basket to be mailed home. They hung precariously through the openings, laughing and joking with her, begging for a last glimpse of leg. She smiled and waved. Not until the train was around the bend did she let her bright smile falter and her straight shoulders sag.

Diane seemed caught by the scene, but when it was over she moved quickly toward her train, which waited on the adjoining track. She handed her ticket to the conductor, who also took charge of her luggage and helped her up the portable steps into the vestibule. She turned to smile, said a hasty good-bye to the three of them, and disappeared into the passenger car as though she couldn't bear to look at them any longer.

Neither of the children seemed to notice anything amiss, but Kay stood watching the empty opening for a minute, more than surprised by her friend's transience. Had she said the wrong thing when she'd urged Diane to think about her own health and the health of her baby? Or had it been the sight of all those young men's faces as they headed for God knows where?

Finally she pulled Billy back from where he was inspecting the wheels, spoke to Millie, who was inspecting the Red Cross girl, and she and the children returned to the station newsstand to await the arrival of the train from Chicago.

The station was still packed with, and smelled of, hundreds of bodies. Restless at standing still, Billy strained against Kay's grip, but she held on resolutely. Heaven only knew how long it would take to find him again if he took off through the crowd.

A glimpse of bright color was rare enough in the surroundings to warrant a second look, but even without the scrap of red perched on her head, Faith Parker would have rated one. Kay smiled uneasily at the sight of Bill's little sister, who seemed to be engrossed in a flirtation with a sailor in dress blues. He was struggling in her wake with two suitcases as well as a seabag, while Faith's delicate build seemed burdened with only a makeup case and a purse tucked neatly under her arm.

Kay knew from experience that there wasn't a delicate bone

in her sister-in-law's body. Tennis, skiing, riding kept her in shape. She was as strong physically as she was strong-minded. Just like her brother.

Millie, who was almost as tall as her mother, spotted her. "Auntie Faith!" she called, waving her arm.

Faith said something to the sailor. Grinning, he edged in front of her, clearing a path.

Setting aside her wariness, Kay smiled and opened her arms as she would have done to her own daughter. After a second's delay Faith hugged her back.

Kay drew back. "Let me look at you." Faith had changed— and she hadn't changed at all. Though now a woman, she still wore a hint of the same look she had worn years ago when she came to live with them, the look of a young girl, younger than Millie, cast adrift by the death of her parents. She wondered if Faith would notice the changes in her.

Bill had not liked it when they received the telegram from Faith telling them that she would be arriving today. He was still concerned about his sister's education. She lacked only one year, he had argued; she could speed that up by attending summer school. Kay had enough to do without having to ride herd on a headstrong young woman like Faith. And, lastly, where the hell were they going to put her?

He had a point there. Kay understood his argument; but she also understood that once Faith Parker had made up her mind, there was no changing it. She had already explained the situation in a letter. Finding another place to live was impossible, at least for now. Faith would have to sleep in the room with the children, she would have to do her part in the hotel, but if she still wanted to come they would be happy to have her.

"Millie? Is this Millie?" Faith said dramatically. "My heavens, you've grown right up. And so beautifully, too."

Millie blushed at her aunt's compliment. "I just cut my hair."

Billy clamored for his share of his aunt's attention. "I'm almost six," he informed her.

Kay turned to the young sailor who stood by with Faith's bags. "Please forgive our rudeness. I'm Kay Parker."

He dropped one of the suitcases he was holding and swept off his hat. What a nice young man, thought Kay.

"That's all right, ma'am. I'm John Harrison. Pleased to meet you."

Faith pivoted, a child under each arm. "John is from St.

Louis, Kay. He was kind enough to help me with my luggage. I hope we can give him a ride.''

Kay wondered if her sister-in-law had arranged this just to annoy her. She did some mental rearranging of the other passengers she was expecting and forced herself to smile. "Of course we can. You'll just fit if Faith holds Billy on her lap.''

"I could ride on the running board!'' offered Billy.

He was squelched by a look from his mother. "I am meeting two other women who were to come in on this train.'' Kay looked around but the human sea was still too thick to pick out anyone traveling alone. "We'll have to wait until the crowd thins out, though.''

"I wouldn't want to put you out, Mrs. Parker.''

"Nonsense, John. I'm lucky enough to have a car and a bit of extra gasoline at my disposal. We'll squeeze ourselves in. Where are you going?''

"The ferry terminal. I'm reporting to East Port Orchard.''

"The ferry terminal is on the way to our hotel.''

"I thought hotel rooms were scarce in Seattle,'' John remarked.

"This is one the navy has leased for the duration to house dependents. We run it ourselves.''

"Run it yourselves?'' He might as well have added, "officers' wives?''

Kay laughed at his astonishment. A lot of things were changing; a lot of things were vastly different and would become even more so. "The former manager stayed on, as did the head chef and a slim housekeeping staff, but we do everything else,'' she explained with a pride she didn't try to conceal and as much for Faith's information as for his. "I'm a sort of liaison to the manager, hence the gas for the car.'' Her attention was caught by the sight of a young woman standing alone in the now-thinning crowd. "Excuse me. This may be one of the ladies that I'm supposed to meet.''

She approached the woman, nicely dressed but a little lonely looking and obviously very tired. "Mrs. Bingham? Mrs. Cabot?''

"Cabot,'' the woman answered flatly. "Are you the hotel manager?''

"Sort of. I'm—''

Her words were cut off with the wave of a gloved hand. "My bags are over there. It was hell finding a porter to get them even this far.''

Kay stared for a minute at the woman and, at her side, the mound of luggage, which she seemed to assume was Kay's responsibility. Not another Valerie, Kay thought with a sinking heart. Lord, deliver me from spoiled children. She indicated the mound with a brusque nod. "You shouldn't have dismissed him then. You have a lot to carry and it's quite a long walk to the car." Ignoring the woman's offended gasp and Faith's raised brow, she deliberately turned away to look for the other passenger she was expecting.

The incoming crowds had dispersed and the only person left by the newsstand was a tall, flamboyant redhead who gave her a questioning smile. She approached Kay slowly. "Are you by any chance Mrs. Parker?" She had a thick southern accent, like honey dripping from a spring hive.

This was the wife of the quiet, soft-spoken Chief Bingham? Kay managed to hide her surprise. Her first impression was that the girl's makeup was much too heavy for daytime; then she realized that the glowing skin, the ripe red lips were Mrs. Bingham's natural coloring. She was tall for a woman and her eyes and mouth were a bit too large for her face.

Kay returned the smile weakly. The girl couldn't be much older than Faith and yet there was a worldliness about her beauty that caused Kay to shudder inwardly. She'd be willing to bet Mrs. Bingham had been around. She just hoped Faith didn't decide to take direction from her. Faith had led a sheltered life.

Just then a man in mufti jostled Mrs. Bingham's elbow, causing her to sway slightly on her extravagantly high heels. He caught her arm to steady her. "I'm sorry," he said. What began as a perfunctory apology changed abruptly as he scanned her face and figure.

His reaction was instant and predictable. Kay acknowledged that the woman was beautiful enough to rate the spontaneous response, but she wasn't amused. Women like this often caused trouble.

"Please excuse me," the man said again in a warm, intimate tone. "Are you all right?"

"I'm just fine," Sydney reassured him in her honeyed drawl. "Think nothin' of it." But she didn't encourage him beyond the simple reassurance; Kay had to give her that.

He seemed reluctant to release his grip but finally, after a moment of dead silence, he recovered and hurried on his way.

The redhead gave Kay an unsteady smile, and Kay sent up another prayer: Lord, save me also from a femme fatale. "Are you ready?'' She tried to be pleasant but inside she was thinking: trouble with a capital T.

"Yes, ma'am.'' She switched her purse from under one arm to the other and reached for her bags.

Suddenly Kay noticed something she hadn't been aware of before. Sydney Bingham's hands were shaking. Though she gave the appearance of being self-confident and in control, there was a definite tremor there. The unexpected sign of vulnerability touched Kay. Femme fatale or not, the young woman was nervous. "We're glad to have you at the Elysium, Sydney. May I call you Sydney?''

"Oh, yes, ma'am, please. I'm not much for formal— formality.''

"Neither are we at the Elysium. We don't have time for it these days. Do you have just the two cases? Good. Come along and meet everyone.''

Thank heavens for the station wagon, thought Kay a few minutes later as she maneuvered into the traffic. She could barely see out over the mound of luggage in the back. She hid her wicked glee at the thought of Patsy Cabot's reaction when she saw the single small closet in her room. The children were chattering to Faith; to give her her due, she had always been a help with them. Maybe it wouldn't be so bad after all.

Faith asked, "Has the commander calmed down yet?''

The children had been distracted by a word from the sailor in the backseat. "He will,'' Kay finally answered, quietly but firmly. "He's disappointed that you would quit school with only one more year to go.''

"I haven't quit,'' argued Faith lightly. "I'm taking a sabbatical for the duration.''

"It's hard to go back,'' Kay warned. I should know, she added to herself. She had quit school after her freshman year to marry Bill. Her intentions were the best; but they'd been married for twelve years now and, though the opportunity to finish school had arisen once or twice, the timing hadn't been right. She'd accepted the fact that she would probably never get her degree. She often wondered if Bill was disappointed in her. Sometimes, in the way he looked at her, she was sure he was. He held great store in education. Her own father and brothers didn't.

In their opinion, shared by most of the people in the farming community in Nebraska where she grew up, if a girl was a good cook and kept a neat house, she would make a good wife, which was what a sensible girl would end up doing, anyway. Her mother had been the one to fight for her when her high school principal had recommended her for a scholarship to go to college.

Bill had never actually said anything about her lack of education but that didn't keep her from wondering how he felt. She also wondered why she had never asked him.

"Do you know yet when his—" Faith was deliberately off-hand "—when the *Shiloh* will leave?"

Kay's own smile wasn't as steady as it should have been. She concentrated for a minute on the left-hand turn from King Street onto Alaskan Way, the wide boulevard that ran parallel to the waters of Puget Sound.

"No. He'll probably come in some night and tell me they sail tomorrow. That's the way it works here."

Faith nodded. " 'Loose lips sink ships,' " she quoted from the latest propaganda poster. "Will he be at the hotel when we get there?"

Kay avoided answering directly. Bill had been gone for two weeks and she had no idea when he'd return. "He divides his time mostly between Sand Point, the Naval Air Station which is close by, and Whidby Island, further up the coast. If he were at Sand Point he would be able to come home every night. It's in the northern part of the city near the university. So he must be at Whidby. Maybe he'll get home by the weekend."

"Ah, the frustrating life of a military wife, never knowing where her husband is or when he'll be back. Don't you ever get jealous?"

God, yes, she was jealous, but she managed to hide it well. Sometimes it wasn't easy. Bill Parker, as handsome as his sister was beautiful, had that appealing sophistication that made women melt in their shoes. Jealous? It was amazing, thought Kay, that their marriage had been as content as it was and had lasted as long. "Faith." There was a warning in the one word as Kay struggled to maintain an even expression. She hoped Faith wasn't planning to start mischief again.

As soon as she'd spoken Faith wished she could take back the words. She was fully aware of Kay's insecurity where Bill was concerned. She had vowed to herself that this time there would be no discord between them. She would get along with Bill and Kay; she would, damn it. She kept her expression amiable, her voice light. "I know, I know. Better you than me. I'm going to marry an accountant," she said, trying to make a joke of her jibe.

Kay raised a brow and grinned, relieved to change the subject. "An accountant? Is there something I should know?"

"Or a lawyer or a banker. Someone who will come home every night to me and the kiddies. I don't want to have to move every three years, or kowtow to the admiral's wife, or nurse the measles and whooping cough all by myself while he's off somewhere."

"Well, I hope you aren't planning an announcement anytime soon. Your brother's resigned now to your quitting school but that would really set him off again."

"Marry me tonight for tomorrow I might be dead? God, no. I have some crazy friends who've done that but I don't intend to marry anyone until this beastly war is over."

Kay was relieved to hear that. One of her unspoken fears for Faith was that she would do just such a thing although she knew that, underneath her rebelliousness, Faith was a good girl. Seattle was filled to overflowing with men, all of whom seemed to have appetites beyond what Faith had been reared to expect. "Just so he doesn't convince you to do anything else, either."

"I don't believe it. My loving sister would deny me the pleasures of sex."

Kay shot a quick warning glance at the children between them, but they were both hanging over the seat, talking to the sailor.

At her sister-in-law's glare, Faith laughed. "Oh, Kay, I'd almost forgotten your good midwestern morality. New York seems positively decadent in contrast to you."

From the backseat Mrs. Cabot interrupted, making it obvious that she'd been listening to the conversation. "You're from New York?" She spoke in a tone that indicated she was surprised to find a civilized person in the wilderness.

Faith met Kay's smile, her eyes wide with amusement, and turned sideways in the seat. "I've spent a lot of time there, yes," she told the woman.

There followed a discussion of schools and do-you-knows that left Kay free to her own thoughts. She hoped Bill would be waiting at the Elysium. Every moment together had become very precious to her.

She'd been honest when she told Faith that she had no idea when the carrier would be embarking; but wives developed a sixth sense about those things. She was certain it was now a matter of days, perhaps even hours. There were a lot of reasons for her feelings. She had learned over the years to read unwritten signs, to hear unspoken warnings. A man began to talk about his affairs, to coach his wife and children about the procedures they should follow if he wasn't around to tell them what to do.

And then there was always the truism—the navy never lets your man stay close long enough for you to get used to having him around. Never.

And good navy wives do not dwell on such gloomy predictions, she reminded herself sternly as she fixed her attention on the others.

She met the hesitant smile of Sydney Bingham in the rearview mirror. The girl hadn't said a word since they'd left the station. Odd that the only quiet person was the one who looked most like a talker. Kay was puzzled by the difference between Sydney and her husband. The chief was quietly friendly, a serious man who seemed a bit of an innocent. There was nothing innocent-looking about his wife. In the bright daylight she looked much younger than she had in the train station; but, strangely, she looked older, too. There was a bleakness in her eyes that spoke of experience beyond her years, of disillusionment and loneliness.

The huge barnlike building of the ferry terminal loomed up before Kay, and she quickly made a sharp turn into the left lane, out of the line of cars waiting to drive aboard. "Take that walkway, John," she said over the sound of a ship's horn, indicating the wooden structure above their heads. "It will lead you to the ferry to Bremerton. It's about an hour's ride. Then you'll have to get the nickel ferry over to Port Orchard. That's just a short hop across the inlet."

The young man had the door open as soon as she stopped, mindful of the cars behind them.

"Call me if you get into town, John," said Faith.

He blushed, obviously pleased at her request. "I will. First chance I get. Thanks a lot, Mrs. Parker. I appreciate the ride. Nice to have met you ladies." He was away with a wave.

Kay ground the gears slightly as she made another left turn and headed back up the steep hill, her thoughts speeding ahead toward the hotel and the hope that Bill would be waiting.

Chapter 7

*Always take the time to study the people around you, Sydney;
learn to judge human nature. Then you'll know what to expect
when you're in an unfamiliar situation.* Mrs. Deveraux's words
came back to her as she looked out upon the landscape.

Well, you couldn't get a helluva lot more unfamiliar than this.
She had finally become accustomed to the sight of mountains
during the trip as the train had passed over and around and even
through them. She had become used to their craggy borders but
was not at all comfortable in their shadow. She didn't like mountains. They were huge and dark and forbidding. Give her a beach
anytime, hot and bright in the summer, and flat. Even the shadows of the Louisiana bayou weren't as scary as those mountains.

Sydney brought her gaze away from the Olympic range visible across the water and contemplated the shiny hairdo in front
of her. Kay Parker had tried—barely—to hide her dubious as-
sessment when they'd first introduced themselves. Well, it wasn't
the first time a woman had looked at her with suspicion, and
she was sure it wouldn't be the last. Still, the older woman's
reaction had surprised her.

Mrs. Parker seemed a . . . motherly sort of woman, thought
Sydney, then she wondered why that word had sprung to mind.
Kay certainly didn't fit the wartime stereotype of a mother.
Magazine advertisements always pictured mothers with round
faces and bodies and a gray halo—always. Kay was slender and
her hair was dark brown with highlights of sunny gold. Her eyes
were wide and honest. Not a beauty, but pretty.

The sister-in-law was the beauty. Faith Parker had the look
of a movie star. Sydney frowned slightly, trying to recall which
one. Jennifer Jones, she decided. That dark hair and those huge
blue eyes, the fine, delicate features and air of fragility would

make every man who saw her want to take care of her. And her clothes were straight out of *Vogue*. She'd mentioned New York. . . .

Sydney sighed enviously. Dressed in clothes from New York she would still look like what she was, a southern farm girl, a cracker, with a passable voice.

Vance didn't seem to mind, though. At the thought of her husband, misgivings returned in a flood. Oh, God, why had she married him? The man was practically a stranger. She could barely remember what he looked like and here she'd come half-way across the country, left everything—she paused in her thoughts—everything? What had she left? Her only living relative was her daddy and he didn't care about anything except where his next dinner was coming from. She made herself think the word. "Alone," she whispered.

"Did you say something, Sydney?" asked Kay Parker.

Sydney met the gray eyes in the rearview mirror. "No, ma'am."

"Please, leave off the 'ma'am.' It makes me feel ancient." She smiled.

"Yes, ma—Kay." She had forgotten that Yankees didn't like the southernism. They preferred a quick, sharp yes or no, reserving the form of respect she'd been taught from birth for their servants to use.

Mrs. Parker—Kay—wasn't rude about the correction. But Sydney Jackson Bingham would never fit in with these people, she realized, desperate for a minute. Never in a million years. She would be an outsider again, like she'd been all her life. The woman next to her, Mrs. Cabot, had held herself as stiff as a board, leaning away as though she was offended by Sydney's very presence. When the sailor got out she had quickly scooted across the seat, as far away from Sydney as possible, to hug the door. I should have worn a hat, thought Sydney. I would have looked more genteel in a hat.

Well, she might be different, but she refused to be a coward. She sat up straighter. She was as good as any of them with their New York clothes and fancy manners. This move, this marriage, was the beginning of a new life for her. She would conform to their edicts, she would learn to get along; but she would not let them make her feel low. If she found herself in an uncomfortable position, she would simply ignore them.

A girl couldn't depend on anyone but herself. That was a lesson she'd learned the hard way. Vance was a good man, they didn't make them any better. She had a future with him, and no one was going to take this opportunity away from her. He knew she'd been hurt by another man; he knew she didn't love him the way he loved her. She had been honest from the start. That was one thing she would never do—lie to herself or anyone else. He'd accepted the truth of it. He'd even entrusted her with all his business. The memory of that last morning in New Orleans restored her confidence more effectively than all her self-sermonizing. Vance had given her a beautiful gift, his faith, and she would never abuse it.

The car stopped. "Here we are," said Kay.

Sydney looked out the car window. In New Orleans, a city of opulent hotels, this one would have been as out of place as a nun in the Roosevelt Ballroom. The exterior bespoke quiet, privacy, and elegance. Instead of the usual maroon awning extending over the sidewalk to protect the hotel guests from the elements, glass doors, almost twice her height and framed in elegant bronze, were set back into the building twelve feet or more. Along one of the resulting walls and bolted to it was a decorative wrought-iron bench; in the other, a smaller door that was half glass. Facing the sidewalk were square granite planters, hip-high, overflowing with baby pink begonias, their dark leaves rich with verdant color in the afternoon sunlight. Over the top of the recess an arc of individual brass letters, flush in the marble facade, spelled out the words, THE ELYSIUM HOTEL.

Sydney felt a momentary qualm, a shiver, as if a rabbit had run over her grave. She grimaced, remembering the first time she had been taken to a hotel—the Roosevelt, as a matter of fact—for dinner. With its lighted marquee, it had looked like one of the places she'd seen in movie magazines, where a beautiful star was being helped out of the car by her handsome leading man as if she were a princess. That night Sydney had pretended she was one, too, as her escort had opened the door for her. He had been charming.

She had held out her hand; she could still feel the warmth of his fingers as they closed supportively around hers. Lord, she had been green. Very, very green.

Nate Bell had introduced her to a part of New Orleans beyond the French Quarter, one that made Clyde Cook's small club seem like a Sunday school picnic in comparison. After the first few breathless days, she had known there couldn't be anything romantic between them, but she'd been swept off her feet by his attention nonetheless.

With the acquisition of polish—such polish as she had garnered—and the experience of the cruel things men do, had come the loss of her youthful enthusiasm. Now only twenty-two, she was sad for the loss. But she had a chance to regain at least a part of that eagerness.

She pretended again. This time she played like she was once again that fresh, innocent girl who had stepped onto the sidewalk into an unfamiliar world. This was a new beginning. She helped unload the luggage, her anticipation of entering this wonderful place growing by leaps and bounds.

Sydney was good at pretending.

"Mrs. Parker, thank goodness you're back." A young girl, maybe seventeen years old, came out from behind the hotel's registration counter with a fistful of paper slips. "The housekeeper needs to talk to you. Mrs. Evans from the Red Cross called. And the people organizing Navy Week want to know if they can set up a reviewing stand in front of the hotel. And . . ."

Faith Parker stood among the mountain of luggage they had finally managed to unload from the car and looked around the lobby, which had been stripped of all but essential embellishments. The walls were decorated with patriotic posters, but no paintings.

Couches and chairs, covered in practical rather than decorative fabrics, were arranged into groups. There were a number of people about. A lone lieutenant slept on a sofa, his head under a tent of newspaper. Little Billy had deserted the adults as soon as they were inside, joining a group of children around what appeared to be a lively game of Chinese checkers. Near the upright piano a very pregnant young woman knitted patiently, glancing occasionally at her watch while a toddler played at her feet. A teenage boy approached the desk and stood waiting at Kay's elbow.

Faith had time to notice something else. Millie watched the boy with all the affected disinterest of a girl with a full-blown crush. She smiled to herself as Millie edged closer.

Finally he realized she was there. "Hi, squirt," he said offhandedly. "What happened to the pigtails?"

It was wonderful to see a girl with pink cheeks these days. But poor Millie. Faith could remember the embarrassment of confronting her first love. She had been about Millie's age and he, like this boy, had been an "older man," all of fifteen.

"I had my hair cut," she informed him unnecessarily but with surprising dignity. "Pigtails are for children."

Just then Faith noticed a striking blonde approaching from across the lobby. She was dressed in toffee-colored, wide-bottomed pants and an exquisite cream silk blouse with flowing sleeves. Park Avenue penthouse, Faith judged. She walked gracefully. Her hair was pulled back into a severe chignon and her chin was held at an assured angle. Only a woman with perfect features would dare wear such a stark style.

"Jimmy," said the woman when she reached their group. "I need you." She smiled at him and spoke softly.

Jimmy promptly forgot all about Millie.

"Do you mind waiting, Valerie?" Kay cut her off. "We need a strong hand with the luggage first. Jimmy can come to you as soon as these ladies are settled." The woman glared at Kay, who returned the look calmly.

The woman flounced off. Faith wondered if the others had noticed the exchange. And she wondered who the beautiful woman was. Obviously she wasn't a friend of Kay's.

Without missing a beat Kay returned her attention to the young woman who had greeted them in the lobby. "Now, slow down, Edna. Mrs. Cabot, Mrs. Bingham, this is Edna McCoy and her brother Jim. Edna bears the brunt of responsibility for messages, as you can tell. And Edna, Jim, I want you to meet Commander Parker's sister, Faith. If you're really nice to her maybe she'll pitch in and give you a hand at the desk occasionally."

Faith forgot Millie and her problems, too. She stepped forward to acknowledge the introduction. Her heart did a plummet. She hadn't given up her ambitions, quit college, and traveled all this way to man a switchboard. She wanted to do something meaningful and hoped that Kay was teasing. But remembering her sister's description of the voluntary duties at the hotel, she had a sinking feeling that she wasn't.

The changes in Kay had puzzled her at first. Her sister-in-law had always been the right kind of military wife, self-effacing and dependable; but Faith could see that her careful conduct was learned, not ingrained behavior. Over the years she'd observed Kay's efforts to do the right thing with the scornful derision of youth. Now, as she noted the rise of Kay's self-confidence and assertiveness, she felt the flowering of respect. She also felt rather ashamed of herself.

Kay was already moving toward the desk, her mind centered

on one question at a time. Removing her hat, she slid it underneath the counter out of sight and turned a large ledger. "You ladies know, of course, about our hotel policy. Manpower is at a premium in this city, so each of us contributes to the running of the hotel by giving of our time, twelve hours a week. I will try to take your preferences into consideration when assigning tasks, but the hotel is full and you may not get your first choice." She smiled before she delivered the bad news. "Or your second. I'm afraid all the favorite jobs are taken." Not even pausing to give them time to complain, she slid the ledger across the desk. "If you'll each fill out the necessary information, I'll get your keys and tell Jimmy where to put your luggage."

In the bustle that followed, Kay spoke softly to Edna. Faith saw the anticipation in her face change to deep disappointment. She wanted to cry out, Don't care so much! Kay was much too vulnerable where her husband was concerned. But it wasn't Faith's place to interfere. Instead she asked calmly, "Was there a message from Bill?"

Kay's look was distracted. "What? Oh, no. Maybe we'll hear something tomorrow. Now—" She turned briskly. "—the keys. Here's the master, Jimmy. You can take the bags upstairs. We'll be right along. Edna, call those people back and tell them we can't possibly talk about Navy Week right now. It's not until October."

Patsy Cabot gave Jimmy McCoy a patronizing smile and reached for her purse. "Let me give you something for your trouble, young man."

"N-no, Mrs. Cabot. No, thank you," the red-faced boy stammered, backing away.

"No tipping is allowed in the hotel, Mrs. Cabot," Kay explained, clearly trying to be kind.

But as Faith watched, Patsy Cabot's face flamed red and her eyes narrowed on Kay. She wouldn't like being mistaken about anything.

"Then you should have told us so," she snapped.

"She just did," Faith put in.

Kay shot her a look, but she was both surprised and pleased by Faith's backing. "I apologize, Mrs. Cabot. Edna, if you'll stay at the desk for a few more minutes while I show these ladies to their rooms, I'll be back to handle the other messages."

Sydney and Patsy were assigned rooms on the fifth floor. Faith followed along as her sister-in-law showed them the way.

"We try to keep one floor for the people without children,"

Kay explained. "This way you won't be disturbed by middle-of-the-night squalling. Sometimes I come up here for an hour or so of quiet. It's almost like a vacation." She produced a key and unlocked the door marked 502, where luggage had already been neatly stacked inside. Then she gave the key to Sydney.

"This is your room. You have a small hotplate but no refrigerator for yourself, I'm afraid. There is a community refrigerator in that alcove." She pointed to a break in the corridor wall. "Also a sitting area, a radio, and the only telephone on the floor. Whoever is closest answers," she went on, indicating the opening a few doors down the hall. "The refrigerator is just for the basics. Milk, cheese, butter, things like that. Most of us keep enough to have breakfast and sometimes lunch in our rooms but take dinner downstairs. The prices in both the dining room and coffee shop are reasonable; we're not trying to make money here. Please keep your refrigerator food well marked. As you both know, food is becoming more precious every day. The penalty for filching is a hangman's noose." She grinned as she stated the warning, but none of them had any doubt that she was serious.

"We'll leave you here to unpack," she told Sydney. "Can you be downstairs in fifteen minutes?"

"Sure."

"My office is the anteroom behind the front desk. Some other new girls arrived yesterday. We'll go over the hotel procedures and your responsibilities in more detail."

Sydney Bingham nodded, seemingly awed at Kay's air of authority. She and Faith, who was also a bit awed, exchanged a smile.

Kay repeated the procedure at room 507. Mrs. Cabot looked dumbstruck when they left her in the tiny room.

They entered an echoing stairwell nearby and descended toward the floor below. "Did you notice her face when she saw the closet space?" teased Faith in an effort to lighten Kay's mood. "It was probably just about large enough for her evening gowns."

"Yes." Kay sighed, a sound that could barely be heard over the sound of their clattering heels on the concrete steps. "Patsy Cabot seems to be another prima donna," she said, giving the door to the hall a definite jerk. Once again they were in a carpeted corridor.

"Another one?" asked Faith.

They came to a door and Kay took a key out of her purse.

"That blonde downstairs was Mrs. Jordan Adair. She manages the coffee shop. I'm surprised she didn't let you all know right away that her husband's father is the United States senator from Illinois." Kay snapped her mouth shut over the sarcasm, frowned, and shoved the key into the lock. "Drat! I shouldn't say things like that. I don't know what's wrong with me lately. I'm becoming positively snide. Valerie Adair is really very nice, and she has the coffee shop running on greased wheels."

She caught the sly grin that curved Faith's lips and chuckled. "I guess I'm jealous," she admitted ruefully. "Bill calls her the debutante. I'll swear the woman never has a wrinkle in her clothes or a hair out of place. She *looks* perfect. She *acts* perfect."

"But you've learned to handle her, haven't you?" Faith asked, prodding gently as she entered the room. Her luggage was there, stacked and waiting. She suddenly wished she had less. "You seem to be in your element."

Kay glanced up to see if Faith was being sarcastic but couldn't find any such emotion in the clear blue eyes. "I'm trying," she conceded. "Valerie's put out because Sydney Bingham's husband is a chief. She doesn't think they should be living here."

Faith was as familiar with tradition as Kay was. "Should they?" she asked, then she held up a hand. "Forget I asked. It's none of my business."

"I can't explain, Faith. I wish I could but—"

Faith interrupted quickly. "I don't want to hear anything even remotely resembling a military secret."

"Lord, neither do I! I don't know why they're here any more than you do. I was told to find them a place."

That surprised Faith. "Well, anyway. I feel kind of sorry for her."

"I know." Kay sighed. "She'll get the cold shoulder from a few of the girls. I hope she's strong enough to take it."

"I have an idea she is," Faith answered as she looked around at the two cramped rooms. Here, the double bed had been pushed against the wall to make room for a dinette set, a couple of easy chairs, a desk, and a cabinet. For the first time she began to wonder at the wisdom of her decision to join them. "So you think Mrs. Adair is perfect-looking? And you aren't?" she asked to avoid having to comment on the accommodations.

"Me?" Kay laughed genuinely for the first time. "To give her credit, though she may have started out like Patsy Cabot, Valerie's adjusted well to a life that must be far removed from what she's accustomed to. And she's an efficient manager,'' she repeated determinedly. "I'm learning to like her."

Handing the makeup case to Kay, Faith picked up her suitcases. "Then I'll learn, too." But I have a feeling Sydney Bingham will need our friendship more, she added to herself.

Kay indicated the open door. "As I told you in my letter, you'll have to bunk with the children. This is our room, and we use it as a sort of living–dining room until bedtime."

When do you have time for each other, wondered Faith as she followed Kay into the adjoining room. Three single beds were lined up on one wall, separated by nightstands. The Shirley Temple doll she'd given Millie for her ninth birthday sat comfortably on the pillow of the farthest bed, and a ragged-eared teddy bear, showing a lot of love-wear, was sprawled against the headboard of the center one. Three small bureaus were placed like sentinels on the opposite wall. There were two straight-backed chairs and a desk, and under one of the two windows was a toy chest.

"Pretty much like another dormitory, isn't it?"

Faith caught the apology in Kay's voice. Instantly she dropped the bags, tossed her purse onto the only bed that wasn't designated, and crossed to hug her sister-in-law. "It's wonderful. You know I love the children. Besides, I'm happy to be with all of you." And she meant it, for once.

Kay sagged, for just a moment, making Faith wonder if the responsibilities weren't too much even for a woman who was used to coping. Then Kay squared her shoulders. "You'll have to forgive me. I put a friend on the train for home this morning. Her husband was taken prisoner at Corregidor. I'm a little down in the dumps." She smiled again and sat on the middle bed, the one with the teddy bear. "I'm glad you decided to come. You know that, don't you?"

"Big brother doesn't feel that way."

"Bill loves you," Kay said gently, hoping that she could finally make Faith understand. "I think he simply feels that he's failed you."

With a snort of disbelief, Faith sank onto one of the chairs and eased her feet out of her shoes. "Failed me? I didn't get that idea at all when he visited the school. I think he's decided I'm just being stubborn again to annoy him. Failed at what?"

"He's always been worried lest you lose anything by the death of your mother and father. They wanted so much for both of you.'' She spread her hands. ''He feels he's let them down; he says they would have made sure you stayed in school.''

''My parents couldn't have known we were going to be plunged into this war,'' Faith argued, disbelieving.

''No.'' A cloud passed over Kay's face so fleetingly that Faith decided she must have imagined it.

''Neither could he.''

''No.''

Faith hesitated. ''Kay, with all that's happened in the world since Pearl Harbor, do you still believe that you should live in Bill's shadow?''

''I don't. I really don't. This job has taught me a lot.''

''For the navy? Bill is in the navy, not you, Kay,'' Faith informed her. ''What if he doesn't come back?'' she added in a softer tone.

''Faith!'' Kay tried to dismiss the fear that surged through her. She would be nothing without Bill. ''We don't talk about such things,'' she said.

''Of course not.'' The sarcastic edge wasn't lost on Kay, but she was relieved that it wasn't directed at her. ''Tell me what's happening on the war front.''

''Certainly you know.''

''I'm not talking about the stuff I read in the papers. I want to know what's really going on. From the Swami.'' She grinned. Her brother often called his wife the Swami because Kay had an uncanny ability to forecast the mind-workings of the military. Kay maintained it was a simple process of elimination and observation. ''Come on, tell,'' Faith urged.

''Well, let me see—the *Shiloh* has been here for two months. The repairs will be finished soon and his squadron will be reassigned back on board. That's no secret. But I'm not sure Bill hasn't already gone somewhere. It would be temporary,'' she mused, almost to herself. ''He hasn't gotten any permanent orders, not even to 'Destination X,' which has become a universal designation for anywhere in the world.

''But he has been gone for two weeks without a word. If he were nearby he would have called.''

Faith didn't interrupt Kay's train of thought or ask how she knew because it was no riddle to her. The instinct of navy wives was indefatigable when there was something going on. And Kay's was more fine-tuned than most.

''The Battle of the Coral Sea was, if not a victory, at least not a total loss. It foiled the Japanese invasion of Port Moresby, the jumping-off place for the planned invasion of Australia. And Jimmy Doolittle's raid on Tokyo was a symbolic gesture, albeit an effective one from the standpoint of morale. But they were stopgaps. Things are about to pick up in the Pacific because we've given up all the land we can afford to give up.''

Her brow furrowed; she went on, apparently rearranging her thoughts as she spoke. ''Nerves have gotten jumpy around here. I understand from a friend's husband who is in the Supply Corps that something's been building for several weeks,'' she said.

One of the first areas to feel heightened tension as materials were stockpiled, then moved, was the Supply Corps. The second area was personnel. ''And a lot of men have been called back to their bases unexpectedly. They've left messages that said not to expect them for a while.''

For Faith that statement needed no explanation, either. The evidence built, almost as though the volume were turned up on the radio, slowly enough that you didn't notice the increase at first, but then, suddenly, the decibel level was loud enough to hurt your ears.

Faith smiled. ''Military wives should be in charge of the intelligence network. You know, men might be in for a rude shock when this war is over. A lot of women who have been content to let their husbands take the lead are going to demand a voice in their marriages and in their lives now that they've learned how.''

Kay hesitated a minute before she said, ''You may be right. Even I've been offered a job.''

''A real job? One that pays?''

Kay laughed and shook her head ruefully. ''Yes, one that pays. The Red Cross is opening a new office and they've asked me to be the manager. I haven't decided yet.''

''Well, well. My esteemed brother might be one of the first victims of the women's war effort. It will be interesting to see his reaction.''

The smile faded from Kay's face. ''Bill has never dictated to me,'' she said stiffly.

''Have you ever crossed him?''

''Faith, please. We're going to be living in close quarters. Let's try not to stir the waters.''

Faith could have kicked herself. ''Is this my bunk, mate?'' she asked, changing the subject.

Kay hesitated. ''Yes,'' she said. She crossed to one of the bureaus and pulled out a drawer as Faith snapped the latches on

her suitcase. "We'll put your things in here. Thank goodness
the kids don't use much closet space."

Sydney hummed lightly along with the music from the table
model radio that helped fill the empty silence. She closed the
dresser drawer on the last of her clothes. She'd used exactly half
the space. Her suitcase was a problem, though. It wouldn't fit
under the bed or on the shelf in the closet. She'd ask. Surely
there was a storage space of some sort. The rooms weren't large
enough to leave it in the middle of the floor.

She looked around. Well, here was her new home—for a
while anyway. Actually the room would have been adequate as
a hotel room, but with the addition of the table and chairs, the
cabinet with the hotplate and space below for food, it was
crowded. An armchair and ottoman, another side chair, a floor
lamp, and a desk took up the rest of the space. The bed had
been shoved against the wall. Clearly an effort had been made
to provide some sense of comfort.

A knock sounded on the door. Her pulse jumped; then she
chided herself for the reaction. She had been able to put her
loneliness out of her mind for a few minutes. That was progress,
wasn't it?

She opened the door to find Patsy Cabot standing there. "The
phone is for you," said the woman shortly. She consulted her
pretty gold watch. "And it's time for our meeting," she added
icily.

"Thank you very much," answered Sydney politely to the
woman's back. She followed her down the hall to the alcove Kay
had pointed out.

"Hello?"

"Honey, it's me."

"Vance," she said, her voice rising with delight and relief at
the sound of his. "Where are you?"

"I'm at the base over in Bremerton, honey. Things are kind
of . . . hectic. I'm afraid I won't be back tonight, maybe not for
a couple of days." He sounded anxious. "Are you all right?
How was the trip?"

"Interesting," she said after a moment's pause for regret.
"Just promise me something, Vance. Don't make me live in the
mountains after the war. I thought that train was going to fall
off the tracks a couple of times."

He laughed, an easy chortle that seemed to scatter his constraint. "I promise. We'll live wherever you want to live. Honey, I've got to go. I'll try to call you tomorrow."

"Vance!" She didn't want him to hang up. She grasped the receiver with her other hand, too, as though to hang on more securely to the sound of a familiar voice. "I—you don't know when you'll get here?"

He heard the disquiet in her voice then. "Honey, I hate it as much as you do. I wanted so bad to be there to meet your train. I'll come as soon as I can."

She felt guilty. "Of course you will, Vance. I know that. I'll be waiting," she told him softly.

He sighed. "Those are the sweetest words I've ever heard. Good-bye, honey."

Sydney replaced the receiver carefully, struggling to overcome her disappointment. She was surprised at how badly she wanted him to be here. Well, she'd just have to get through by herself for a little while longer.

Chapter 8

In room 511 Valerie Adair sat on the edge of the bed and poured a scant measure of golden liquid into an etched balloon glass. The fiery cognac would take hold quickly, lulling her jittery nerves, soothing her temper. Jordan would be here soon, and she had to be able to face him, calm, collected, in control of herself.

Each confrontation she was forced to suffer with that nobody, Kay Parker, left her unsettled. The fine French brandy helped, though lately it seemed to take more than a sip to calm her. Still, she apportioned her supply carefully because there would be no more until this bloody war was over.

An hour later Valerie watched her husband knot the black tie neatly under his collar. He had arrived after being gone since last week, to shower and shave, and tell her he was leaving again. She wasn't pleased. "Surely, Jordan, you could take one day off."

"I told you, Valerie—"

She interrupted. "I know, I know. 'Things are really busy right now.'" She sighed and looked around at the room. She had managed to bring a modicum of elegance to the cramped space that amazed even her. The addition of a leather wing chair, a touch of chinoiserie in the new lamp, and few other well-chosen accessories had done wonders. "I understand there's a chief petty officer moving into the hotel," she told Jordan.

"Yes, I met Chief Bingham when I was out at Sand Point the other day," answered Jordan.

"At Sand Point? When? I just don't understand it, Jordan. Why would Kay Parker allow an enlisted man and his wife to move into the Elysium?"

Jordan sucked in his breath. Damn. He was going to have to

be more careful. He didn't want any speculation about Vance Bingham or his own relation to the man.

Jordan's desk in the judge advocate general's office was in the Federal Building a few blocks away, but he spent little time there. He had been at the Naval Air Station to greet the chief when he arrived, to help him unload the equipment he'd brought from New Orleans, and to direct him to the space that had been set up for his work. Until the testing on Bingham's radio device was concluded and, presuming it performed properly, production began, security was critical. "What difference does it make, sweetheart?" He met her gaze in the mirror.

"I don't like it. It goes against navy policy." She played with a loose strand on the chenille bedspread and thought about mentioning Kay's continual rudeness to her. But she decided not to complain right now. She kept her gaze on his. "The chief and his wife are newlyweds."

"Really? I'm sure Kay had a perfectly good reason for allowing them to live here," he added blandly.

Her blue eyes narrowed. "You know something about this, don't you?" she asked without rancor.

He shrugged into the jacket of his uniform and crossed the room to lift Valerie's chin. "If I did, I wouldn't tell you." He forced himself to smile, kissed her, and reached for his hat. "Gotta go. Walk down with me?"

Valerie glanced at her watch and sighed. "Yes, it's time for me to go, too. The lunch crowd will be gathering soon," she said, realizing that she spoke of the people like cattle congregating at a water hole. She rose, screening a giggle with a small cough, tucked in her silk blouse that didn't need tucking, smoothed her neat blond chignon that didn't need smoothing, and headed for the door. When Jordan didn't move she glanced back at him.

He thought he'd heard a voice in the hallway, soft laughter. How odd. He mentally shook himself and joined her with a smile. As he laid his arm over Valerie's shoulder he couldn't help comparing her to the woman who could almost meet him eye to eye. Again he banished the forbidden image. He had to get hold of himself. He had suspended all thoughts of her from his mind months ago, since he'd resolved to break off their affair. But once in a while she crept in without warning and left him with an empty, desolate void inside and an overwhelming feeling of guilt. He and Valerie left the room together.

The hallway was empty. There were voices in another room

further on. He closed and locked the door behind them. "Do you know, Mrs. Adair, that I'm very proud of you?" he asked softly and determinedly on the way downstairs.

Valerie smiled. Yes, she knew. Jordan had told her often enough. What surprised her was that she was also proud of herself. "Didn't think I could do it, did you?"

"I knew you could do anything you set your mind to; I didn't know you would do it so well. Admit it, sweetheart. You're happier, too."

Playfully she poked him in the stomach with a small fist. "I hate people who say 'I told you so.' "

"Did I say that?" he asked innocently.

"No, but you thought it."

"Are you happy, Valerie?" This time his question was serious. "Do you miss Chicago?"

Valerie hadn't totally put away her wariness. "Honestly?" When he nodded, she mused, staring into the middle distance beyond his shoulder. "Yes, sometimes I do," she admitted quietly. She laughed. "But I don't miss the bridge foursome, except for Peg." Then she sobered. "Or the mire that had our marriage so bogged down. When we go back it will be different, Jordan. I will be different."

"What if we decide we don't want to go back?" he asked after a moment.

"Oh, Jordan, for heaven's sake don't start that again," Valerie ordered sharply, her good mood totally ruined.

Faith entered the small anteroom off the office and took a seat on the back row. When Kay began to speak she listened with half an ear as she allowed her gaze to wander over the dozen other women in the room. She was still a bit preoccupied by the changes in her sister-in-law. For a minute she felt an odd pang of loneliness, missing school, her friends, the life she'd left.

"This hotel is an example of what our lives are like today," Kay explained. "While you live here you will probably be called on to do things for which you are inexperienced and unprepared. You may not think it is fair of us to ask it of you. But there is no alternative. If you want to be near your man, you have to help. Now that you've seen the closets, you will be searching for other accommodations." She paused for the laughter.

"I urge you to remember how fortunate we are. Our sisters in Europe have lost their homes, their families, in some cases their national identities. Our country needs us, our men need us, and our children need us. If you don't like the circumstances, as I said you are free to look for other accommodations. But if you stay at the Elysium you will be expected to help us keep it going. And we have a waiting list. If you decide to leave we can fill your room immediately.

"Now, for specifics. This hotel has five floors. Each floor, excepting the first, has twenty-one rooms. That's a total of eighty-four rooms. You will be expected to give twelve volunteer hours a week. If you have outside jobs in the defense industry, that number is reduced to eight. If you want to work in the cosmetic department at Frederick and Nelson, which is a local department store, you still have to give us the twelve hours.

"It should work out to 1008 man—or, in this case, woman—hours. With the exemptions for defense work it actually comes to about nine hundred. Now, nine hundred hours seems like a lot until you do the math. We have two eating establishments which are open from six A.M. to midnight. That works out to 252 hours a week if we only had one person working in each of them, and it takes at least three. Juggling schedules and cutting back during the less busy times we barely scrape by. We have a few wonderful souls who give more time than they are asked for. But we'll soon be opening the coffee shop twenty-four hours a day. I'm explaining this to you so that you'll understand the importance of doing your part. If you don't, someone else will have to do it for you."

She consulted her notes. "We are on dimout regulations—lights out when you leave a room. Blackout shades drawn before sundown. And we have air-raid practice about once a month, sometimes more often. The basement is our designated shelter. Conservation of all our resources is a must. Elevators are only to be used when necessary to carry heavy loads. We are facing some shortages, so don't complain about the food, please. Some of you girls, the ones from the East, will be familiar with gasoline rationing. I have it on good authority that rationing, both gas and food, will begin here on the West Coast in the fall—or as soon as the coupons are printed and distributed. Then we'll really have something to complain about." She smiled.

"You're each responsible for the upkeep of your own rooms and the alcove sitting room on your floor. I recommend you talk to someone or check the bulletin board on each floor for cleanup schedules. Our housekeeping staff cleans the lobby, the dining room and coffee shop, and the corridors. If the aircraft plants go any higher with their salaries, we will lose some of our ranks and have to take their jobs over as well. Now that school is out we have two extra employees, Edna and Jimmy McCoy. They're high school students, the children of one of our company, Lieutenant Commander James McCoy. Edna mans the switchboard and Jimmy helps out in a hundred ways around here.''

Faith shifted in her chair, awed by the organization it took to run this hotel. Kay went on. ''Children. If you have destructive kids you'd better keep them under lock and key,'' she said, drawing another laugh. ''You'll be personally responsible for any repairs to furniture. I don't mean simply reporting the damage and paying for it; I mean the actual work. If a child jumps up on a coffee table in the lobby and breaks it, you must see to having it repaired. If he takes his kiddie scissors or crayons to a chair you must have the piece cleaned or reupholstered. Most of the local craftsmen have hired on at the shipyards and, believe me, it isn't easy to find an upholsterer in this city. Broken crockery isn't too hard to replace—yet.

''You all know that the families with children live separately from those without. Some of the mothers have worked out swapping sitters, but there is a wonderful service at the YMCA only a few blocks from here.''

She shuffled through her notes and smiled at the assembled group. ''One last matter: our luxuries are irreplaceable. There is a good console radio in the lobby and one on each floor, as well as small table models in your rooms. Please treat them as though they were made of fine crystal. Don't allow small children—say under eight or nine—to tune them. Now that school is out it will be a problem, I know. We have no objection to the 'Green Hornet' or 'Henry Aldrich,' but just use common sense. And the piano in the lobby is for the enjoyment of everyone, so don't let the kids drop their toy soldiers in among the strings.''

As Kay squared her papers and slid them into a file folder, Faith speculated again about the positive changes in her brother's wife. Kay's speech, sparked with humor, revealed tact, which she had always shown; and command, which she had not. She undoubtedly was tapping resources she hadn't used before. Now, faced with these additional responsibilities, she'd become quite pragmatic and businesslike.

Faith's thoughts were distracted by Kay's suggestion that they all go to lunch together to give themselves a chance to get to know one another. ''If you have any questions, please don't hesitate to ask for clarification. And we welcome your suggestions. This project is only two months old and we want it to be successful, don't we?''

As they left the room Faith found herself beside Sydney. On impulse she said, ''Why don't we take a walk after lunch, Sydney? I'd like to explore a bit; would you?''

When she saw the smile of pleasure, Faith was glad she'd asked. ''Yes. I would love to, thanks.''

The coffee shop was noisy with the clatter of crockery and the click of heels on the tile floor. There were a dozen or so tables and a camelback-shaped counter protruded into the room. Most of the chairs and stools were filled with chattering women and children.

Valerie looked around from her perch on a high stool behind the cash register. As the group entered she smiled a warm welcome. ''I'm Valerie Adair, the manager of the coffee shop,'' she said to the new arrivals. ''I hope you're ready to start right to work. It's very difficult to make this place run smoothly when I can't get enough help.''

Faith could imagine the woman making such a statement about the appalling servant situation in peacetime. ''Bossy from the cradle, I'll bet,'' she whispered in an aside to the redhead next to her. ''She would probably never play unless she could be 'it.' ''

When there was no response to her remark she smiled at Sydney, willing her to share the joke. The sight that met her eyes was a shock. The woman looked as though she was about to faint.

Faith took her arm. ''Sydney, are you all right?''

''I'm fine,'' Sydney assured her, but her voice sounded weak.

''You aren't fine at all. Come and sit down.'' Ignoring the fact that the closest table was occupied, Faith pulled out an empty chair and thrust Sydney into it. ''Put your head between your knees,'' she ordered.

The others had noticed the commotion by now. Kay came over to them, followed by Valerie Adair. The color returned to Sydney's face with a rush when she realized she was the object of all eyes. ''I'm all right,'' she insisted. ''Please, really.'' She resisted Faith's efforts to push her head down.

''You don't look fine,'' Kay observed. With a worried frown she knelt beside them.

''I'm fine, really,'' Sydney assured them all. Adair. Adair. The name repeated like a cadence in her mind. ''I didn't sleep much on the train. Maybe I'm a little tired.''

"And hungry as well, I imagine. I know I am. After lunch you can lie down for a while. We're not quite the slave drivers I implied earlier. You don't have to start your volunteer duties immediately. Take a few days to get accustomed to the hotel. A week if you need it."

Valerie seemed about to protest, but Kay fixed her with a glare.

Sydney regretted the confrontation, regretted anything that brought attention to herself right now. She needed to get away from here. "Oh, no. I'm sure I'll be fit as a fiddle tomorrow."

The southern expression brought a smile of derision to Valerie Adair's mouth.

Sydney didn't miss that reaction, either, but it was no surprise. She'd be damned if she let it get her down. Right now, though, she desperately needed to be alone. This whole situation might have taken on the aspects of a nightmare, but she would handle it as she handled all the other nightmares in her life. Besides, Vance would be here soon. She clung to the thought; she could depend on Vance.

Kay kept a hand on her arm as she rose. "Are you sure you're all right?"

"Oh, yes," Sydney assured them hastily. "If you'll excuse me for a minute, though, I'd like to run back upstairs. Please don't wait for me."

"I'll check on you later," said Faith.

Sydney looked at her for a minute, confused. Then she remembered their promised walk. "Sure."

Kay stayed with her until they reached the door, then Sydney gently loosened her arm from Kay's grasp. "Thank you," she murmured.

She left the coffee shop, walking straight until she thought she was out of sight, then she bolted in the direction of the elevators.

Valerie and Faith had approached Kay. "I wonder what upset her?" mused Valerie. She turned to Kay and arched a severe brow in disapproval. "You haven't told them about not using the elevators yet?"

"Honestly, Valerie. The girl is obviously ill," snapped Kay. She looked beyond Valerie's shoulder. "You have a line forming at your register," she added with a note of satisfaction.

* * *

Sydney sagged in relief against the closed door to her room. Why, out of the hundreds of places in Seattle to be quartered, did she happen to end up here?

After a minute she stalked to the bed and stood there glaring at it. Then slowly, she deflated like yesterday's balloon, crawled onto the bed, curled into a self-protective ball, and let the tears come. They were hot tears, tears of regret and remorse, even tears of self-pity, but they were also tears of fury and frustration.

Fate wasn't cruel; it was bloodthirsty. She'd known Jordan was going to be in Seattle but how in the world had she ended up living at the same place he lived—with his wife? His absolutely gorgeous wife. In the split second before she'd discovered the woman's name, Sydney had felt the influence of Valerie Adair's lovely, welcoming smile and responded agreeably to it.

Her only comfort was that Vance hadn't been here to see her practically keel over in shock. If he had been present, she would have had to furnish explanations that would bring a lot of unhappiness to everyone. Vance was broad-minded; he had accepted that her feelings for him were unconventional. He knew she'd been deeply in love at one time and that the loss of her love had left her devastated. But even Vance would find it tough to accept that her former lover was living right here, in the same hotel.

Her reaction was simply a shock, she repeated, and she would not let this situation destroy her plans for a new life. As long as she didn't delve too deeply into her feelings, as long as she could function on a superficial level, she would be all right.

A year ago she would have been devastated, but now she could handle it. Determinedly she bounced off the bed and crossed to the bathroom, where she splashed cold water on her burning eyes. She had only a short time before she had to come up with a likely explanation for Faith Parker.

I've lived through worse, she reminded herself, much worse. I'll survive this.

She'd look for another place to live. Kay had said the city was crowded, but someone had to leave sometime. If she could find the place they'd just left *from*, her problems would be solved.

If that didn't work she would find something to do with herself, a job. Vance was bound to be gone a lot. The twelve volunteer hours a week wouldn't be enough to keep her busy. She would look for something beyond the walls of this hotel. She didn't belong, that was obvious. All the other girls were married to officers. Why had they even allowed her beyond the front door? She wished with all her heart they hadn't.

She groped for a towel. When she raised her head, the mirror reflected her swollen cheeks, puffy eyes, and red nose. A choked sob of genuine laughter escaped through her lips. She had never been able to cry without looking like the south end of a north-bound pig when she was through.

Disgusted with fate but amused at herself, she threw the towel at her reflection, reentered the bedroom, and reached for her makeup case.

A few hours later Sydney and Faith again entered the lobby from the street, laughing together. Sydney had enjoyed the walk. It cleared some of the cobwebs out of her brain and she felt better. She had enjoyed Faith, too. She was an interesting girl.

As she had observed in the car this morning, Faith was sophisticated in a way that only New Yorkers are sophisticated; but she was also relieved to notice that when the posture slipped, Faith was very down to earth. She laughed a lot and Sydney liked that.

Edna McCoy hailed Faith the minute she saw them.

"Goodness," said Faith. "Do you ever go off duty?"

The young girl laughed. "Not often. You had a call from—" She consulted a slip of paper, then held it out to Faith. "John Harrison. He wanted to know if you would like to take in a movie Saturday night. That's his number. He said he'd be there for a little while."

Sydney grinned. "That was a quick conquest."

Faith grinned back. "Wasn't it, though? I'd better call before he gets away."

Sydney said good-bye and returned to her room, using the stairs this time. Faith had told her about the elevator rule and the odd animosity between her sister-in-law, Kay, and Valerie Adair.

Sydney kept her amusement to herself. If Faith thought *that* was animosity, she should see the anger that would erupt if Valerie ever found out who *she* was—Jordan Adair's ex-lover.

Or maybe Valerie didn't know anything about her. Maybe Jordan had never admitted being unfaithful. Her heart still caught in her throat at the thought of his name.

Peeling off her jacket, she began on the buttons of her blouse. When she was naked she reached for the robe she had hung up only a short while before and decided to take a nap. The feelings buried deep inside her must not be visible on her face if Vance should arrive unexpectedly.

Jordan.

"Oh, Jesus." The word was half prayer, half curse. How would he react when he saw her? At least she had the advantage of knowing he was here. At least she had some warning. He wouldn't have any warning at all.

Or would he? Vance had told her that he and the lieutenant would be working together. Surely he had mentioned his wife. She stripped back the covers and climbed into bed.

Regardless of whether Jordan knew or not, she should try to find a way to have a few private words with him. Perhaps she could linger casually in the lobby and intercept him. But she had no idea what his schedule was. Military men didn't exactly keep regular business hours, she reminded herself wryly. She could be stuck in the lobby for days, waiting.

On the other hand it might be interesting to see just how Jordan would react to seeing her again. He had loved her, she knew, but he'd left of his own accord. Maybe he wouldn't care.

Closing her eyes, she burrowed her head deeper in the pillow.

She'd often wondered what Jordan would have thought if they'd met for the first time at the club where she sang. In the tight lamé dress, her red hair wild around her shoulders, the freckles across her nose hidden by heavy stage makeup, she was quite another person from the scrubbed-faced, ponytailed, blue-jeaned figure that met him at the door of Mrs. Deveraux's house with a paintbrush in her hand.

It had been early spring, a year ago. Sydney enjoyed Mrs. Deveraux's yearly custom of spring cleaning. She didn't mind helping because her mother had always done the same, though certainly not to the same elaborate extent.

In preparation for the long hot summer to come, the heavy velvet draperies came down, to be replaced by curtains made of light cotton; the upholstered furniture was slipcovered in white duck; and the huge carpets were rolled up and stored in the attic to be replaced by small area rugs on the polished floors. The porch railings were whitewashed and the floor-length shutters scrubbed until the paint showed blue-black.

For Sydney the immediate reward of the lighter, cooler atmosphere was a lightened mood.

"Are you Lieutenant Adair?" she asked the handsome man in uniform who stood on the other side of the screen door.

He leaned forward and narrowed his eyes to see into the cool, shadowy hall. "Yes, I'm Jordan Adair. I called about a room. Is your, ah, is Mrs. Deveraux at home?"

She laughed, the husky laugh that always got positive results from men, and held the door open for him. "If you were going to say 'mother' thanks for the compliment. I'm Sydney Jackson, one of the boarders."

"I'm sorry," he responded, not moving.

"Don't apologize. I can imagine how I look. I was painting the back porch. Mrs. Deveraux is out right now. She asked me to show you to your room." She waited for a minute, still holding the door. He didn't look like a man who lost his composure often, and she had to fight the impulse to laugh. "Would you like to come in?"

"What? Oh, yes, thank you." He lifted a bag from the floor at his feet and crossed the threshold, never once taking his eyes off her face.

As the man took a step, Sydney suddenly had a chilling premonition, a feeling that something was about to happen that would change her life forever. The gris-gris are gonna get you if you don't watch your step, she warned herself. She shook her head to throw off her crazy reaction to the broad-shouldered stranger.

Lieutenant Jordan Adair was taller than she was, but not much. He had blond hair and beautiful blue-gray eyes. His jaw was firm but not belligerent. All in all he was quite a man.

But Sydney knew a lot of men. "Just let me get rid of this," she said brandishing the brush, "and I'll take you upstairs."

She could feel his eyes boring into her back all the way down the long hall to the kitchen. The crazy feeling wouldn't be thrown off.

At first he seemed to avoid her, but it was hard to remain aloof at Mrs. Deveraux's boardinghouse. The boarders were like a loosely knit family. On the evenings she didn't work, Sydney often played the piano in the parlor. Lieutenant Adair seemed to enjoy her music but, she noticed, he didn't smile often. When he did, the smile just sat on the surface of his eyes.

She wasn't sure when she first realized that he was no longer avoiding her. Suddenly he was always there—at Mrs. Deveraux's, at the club. When he wasn't working, or she wasn't, they went for long walks, picnicked by the river, or dined in splendor at one of the downtown hotels. An affinity grew between them, one of those rare forms of communication. Their eyes would meet after a chance remark and she knew exactly what he was thinking. He began to laugh, and the sight was glorious. He threw off his constraint and looked years younger. He told her later that she was like a bright, warm blaze to a man whose nature was chilled by a lifetime of tradition and formality.

Over the next few weeks, Sydney fell more and more deeply in love with him and he, with her. At last their physical desire could be denied no longer. Their lovemaking was golden. And brief. The affair lasted less than a week longer.

She knew immediately that something was very wrong, for his restraint returned with intimacy. Except for the hours in her arms he became again the reserved, detached man he'd been when he arrived. She didn't have to ask what was wrong. He would tell her soon. She knew him well enough to know that when there was a problem he liked to bring the facts out into the open and solve it.

Of all the guesses she might have made, the truth would have been the last of her suspicions. She knew without a doubt that Jordan was an honorable man, ethical and highly principled. For him not to admit to being married was inconceivable.

She had been defeated—and unforgiving.

Only with time and distance had she been able to steel herself against the pain. She'd vowed never to love again.

And now here she was, the distance and the time obliterated, unsure what would happen next.

Chapter 9

Saturday, June 6th, 1942

Kay Parker thought of the weekly meeting with the hotel manager, Charles Wagner, as an endurance contest. It was becoming difficult to hold her tongue against the cynicism of the representative of the owners of the Elysium Hotel. Charles was abdicating more and more of the responsibility to her as the weeks went by. She didn't welcome the obligation.

He was waiting for her in his office, the one place in the hotel that hadn't been stripped of embellishments. He lounged in his high-backed leather swivel chair. She bridled when she saw that he was reading a book, his distinguished gray head bent forward in concentration.

When Kay entered he placed it on his desk, open and with the spine up. A novel. When was the last time she had had the leisure to read a novel?

"Good afternoon, Charles," she said, taking the chair across from him. She held out a sheaf of papers. "Here are the figures from the coffee shop. Has Maurice—?"

"Yes, yes." He waved away the question as he took the papers she held. "Maurice has given me the dining room receipts. I'll look these over. Anything else?"

Kay looked at him in slack-jawed amazement. "Well, of course, there is something else. Several things, as a matter of fact. The payroll checks, the broken lock on the alley door, the orders for next week, the housekeeper's request for a raise, the promise of rationing, the—"

He passed his fine-boned patrician hand over his smooth hair. "Please, Mrs. Parker. You have the authority to decide upon

112

the raise and to find someone to fix the lock. If my information is correct, rationing won't go into effect for a few months.''

"Yes, but Maurice is already worrying."

"Maurice isn't happy if he's not worrying. I will sign the payroll checks as soon as you have prepared them."

"Me? I'm not a bookkeeper. Where is Theresa?"

"My secretary has quit," he announced, seemingly untouched by this devastating piece of news. "The lure of more money at the bomber factory was too much to resist," he explained.

Kay, who had been leaning forward, subsided against the chair back with a loud sigh. "Charles, I can't do everything."

He fixed her with a bland stare. "I'm afraid you'll have to."

Most of the time Kay felt compassion for the poor man. Having been wounded in the last war, he was unfit for service and she was sure that rankled. His elegant hotel had been stripped almost bare of its beautiful prewar appointments. He could go on for hours about the particular piece of furniture that sat in the foyer on the second floor or the antique garniture that had been displayed on the mantel of the lobby fireplace.

And now a passel of women and children had moved in for the duration. At first he had been helpful. Back in April when they had arrived he seemed to take a genuine interest in the experimental situation. But this last remark took the cake. Kay's patience evaporated like the morning fog.

She stood up. "Charles, I'm sure you would have preferred a position on the front lines to managing a hotel using women who know nothing about the business. But don't ever whine to me again about the sins of the volunteer staff. They're doing more than you are." She spun on her heel and left him.

Usually on Saturday, when she finished with Charles, she looked forward to the second weekly meeting, one with Maurice Beaumont, a wonderful sugar dumpling of a man. Today, however, might be an exception.

In addition to her anxiety about Charles, there was another matter that bothered her. Maurice simply took no notice of wartime shortages. He was an artiste, he vowed. How could he produce masterpieces without adequate provisions? She had argued but had yet to convince him that preparing good hearty food for hardworking people was a worthy challenge to one of his stature and a masterpiece in itself when faced with shortages.

Maurice didn't see it that way at all. She just prayed he wouldn't quit when rationing became a reality in the fall.

* * *

"Maurice, can't you talk to him?" asked Kay, pacing rest-lessly in the chef's small office next to the kitchen. "I can't run a hotel all by myself."

Maurice smiled, showing the dimples in his round cheeks. "It seems to me that's exactly what you've been doing for the last month."

"But I didn't have the ultimate responsibility, don't you see?"

Maurice frowned. "Yes, Kay, I do see. And I think since you're doing Charles's job, you should be getting his salary. If the owners knew what was going on, I'm sure they would agree with me."

"But they mustn't know. This project is still fairly experi-mental. If things don't go well here it could jeopardize the pro-gram nationwide."

A full, rich laugh shook Maurice's ample belly. "Kay, Kay. Only you would try to take on the responsibility for the whole country."

She gave him a wry smile. "I do, don't I?"

"Why do you?"

Maurice watched her pretty face take on a concentrated look. When she spoke it was with slow, soul-searching intensity. There was vigor and strength in this woman, but she didn't recognize those things in herself.

"I don't really *want* to, you know." She shrugged. "But since I was a little girl back on the farm I've had this need to make sure everything ran well. It's a compulsion, I suppose." She thought for a minute. "Will you talk with him, Maurice?" she asked at last.

"I'm not sure it will accomplish anything, but I will try. Charles is a lonely man. Bitterness and loneliness are a poor blend. I'll talk to him, but I think you'd better learn as much as possible in a short period of time."

"But the owners—"

"The owners have a good deal going. The government is paying them top dollar on the lease. If Charles is a manager in name only, they aren't going to care."

Kay folded her hands in her lap. "Then I suppose it is up to me," she said after a minute.

Maurice laid a hand over hers. "I'll help as much as I can."

A small glimmer of amusement enhanced her grateful ex-pression. "Even to not having an artistic fit when rationing starts?"

"That's blackmail!" he protested. But he smiled back. "If you will do something for me."

"That's blackmail, too," she countered. "What is it?"

"Isn't Jimmy McCoy on a salary?"

She was puzzled at his sudden seriousness. "Yes. He and his sister are earning extra money for college that way."

"And isn't he supposed to help out in my dining room as well as in the coffee shop?"

"Of course. Why? Isn't he doing his job? I'm surprised. I thought Jimmy was a dependable young man."

Maurice shook his head in contradiction. "No, that isn't what I mean. He does a very good job—when he's available. But Mrs. Adair keeps him tied up all the time. I needed some supplies moved this morning and I asked him to help. She was rather put out by my request. She doesn't like the boy to leave her side."

A smile wandered over Kay's face. Maurice was convinced that Valerie had a vendetta against him. "I'm sure she's not deliberately trying to annoy you, Maurice. She's simply accustomed to having her own servants."

"It's almost as though she has a halter on him."

"I'll speak to her, make sure she understands she isn't to monopolize his time."

"Thank you," said Maurice with dignity.

Kay sighed. Maurice's pride only added one more task to her already long list of things to do.

Chapter 10

Only five days had passed since she'd arrived in Seattle, and yet Sydney felt at home. She made her way through the crowded lobby toward the entrance to the dining room. She saw enough of the coffee shop during her volunteer hours, so tonight she intended to splurge on a leisurely dinner even if Vance wasn't here to share it with her. He had called again this afternoon and promised he would be here tomorrow. Well, he'd practically promised.

A group of young women broke into laughter as she walked by. She hurried past them, wondering if they were laughing at her.

Don't be silly, she admonished herself. They don't even know you. Though she was not familiar with military protocol, it had quickly become obvious to her that some of the other women disapproved strongly of her presence in the hotel.

She had to get over this tendency to be self-conscious because of her husband's status. The navy must have had a good reason for putting an enlisted man in with the officers. At first she had wondered if Vance had been ordered to live at the Elysium. The next time he'd called she asked if there was a rule against her looking for another place, and he had laughed.

"We're free to live anywhere, honey, as long as I show up for duty." He was quiet for a moment. "Are you unhappy there?"

"No." Her denial was too quick. "Not unhappy, Vance, just a little lonely."

"Well, if you can find us another place, we can certainly move. Good luck."

116

In her spare time she had explored the city looking for another place to live and found that Kay hadn't exaggerated when she'd told them at the orientation meeting that housing was at a premium.

Now that Sydney had accepted the hotel as the place where she would live, she had vowed to adjust. She wouldn't question the motives of the United States Navy but she would stop and think before she opened her mouth. With a smile of amusement, she thought back to Mrs. Deveraux's lightly veiled instruction concerning the rudiments of correct behavior. Surely some of the lessons had been effective enough to keep her from embarrassing herself.

"Things are quiet tonight," observed Kay as she and Faith entered the dining room. Only a few tables were taken. They had fixed a supper of scrambled eggs for the children and left them listening to the radio. Sunday was their favorite night. Charlie McCarthy came on Sunday, and was followed by Eddie Cantor and then Jack Benny.

The two women were just starting on their soup, a delicate, flavorful terrapin—thankfully there was no shortage of those— when Sydney entered. "May I ask her to join us?" asked Faith.

Kay only hesitated for a fraction of a second. "Of course."

Faith rose and approached the redhead. "Kay and I are over here, Sydney. If you weren't planning to meet anyone would you like to sit with us?"

Sydney gave a laugh that was too loud in the hush of the nearly empty dining room. "I don't know anybody to meet," she said, following Faith back to the table.

The sound of laughter drew Valerie Adair's attention. At another table she listened with half an ear to Patsy Cabot's monologue and watched the interchange. She was somewhat amazed to see that Commander Parker's wife and sister were going out of their way to be nice to that floozy-looking woman. One way or another she was going to find out what was so important about a lowly chief and his wife.

Jordan was supposed to be back tomorrow. She would make him tell her. Or maybe she could find out for herself. Perhaps she should join their little group for dessert.

"Have you heard from your husband?" asked Kay when Sydney and Faith were seated.

"Yes, he called this afternoon from Bremerton. He was real busy with something. He said he wouldn't get here tonight, but maybe tomorrow."

"I haven't heard from Bill at all," Kay said quietly. "It's been almost three weeks." She had a thought. Captain Conway had told her that Chief Bingham was to be stationed at Sand Point, but he had called from Bremerton . . . ah, well. The men moved about a lot in the area. Even Bill went back and forth regularly from Sand Point to Whidby Island further north.

A waitress approached and set a bowl of clear soup before Sydney. "Good evening. Tonight we have poached salmon or grilled chicken."

Sydney recalled that the dining room menus were limited to two entrées. The accompaniments were the same for both. "I'll have the salmon."

"What would you like to drink?"

"Coffee?"

The waitress smiled. "You're lucky tonight. We have some." She went off to fill the order.

Sydney unfolded the large napkin across her lap. "Is she a volunteer, too?" she asked.

"Yes. That's Marie Clifford. I think she's from Kansas"— Kay frowned—"or is it Missouri?"

"I don't see how you remember all the names, much less where they're from," said Sydney.

"Basic training for a navy wife," Kay explained succinctly. "It's expected."

Faith made a face. "Along with a hundred other expectations. But you probably know all about them," she added to Sydney.

"No, I'm pretty new at this," Sydney admitted. "We haven't been married long."

"Kay will show you the ropes and tell you the rules. Never question orders; never correct a superior's wife or chastise his children, no matter what rotten little brats they might be; never have more than one drink; never forget that you're an example to the civilian population, and on and on, ad nauseam."

"Faith." Kay's voice held a warning.

"That's why I don't intend to be one," Faith went on as though Kay hadn't spoken. "The worst part of it all though, Sydney, is never having a place that's home."

"I wouldn't like that," Sydney admitted. She wondered at the tone of Faith's remarks. The girl hadn't shown this bitterness the other day when they walked together. But she hadn't seen Faith since except in passing.

"It isn't so bad," Kay interjected, her voice not quite convincing. "You get used to it. And you get to see a lot of the world."

Sydney didn't comment. She wanted a home of her own. Vance shared the dream; they had spoken of it at length. She didn't care how much traveling she was able to do, she would always want a place to come home to.

"Times are changing, Kay. You're crazy to put up with all that foolishness. Excuse me, Sydney. We aren't being deliberately enigmatic. My dear brother has forgotten that we live in a democracy. He puts rather harsh demands on his wife. My own relationship with him doesn't always run smoothly because I refuse to kowtow to him."

Kay wisely chose to keep silent.

Sydney could almost see Mrs. Deveraux's disapproving frown. Never air your dirty linen in public, she would have said. Kay was clearly embarrassed. Sydney wondered if she could diffuse the situation before it became a full-blown argument.

"That's all right. I never had a brother—much to my daddy's regret—but I'd probably fight with him, too." She smiled at Kay and changed the subject. "M-m-m, this is delicious soup. I'm glad I didn't decide to eat in the coffee shop."

Kay looked a little surprised, but she answered the smile.

"I'm glad you didn't, too," said Faith. "Kay and I were saying this afternoon that we'd like to get to know you better."

"Me?" Sydney murmured. But she was pleased. Despite being in Jordan's vicinity, she knew she'd been right to come here; she and Vance were going to be fine. "I'm looking forward to knowing both of you, too."

There was silence for a few minutes while the women finished their soup. When the bowls had been removed Sydney asked, "By the way, Faith, did you get in touch with that nice boy from the train . . . what was his name?"

"John Harrison? Yes. I called him back Tuesday. We had a date for last night. But he called again Wednesday and cancelled it. I heard that his ship has already left."

"You could hear a hundred stories but there's no way of knowing for certain," said Kay. She went on to explain to Sydney with a wry chuckle. "I forgot to mention in our meeting the other day that rumor and gossip is another major industry here in Seattle."

"It's pretty major anywhere, isn't it? I guess curiosity is natural, to want to know where your friends and husbands are going."

"It's also very dangerous." Kay was totally serious now. "There are a lot of people who would have no scruples about reporting troop movements to the enemy. Especially in a place like Seattle."

Sydney thought Kay was overly cautious, but she said nothing.

They had just begun on their dessert, bread pudding with hard sauce, when Valerie Adair approached their table. She had her coffee cup in one hand and her dessert plate in the other. "May I join you?" she asked, indicating the empty chair.

Sydney kept a straight face as Kay said, "Of course."

It hadn't taken Sydney long to see through Mrs. Jordan Adair. She walked on eggshells when the woman was close, held her breath every time she saw her.

She didn't *want* to sit here and talk to this woman. So why the hell should she?

Because you promised yourself you would learn to fit in. She mentally prepared herself for any mention of Jordan Adair.

Valerie, though, was more interested in Sydney's husband—in where he was from, in what he did before the war—than in her. Which seemed odd.

It must have seemed odd to Kay, too. Every time the conversation tended to drift toward the subject of Vance, the older woman redirected it, either by a reference to the coffee shop, the weather, or another bland topic.

Bill was once again in the reconnaissance aircraft in the nighttime sky above Dutch Harbor, but this time he was headed for Seattle. Normally he didn't allow thoughts of his family to distract him from his job, but as he settled the plane on a straight course he let his mind wander to his wife and children. And his sister, Faith. He had mixed feelings about Faith.

He loved his sister very much, and he was really looking forward to seeing her; but he didn't intend to let her give Kay a hard time. She was to have arrived last Tuesday, the day he'd spotted the disturbance on the ocean's surface and reported the first carrier sighting off the Aleutians. One of the other recons had seen a second carrier, one cruiser, one destroyer, and one transport. It was corroborating proof that this was definitely a secondary force. True to Nimitz's prediction, the major battle had taken place at Midway, but the clash at Dutch Harbor had been pretty bad.

What was today? Sunday? His memories of the battle just

lived through were vivid, but time and perspective were blurred by lack of sleep.

The battle for Dutch Harbor had been a violent four-day slice of war. The mist and rain were so heavy that only the commanders of the spot knew what course the battle was taking. Finally the Japanese, unable to land a force at Dutch Harbor, had withdrawn into the impenetrable fog. The available American planes had searched for hours but found no sign of the enemy carriers.

Had the base not been on full alert the result would have been much worse. Thank God, there was sufficient warning—no Pearl Harbor here, he thought.

But there had been no clear-cut victory, either. The protective force had held, but they had been unable to take the battle to the enemy. The invaders had suffered only light damage after having abused one American ship and blown up many of the fuel tanks at the base.

The enemy had also landed approximately 1800 men on two islands further along in the westernmost Aleutians. The country didn't know of the occupation yet; Bill supposed the thunder surrounding Midway would drown out any outcry for a week or two.

It was a sobering thought. American soil was in enemy hands. The tiny islands of Attu and Kiska, really no more than big rockpiles, were only 800 miles from the base at Dutch Harbor. And the Japanese were digging in; God only knew when the navy would be able to rout them out again.

Meanwhile, the all-out battle, using the full power of the Imperial Navy, had gone on as expected at Midway Island. The first decisive naval battle of the war in the Pacific was over except for the mopping up.

Six months from the day Pearl Harbor was bombed, the United States had finally dug in its heels and refused to give up any more land in the Pacific.

When he heard the news Bill was jubilant; they all were. Holding the Japanese off at Midway had been vital. The country didn't know how vital it was. But they would find out and morale would jump.

The toll was high. The casualty lists hadn't been released yet, but he knew they would be heavy. The victory was worth it.

At first the sparse reports coming in from Midway hadn't been good, but on the third day the boys had been able to turn the battle around. Navy pilots—fighter pilots, torpedo plane pilots, and bomber pilots—had given the Japs hell.

Like the Battle of the Coral Sea in April, this had been an indication of change in naval warfare. The ships never came within sight of each other; the battle was carried on wholly by the naval air forces.

Word had also reached them that there was another prong to this offensive. Japanese submarines were tracked near the coast of Brisbane. Allied planes were still fighting off that assault.

Now Bill was on his way back to the base at Sand Point to report on the conflict at Dutch Harbor, Unalaska, and the condition of the base there. What was he going to say? In his opinion the Japanese presence in the Aleutians was a dangerous threat to the Pacific Northwest. Maybe more so since the enemy had been shown very dramatically that they weren't going to break through via the Midway route.

The base had to be strengthened, the perimeters reinforced against encroachment. The small force on Attu and Kitka would have to be contained there. No advancement must be permitted, not even to the next rock.

The men aboard the plane, some of them wounded, were deadly quiet behind him. With a struggle he fought off the weariness that threatened to overtake him. The crew was tired, too, and tired men made mistakes. Even on the way home. He reached for the thermos of hot coffee beneath his feet, poured himself a cup, and passed the rest around.

The console model Philco radio in the lobby was always the center of a crowd during the news hour. The volume varied from a soft drone to a sharp tone, depending upon the immediacy of the story. Tonight the atmosphere was quick with an underlying excitement. The radio blasted away.

As they left the dining room, Kay heard someone say the word "Midway" and hurried over. Faith and Sydney followed quickly, Valerie more slowly.

The newscaster was attempting to remain calm, but he could hardly keep the elation out of his voice. "The battle began three days ago, on June 4th. Our boys were outnumbered and outgunned from the beginning. The invasion force was said to be the largest assembled by the enemy since Pearl Harbor," he said. "Casualties were high."

Kay caught her breath.

"Those Japs really like to get up early," the man went on.

"At 4:30 A.M. Midway time, the first wave of the attack took off from the carriers. One of our boys spotted the planes and sounded the alarm. The island base was ready for them. From then on it seemed to be an aircraft battle. These details were provided hastily but we hope to have more news soon. To repeat, the American forces have won a decisive victory on the island of Midway in the Central Pacific. Stay tuned to this station for the complete story. We return you now to your regular program."

As the newscaster's voice faded to be replaced by a commercial announcement, the lobby seemed to erupt in joyful celebration. Jimmy McCoy put two fingers at the corners of his mouth and let loose an ear-splitting whistle.

"Can you picture that?" squealed Edna McCoy over the din.

"We finally won a battle!" added Jimmy.

Edna looked to Kay. "Where is Midway Island, do you know?"

"Yes, I do." Kay could hardly contain her agitation. Heavy casualties. Why hadn't she heard from Bill? Logically she rationalized that he wouldn't have been sent to Midway on a temporary duty assignment, logically she knew that personal communication was always the last to be handled, but instinctively she was afraid.

She reached out for a hand; it happened to be Faith's. She squeezed hard. Here was the explanation for the disquiet they'd all been feeling. Midway would be a decisive battle, a big one. Maybe *the* biggest. Keep steady, she reminded herself. "Why do you think they call it Midway?" she asked lightly. "It's right smack in the middle of the Pacific Ocean."

"That's what the newscaster said. Can Jimmy and I look on your map?"

"Certainly, come on." She led the way toward the stairs.

Faith beckoned for Sydney to accompany them. "Let's go. Kay has a world map on the wall of her room," she explained.

"Mama! Did you hear?" asked Millie when they entered.

Billy, dressed in his pajamas, was dancing up and down in front of a huge wall map, stuck all over with small pins—red ones, blue ones, yellow and white ones. "Look, Mama. There's Midway. I found it all by myself. The Japs tried to take it, but we beat them off. They lost a lot of ships and planes and carriers. Can I put the tack there?" He and his sister had been listening to the radio, too, and another newscaster was repeating the story.

Billy was allowed to put a red tack in the map on the tiny

island. Then he climbed on the bed and wiggled to make himself comfortable.

"I'll put on a pot of coffee since we don't have champagne to celebrate with," Kay said as she busied herself at the hotplate.

Jimmy and Edna had to leave, and Sydney offered to, but Faith vetoed that. "Why go back to an empty room?" She indicated a chair at the dinette table and sat down herself. Millie and Kay joined them there while they waited for the coffee to perk. They all examined the map again. Faith and Kay got into a discussion about the tiny island in the middle of the Pacific. While they drank the coffee they speculated about the battle from every conceivable view. Kay was impatient that they would have to wait for the morning papers to get details.

"Isn't it wonderful that we held off the Japs?" Millie commented to Sydney.

Sydney agreed with the girl that it was wonderful that a battle had been won, but she didn't admit that she had no idea what all the pins in the map meant. She was uncomfortable; for the first time she felt guilty and a bit humiliated as well when she realized that both of the Parker children knew more about this war than she did. She listened carefully and, after a few minutes, she realized that each pin represented a battle front, or the movement of a military unit, an army, a navy, or a friend or relative that Kay or Faith wrote to regularly.

Kay finally broke off the revelry and barked a bedtime order to the children. They said good night and followed her into the next room.

The connecting door was open and Sydney could see the barrackslike setting. Though the carpet on the floor was the same drab, practical green as her own, though the draperies were the same maroon and the bedspreads the same chenille, these rooms, stamped with a homelike atmosphere, made her feel lonely. Both rooms were neat, but the large colorful map did a lot to disperse some of the barren atmosphere in here. The children's toys, except for a few strays, were relegated to a big cardboard box, but even that jumble added warmth.

The table between two easy chairs was piled high with issues of *Newsweek*, *Life*, and *Collier's*. Both bedside tables held books and boxes of Kleenex. On one was a glass ashtray and a clock; on the other, a doily that looked as if it might have been crocheted by someone's grandmother.

It was nice, the comfortable mood in the two rooms, thought Sydney. Through the doorway she could hear Billy repeating the same prayer she had learned as a child. "Now I lay me down to sleep. . . ." Unexpectedly she felt tears burn her eyes and blinked them away. It all reminded her of her home before her mother had died. Soft conversation, warmth, a sleepy child. She hadn't thought of her mother in a happy way for a long time.

Faith noticed that Sydney's eyes had taken on a suggestion of homesickness or nostalgia as she watched Kay and the children.

"What are you thinking of? Home?" she asked with a small smile.

Sydney laughed, but there was no humor in the sound. "Not home. I was thinking of my mother."

"It must be hard to be so far away from her."

Sydney gave another low, sad chuckle. "Yes. She's been dead since I was twelve."

Faith felt her own heart contract. "My mother died when I was that age, too. That's when I moved in with Kay and Bill."

"You were lucky to have someone."

"Where was—" Faith broke off. "Forgive me. It's none of my business."

Sydney sipped her coffee. Carefully she set down her cup. "That's all right. My daddy . . . changed after my mother died. I ran away from home when I was sixteen."

Faith tried to imagine herself alone, on her own, at that age. She couldn't. "How awful for you," she said.

Sydney shrugged. "It could have been worse," she mused. "If it hadn't been for Mrs. Deveraux, it would have been." Much worse. She told Faith briefly about her arrival in New Orleans, finding Mrs. Deveraux and the boardinghouse.

Faith spoke again, changing the subject. Despite her protest the southern girl was feeling homesick. "Do you write to any boys in the service?" she asked.

"I don't know any well enough to write," Sydney admitted.

"I'll bet you do. My roommate and I got some names out of the paper. I write to Kay's brother, too." Kay had a brother overseas, in North Africa.

Sydney thought of Bobby Dick. He was the only other serviceman besides Vance that she knew personally. "I do have one friend. He's in flight school."

Kay had returned to the room. She was picking up toys. At the mention of flight school she paused and said, "Oh? Where?"

"In Tuskegee, Alabama."

Kay looked blank. "Where?" she repeated.

"That's where the army just set up a school for Negro pilots."

Kay hadn't heard about that, but she was clearly pleased. She tossed the toys into the large box and joined them at the table. She asked a lot of questions that Sydney was unable to answer. "Good for the Army Air Corps," she stated finally. "I've always felt that the navy policy is archaic."

Sydney smiled; she could agree with that. She remembered how hard he'd tried to be admitted into a navy program. "Bobby Dick loves airplanes. He'll make a good pilot." It was gratifying to be able to make a contribution to the conversation. Silently she thanked Bobby Dick. "I'll write to him soon."

Later as Sydney lay in her own bed she made another promise to herself—to learn more about what was going on in the world. She would read magazines and back issues of the papers and ask questions. Tonight she'd felt like an ignoramus, but she wouldn't feel that way again. From now on when people started talking about the war she would have something to add.

She decided to make some changes in her room, too. Make it warmer, more inviting with a nice lamp, with a map of the world like Kay's.

And a checkerboard!

Vance loved to play checkers; he said it was more of a challenge than chess was. When she'd met him, Sydney didn't know how to play either game. Mrs. Deveraux had been a better opponent than Sydney, but he'd seemed to enjoy teaching her on the old board in the parlor in New Orleans.

Vance would like a checkerboard. She also reminded herself to write and assure the old woman that she had arrived safely.

When Sydney fell asleep that night she was happier than she'd been since she arrived in Seattle.

Chapter 11

Monday, June 8, 1942

Sydney wiped her damp palms on her skirt and opened the door in answer to an emphatic knock. The man who stood there seemed taller, thicker, than she remembered.

The khaki uniform distinguished him. This was her husband, she reminded herself, yet he seemed like a stranger, standing there, broad shoulders at attention, his hat tucked under his arm. She barely knew him. Her heart thudded loudly in her chest. Married one day, what could she have been thinking of? He cocked his head and grinned. That reassured her only slightly.

"Honey." There was a world of emotion in that one word as Vance came through the door and dropped his seabag.

She closed the door and leaned against it. "Vance, how are you? You're looking good." The mechanical greeting had the effect of stopping him in his tracks.

"You're looking good, too." His eyes wandered down over her yellow blouse and tan skirt; then they returned quickly to her face as though he'd been caught doing something improper.

Sydney cursed herself silently. She felt wicked, hated herself for the stiffness. Why couldn't she be natural with him?

He turned away. "So this is home." His presence dwarfed the room, making everything in it look smaller. She could sense his impatience, his eagerness, and the awareness did nothing to allay her anxiety.

"Did—" She cleared her throat. Had he noticed her nervousness? "Did they give you your key downstairs?" She took a step away from the door, watching as he opened the closet, tried the new lamp, looked in the bathroom.

"Yeah." He was back, bouncing on the bed, testing the mattress. "Hey, a checkerboard!"

The board was folded, and the wooden box of checkers sat atop it on the table beside the bed. He opened the box, took out a red piece, examined it carefully, and replaced it in the box.

"Yes, I went shopping this morning. I thought you might enjoy . . ." Her voice sounded indifferent even to her own ears. She let the statement trail off, unfinished.

He centered the box on the board, the board on the table, and then looked up, meeting her gaze head-on. "Are you nervous, Sydney?" he asked, the casual note of the question belying the hurt expression in his eyes.

Guilt overtook her. She opened her mouth to deny the accusation. "Yes," she said instead. "I'm not sure why, but I guess I am."

"Me, too."

"You?" Vance nervous? He was always totally in control. It was hard to believe, but she felt comforted by his confession. Slowly she approached the bed and he rose to meet her. They stood there, time suspended for long seconds as they looked at each other.

The scent of his after-shave lotion reached her nostrils. It was what he always wore. She smiled at the familiar reminder and raised her hands to his arms. "I'm glad you're nervous, too. It keeps me from feeling like such a ninny." The worsted sleeves of his uniform jacket were rough under her fingers; the texture was something tangible to hold onto and dear.

His fingers barely skimmed her waist. He seemed to be holding his breath.

Slowly the stiffness ebbed from her, slowly she smiled. "Welcome home, Chief."

Sydney was glad she'd waited for him in the room, because the sort of kiss he bestowed on her wasn't the kind you'd want to share in public—at least, not a public filled with officers' wives. Then she wondered why she'd thought that. This man was her husband, and she didn't give a damn what a group of prissy-assed women thought about where or how he kissed her. She wrapped her arms around him and responded ardently to the kiss. And Jordan Adair's image didn't force its way into her head.

He backed her against the bed. The kiss was becoming more insistent.

Sydney squirmed and he relaxed his hold a fraction. "I've

missed you, honey." He smoothed a strand of hair away from her forehead. "I've missed you like hell. Sometimes our wedding seemed like a dream. I couldn't really believe you were my wife. But you are and you're here." He chuckled. "And I'm finally here, too."

He was tugging her blouse out of the waistband of her skirt.

"Vance, wait. I have to go to work in a few minutes."

"Work?" A frown descended over his features, blotting out the happiness like a black cloud.

"Yes, work," she teased. "You do remember telling me that I would have some volunteer duties in the hotel? Well, priority has placed me at the bottom of the totem pole." She glanced at her watch. "I've got to be downstairs in a few minutes."

"I thought . . . well, damn it, I just got here! Can't they let us have some time alone?" He whirled on her. "Did you ask?"

"No. It's only for two hours, Vance. I'm not complaining."

"Well, I sure as hell am." He surged to his feet, dropping her hand and heading for the door.

"Vance, please. I don't want you to get into trouble. These are officers' wives here."

"There won't be any trouble, I promise you," he answered grimly. "Stay here. I'll be back in a minute."

She stared after him, hoping his interference wasn't going to make her life any more difficult than it already was.

Vance ignored the speculative looks he received from several people in the lobby. There was no gold braid on his uniform. They'd get used to seeing him there, but it would take a while. He thought of just packing up Sydney and himself and walking out. But where the hell would they go? There wasn't a corner of the Puget Sound area that wasn't packed to the rafters.

Still, if things got uncomfortable for his wife, he would do just that. If he had to, he'd buy a car and they'd sleep in it. For a brief moment he regretted not having accepted the officer's commission he'd been offered, but the regret passed quickly.

Sydney would have been more comfortable living in the Elysium if her husband were an officer, but even his love for the redhead couldn't change how he felt. He was only interested in his inventions and didn't want the responsibility of leadership. To be left alone to do his work was all he wanted. And he was.

At the thought of the top-secret work he was doing, his mind, like a race car, promptly picked up speed and veered toward a problem that had been bugging him all weekend. The difficulty of swiftly changing distances, a different audio filter . . .

The door to the small anteroom behind the desk was closed. Vance set aside the random reflections, approached the door, and knocked.

"Come in."

He recognized Kay Parker's voice. When he entered in response to her call, he found her at a desk covered with accounting sheets, her chin propped on one hand. She looked tired but at the sight of him her smile of inquiry became one of genuine welcome. "Chief Bingham. How nice to see you again."

He didn't return her smile. "Mrs. Parker—" he began.

She interrupted, a worried look on her face. "Kay, please."

"Kay," he acknowledged. "You know that I shipped out the day after Sydney and I married."

"Yes."

"Well, I'd like a few hours alone with my bride. You know how it is, Mrs.—Kay. If you'd been separated from the commander so soon, you'd want some time alone and he'd want to be with you. I understand that Sydney has volunteer duties; she's more than willing to do her part. But I would like this first night with her."

"Of course, I understand."

"Well, for some reason Mrs. Adair doesn't. She's got Sydney working in the coffee shop tonight. I asked her to swap but she wouldn't even consider it. Mrs.—Kay, I know I'm only a chief petty officer, but—"

"Chief Bingham, we all know who runs the navy," Kay said with a placating smile.

But he was not to be placated. "She was—" He groped for a word. "—firm about it."

In fact she was quite rude, Kay silently finished for him. She could imagine the scene. "Sometimes Mrs. Adair is overly protective of her province. It's a demanding job."

"I'm not questioning her ability, just her compassion. Will you intervene?"

She hesitated. "Are you sure you want me to?"

He thrust his hands into his pockets. "Kay, I brought Sydney here. I'm responsible for her happiness. If I could find other quarters, I would, but we both know that's impossible."

Kay remembered Captain Conway's admonition, relayed by Bill, to keep the chief happy. She also remembered the early days of her own marriage, when she and Bill were young and passionate, impatient to be together. After thirteen years the youthful impatience had faded somewhat, but she still remembered vividly. And, she told herself, the avid, breathless emotions had been replaced by finer, deeper feelings. If they weren't as strongly passionate, well, that was normal, wasn't it?

Yes, she could sympathize. She could admire the chief, and she could even envy his wife. She dropped the pencil she'd been holding and linked her fingers. "Very well." But she felt compelled to add a caution. "My interference will probably complicate things for Sydney."

"Sydney can take care of herself. The only reason she didn't tell Mrs. Adair to go—" Again he seemed at a loss. "—jump in the lake, was that she was afraid it would come back on me somehow."

Kay hid a smile. The more she was around this man, the better she liked him. She wished she could say the same about his wife. Not that she *dis*liked Sydney, but she was wary of her worldliness and of her growing influence on Faith. "And aren't you afraid it might?" She knew the answer before she asked the question.

"At this point, I don't give a damn."

Kay allowed her smile to break loose. "Consider it done, Chief. Your wife is a very lucky woman."

But the smile had faded by the time she crossed the lobby to the coffee shop.

Regular navy wives, the ones whose husbands made the service a career, realized that they had more influence than was perhaps desirable. Men who were gone a large percentage of the time, be they salesmen or soldiers, usually relied on their wives, not only to keep things going while they were away, but also to keep them up to date on what was happening in their families, their communities.

If a military wife was the spiteful type, ideas could be planted easily and surreptitiously over the dinner table, ideas that might later end up as a recorded part of a man's fitness report and have a weighted effect on his next promotion, even his career. Thank goodness, not many women succumbed to the temptation. But there were always a few who, because of some slight, a personality conflict, or simple dislike, did.

The civilians who suddenly found themselves cast in the role of service wife seemed more tempted by the illusion of power. Maybe they would have behaved the same way had they remained in civilian life.

She had an idea that Valerie Adair would have been a driving force in Jordan's decisions even if he were still in Chicago practicing law. Jordan seemed to accept that, which surprised Kay. When they'd first met she hadn't thought he'd be the type to let his wife influence his choices. You never knew.

Sydney was wiping a table in the far corner. She looked up with a worried frown.

Kay smiled reassuringly and asked Valerie for a word in private. The two stepped into the small cubbyhole behind the register that served as an office.

Valerie took the chair behind her desk and waved Kay into the chair opposite. "What can I do for you?" she asked coolly.

"Two problems," said Kay with equal aplomb. "First, Maurice is complaining that you seem to be monopolizing Jimmy McCoy's services." She was surprised to see color seep into Valerie's cheeks.

"There is a lot more to do here than in the dining room. I need Jimmy."

"I'm sure that's true. But occasionally Maurice needs him as well. He tells me he has been trying to get some stock moved for two days. Surely in that time there has been an opportunity for you to get along without him for a short while."

Valerie gave quick short nod. "Very well. I'll see that he spends a part of each day with Maurice."

"Thank you. The second problem concerns Chief Bingham and his wife."

"Here for less than a week and she's already trying to get out of her duties."

"I was under the impression that it was he who made the request."

"Yes, he did come by. But I know that kind of girl, Kay. Give her an inch and she'll try for a mile. She put him up to it."

"No, as a matter of fact she didn't." Kay leaned back in her chair and eyed the other woman thoughtfully.

"Sydney isn't familiar with navy custom. She wouldn't ask for a special consideration because she thought it might come back on her husband. Which, of course it wouldn't, would it, Valerie?"

Valerie met her eyes. "No, of course not."

"The Binghams had been married for one day when he had to leave her in New Orleans. I think another day or two for a belated honeymoon could be tolerated without the coffee shop falling apart, don't you?"

Valerie shrugged. "It's your decision."

"Right. It is. And I've made it. Sydney can swap with one of the other girls."

The sound of Vance turning the key in the lock was very loud in the silence. Sydney entered before him and kept walking. Though it wasn't completely dark, she went to the window, drew down the blackout shade, and closed the heavy draperies. Her nervousness had returned, and she had an idea that his had, too. At least she hoped that was all it was.

They had eaten at one of the seafood places down on Alaska Way. Vance had been very quiet throughout the meal. "I enjoyed dinner," she said.

Behind her Vance clicked on the light. Instead of answering he looked around and thrust a hand through his thick hair. "This is not much of a room. You had more space in Mrs. Deveraux's house." His voice held regret and apology.

"No! It's a great room," she blurted, returning to his side. She took a breath. "Well, it will be," she amended.

"Yeah." He didn't sound convinced.

"I'm going to add some homey touches. I bought the lamp just this morning, you've seen the checker set, and I have some other ideas." She paused. "We're lucky to have this room, Vance."

"And you have to work in that damned coffee shop to earn the privilege." He took off his coat, tugged at his tie, avoiding her eyes during the process.

"Is that what's bothering you?" she asked.

He shrugged and said, "I should take a shower."

As Vance ran a hand over the lower part of his face, she could hear the rasp of skin on beard over the drumbeat of her heart. This is my husband and he isn't a stranger at all. "Vance?"

He raised a brow in inquiry.

"I'm very glad to be here, with you."

The statement stilled his hand. He searched her expression for any sign of deception. "Do you really mean that, Sydney?" he asked quietly.

She smiled and helped him with his buttons. "Yep," she said. "And I think the shower's big enough for two, don't you?"

His arms came around her with an almost desperate grip.

Bill propped one stiff arm against the bulletin board, ignoring the still-jubilant air of the men in the offices. The battle at Midway was on the minds and lips of everyone. His other hand, thrust into his pocket, was knotted into a fist. His eyes, already tired and red from flying all night, burned anew with sorrow and anger as he read the first casualty list from the battle. Goddamn! Gorman and Jones. Good men, good pilots. Gorman's son, Henry, was the same age as Billy.

But his outrage was born of the other notice. He'd just read that Caster had been given command of his old squadron. He supposed he would be back to training pilots.

Frustrated to the length of his patience, Bill left the administration building and strode across the grassy quadrangle and down the street toward the Sand Point Officers' Club. Though it was not yet noon, he needed a drink. He noticed neither the young swabbie who saluted him nor the sober-faced officer with four stripes on his epaulets who followed about fifty yards behind him.

After years of training pilots and testing planes Bill had finally been assigned last January to a fighter squadron aboard the aircraft carrier, USS *Shiloh*. The pleasure hadn't lasted long. When the *Shiloh* took the destructive hits that crippled the ship and sent it here for repair, his squadron had been sent to New Guinea until it could rejoin the carrier. He'd gotten four Zekes— Japanese Zeros as they were known to the public—those magnificent fighter planes produced by the Mitsubishi Company, while flying out of the island country. They were faster and much more maneuverable than the navy's Wildcats . . . ah, hell. It didn't bear thinking about.

Then had come the orders to Seattle. He had pleaded to remain with his squadron in the South Pacific. But he'd been told very firmly that he was more valuable to the navy here. Hell, he knew that there were pilots to be trained, but someone else could do that. He'd also been assured that it was his experience, not his age, that had led to the decision to bring him back. He wondered about that. He was almost forty-two. Most pilots his age had been relegated to desk jobs.

He hadn't raised a stink when the orders were reaffirmed. He hadn't raised a stink, either, when they'd placated him with the recon mission at Dutch Harbor when he'd rather have been flying at Midway.

He knew planes, he'd tested them for enough years and he'd been flying, testing, for so long, he could spot a problem through his fingertips. He would even give up the chance to test the new F6F fighter, the plane that was being touted as the one that would defeat the Japs. They needed one. Even if they tested the prototype for the new plane this month, it would still be next summer before any of them saw battle.

But, hell, he wanted to be out there with his buddies and with the men he'd trained.

Now it sounded like they were threatening to take him off the carrier permanently, to keep him Stateside for the duration. And that he couldn't handle.

He reached the red brick building and took the shallow steps three at a time. He slapped the swinging door, sending it crashing against the wall.

The interior was charcoal black after the glare of sunshine outside but he knew the way. From the jukebox the mellow tones of Glenn Miller's orchestra playing "In the Mood" wound through his mind like a slimy slug. He wanted to hit something or somebody, and he felt misguidedly that the music should match *his* mood. His long legs ate up the distance to the bar. "Scotch on the rocks," he growled at the steward. "Make that a double."

"I see you got the news," said a voice from behind him.

Bill swung around to face Captain Douglas Conway. For a minute he couldn't say anything. He simply stared into the cold gray eyes that met his without flinching. This was the man responsible for the detested orders. "Yes, sir."

"Join me, son."

It was an order. Bill thought briefly about ignoring it. He finally shrugged and picked up his drink.

"Take a coffee break, sailor," said the captain to the steward.

Puzzled, Bill watched as the officer scanned the tables. He seemed to be looking for a place to sit, which was ridiculous because they were the only two people, aside from the steward, in the room.

Finally he led the way to a table in the corner and took a seat with his back to the intersecting walls. "Have you been home?" he asked conversationally. His eyes were on the steward.

"No, sir. I just landed about an hour ago. And saw the bulletin board. Caster's taken command of my squadron."

The young man left the room and finally Captain Conway gave Bill his attention. "Yes."

"A desk job, then?"

"Christ, no! Bill, before you go flying off the handle and live up to your moniker, let me tell you that what you're going to do is much more important."

Bill gave a harsh laugh. "That's what they say to everyone just before they ground them."

The older man's eyes narrowed dangerously. "We all do the jobs that are necessary to defeat our enemies. Sometimes they aren't the glory jobs."

The captain had hit a sensitive nerve and suddenly Bill was embarrassed by his own outburst. "I'm sorry, sir. If you think glory-chasing was my motive for the protest—" He heard the stiffness in his own voice and broke off midsentence.

"Of course it wasn't," the captain said. "I don't know where the hell you ever got that idea you weren't going to fly. I know you're in your forties but your last physical certainly denies your age. Why would the navy ground one of its best pilots, who is also as healthy as a horse?"

Bill kept silent, but his blue eyes narrowed.

"You aren't the only man who can lead a squadron but you are the best man for a job we have for you. Have you met Chief Vance Bingham?"

Bill hid his surprise. Maybe now he was going to find out what made the chief petty officer so important. "No, sir, but I know of him," he answered. "He was looking for quarters, I understand. You suggested that Kay find a place for him and his wife at the hotel. But I left for Alaska before they arrived."

The captain folded his arms on the table before him. "Before the war Vance Bingham was a mechanic. He had a small auto repair business in Pittsburg. But his hobby is shortwave radios. He sensed the war was coming and had some 'jackanape inventions'—as he called them—that he thought might be helpful. This happened long before Pearl Harbor, by the way. The navy saw the promise in a couple of his devices. He enlisted and they sent him to the communications center in New Orleans. Evidently during the tests there, they discovered that one of these inventions is pretty effective in keeping the enemy from intercepting radio transmissions between ships."

Bill caught his breath, his mind making the logical leap from ships to planes. A smile began to grow on his face.

The captain read his thoughts. "Yes, he's now trying to adapt it for use in planes. We've named it Vocat."

" 'It calls,' " Bill translated the Latin word. "God! What a discovery!" His drink was forgotten as he leaned forward and instinctively lowered his voice. "This might be just the advantage we need until the F6F gets to us. How does it work?"

"I don't pretend to understand electronics except in any but the most basic way, but it is some kind of voice encryption. The transmitter not only uses inverted frequencies, but also splits them into separate bands. It takes a sophisticated receiver to decode the transmissions on the other end. I heard from the skipper on one of the ships out of New Orleans that to the enemy it sounds like a recording being played backward at half speed.

"Is it ready for testing?"

"Not yet. Soon. Security is our main concern right now. We're sending Bingham to Hawaii on a destroyer, the *John Tuggle*. It sails the first week in July. We hope that will divert any speculation that what he's doing is associated with the air wing. He'll finish the models there in a remote facility near Hilo on the island of Hawaii.

"The *Shiloh* will be ready to sail about a week later. You'll be on board with four other pilots of your choosing, ostensibly a part of the fighter squadron but in reality as an independent group. The carrier will make a stop at Hilo where Bingham will be waiting to board with his radio devices. The Vocat won't actually be installed on the planes until the carrier leaves Hawaii. You'll carry out your tests and report as quickly as possible. We want this thing ready to go before the major push for the Solomons."

"We'll be testing four units?" He was already selecting and dismissing candidates in his head. Cody Bristol, of course. Maybe Mason.

Conway nodded. "Another man in your hotel is working on the production end. Lieutenant Jordan Adair used to do some scouting for the War Production Board and for the Truman committee; he has good contacts in industry. The manufacturer he has picked will be ready to go into production as soon as they hear from you and Bingham that the tests are complete. Bingham will be flown back to Seattle to get right to work."

Bill's gaze sharpened at the name of the senator from Missouri. He recalled that he was to meet with Truman while he and Kay were in Washington, but of course, the attack on Pearl Harbor postponed that meeting indefinitely. "One question: Why don't we test it here in this area?"

"There are several reasons, the most important being Bingham's insistence on actual battle conditions. He says that there may be interference he hasn't counted on." The captain ticked off on his fingers. "The others are the fact that the thing isn't ready yet. From what I understand Bingham will be pushing it to be finished before the carrier picks him up at Hilo. And security. Our intelligence types have picked up on a rumor that maybe the enemy suspects we're working on this.''

That brought a grim look to Bill's features. "If the enemy gets wind of this they'll do anything and everything to get their hands on one of the Vocats to study.''

Conway nodded. "Of course, that's one of the facts of war. But it will take them a few months to figure how it works, and those might be the few months we need. So until it is operational we have to keep the lid on it and screwed down.

"We're not testing a plane here, Bill, but I want you to wring her out just as if we were. Work this device hard during the testing," Conway added, the seriousness vibrant in his tone. "Because if there are any bugs we have to know before we start production. That's important. We don't want to load any useless material on our planes.''

Bill knew how important it was.

"The man's a genius, Bill. Some people are comparing him to William Friedman.''

Friedman was the director of the Signal Intelligence Service. Bill couldn't conceal his surprise. And now he was more curious than ever to meet Vance Bingham. This explained the high-powered support this man was drawing on. He knew of, but had never met Friedman, who had built the "Purple" cipher machine that decoded Japanese diplomatic communiqués at the beginning of the war. Friedman's work had been "top" secret, a new classification by the government for work that wasn't to be seen except by the most important eyes. If Bingham was in that league . . .

"Bingham has other ideas—well, I don't know the specifics, but the Pentagon has more or less turned him loose to work on whatever he chooses. This war will be a long one; they think his ideas can help shorten the time by possibly a year or more. God knows, we need all the help we can get.''

"Midway—''

"We'll be celebrating Midway for a long time, but it was only a beginning. We need a hundred, a thousand Midways, if we're going to win. And we *have* to be technically superior. The Germans are doing experimental work. They've given the Japanese a lot of their . . .''

Captain Conway's grave commentary trailed off, halted by the arrival of a group of men on their lunch hour. The steward must have been waiting just outside the door, for he returned in the wake of the men, hurrying to take their orders.

Bill subdued the excitement he felt at this revelation. Communications was a major problem among pilots. A command not to break radio silence under any conditions, so as not to alert the enemy to the squadron position, left pilots dangerously handicapped. He sensed that Conway wouldn't continue this discussion until they were alone again. "Have you heard anything about the new plane?" he asked, shifting smoothly to an innocent topic.

The captain picked up on it. "We're pleased with the modifications." The navy had great expectations for the proposed fighter Grumman was developing. The plane, called the Hellcat, was supposed to be more of a match for Japanese planes than the F4F Wildcat that the navy was flying now. But the new plane was plagued by problems. They'd had to modify the prototype several times, hence the 3A addendum.

"Grumann's working night and day now that the New York plant is finished," Conway went on. "But it will still be a year before the new plane sees action."

Bill nodded. "Yeah," he said.

Conway hesitated, then added, "Bob Hall is going to test this month."

Bill smiled at that. His disappointment at not getting to test this prototype was ameliorated by his enthusiasm over the Vocat device. "Bob's a good man," he commented mildly. "It's a shame we don't have one or two of the Mitsubishi engineers working for Grumman."

"The Zeke is twice as responsive," Conway agreed. He grinned. "But we've got superior pilots."

"Naturally," agreed Bill, wishing to God that was true. Japanese pilots were damn good; and spurred by their reverence for their emperor, they were willing to commit religious hara-kiri for the Empire. He shook himself. "Tell me what reports we're getting from Midway."

"I'll get it," shouted Billy in response to a knock at the door of the living room.

Faith laughed and continued to fold from the pile of clothes on the middle bed. "Where on earth does he get all that energy?" she asked Kay.

Kay handed Millie a stack of towels. "Put these away, please, honey." Millie headed for the bathroom.

"Daddy!"

At her daughter's call Kay ran through the connecting door. She paused at the sight that met her eyes.

"Forgot my key." Bill looked exhausted, his face was tired and lined, his uniform a wrinkled mess, but he smiled. Suddenly the sun had come out. She walked forward into his arms.

The children danced around them while he took his first kiss, a deep and thoroughly satisfying one.

Faith stood at the door to the connecting room, waiting, renewing her vow to be on her best behavior.

Bill looked up. "Good Lord, you get prettier every time I see you," he said, grinning. "Come here and give your big brother a hug."

Her laughter was light, like a song, as she came to them.

Kay lay in the curve of Bill's arm. The muted sounds of giggles beyond the connecting door clashed with the mellow music of Benny Goodman coming from the radio. Go to sleep, she instructed silently.

"Since Faith is here to take care of the kids I thought we might take a couple of days and go up to Victoria," said Bill softly. "Would you like that?"

"Oh, yes. I'd like that very much. When could you get away?"

He chuckled. "When could *you* get away? Since you've become the businesswoman, you're busier than I am." The words were uttered with the slightest tinge of restraint.

It wasn't true, of course, but Kay knew that her husband was impatient. A pilot, a career navy officer, couldn't react otherwise in time of war to this enforced idleness. Idleness wasn't the right word. The navy wouldn't be keeping him in the States for no reason. He was training pilots, trying to help meet the quota set by the Secretary of the Navy.

He wasn't testing.

She always knew when he was testing. The adrenaline flowed, and he came home exhausted and with grease under his fingernails, but exhilarated. For Bill wasn't content to report on glitches in the planes he tested, he had to get right in there and show the engineers what was wrong.

She raised herself on an elbow and looked at him through the pitch-black darkness. "I'll make arrangements to go anytime you say."

"Sometime next week then. I'll check the dates. We'll take the ferry up and spend a night or two at the Empress. It will be nice not to have to whisper when I want to make love to my wife.''

She laughed softly. ''It will be wonderful.'' She paused. ''You'll be leaving soon then.'' It wasn't a question.

He pulled her back into the crook of his arm. ''Is that the only time I make love wonderfully? When we're about to be separated?''

''Mostly.'' When he gave a mock growl she allowed a teasing tone to color her whisper. ''Well, no, but things have a way of heating up then.''

He sighed. ''Kay, I've got—''

''A lot on your mind,'' she finished for him. ''I know, honey.'' He refused to discuss his job—it was a silly superstition, one of several—but she hated the thought of being left out. She supposed that was why she'd become so good at guessing. ''This will sound selfish, but I'm glad you weren't at Midway.''

''How do you know I wasn't?''

''Because you didn't take your tropical uniforms. You must have been on temporary duty somewhere, but I figure you were north of here.''

His wry laughter reached up through his chest to tickle her cheek. ''I can't talk about where I'm going, but I don't suppose there's a rule about telling you where I've been.''

She raised her head to stare at him. ''You weren't!'' she said accusingly.

''No,'' he said. ''I wanted to be but I wasn't. They gave me a consolation mission.'' He proceeded to explain briefly about the attack on Dutch Harbor in Alaska. He didn't tell her that the Japanese had landed on the Aleutians. Or that they were still there.

Kay was silent during the recounting. The news reports had mentioned Alaska but had drastically played down that battle in light of the victory at Midway. But she couldn't get the picture of Bill out of her mind, flying his reconnaissance aircraft high above the fighting. A few moments ago she had felt left out because he wouldn't talk about his job; now she wished he hadn't. Her silence continued after he was finished.

Finally Bill spoke again, distracting her, ''To return to our original subject, I seem to remember a lot of heavy breathing and innovation while we were in D.C.''

He was right. But the atmosphere in Seattle was different, especially in light of what he'd just told her. In D.C. he had a job to do, convincing Congress and BuOrd of the need for testing. It was important and he did it well, but it didn't cause the distraction that his duties here caused. The timeliness and focus on the present to the exclusion of all but rote emotions, hadn't been present in Washington, and it robbed them of the closeness that she needed right now. But she didn't know how to talk to him about it.

Sex and sentiment weren't subjects they discussed except in the vaguest of terms. When a man was about to go into a danger zone, the slightest distraction could cause him to lose the edge, the edge that fighter pilots claimed was so important. So, knowing she wouldn't, couldn't make demands, she reverted to the old teasing terms. "Bill, that was six months ago."

Bill began to nuzzle her neck, ready to rectify the situation when a laugh from the next room caused them both to sigh. "Don't those kids ever sleep?" he said gruffly as he fell back on his pillow.

Kay dropped the arm that had crept around his neck. "They're still excited about Faith's being here."

When she got no reply to her observation she went on. "I'm excited about her being here, too."

She felt him smile. "She looks wonderful, doesn't she?" He hesitated. "How are the two of you getting along?" he asked.

"Fine. She's changed; she's a lot more mature than she was the last time we saw her."

"I'm glad," he said, the relief evident in his voice. "I wish she'd stayed in school."

"I know you do, darling, but she's promised to go back to get her degree and you know that your sister never makes promises lightly."

He chuckled. "Yeah. Remember the time you took her to the Change of Command ceremony in Jacksonville? We warned her she would be bored but she wanted to go, and she still wouldn't swear to behave because she was afraid she couldn't keep her promise."

Kay nodded against his shoulder. "But we took her anyway. She fell sound asleep right in front of the admiral. She wanted to be near you, Bill. That was soon after your parents were killed. She needs that now, too."

Bill's arm tightened around her shoulders, his deep voice rumbled under her ear. "Maybe you're right, honey. Hell, I know you're right. Being together as much as possible is what we all need right now."

Chapter 12

Wednesday, June 10, 1942

Vance's two-day pass was almost over. He grumbled to himself as he thought about reporting back to the base at midnight. Tomorrow he would be thrust back into the preparation for sailing aboard the USS *John Tuggle*. He'd arrived in Seattle to find that the navy had set up a workplace for him at Sand Point. The security was better there; but it meant that, as his departure date drew closer, it all had to be moved to the destroyer's berth at Bremerton. So he was back and forth a lot, wasting valuable time in travel across Puget Sound.

But at least, after one chore was finished, he and Sydney would have the rest of today. He was on his way to the main kitchen to help Maurice decide if one of the old appliances could be saved despite a balky thermostat. The job should take about an hour. While he was working in the kitchen, Sydney was going to meet Faith for a trip to Pike's Market to buy some fresh fruit.

Sydney descended the stairs to the lobby at her husband's side. Her heart sank as she looked across the lobby. Jordan. If they continued in the direction they were moving, their paths would intersect just near the front desk, where Valerie was once again in a heated discussion with Kay. Sydney's footsteps slowed; her fingers tightened on her husband's arm.

Vance misunderstood the response and laid a reassuring hand over hers. At the same time he caught sight of Jordan himself. His expression lightened with pleasure. "Lieutenant Adair."

Jordan turned, the beginning of a smile forming on his face. His gaze slid from Vance to the woman at his side. "Sydney!" His reaction, involuntary and uncontrollable, was clearly shocked.

The tableau seemed frozen in time. Three other pairs of eyes were suddenly fixed on Sydney. She would never forget the varying degrees of amazement reflected in each expression. Kay, behind the desk, was surprised. Vance was interested and Valerie was stunned.

"Jordan Adair!" Sydney moved forward with her hand outstretched. "How nice to see you again."

"You know this woman?" blurted Valerie.

Clearly it was an accusation, not a question at all; and Jordan recovered quickly under its intensity. "Of course I know her. This is Sydney Jackson. She lived in Mrs. Deveraux's boardinghouse. You remember, don't you, Valerie? I told you about the charming lady in New Orleans who rented out rooms."

Valerie subsided, but her gaze was wary and suspicious as it skated from Sydney to her husband.

"Lieutenant," said Vance by way of greeting. He shook the hand Sydney had quickly abandoned. "Her name is Sydney Bingham now," he explained. "I'd heard that you roomed at the same boardinghouse." His mouth tilted in a half smile. "Small world." As he spoke Vance interposed himself smoothly between Sydney and Valerie.

Sydney was relieved, and a little surprised at his protective ploy. Despite her embarrassment and shame at this unwelcome reminder of the past, she was also aware that none of the emotions churning through her included despair at the sight of Jordan.

"Yes, it seems to be," acknowledged Jordan. "How are you, Chief?"

"Happier now that my wife has arrived and I've had a little time to spend with her." He draped his arm across Sydney's shoulders and shot a telling look to Valerie, who avoided his gaze.

The uncomfortable moment threatened to stretch to an extreme when, to the relief of everyone, Maurice came bustling up. "Vance, are you coming? I'm really worried about the oven. The thing won't heat at all now."

Jordan Adair watched the two men leave. He was badly shaken by the encounter, but he managed to conceal his shock under his natural reserve. When Vance had arrived last week he'd talked superficially about his marriage, his new bride, but they had so many other things to settle, he never mentioned her by name. Damn it. If he had just known, he could have prepared himself. Instead he felt like fate had dealt him a punch to the gut.

He said a polite good-bye to Sydney and returned to his wife. He didn't like the expression on her face. She was suspicious as hell and with perfectly good reason. If she but knew the truth.

Sydney Jackson—Bingham, he corrected himself—was more to him than just an acquaintance he'd met in a rooming house. Much more. At one time she was his life. Leaving her had been like losing a part of himself.

Leaving? He laughed, silently and without humor. Hell, she'd thrown him out when he'd finally admitted his offense. But she couldn't be blamed; he hadn't played fair from the first. Why hadn't he told her he was married? He, who had always prided himself on his honesty, had been dishonest with the woman who meant the most to him. And he'd hurt her, badly.

His marriage had been in trouble for a long time. The extended work he had to do in New Orleans was a welcome hiatus from the cold mausoleum he lived in with Valerie. The weeks spent there, with Sydney, were like a glimpse of heaven.

But all this was in the past. Valerie was really making an effort to save their marriage; he had to give her that. She deserved his support, his love.

So how the hell was he going to stand having Sydney here?

Sydney was gratified to be free of the hotel. Her emotions were unsettled, flitting lightly, like butterflies within her, and she felt that with the wrong word they might just fly out and scatter all over the street. Faith didn't say a word as they walked briskly down the hill in the direction of the market.

It was over. The confrontation she'd dreaded was finished, and she'd survived. She didn't think Vance had noticed anything amiss. If he had, and if he questioned her later she was confident that she could manage a graceful explanation. If anyone had marked the tension in the exchange, it would be Valerie. Shrewd, sly Valerie. Valerie was Jordan's problem, thank God.

The physical exercise helped calm her, and by the time they reached the market her unsettled emotions were settled again.

It was an unseasonably hot day for Seattle. They reached the temporary market at the corner across from the burned-out shell of the original, using handkerchiefs to fan their faces. Stalls were filled with a myriad of goods, from fresh produce to fish to dried fruits. The conversation was limited to the condition of the produce as their shopping baskets gradually filled. They paused at the balustrade to catch a breeze from the waters of

Elliot Bay. The Olympic mountains hovered beyond Puget Sound.

"This is a beautiful city, isn't it?" said Faith.

"I don't like mountains," Sydney answered.

"Why on earth not?"

Sydney thought for a minute. "I don't really know. I guess—they seem to crowd and bunch up on you. We don't have mountains in southern Mississippi or Louisiana. I like the flat land where you can see what's coming."

Faith laughed. "Makes sense, I guess. By the way, Sydney. I'm going to the hospital tomorrow to sign up for volunteer work. Would you like to go with me?"

"Sure," said Sydney instantly. Anything to keep her away from the hotel after Vance left. The less she saw of Valerie and Jordan Adair, the better. "Just let me know when."

A wizened old man held out a basket of beautiful red apples for their consideration. Faith stopped to bargain, and Sydney wandered forward a few steps. The apples brought back a childhood memory—a book—the poisoned apple in the fairy tale, "Sleeping Beauty." In her imagination she could see the picture of the wicked witch with the long fingernails, enticing Beauty to eat the luscious fruit. Despite the heat Sydney shivered. The witch took on the features of Valerie Adair.

Suddenly the absurdity of her thoughts hit her and she laughed. "I'm going to get out of this sun, Faith, or I'll be a mass of freckles. I'll wait for you under the next shed," she said, and moved out into the shade.

"Sydney?" The sound of her name made her pause, but somehow she wasn't a bit surprised to find Jordan at her elbow.

She turned, glancing over his shoulder to locate Faith. There was no sign of the younger girl. "Hello, Jordan," she said calmly.

His eyes were shadowed by the brim of his hat, but she could see the wariness in them. She shared the same guarded feelings. Actually seeing him was both harder and easier than she'd expected. Now that she had the leisure to look carefully she noticed that he looked like the very devil; he'd aged in a year. Not unattractively but definitely. The observation threatened to rouse her compassion, but she determinedly put it aside. His next comment made the effort easier.

"What are you doing in Seattle? Did you follow me here?"

Her jaw dropped at the audacity of the question. To her great relief, anger submerged the softer feelings she'd experienced when she'd first seen him. She clamped her teeth together and spoke through thin lips. "Just who the hell do you think you are?" She didn't mean to sound quite so harsh, but she was hurt. How could he think she would deliberately follow him?

He took her arm. The physical contact startled them both, and he immediately dropped his hand. "I didn't—ah, hell, Sydney! It was a shock to see you, that's all. I didn't know who Vance Bingham married."

"Well, now you do." She paused. "And you'll notice I'm telling you this right up front."

He didn't miss the message. "Does he know about us?"

She stared at him. "God, you have a lot of gall, don't you?" He waited for her to answer. Finally she sighed. "He knows there was someone. He doesn't know who it was."

He shoved his hands into his pockets and turned to look out over the water. "Damn! Of all the bad luck."

"Yes, isn't it?" She heard her own voice shake, bringing his gaze back to her, and this time it was her turn to swing away from him, pressing the fingertips of one hand to her temple. She felt the dampness there. The smell of fish was overpowering, and the unseasonable heat was worse under the metal roof of the shed. The lack of movement in the air made her short of breath. "Dear God, why am I going through this again? I don't know why you followed me, Jordan, but please leave me alone."

Jordan was suffering, too. Her face had haunted him day and night for over a year. He'd tried to forget her, but he knew now that he never would. But he could do one thing for her. He said, "I had to talk to you."

She was really surprised at his manner. She knew him well enough to know that Jordan Adair seldom lost his composure. His agitation was the tiniest bit flattering, she admitted. She tried to bury her curiosity. This man had left her feeling cheap and degraded at a time in her life when she was just beginning to recover her self-respect. Now what did it matter? "We said everything we have to say to each other a year ago," she told him. "I can't see that we have anything else to talk about."

"But this is a different situation. Now you're married to a man that I have dealings with. We live in the same building. We'll see a lot of each other."

"You're Vance's lawyer." She didn't like his inference that she couldn't handle the association.

"I handle some of his business," Jordan said evasively. He

saw in her eyes that she despised him. Maybe it was better this way.

She took a breath and said lightly, "Well, that's the only contact we have to have, isn't it? My, it's hotter up here than I expected. With this humidity you'd think you were in New Orleans."

He ignored her attempt to change the subject. "Sydney, we can't avoid seeing each other, and Valerie's already suspicious."

"I don't know why." Her mouth twisted into a parody of a smile. With her handkerchief she blotted her forehead. "You needn't worry, Jordan. I won't bring your dirty little secret to light." In self-defense she went on, "I never set out to have an affair with a married man."

He watched her beautiful green eyes, always so full of life, dull under the pressure of guilt. God, how he wished he could turn back the clock, bring back their love. Vance and Valerie be damned! But even as he wished, he knew it could never be; she had no feelings for him anymore. "I know," he said quietly. "And I never deliberately set out to deceive you."

She bit back a retort and continued as though he hadn't spoken. "I'm not very proud of myself, you know, for falling in love with you. But it's certainly over now and as far as I'm concerned it never happened."

He closed his eyes, then opened them again. For the first time she noticed the opaque emptiness in them. "I've bungled this badly, Sydney," he said, in a low, regretful voice.

She swallowed hard and tossed her head. "You sure have, Lieutenant, but that's nothing new. Now I wish you'd disappear."

He opened his mouth to reply, but Faith interrupted before he could speak. "Are you finished with your shopping, Sydney? Why, Lieutenant Adair, I didn't recognize you from the back."

Jordan looked at her. "Faith, isn't it? Bill Parker's sister?"

She laughed lightly. "Yes. But someday I hope to be known as myself."

He looked at her as though he hadn't the slightest idea what she was talking about. "I have to be getting to the base. Ladies," he said. Touching the bill of his hat, he left them.

"Well!" she said. "What was that all about?"

How much had she heard? Sydney shrugged. "Nothing. Are you through with your shopping? I'd like to get out of this heat."

"Yes, I'm finished." She seemed about to say something else, but Sydney had already begun to move through the crowd.

As they climbed the hills toward the hotel Sydney kept expecting her to say more, to cross-examine her about the scene she had witnessed. But Faith kept her peace.

That was a good thing because Sydney was afraid her response to any questions right now wouldn't be in keeping with what Mrs. Deveraux had taught her about polite behavior. By the time they reached the entrance to the Elysium, Sydney was drenched with sweat.

There weren't enough chairs for everyone in the alcove around the radio, so some of the women sat on the floor, others perched on the arm of a chair. Several of them, the restless ones, wandered back and forth to their rooms to return with knitting or mending, sometimes cups of coffee, which they handed around.

Sydney was on the floor, her legs curled under her, at Vance's feet. They sat a little apart from the others. She'd been reluctant to join the group at all but Vance had seemed to want to, so there they were. All day they had figuratively tiptoed around each other, being overly polite. That was not the way she was accustomed to behaving around her husband. He was one of the few people with whom she could totally relax, be just herself.

Jordan avoided looking at her as painstakingly as she avoided looking at him. While she tried to remain calm she was nervous of the impending encounter with Vance. He loved her, she knew, but she wasn't sure his love was strong enough to survive the burden placed on it by Jordan's nearness. And, she discovered with peculiar intensity, she wanted it not simply to survive, but to flourish.

Edward R. Murrow's voice, amplified by the volume turned up all the way, echoed down the hall. He was broadcasting from London, quoting from an Air Ministry report on results of the bombing of Cologne, Germany. The allies had devastated eight square miles of that city on May 30th and two days later 1,000 bombers had raided the city of Essen and the Ruhr River industrial area nearby.

"And that's the way it is," Murrow ended as usual.

The announcer encouraged the listener to "Call for Phillip Mor-ees." Valerie reached out to lower the volume. "I'm for bed," she said to no one.

Vance took Sydney's hand, and they headed toward their room. They had to pass the spot where Jordan was standing. "Good night, Lieutenant."

"Good night, Vance, Sydney."

Sydney murmured a response, avoiding his eyes as she passed. When they reached their room and the door was closed behind them Vance brought up the subject she'd been dreading. "So, you knew Adair pretty well in New Orleans?" he asked casually.

"Yes," she answered, trying not to think about how heavy her heart felt. "You know he stayed at Mrs. Deveraux's."

"How long was he there?" His tone was still casual but there was another, deeper note of something else.

She looked at him and prepared herself for a clash. He knew. There wasn't a doubt in her mind that he knew, and if he pushed for it she was going to tell him the truth. She owed him nothing less. But she dreaded his reaction. What if he decided she wasn't worth forgiving? "Off and on for several months. Why? Is it important?" she asked, then held her breath waiting for his answer.

He smoothed her hair back from her face with a gentle touch. "You tell me, sweetheart," he asked with a small, detached smile. "Is it important?"

Responding to her instincts she moved forward into his arms, wanting to erase that look from his face. She couldn't bear to see the slightest sign of pain in his eyes. Not Vance. She shook her head. "No." Her own smile was born at the corners of her lips, rose to light her eyes with appreciation for this wonderful man she had married. "It isn't important to me—not one bit," she whispered, her voice husky but adamant. "What's the absolute last ferry you can take to get to the base by midnight?"

He held her away and lifted one brow in amused inquiry. "The one that leaves at eleven-ten. Why?"

"I'll try to see that you don't miss it but I'm not making any promises," she said as she eased gratefully into his warm, loving embrace.

The next morning Valerie was prepared for an encounter with Sydney Bingham. She wanted to know more about New Orleans and about just how friendly her husband had been with the tacky Southerner. The woman took gaudy to new extremes. Her favorite color seemed to be green and with that red hair she looked like an overgrown Christmas tree.

Last night Valerie had merely been hurt when she couldn't get an acceptable explanation out of Jordan. Obviously some kind of friendship had developed between him and Sydney. But he continued to dismiss her questions as though they were the least of many important things he had on his mind. This morning he'd grown impatient and had brushed off her renewed demands as though she were a pesky fly. His attitude had irritated her to the point that she'd aired all the gripes she'd kept so carefully to herself over the last weeks. She presumed he'd hear about this encounter, too. And take her to task for it.

Sydney was on the way to the laundry room in the basement when she was confronted by the beautiful blonde.

"I would like to talk to you," said Valerie.

Sydney felt at a definite disadvantage with her arms full of dirty clothes, but she nodded. "Sure. I'm on my way to the basement. Do you want to come along or can it wait until I'm finished?"

Valerie seemed to waver. "I'll come with you," she said finally.

The old wringer washer had to be filled with a hose, giving Sydney time to think. She made the connection from the faucet of the sink and turned on the water, adding soap powder and swishing it with her hand before she dumped in the clothes. She was good at pretending, wasn't that what she always told herself? So, she would pretend nothing had ever happened between her and Jordan.

She dried her arm and hand with a towel that she then added to the load. "Now, what can I do for you?" she asked.

Valerie took a pack of cigarettes from the pocket of her skirt. She lit one for herself and replaced the pack pointedly without offering one to Sydney. Everyone shared their cigarettes; it was a deliberate insult, almost as though she hoped Sydney would be offended and therefore make an undisciplined comment. Sydney shrugged off the bait.

"I was quite surprised to find that you and my husband had met in New Orleans."

"Were you? New Orleans is a small town in many ways."

"Jordan was fond of your landlady."

Sydney gave a reminiscent smile. "Mrs. Deveraux is a wonderful lady. She's easy to be fond of."

Valerie inhaled deeply from the cigarette and let the smoke out in a long stream. "I believe she is from a prominent New Orleans family."

Meaning: what were you doing associating with her? "Yes, I believe so."

"Jordan mentioned that he was very comfortable in Mrs. Deveraux's home."

"He seemed to be happy there." Sydney shrugged. "But then he's a nice man. He wouldn't complain if he weren't."

"That brings me to the point I want to make." Valerie stubbed out the cigarette in an ashtray, impatiently, as though she wanted to get on with the purpose of this interview. "Sydney, I noticed today that there was a certain amount of—how shall I say it—embarrassment when the two of you met yesterday morning. I have been aware for a long time that a lot of girls mistake Jordan's kindness for flirtation." Her voice became colder, more threatening. "I hope you won't make that error. After all, even if he were free, which of course he's not, you are not exactly his social equal."

Sydney stared at her, jaw agape, unable to believe her ears. Finally, at a loss, she shook her head. "You know, Valerie, you're a real bitch." She broke off, embarrassed to have been goaded into the off-color designation. "How in the world did Jordan ever get stuck with you?" she asked in wonder.

"He 'got stuck with me' as you so crudely put it, because we're alike. Dignity and pride and tradition are important to us. And background and family. We like the same things, we have the same friends, the same ambitions."

For the first time in the course of this conversation Sydney was tempted to set Valerie straight. She had to bite her tongue not to speak. It took all her power of restraint not to blurt out the truth if only to take this woman down a peg. She was horrified to discover that she wanted to hurt, to wound, Valerie Adair. Calling her a bitch had rolled off her like water off a duck's back. But there were other things she could say.

Valerie didn't even *know* her husband, much less share his ambitions. She could tell her about a Jordan who had been her friend before he was her lover, a relaxed, open Jordan, free of the social strata she coveted so. A man who, once he rid himself of the bonds of restrictive tradition, laughed and teased and played with energy and enthusiasm. A Jordan that this woman would never see.

But of course she couldn't. She suddenly felt even more sorrow for Jordan, condemned by his honor to a life with this cold, unbending woman.

The silence was broken only by the washing machine, singing a rhythmic chorus behind Sydney. A swish, a swish. I wish, I wish. I wish—what? That things had been different? Of course. But they weren't different. And human beings had to accept life as it was handed to them.

Sydney looked appealingly at Valerie. She opened her mouth to speak, then closed it again. At last the right words came to her—at least she hoped they would be the right words. "Valerie," she inquired gently. "What have you ever done *for* your husband? He doesn't want to go into politics, you know."

"Did Jordan tell you that?" Valerie put the emphasis on the personal pronoun.

Sydney wasn't intimidated. "We talked, yes. I think Jordan is a fine man just as he is. Try putting him before yourself for a change."

Valerie opened her mouth to answer, but she couldn't seem to form any words. Her eyes narrowed dangerously; her face infused with blood, quite alarming Sydney, who watched helplessly.

Suddenly the woman's hand snaked out and she slapped Sydney with enough force to rock her on her heels. Then she clamped her lips together and whirled around, running from the room.

Sydney stood there like a rock, stunned into immobility, not even mindful enough to be angry.

The slut! The ridiculous-looking slut, thought Valerie, her fists clenched in fury as she stomped back upstairs. Her suspicions were confirmed, but as she approached the door leading to the lobby, she made a conscious effort to wipe all traces of anger from her face.

Suddenly, without warning, her head began to throb, the low beat of her pulse hammering loud in her ears; her vision blurred. She put a hand to her forehead. Her skin felt hot, scorching hot.

She sank down on the top step, leaning against the cool concrete wall. A minute, that was all she'd need. A minute to compose herself.

Sydney had caused it. How dare that tramp question her relationship with Jordan? Who the hell did she think she was to talk to her betters that way?

What had she done *for* her husband? the redhead had asked. Sydney and *her* husband shouldn't even *be* in this hotel.

What in the world was wrong with her? A few scathing, chilling comments should have put the girl in her place.

Instead she had completely lost control.

Valerie dragged herself up off the step and smoothed her skirt. She tucked a stray wisp of hair into her chignon.

The coffee shop was almost deserted. It would be a good

time—she turned to scan the lobby. A pleasant smile curved her lips as she spied her objective. There was always one person she could depend on to treat her the way she liked to be treated.

"Oh, Jimmy, there you are. I need your help." She widened the smile and cocked her head to one side. "Please?" she added innocently.

The boy was listening to the radio with the little Parker girl, but at her request he turned red and hurried to her side. His immediate response to her request was gratifying to Valerie's wounded spirits. The boy worshipped her.

Chapter 13

Friday, June 19th, 1942

Faith and Sydney were becoming good friends, which surprised both of them.

They'd signed up to do hospital volunteer work twice a week; but, that first day, it had taken neither of them very long to realize how understaffed the place was. Once they realized the need and finished the short training course, they tried to fit in as many additional hours as possible and ended up volunteering at least five times a week.

Faith liked Sydney, liked her gentle open humor, liked her breezy manner. Maybe because they had both lost their mothers when they were children, maybe because they were close to the same age—Sydney, twenty-two, to her twenty-one—or maybe just because they were very different, and found the differences interesting, they had developed a quick friendship in these past three weeks.

They climbed the last hill on their way to the hospital, talking about their plans for the weekend. Kay and Bill were taking the midnight ferry to Victoria for the weekend, and Faith had agreed to keep the children until Monday morning. She glanced sideways at Sydney. "You want to help?"

Sydney didn't know whether Vance would get leave or not. "If Vance isn't here, sure."

"I guess it's only fair to warn you—I told Billy that you played the piano," she confessed, holding the heavy glass door for Sydney to precede her.

Faith had been surprised and pleased recently when she walked into the lobby and heard Sydney playing for an impromptu, stand-around singing group. She had played every-

thing from blues, to swing, to church hymns. The conviviality
and applause was warm, and she saw a number of people come
up afterward to thank Sydney. In Faith's opinion that sort of
thing was just what was needed to counter some of the Spiteful
Nellies and encourage people to accept her for what she was, a
very nice girl. "He's planning to ask for a performance," she
cautioned lightly.

Sydney grinned. "I hope I can remember some kids' songs."

"Billy's favorite song is the 'Beer Barrel Polka.' "

As they approached the double doors leading to the ward,
Faith decided to pry a little bit further. "You're really good,
Sydney. And very versatile. Do you play by ear?"

"No, though I can pick out some songs. My mother was a
piano teacher. And I used to sing in a club in New Orleans. But
that's all in the past." To change the subject she asked, "Do
you play?"

Faith wanted to ask more, but the closed look on Sydney's
face told her to let go the issue. "Not a note. It's hard to take
lessons in anything if you're always moving around," said Faith,
hearing a mark of sadness in her own voice and seeing Sydney's
surprised look in response to it.

Both Faith and Sydney had been shocked when they first
entered the cavernous room that was Ward 2A and were assaulted by the smell. Curtains gathered onto movable metal
frames provided privacy only for the most severely injured.
Overhead fluorescent fixtures burned all day long, casting a harsh
light over everything.

Today the ward was active with movement—nurses, doctors
rushing from bed to bed—yet the patients were strangely quiet.
Sometimes they were greeted with good-natured wolf whistles
and catcalls. Today the men still watched them, but they were
subdued, the only animation a longing, a yearning in their eyes.

They soon learned the reason. A hospital ship had docked
this morning with casualties from the Battle of Midway, dis-
patching over seven hundred wounded men. The beds had been
crowded together allowing the addition of five more beds to the
thirty-five that were already here, and there was a spillover of
patients into the adjacent solarium.

"The hospitals in the area are filled to capacity," Sylvia Wallace, the ward nurse, told them. "We've taken two hundred new
cases in this hospital. You girls will have to put off the letter
writing today and help us out."

One battle, thought Faith, one battle that halted the progress of the enemy, and this was its toll. Dear God, what would it be like when . . . "We haven't even started taking back the stolen land yet," she said absently, looking out over the ward.

The nurse understood the direction of her thoughts. "No, we haven't. This many wounded, so many others dead, and we've only begun."

"What do you want us to do?" asked Sydney.

Mrs. Wallace sent them on their way with a list of instructions. Faith rolled out the juice trolley, filled a large bucket with ice, and set off down the right-hand side of the aisle between the beds. Sydney gathered up an armful of clean bed linens from the storage closet and began on the left.

Making beds with the patients in them wasn't an easy job, and when some of the patients were in excruciating pain it wrenched at Sydney to have to shift them. A nurse was usually available to lend a hand, but this morning they all had their hands full with more critical tasks.

She approached the first bed in the row and searched her mind for the youngster's name; she prided herself on not having to look twice at the chart hanging from the footboard. The name floated easily up through her memory—Rex Suldane. Rex had lost a kidney to the surgeon's knife and had to be kept in bed. She knew it was painful for him to move but he obligingly curled to one side while she rolled the soiled sheets against his back and replaced them with a fresh bottom sheet, top sheet, and blanket, making the bed neatly in a vertical half. Then he rolled back, and she moved to the other side to strip the soiled sheets away and finish arranging the fresh ones.

When the staff had shown them how to change sheets with the patient in the bed Sydney had been uncertain whether she could ever manage such a feat, but it was easier than it looked. Now she was able to make a bed in three minutes flat, even if the patient was comatose.

Fifteen minutes later Sydney approached her last bed, which was filled to overflowing with one of her favorite patients, Howard Lewis from Estaboga, Alabama.

"Ha'ard," as he called himself, was an air force mechanic, a huge, farm-bred young man, at least six foot four. He had the open face and guileless expression of a country boy. He had been wounded in the thigh and gave a lot of thankful prayers that the bullet hadn't been a few inches higher. The thigh bone was shattered, but the doctors had done some miracle repair work and Howard would fight again. He'd be out soon and headed back to God knows where. He had graduated from crutches to a cane since Sydney had begun coming here and would soon be removed from the ward to a recuperation center for ambulatory patients. She would miss him.

Now he groaned. "You're here early this morning, Sydney. We ain't even had breakfast yet. You know a farm boy ain't no good till he's had his coffee."

She grinned at him. "Quit griping and I'll find you some coffee as soon as I finish making up your bed." She grabbed the dark blue robe off a nearby chair and tossed it at him.

He laughed and sat up with an effort, shrugging into the robe before swinging his legs off the bed.

She helped him with his slippers and handed him the cane. "Do you need a hand?" she offered as he got unsteadily to his feet.

"Nah. I'm gettin' good at this. I'll be out in the solarium when you find that coffee." He sobered. "Did you hear about the hospital ship comin' in this morning?"

"Yes, I did."

"Poor bastards."

She started to reply when a scream from the other side of the room sent a chill up her spine. She dropped the sheets and hurried over to the patient. Bile rose in her throat as she reached his side. His eyes had rolled almost completely back into his head, the tendons in his throat were like knotted ropes straining to break loose. Another high-pitched wail came through the dry lips. She could see that in his thrashing the boy had pulled a drainage tube from a gaping wound in his stomach. The stench was almost overpowering and she swayed. Recovering quickly she raced for the door. The nurse was in the hall. "Get a doctor," Sydney called, then hurried back to the bedside. She grasped his bicep and began to talk to him. "The doctor's on his way. Hang on, just a minute more." The boy was strong, and she feared she couldn't hold him on the bed much longer when the doctor appeared. Sydney had never been so glad to see anyone in her life.

He spoke to the woman in white at the other side of the bed. "Nurse, prepare a morphine injection."

"Can you hold him," the doctor barked at Sydney. "Or should I get someone else?"

She swallowed. "I can handle it," she assured him.

When the patient had finally been artificially calmed and the tube replaced, the doctor thanked her curtly and told her she could return to her duties. He instructed the nurse to replace the dressing but, when he was out of earshot of the boy, he added, "Don't spend too much time on this one. He won't last."

Sydney caught her breath and looked briefly into the doctor's eyes, searching for a sign of compassion. His expression did not change. He returned her look with a fleeting frown, then moved to the next bed. She stared after him, wondering how on earth he could be so cold-blooded.

The nurse watched her reaction for a minute, then spoke softly above the patient. "They see so much; they can't let themselves care too deeply."

Sydney knew she should keep silent, but she couldn't. "That's a piss-poor excuse for a lack of heart," she said, speaking to his back just loud enough for him to hear. "I hope to God if my husband is injured in this war, he won't be treated by a man like that."

She stomped out, muttering under her breath.

Faith and her trolley were in the hall outside the solarium. One look at Sydney's face and she came over. "Sydney? What's the matter?"

"Nothing, I'm just mad, that's all. I'm going to get a job, a real job, then I'll have an excuse not to come here anymore."

Faith laid a placating hand on Sydney's arm. "Sydney Bingham, you don't mean that! The men love you."

Sydney shook her head ruefully. She turned her face to the wall to hide her tears. "Don't pay any attention to me; I'm just spoutin' off." She spoke huskily, heavily. "Even if I do go to work it won't be until Vance leaves. And I'll still spend some hours here. It's just that sometimes it gets to me."

"I know what you mean," agreed Faith. "The boys—"

"Not the boys!" interrupted Sydney, gritting her teeth. She recounted the scene with the doctor.

To her surprise Faith didn't jump in to concur that the man was a monster. Instead the younger girl was thoughtful for a long minute before she finally answered. "He sounds heartless, doesn't he? But put yourself in his place. There is only so much one person can do and hundreds of boys waiting for help. It must be so frustrating not to be able to save them all; I think some of the doctors, and the nurses, too, have to build a wall of indifference just to get through the hours. I would go insane within a very short time."

Sydney wasn't sure she agreed, but she was impressed with

the younger girl's thoughtful answer. "I guess I tend to fly off the handle, don't I?"

Faith gave her a quick hug. "Not at all. You're a warm, generous person, that's all, and you hate things that aren't fair."

"And war is the most unfair thing there is."

Faith didn't have to reply.

Bill and Kay stood behind the double chains in the stern of the boat, on the lowest level with the automobiles. With a ponderous grumble of its engines, the midnight ferry fought to break the invisible bonds that held it to the dock. The wake surged in confusion as though unsure of which way it wanted to curl. Finally the vessel caught its rhythm, the wake settled into twin contours, and the dark waters accepted the heavy consignment. Tons of weight displaced a considerable amount of water but the infinitesimal flux was noted only by the gods who measure such things.

They continued to watch until the darkness collected around them and the illuminated figures on the pier were toy-sized. Soon they would climb to the top deck, to the tiny cabin assigned to them for the voyage. At dawn they would be in Victoria.

A fine spray hit them in the face, and they both laughed. He pointed with his thumb, asking if she wanted to go topside.

Kay looked for an indication of his wishes. His face was lined with weariness and the tension was there, under the surface of his smile, but he seemed content for the moment. She shook her head. She loved this exhilarating feeling of wind and water, sky and stars.

The ferry moved from the relative protection of Elliot Bay into Puget Sound. Without the wind-breaking hills of the city to protect the craft, the gusts became more high-handed. One picked up Kay's skirt and tossed it immodestly over her derriere. She slapped it down. Laughing, Bill backed against a bulkhead and pulled her close, wrapping her tight in his arms from behind. She leaned into him.

They stayed like that for a long time. At first Kay was comfortable; but then, slowly, almost insidiously, anxious, unwelcome feelings began to form within her, and she shivered under their intrusion.

She fought squarely against the feeling that something might happen to Bill before they could be together like this again. This wasn't the time to worry about tomorrow; this was the time to revel in what she had now. It was a dangerous world, and he performed a job that grew more dangerous every day. She tried to block the anxiety, savoring each beat of the heart under her shoulder, each breath that made her part of the movement of his broad chest. Suddenly she turned in his arms, reaching around his neck to pull his face down to hers. She saw the flash of surprise in his eyes, but she ignored it. Her mouth was demanding.

Bill grasped her tightly as though he were reading her mind. He kissed her back, a quick, hard kiss, then he led her upstairs.

The next morning, they wandered through the magnificent gardens surrounding the Empress Hotel. Victoria was a charming city, quaint, a bit old-fashioned. It satisfied Kay's imaginary picture of an eighteenth-century English village. Many of the streets were brick and narrow, which invited a leisurely saunter. The flowers were magnificent, almost unnatural this far north. As opposed to Seattle, so noisy and busy, so filled with industrial influence, Victoria was the perfect place for a romantic interlude.

Bill was in a good mood, too. On impulse he stepped off the path and picked one of the flowers, a glorious pink peony, which he presented to her with ceremony.

Kay accepted the blossom and raised it to her nostrils. She let her lips curve into a smile. "Thank you, sir, but I don't think you're supposed to—"

"What do you think you're doing, young man?" The squawky voice came from somewhere behind them, but they didn't wait around to see who it was.

"Let's go!" Bill grabbed her hand and they went running toward the harbor, laughing like two kids. Kay held onto the flower.

Kay hesitated to bring the mundane into the weekend but she needed to broach the subject of the Red Cross job to Bill. As they walked she explained the offer, still unsure herself of what she wanted to do. "The Y has a good program of day-care," she finished.

He had listened quietly, occasionally asking a question. Now his expression hardened as he thought of his children staying at a day-care facility every day. What if he got a quick leave and spent it alone because Kay had to work? Finally he drew a deep breath. "If you're asking what I'd prefer: stay home, take care of the kids, keep the home fires burning."

Kay didn't realize that he was really angry. She laughed. "Just like that?"

"You asked," he reminded her with a snap. "You wanted me to make the decision? Okay, don't go to work."

Kay was both relieved and resentful. And more than a little angry herself. "A lot of wives are working, Bill. We want to do our part to help win the war, too."

"You are doing your job," he answered. "The most important job there is."

Kay sighed. Maybe she shouldn't have put it to him now, while they had only these few hours together. If she read the signs right, he was definitely leaving very soon. "Bill, I don't want you to worry about me when you leave." She shook her head, helplessly trying to understand. "I thought you would be pleased. You've encouraged me to be independent."

"So now you're independent, you don't need me anymore?"

She was stunned. "How can you think that? To be honest I dismissed the idea immediately when it was put to me. But I just thought I'd mention it."

He shot back his sleeve and glanced at his watch. "You wanted me to be honest, didn't you? Look, I've got to find a phone and check in. Shall we meet back at the hotel in an hour?"

She nodded. "Yes, all right." He was not only being honest, he was being overbearing. She turned away.

Bill watched her go, feeling like a jackass. Hell, he wanted her to be self-sufficient and secure. Then why did he feel threatened by this? He took a step to follow, then he muttered a curse and stalked off in the opposite direction.

Kay's brows furrowed in perplexity as she shopped. She went to the chocolate shop to buy the famous Victoria Cremes for Billy. At another shop featuring imports from England, she bought a lovely mohair shawl for Faith and Shetland sweaters for her and Millie.

Her thoughts were spinning even as she counted out the money for her purchases. Perhaps she should consider the job even over Bill's objections. Perhaps she owed it to her children, herself. Faith certainly thought so.

Many women, who in the past had stayed home to keep the home fires stoked and the hearth polished, were taking an active part in this war effort. The newly formed women's services were turning away applicants.

As long as the war continued, Bill should realize she would

have to think for them both. And who knew when this war would be over? Months, perhaps years from now.

When they met again later, his expression had eased but he was still less than happy. She couldn't shake this feeling that he hadn't given her a fair hearing. She would have to make choices while he was gone. Why couldn't he allow her to make this one?

He could have said, Do what you think is right, Kay, and trusted her.

"Gimme that Jersey bounce. . . ." As they moved to the syncopation of the swing tune, Bill's hand was hard against Kay's back. He smiled suggestively, knowingly, his hips moved against her just before he spun her away.

They were dancing in the beautiful ballroom of the hotel. She knew they made a nice couple. She wore the white dress he'd bought for her in Washington. He wore his white uniform.

Kay's heels tapped a staccato, her skirts whirled around her ankles, before she took the step to bring her back against him. She threw her head back and laughed in pure delight.

The music throbbed around them with an urgent jitterbug beat, so incongruous in the ballroom of the old Empress Hotel. The orchestra seemed to have taken on the responsive mood of their audience, the reckless, carefree mood that held a hint of frenzy.

As Kay looked around at the other couples on the floor, she saw her expression mirrored in a dozen other faces. A desperate, hungry expression. A frantic, hurry-up look. The war. The war had prompted the emotion, in herself and in the others. But for this moment she felt young, and carefree, and happy. She would guard that feeling, revel in it. Later there would be plenty of time for missing him.

The music switched suddenly to a slow rhythm. Bill gathered her against him and her euphoria faded like the fog on a sunny day. Kay felt the burning sensation behind her eyes. Her throat closed. She concealed her face in the angle below his chin. His skin was damp; she put out her tongue to taste him.

He jerked as though he'd been stung and peered down into her eyes.

She gave him a helpless smile.

In their room, they let their hands and lips speak for them. With slow, sliding movements they undressed each other and made love until the first light of dawn seeped in around the edges of the window shades.

Chapter 14

Saturday, June 20, 1942

The children were especially restless tonight. Billy's usual bedtime was at seven-thirty, Millie's at nine. It was now nine-thirty, and neither of them seemed inclined toward sleep. Millie was cutting paper dolls out of the Sears Roebuck catalog. Billy was playing the piano on the edge of the table, his little fingers moving in time to his firmly nodding head. He sang:

> "Oh, we ain't got a barrel of—mon-ee,
> Maybe we're ragged and—fun-nee.
> But we'll travel along, singin' our song,
> Side by side."

Thanks a lot, Sydney Bingham, thought Faith. She'd listened to that song, usually with dining table accompaniment, at least a hundred times tonight. It had been fun, though, all of them spending last night around the piano, singing along.

> "Oh, we don't know what's comin' to—morrow,
> Maybe it's trouble and so—rrow. . . ."

Faith yawned wearily and eyed the messy rooms. She'd have to straighten up before she could seek her own pillow. "C'mon guys," she urged, breaking into the song and heaving herself out of the easy chair. She grabbed a dump truck and a model airplane and headed for the toy box in their bedroom. "Help me with this stuff. You know what your mother would say about your staying up past your bedtime. It's time to give in. You have to go to the Y tomorrow while I'm at the hospital." Because of the heavy influx of casualties she had agreed to work on the ward all weekend. But her feet were complaining.

She had also accepted a part-time job in the office of the hospital beginning Monday. She had intended to look for a job, but this one seemed to have found her. Clerical work wasn't what she was trained for or wanted to do for the rest of her life, but it was a job. Her main reason for leaving school was to help out the war effort and this was where she was needed. She could type, after a fashion, and filing shouldn't be too difficult to learn.

"Bleh-h," said Billy, sticking his tongue out as far as it would go. "I hate that old place."

Millie smiled that enigmatic little smile. "Me, too," she agreed.

"Now that's a story," accused Faith lightly. "You had a good time today. You both enjoyed being around the other kids." They were trying to set a load of guilt on her shoulders, and she wasn't going to accept it.

"Are you going to teach a sewing class like they asked you to? Can I come?" asked Millie.

Faith wondered about that. She would love to do it. She had some rather original ideas for remodeling outdated, unworn clothes. "If I can find the time you'll surely be included, but I could teach you to sew right here, you know."

"It wouldn't be the same as taking a grown-up class."

Faith smiled and shook her head at the logic. "All right, you can take the class. Now, what about bed?"

Millie was the reason for the late night in the first place. She was in a playful mood tonight and that alone would have been reason enough for her aunt to indulge her; but the child was also bothering her brother, Faith noted with glee.

Faith had been disturbed from the moment she arrived by the attitude of her beloved niece. Millie had been much too nice to Billy. It wasn't natural and besides, her benevolence was threatening to turn the little whirlwind into a tyrant.

When Faith had commented to her sister-in-law about her observations, Kay had agreed and confessed that she didn't know what to do about it.

"Millie has been like this for several months, ever since the *Shiloh* was attacked and we didn't know whether Bill was okay," Kay had told her. "I didn't handle the situation so well. Now it's almost as though she's afraid to make a mistake, afraid something awful might happen. I can understand it but I can't combat it."

Millie's voice interrupted Faith's thoughts. "All right. But if you think I'm going to bed before *him*, you'd better think again."

Billy thought the statement was hilarious and he erupted into loud laughter. He ran circles around Faith's skirts until she scooped him up and sat down with him on her lap. "Sh-h-h. Billy, you'll wake up everyone on the floor."

"Good! Then we'll all stay home tomorrow."

"Don't count on it," Millie answered wryly as a knock sounded on the door. "I'll get it, Auntie Faith. They've probably called the MPs to haul Billy off to the brig for disturbing the peace."

The child opened the door and shrieked, "Cody!"

Faith swung around, releasing her squirming nephew. Both children began to squeal. "Cody! Cody, Cody. When did you get here?"

"Where have you been?"

"Dad and Mom are gone to Canada. We're staying with our Auntie Faith."

"I've cut my hair."

At first Faith couldn't see the man who laughed in response to the jubilant greeting. Down on his haunches, he was effectively camouflaged by a flail of arms and legs. "Canada? Did he go AWOL? Cut your hair? What'd you want to go and do that for? I liked the pigtails."

"Oh, Cody, they were so childish."

"My daddy wouldn't desert. They've gone on a 'cashun."

The man stood up and the children slid off him to the floor like raindrops off a polished car. When he spied her he seemed taken aback for a minute. "Well, well, what have we here?" he drawled. "Millie, you promised you'd play matchmaker, but I didn't expect you to do such a spectacular job of it. She's perfection."

Faith had stood quietly during the exchange but at his words, and Millie's giggle that followed, she raised her chin to a point just shy of haughty.

Good Lord, he was gorgeous. Tall, strongly built, he had thick hair, a rich brown color. His face was tanned and his eyes held humor in their hazel depths.

And he knew he was good-looking. The proof was in his confident stance, legs apart, arms folded, a sneaky little smile on his lips, never doubting his welcome when a halfway attractive woman was in the room. The thorough study that accompanied his statement left her feeling very warm, and more than a bit uncomfortable. What nerve!

The children each took a hand and dragged him across the room to her as though presenting a treasure for her inspection.

"This is our Auntie Faith," said Billy.

Or maybe, Faith amended her thoughts, she was being presented to *him* as a favorite treasure for his inspection. What had he said? Millie was going to play matchmaker? She couldn't imagine that, even in jest, he would allow that—or need it for that matter. Women probably fainted at his feet. Well, not her.

"Stupid!" said Millie heatedly to her brother. "Don't you have any manners? You're supposed to introduce the gentleman to the lady. Auntie Faith, I would like you to meet Ensign Cody Bristol, one of the men in Daddy's old squadron."

"From Texas," put in Billy.

"Cody, this is Daddy's sister, Faith Parker."

"Emily Post, watch out," he said with a grin, gently ruffling Millie's hair. "How do you do, Miss Parker?" he said formally. The grin, the gleam in his eyes, suggested that she share his amusement. "I've heard a lot about you from your family. It's a pleasure to meet you at last." He lifted a brow in Millie's direction. "How'm I doin'?" he asked out of the corner of his mouth.

Millie giggled again. "Pretty good."

Faith would have known that Cody Bristol was a pilot if she'd met him on the street. The cocky stance, the smile, the confident demeanor were all worn more consistently than the uniform by most of the fighter pilots she'd met. The man who stood before her might as well have been a carbon copy of her brother. She tried to tell herself that was no recommendation. "How do you do," she answered with an equal, if not as playful, formality and no grin at all. "Would you like to have a seat, Mr. Bristol?"

"Cody, please."

Faith nodded, but she didn't return the offer of intimacy. He politely took a seat.

"Cody flies fighters, too," put in Billy. "F4F Wildcats. Like Daddy."

"Yes, I'm sure he's just like your daddy," Faith said wryly, earning herself a raised brow.

"Thank you," he said, pretending to misunderstand.

He fixed her with a stare that made her squirm.

Cody's gaze kept coming back to her while he talked to the children. She was unhappily aware of how she looked. Her hair was bunched at the nape of her neck, tied haphazardly with one of Millie's cast-off ribbons. She'd long ago eaten off her lipstick. She'd exchanged her volunteer's uniform for a pair of faded shorts and a halter top. She didn't like feeling at a disadvantage, didn't like it one bit. He could at least have called from downstairs instead of just popping in.

He'd gotten Millie and Billy all stirred up again. She watched and listened to the three-way conversation, conveniently forgetting that they'd already been stirred up. Finally she'd had enough of the sly glances. "I hope you won't mind losing your audience, Mr. Bristol, but the children must go to bed now. They have to get up early tomorrow," she said abruptly.

Conversation stopped and she finally ameliorated her manner with a smile. She'd expected an argument, not the sad accusation she saw in Millie's expression. Billy just hung his head.

But Cody responded immediately, showing a perception she wouldn't have thought him capable of. "Look what time it is." He glanced at his watch, then held it out for them to see and gave a mock growl. "Why, you little devils—you get in your bunks right now or I'll put you on report."

Billy crawled onto Cody's lap and curled his arms around his neck. "Will you come back to see us soon?" he asked sleepily, laying his head on the broad shoulder. "We've missed you and Gladys a lot."

"Billy!" admonished Millie.

"What?" said Billy. "Oh, yeah, we're not supposed to mention Gladys."

The man's arms encircled the slight body with a gentleness that brought a lump to Faith's throat. How odd that a man like this could be so patient with children. Who was Gladys? Was he married; did he have children? Why did she care?

He didn't wear a ring, but a lot of men didn't. He didn't have the right to look her over like a side of beef at auction under any conditions, but especially not if he was married.

"That's okay. And of course I'll come back to see you. I've missed you two devils, too," he said softly.

Faith noticed for the first time the lines of weariness that framed his eyes. She felt guilty when she saw them.

He spoke to Billy again, still in that quiet tone. "Now, it is past your bedtime."

Billy nodded. "Okay," he said but he made no move to leave the shelter of Cody's arms.

"Maybe you'd better tuck him in," suggested Millie. "He's been pretty wound up tonight."

He grinned as he rose. "Do you need to be tucked in, too?"

"You know perfectly well I've been too old for that for a long time."

Cody had reached the connecting door. He looked inside to see three beds lined up like neat soldiers. "You're never too old to be tucked in, are you, Auntie Faith?"

The suggestive tone of voice, the sexual awareness in his eyes as they traveled over her wiped out all the kind feelings she had begun to have as she'd watched his tenderness with the children.

She moved restlessly around the room as she listened to the murmurs, the rustle of the covers. After a few minutes all was quiet.

Cody stood beside the open door but out of sight for a minute. He needed to pull himself together before reentering the room where Bill Parker's sister waited. He'd flown in from New Guinea, come straight here from the field to say hello and to report to Bill, whom he knew would be anxious for first hand news from the squadron. He was tired, the memories of war too fresh.

He needed time to put a cap on his irritation—and his attraction. He'd already been fifteen rounds with one girl like Faith Parker. Billy's sleepy and inadvertent mention of Gladys had brought back an ache in the region around his heart, the kind of ache he wouldn't allow to govern his life again. His former fiancée was a snobbish, self-centered little bitch, and he wasn't about to fall for another one.

Hell, he didn't need to be attracted to any girl right now. But damn, if he wasn't attracted already. She was beautiful, with those luscious legs and that delicate, Snow White beauty of fair skin and black hair. The same beauty was only a promise in Millie but, he knew, it worried Bill to death.

He entered the room and stood, feet apart, in front of her and planted his fists on his hips.

"Are you sure you're Bill Parker's sister?" he demanded. "The same Bill Parker I know?"

She inhaled deeply, annoyed at his sarcasm, but also feeling guilty that she hadn't been very hospitable to this friend of Kay and Bill. "I'm sorry if I'm not exactly sociable, Mr. Bristol." And then Faith made the mistake of the month, the year. She, who prided herself on not making excuses, said, "I'm very tired tonight."

His voice was very soft. "Oh, really?"

She realized her mistake immediately. Daddy's old squadron, Millie had said. New Guinea, she thought. How could she complain of being tired to this man to whom exhaustion must be a natural condition? "Ohmigod—" she began.

Cody interrupted. "I'm just sorry that you chose to be unsocial in front of a couple of kids I happen to like very much. You stuck that pretty nose in the air and kept it there."

Faith's chin dropped at the accusation in his voice. "I really am sorry."

"If you'll excuse me, Miss Parker." He picked up his hat and anchored it precisely on his head. "Good night."

He left, resisting the urge to slam the door in her face.

Chapter 15

Monday, June 22, 1942

Spaghetti was something that could be prepared fairly easily on a two-burner hot plate. Kay didn't often attempt major cooking in the room, but Cody was having dinner with them tonight and he loved her spaghetti. Maybe the dish would make up for the welcome, or lack of welcome, he seemed to have gotten from her sister-in-law the previous evening. She'd thought Faith had matured but it seemed, from her description of the encounter, that the maturation wasn't totally consistent.

Bill had a great deal of respect for Cody's ability. He had pronounced Cody a hotshot pilot with a brain, the highest compliment her husband could pay, meaning Cody took the chances he had to take, but he used his head. From the time he was in flight school under Bill, they had always treated him like a member of the family; the children adored him. It was a puzzle to her why Faith and Cody had reacted with such antipathy toward each other. Kay had never seen Cody lose his good humor with anyone.

When the ferry docked this morning, Bill had gone straight to the base. He'd called back at noon to tell her that Cody was in town. She hadn't revealed that she already knew, but she had quickly agreed to his suggestion that he invite Cody for dinner. Maybe if Faith could see how much they all liked Cody, how well he fit in with the family, she would change her opinion about him.

She stirred the thick tomato sauce again and brushed a sweat-drenched curl away from her face. The electric fan, oscillating bravely but in vain, failed to dispatch the steam rising from Maurice's pot.

The trip to Victoria had been a wonderful break in the routine of their lives; but now she was back to reality. She continued to ask the question: Didn't she have a responsibility to herself? Faith had taken a job, working part-time at the hospital. Why shouldn't she?

She set the spoon on a saucer and sank despondently into a chair. The job at the Red Cross was looking more and more appealing. She hadn't quite made up her mind about taking it. If she did, there would be more responsibility—but of a different kind. The difference was she would get paid for it. Money wasn't a factor in the decision except as a measure of her worth. But wasn't that important?

Still she hesitated because of three other elements—the idea that she would be doing it over Bill's objection, the children's welfare, and the hotel.

She propped her feet up in the chair opposite and thought hard. She would have to give up managing the hotel, but, after the incident last night, heaped on others, she would gladly relinquish that one.

While she and Bill were on their way back from Victoria, there had been a robbery on the third floor. She'd been met upon her return this morning by a dozen people ready to tell her all about it. In the past they had been rather slack about security; someone was always at the front desk, that was about it. Now that policy was in question, and she had to do something about it immediately.

Maurice, when questioned by the police, regretfully admitted that he couldn't be certain that the entrance off the alley was locked securely. He thought so, but he couldn't be sure.

Kay had explained to the police that they couldn't set a curfew; too many people came and went at odd hours. The lieutenant understood. The problems were the same all over the city. He promised to increase the patrols nearby and she promised to implement his recommendation that there be two women on duty in the lobby at all times.

If Kay decided to accept the Red Cross job, Valerie was the logical choice to take over the hotel. Val was born to administrate. Her books were spotless, her coffee shop ran like a well-oiled engine. Kay shook her head. The woman would be a tyrant. She intended to recommend to Captain Conway that, if he didn't want a mutiny on his hands, the navy should appoint someone else.

The children were another consideration, as Bill had pointed out. But though they'd protested, they hadn't really seemed to mind staying at the Y while Faith was at the hospital. Protest was a ritual of childhood; they would adjust.

Which left the subject of Bill—well, Bill wasn't going to be here. If she decided to go against his wishes, she would have to cope without his approval.

Kay got to her feet and went to the window, grateful for the restorative beauty of the scene before her. One advantage to living this high was the view of the sound and beyond. As darkness approached, the Olympic Mountains were silhouetted by the setting sun, their snow-covered points reaching up toward the violet sky. In the distance she could see a ferry and the sight brought a smile to her lips.

"Boy, there must be something in the water in Victoria."

She hadn't heard Faith enter the room, but she chuckled at the comment. "It's a beautiful city," she said innocently. "Flowers everywhere. A steak for dinner. You should make the trip sometime."

"Well, it certainly did a lot for you. You look rested and years younger."

"Is that to say I looked like an old hag when I left?"

Faith bent over the steaming pot with the spoon. "Not a hag, just tired. Um-m, this is delicious."

"How was your first day on the job?"

Faith thought for a minute. "Interesting," she answered.

Kay laughed. "That's my euphemism for boring. By the way, I didn't have time this morning to thank you properly for keeping the kids."

"You're welcome. They're not too happy with me right now, but we got along fine." She spooned up another taste of sauce. "Why are you cooking like this tonight? Not that I'm complaining. I've always loved your spaghetti."

"Cody is coming for dinner. It's his favorite, too."

The spoon stopped halfway to her mouth. "Uh-oh. I'd better make myself scarce."

Kay met and held her gaze. "I'd rather you stayed."

"Why? I told you we didn't exactly hit it off."

"You want Bill to see you as an adult? Then behave like one."

Faith bristled at that. "I thought you had decided to quit telling me how to behave."

"I had. Believe me, I don't need the responsibility for anyone else. But Cody is a friend of ours. We'd like for him to feel welcome in our home." She glanced around at the cluttered rooms. "Such as it is."

Faith looked into Kay's clear eyes; she was the first to look away. Kay was right. She had acted like a juvenile. A lot of girls her age had husbands and children of their own. A lot of girls her age were widows. And she was making an issue over a personality clash. "All right," she agreed quietly. "I'll be the perfect little hostess for your guest."

"It won't be hard if you let yourself like him. Cody is a fine man."

"He's too much like Bill for me. Who is Gladys?"

"Oh, my God. Who in the world mentioned Gladys—as if I didn't know?"

"Billy was sleepy. It just slipped out. I thought Millie was going to go through the floor."

"Gladys was Cody's fiancée."

"Was? Is she dead?" She felt compassion swell within her.

"For a while I wished she were," said Kay bitterly. "No, she just decided he wasn't good enough to wait for. She was the daughter of a Dallas oilman, absolutely beautiful, educated back East, made her debut in New York City, and the term 'spoiled rotten' was coined for her. Cody was stunned when she started after him, and he fell like a ton of bricks. She introduced him to a way of life he'd never experienced before." Kay stopped for a minute, thinking about the man who was like herself to a degree. She'd been reared on a farm, Cody on a ranch, but neither of them had been exposed to urbaneness. "I'm not sure it was ever truly love."

She sighed and went on. "Gladys liked the picture of Cody in a uniform, but she wanted him to stay out of the war. Without consulting him she made arrangements for him to work for her father, using his position to get Cody out of the service. When he refused the job she'd set up she married someone else. And sent his ring back afterward with a polite little note."

"A note?" Faith couldn't believe her ears. "She sent him a note?"

Kay nodded. "He might seem arrogant to you now, but it's a protective façade. He doesn't want to be hurt again." She smiled indulgently. "Most men are vulnerable, Faith, despite what they would like you to believe."

"I can understand what a blow it must have been."

"It was. Now he vows, like you, not to get seriously involved until this war is over."

"He's much smarter than I suspected," said Faith with a wry smile. "I promise to be nice."

"Good. Now, how about grating some cheese to go on this spaghetti?"

When the men arrived the children greeted them jubilantly. Bill handed out the gifts they had brought back from Victoria.

Faith had already witnessed the children's fondness for Cody. Now she watched the way he interacted with Kay and Bill and they with him. Kay was warm and affectionate; Bill, genial. She was the one who felt like an outsider. And, she recognized suddenly, that was no one's fault but her own.

She was a grown woman. She had quit school and asked to join the family in Seattle. The last thing she wanted to do was cause dissension.

If she didn't allay the conflict with Cody, Bill would be bound to notice. It would be another bone of contention between them; though she was often at odds with her brother, she loved him dearly. She waited for a moment when she could have a private word with Cody.

Finally it came. Bill was mixing drinks and Kay was preparing a pot to cook the spaghetti. The children had been sent to bring in the table from the next room. She approached the window where Cody was standing.

"Cody, I apologize for last night."

He turned his head to look over his shoulder and down at her. "Oh? Did Kay reprimand you?"

"Certainly not! She just—oh, forget it!"

She started to turn away, but he caught her arm. "She just what?"

He didn't restrain her; she could have pulled away at any time, but the feel of his hand was warm and pleasant. She knew, beyond doubting, that he wouldn't appreciate Kay's having told her about his fiancée. "She just explained how close they felt to you. 'Like one of the family,' she said."

"That's very kind of her."

"She was upset with me. I was upset with myself," Faith admitted.

"And Bill?"

Her chin came up. "Bill doesn't know. Unless you told him." He smiled and for a minute she wondered. Then she said, "And he would have done his big brother act if you had."

He turned to rest his shoulder against the window frame.

"Your secret is safe with me." He smiled, a slow, lazy smile and crossed his arms over his chest. "Tell me about his act."

She shrugged. She didn't want to like the smile, or anything else about this arrogant man, but she didn't want to call a halt to the conversation, either. "Bill tends to think he knows what's best for everyone around him."

Retaining the smile, Cody extended his hand to a point behind her. Her gaze followed the action as he took his drink from her brother's hand. She met Bill's bland expression. "Well, you do."

"You have to admit, Faith, that I do have a few years of experience on you."

"I admit that. But you don't know a thing about women."

Bill lifted his glass to drink from it. "I know what I need to know about women; but girl-children confuse me."

Faith caught back what would have been a knee-jerk response and looked at her brother curiously. "Are you trying to provoke me?"

His eyes narrowed with a hint of respect. "I suppose I am. Sorry. Suppose we put our sibling rivalry on the back burner for the duration."

Faith lifted her glass in a toast to him and grinned. "Agreed. I do love you, brother, even when you're exasperating."

With his free arm he pulled her close for a hug.

The children were back, struggling with the table. Faith went to lend a hand.

Bill Parker had been in a strange mood all evening. Faith's comment about his inadequate knowledge of women had given him pause.

He sat in his easy chair and lit a cigarette as he studied the ones in this room. Remembering the argument he'd had with Kay in Victoria, he decided Faith had a point.

His wife wanted to take a job. He didn't like the idea worth a damn, but he recognized his reaction for the selfish impulse that it was. When she'd tried to talk to him about it, he'd broken one of his own rules: If what you have to say is right, it's likely to be as right in twenty-four hours, and a good deal more wisely said.

The old feeling that a man should take care of his family reared up inside him. He deliberately tamped it down. War provided exceptions to every rule, even the one that said: Every ship must have a captain whose word is final.

He frowned, looking at Millie. There were changes there,

too. She was unquestionably growing up. His little girl was wearing a dress that he thought was much too sophisticated for her. When he'd protested he'd gotten a patient look from his daughter and an amused one from his wife. And there was the matter of the bra. Kay had warned him, but he hadn't been prepared for that.

His eyes slid to Faith. She didn't have any more growing up to do. His baby sister was an extraordinarily beautiful woman, he realized, without brotherly bias. He felt old as he looked at her. Where had the years gone? Even Billy, always a bundle of high-powered energy, was unusually subdued and mature tonight.

He smiled to himself. Kay had probably threatened him within an inch of his life if he didn't behave.

Kay. She was his anchor. His thoughts wandered back to the summer they'd met at the Officers' Club in Corpus Christi. She was barely nineteen; he hadn't known that, of course, or he wouldn't have pursued her. He had been twenty-nine.

She was so pretty—maybe he would have, at that. She was visiting her college roommate, the daughter of his commanding officer. He'd been surprised by her intelligence, her vivacity. She was different from the girls he'd known, those girls who were impressed by the fact that he was a test pilot, thought the job was daring and glamorous. You could see it in their eyes— a sort of glazed-over sparkle. They didn't give a shit about what he was like as a person. But Kay—ah, Kay was different.

Bill stubbed out his cigarette. Should he have encouraged her to take the job with the Red Cross?

Their position in this war was more critical than the most pessimistic civilian thought it was going to be. If the law of averages for pilots held he very likely could be one of the hundreds, thousands, of men who were dying every month.

Kay and the children would not want for money. She'd have more than the pension the navy would provide. There was an income that he and Faith shared from their parents' estate. Of course, when the war was over, who knew what it would have cost? Taxes had already gone up, and surely would do so again. Inflation was rising. He remembered his parents' complaints after the last war.

If he were killed how much would it cost Kay to build a house somewhere? To send the kids to school? And besides money she would need something to fill her days, and confidence in her ability to function without him. Her volunteer hours wouldn't provide that. She would need the assurance that she was worth enough to be paid for her work.

Kay came over and sat on the arm of his chair. "You look like a man absorbed in deep thought." Kay laid her hand on his and spoke in a soft tone, inaudible to the others.

He covered her hand with his. "Not too deep. I've been reconsidering what you said about going to work. Maybe it would be a good thing."

"But you said—" Kay's eyes widened in genuine surprise.

His answering smile was rueful. "I know what I said and I'm sorry. I didn't take time to think. It was a selfish, knee-jerk reaction, honey. Little woman by the home fires. But this world is different; it may never be the same. You must do what you want to do."

She didn't tell that she'd already decided to do just that. Not the job, that wasn't finalized in her mind, but to do what she wanted to do. Still it was nice to have his approval. She leaned forward to place a kiss on his brow. "Honey, would you run down the hall to the refrigerator and get the butter while I slice the bread?" she asked sweetly.

The rest of the evening passed rather quickly.

The children were helping Kay clear the table, the men were enjoying a cigarette, and Faith had just poured herself another cup of coffee when the air-raid siren sounded.

Coffee sloshed from the cup to the saucer and onto her hand. Millie dropped a plate of spaghetti.

"Damn," said Kay. "Another alarm." She glanced automatically at the blackout shades. Air-raid drills were becoming a fact of life during this war, but the sound of the siren never ceased to unnerve her. She didn't hurry, however.

Bill headed for the door. "I'll call the base."

Cody nodded. Even when it was only a practice raid, all military personnel had to check in.

"I'd better be going anyway. Kay, thanks for the dinner. It was delicious as usual."

Kay smiled. "We'll see you later, Cody." The children came for a good-bye hug.

As he was leaving he took Faith aside. "Are we friends?" he asked in an undertone.

"Yes," she said, smiling. There was no reason not to be friends.

"Then how about dinner Saturday night?"

At once her wariness returned. "The Victory Caravan arrives Saturday. I'm selling bonds at the rally from five to seven."

"Why don't I meet you there afterward?"

She walked to the door with him, delaying her answer. "Okay," she agreed, not really sure why. "I'll wait for you at the booth. What time?"

He drew her into the hall. When she saw his expression she answered her own question with a wry smile. "Whenever you get there, right?"

"Right. I'll try to make it by seven."

He hesitated for a second then bent down to brush her lips lightly with his. The kiss surprised them both.

"Cody." Bill leaned his head out of the alcove. "Come here a minute, will you?"

Cody looked puzzled but he complied immediately. Faith followed him down the hall. Other couples were beginning to come out of their rooms, to drift toward the stairs. "How tiresome," she heard someone say.

Bill was still speaking into the phone, but when he saw Faith he put his hand over the mouthpiece. "Sis, why don't you go on downstairs?"

Faith opened her mouth to protest until she saw her brother's face. He was white as a sheet. "Wh-what is it?" she stammered.

He ignored her, speaking to Cody instead. "Get the car keys from Kay. And my uniform jacket and hat."

All at once Faith realized what was going on. "Oh, God. It's a real air raid, isn't it?"

A man in uniform came out of a room behind them in time to hear her remark. Bill ignored the man's curse; he grabbed her arm. "Help us, Faith. Before you go down to the shelter check and see if Jordan Adair and Vance Bingham are in the hotel. If they are have them meet us at the entrance quickly."

She whirled and ran down the hall toward the stairs, the siren still screaming in her ears.

The four men piled into the station wagon. Before the doors closed Bill let out the clutch and floorboarded the gas pedal. The car went careening off down the street with no headlights, toward the base of Sand Point.

The next afternoon the four men assembled again. This time they were joined by Captain Conway in a small building that had been assigned as a workroom for Vance Bingham.

From Cody's point of view, it was interesting to observe the other three. He'd noted that the relationship between Bingham and Adair, though professionally faultless, was personally detached and aloof. He was surprised by that; they had evidently worked very closely for a number of months. Bill didn't particularly like Adair, either, Cody could tell. He himself didn't warm up to the senator's son.

Though he was nice enough, Jordan Adair seldom showed any animation. He needed to relax a little, but he couldn't seem to unshackle himself from the iron control and self-possession that were so much a part of him.

"The attack was real, all right," the captain was saying. "There was one raid on Vancouver Island, Canada, and a Jap sub shelled the military depot at Fort Stevens, Oregon. The fort sits on an estuary of the Columbia River. Until yesterday there has not been an attack on a military installation in the United States since the War of 1812."

It was a sobering thought, and the men met it with silence. They had already discussed the seriousness of the shelling.

The captain went on. "It seems to have been a random attack but it fuels the arguments of some who claim that the Japs make regular forays into Puget Sound. We're taking no chances. This area, 150 miles of coastline and the entire sound, is now on total blackout."

He turned to Vance. "The destroyer is scheduled to leave July fourth."

"I'll have all my equipment together and be ready, sir."

"That's all then," said the captain.

Bill stood and stretched. "Are we ready?" he asked Jordan. He'd told Cody that the other two men he'd selected to be on the testing team, Mason and Jersey, were due in today. Cody was to wait here at the base and brief them. Now he spoke to the chief. "We're going back to the hotel, Vance. Do you want a ride?"

Vance shook his head. "I'm going to work for a while longer. I'll catch the bus in later. Will one of you tell Sydney?"

On the way back to the hotel Bill asked a question he'd been wanting to ask ever since he'd met Jordan Adair. "Just what the hell is it you *do*, Adair?"

Jordan laughed and for the next five minutes Bill got a lecture on basic economics as applied in wartime. "The profit motive is the difference between us and the Japanese and Germans. They're working slave labor; we're working free men," Jordan said.

Bill made a left-hand turn and gave a noncommittal grunt.

"The only way we're going to win this war is to let private enterprise have the initiative to do whatever it takes," Jordan went on. "Boeing, Lockheed, they're all responding. Henry Kaiser is working on a ship that can be completed, from the laying of the hull to the launching, in only a few days. Calls them Liberty Ships. He's going to make a fortune—while at the same time we'll get the ships we need."

Bill's eyes narrowed. "I agree about our preparedness but I don't agree that the only way we'll win this war is to let the big industrialists make a lot of money," he said. "We'll win this war because Americans are basically a patriotic people who value their freedom."

"Of course they do. I'm not saying that patriotism doesn't enter into it. And the average American man on the street is going to make money, too. A helluva lot of money. Look what's already happened to wages. One thing the people of this area don't have to worry about is money.

"But the big boys with the bucks have to be willing to produce, too, and they won't do it without incentive, which Congress is now giving them. Look at the kinds of planes, the kinds of weapons you were using on December 6th. You have better weapons already, and why? Because millions of dollars will be made on this war."

Bill persisted. He didn't like this argument or Jordan Adair's cynicism. "The planes and ships wouldn't be worth a damn if there weren't people willing and ready to man them."

"You're an idealist. I have no quarrel with that but I still say let the manufacturers reap the profits, as long as they furnish us the matériel we need at the same time."

"The enemy attacked and our people responded with a broad show of patriotism," Bill continued, stubbornly sticking to his own philosophy.

"I'm not denying the work ethic, and the basic goodness of the people will be the deciding factor. But the profit motive is there and it's vital right now."

"I agree it's vital, but let me play devil's advocate for a minute. After the war, what then? What happens to the defense contractors? Do you think a politician is going to vote to eliminate—say—a Lockheed plant from his district? With all the jobs a company like that furnishes?

"Jordan, if you were a military man you'd know that it's easy to bestow power; it's not so easy to take it away. After years of war, in which huge profits are made, do you think the monster manufacturing machine will quietly return to its cave, back to business as usual?''

A long silence followed his question. Jordan considered. ''Congress still controls the spending dollar,'' he said, but he knew it was a weak argument.

Bill laughed aloud. ''It isn't me who's the idealist, Jordan. It's you, if you think that way. Maybe you'll have to do like your father, run for office yourself. Maybe you can help control this huge monster.''

''I have to admit, you've given me something to think about,'' Jordan said quietly. Then his expression slipped into rigidity. ''But politics isn't for me,'' he stated positively.

The fierce answer surprised Bill. He'd heard Kay say it was Valerie who wanted the career in politics, but he'd assumed that Jordan was presently lukewarm and would eventually agree. But this man looked like one who would fight the idea with everything in him.

Chapter 16

Saturday, June 27, 1942

Sydney walked down the hill on her way to the shoe repair shop near the hotel. The day was cool and overcast, but the clouds were too high for rain. The weather in Seattle was as capricious as a fickle flirt.

She had walked for only a block or two when she suddenly had the feeling that she was being watched. She turned to look behind her but no one seemed to be paying any particular attention. The feeling persisted, though she tried to dispel it through reason. Who would be watching her? She shrugged her shoulders and turned right at the next corner.

The small shop, snuggled between two dignified office buildings, was distinguished by an ambitious sign. Tall gold leaf letters across a window smeared with dust and grime proclaimed this to be the KING COUNTY SHOE REPAIR. As she entered, the smell of raw leather and polish stung her nostrils. One customer was pleading with the burly, smeared man to save what he could of a pair of brogans, and four other people were lined up at the counter. While she waited her turn she watched the passing crowds through the window but she saw no one who was even faintly familiar.

At last the burly owner got to her. She handed him a pair of Vance's regulation shoes and a pair of her own black pumps, explaining that both pairs needed new heels and a polish as well.

"From the South are ya? Wouldja want taps on these?" He held up her pumps.

"Taps?" she asked. "No, I don't think so." Why would she want noisy taps on her shoes?

"Everybody's getting them. Makes your shoes last longer," advised a woman behind her in the line.

"Leather taps is what I mean," added the cobbler, noticing Sydney's dubious glance at the woman.

"Can you show me?" She was still doubtful.

He grimaced, as though she were some kind of fool, and plucked a small packet from his workbench. He opened the envelope and shook two little scraps of hard leather into his palm. "They go on over the heels to keep them from wearing out as quick."

Well at least they weren't metal. "Okay. Taps, too. When can I pick these up?"

He tore off half of two bright orange tickets, handed two halves to her and stuffed the others into the toes of the shoes. "I'm real busy. Check back."

She would have liked to try to pin the man down to a definite time, but the people behind her were growing restive so she simply nodded and moved away from the counter. She stowed the orange cardboard pieces in a pocket of her purse and left the shop.

Suddenly the feeling was back, causing a definite itch between her shoulder blades. This was ridiculous. She swung around sharply and searched the crowds.

She caught her breath when she spotted Valerie Adair coming toward her. When the blonde saw Sydney, her pace slowed slightly. But Valerie's presence shouldn't account for the feeling.

Valerie stopped when she reached Sydney's side. "I understand that the *John Tuggle* is leaving a week from today. Isn't that your husband's ship?"

Sydney tried to hide the jolt of shock the news gave her. Vance leaving? Why hadn't he told her? She felt a panicky fear at the thought of Vance, on a ship, in the middle of a battle.

She grabbed Valerie's arm and pulled her out of the pedestrian traffic. "Are you crazy, Valerie? To announce something like that in the middle of a public sidewalk. Troop movements are secret." She had a sudden mean thought; she could probably turn Valerie in for this. The senator's daughter-in-law wouldn't be punished, but she would be uncomfortable for a while. Sydney dismissed the temptation almost as soon as it arose.

Valerie had the grace to look embarrassed but she went on huffily, "All I wanted to tell you was that if Vance has any leave before his ship sails, you can take time off."

Sydney was surprised by, but wasn't about to question, the

woman's generosity. She was just relieved that there wouldn't be another confrontation between Vance and this woman. She had another thought and a smile formed on her lips. Valerie was smarter than she'd given her credit for being. If Sydney was occupied with her husband she wouldn't be around Valerie's. Little did she know. "Why, thank you, Valerie. That's very generous of you," she said sweetly.

"You can make it up later." Valerie gave a regal nod and moved on.

Sydney choked back a laugh.

Neither of the women noticed the smile on the face of the tall, extremely neat man who had been hidden in a nearby doorway. He had overheard everything.

Sydney had left Vance sleeping, but he was dressed and ready to leave when she arrived back at the Elysium. "Hi, honey. Did you decide where you want to spend the day?" he asked.

She didn't answer. She simply went to him and wrapped her arms around his waist, seeking an antidote to her uneasiness, her fear. The creepy feelings she'd had and her negative conversation with Valerie slowly began to fade under the reassurance Vance offered with only the warm strength of his arms.

"Anything I can help with?" he asked quietly.

She hesitated. "No," she answered. "I'm just thinking that these forty-eight-hour passes aren't a lot but they're better than nothing. I'll miss you when you leave for good."

"And that will be very soon."

She looked up. "I know. One week. Valerie Adair just told me."

Under his breath he muttered a descriptive word for busybodies that brought a smile to her lips.

"I wanted to straighten out all that mess about volunteer hours before she got started on you again."

"Vance, I wish you would stop trying to protect me from Valerie Adair. I can take care of myself. Now, when do you leave?"

"Next Saturday. The fourth of July. We've gotten a hurry-up order from Washington," he explained.

"I won't pretend to know what that means."

"The device. I'm still working on some of the bugs." He sighed wearily.

Sydney was dying to know more, but she realized information

could be dangerous. "Don't tell me about it. Just answer one question for me. Will it help get this war over quickly?"

"It won't win the war all by itself but possibly it will help. At least until the Japs get hold of a plane equipped with one and figure out how it works."

"Can they do that?"

He laughed, but there was no humor in the sound. His face took on a thoughtful expression when he added, "The Japs aren't as backward as our politicians would like us to believe, honey."

They had Maurice pack a picnic for them and spent the day at the crowded beach on Lake Washington, an inland lake east of the city.

The water was cold but the sand and the sun were warm and wonderful. Vance worried that her fair skin would burn, so—to her amusement—he spent the afternoon applying and reapplying suntan lotion. They lay in each other's arms, whispering, giggling like children. They also received numerous looks of disapproval, but Sydney didn't give a damn. She delighted in her husband's attention.

It was almost dark when they returned to the hotel to dress for dinner. Vance was in an exuberant mood. He even greeted Valerie Adair with a cheerful hail as they passed her in the hall.

"Vance!" hissed Sydney. "The woman will think you're drunk!"

"I am. I'm drunk on love," he proclaimed.

Sydney shook her head but she laughed. She'd never seen him in such a mood.

As he closed the door he spun her around and swatted her bottom affectionately. "Now, get your glad rags on. We're going out for a really big evening on the town. Wear that greeny thing."

"Yes, Chief." She grinned over her shoulder. What Vance called the greeny thing was a prewar evening dress with yards of chiffon in the long skirt. She called it her dancing dress. He *was* planning a big evening.

The Hollywood Victory Caravan was making a three-week sweep across the country to raise money for Army and Navy Relief. Faith had heard reports that the ten-car train was a success beyond the estimate of anyone in on the planning. The seats were five dollars apiece. The audiences were averaging three thousand in number and the only problem seemed to be over-enthusiastic fans.

And no wonder, thought Faith, as she stood behind her war

bond booth with Kay. The rally itself had been a huge success and so had their booth. Faith had wondered, because of blackout restrictions and the shelling of the fort in Oregon, but neither event seemed to have had an effect on the turnout of people who had come to see the stars.

And the stars were out tonight. Cary Grant, Joan Bennett, Jimmy Cagney, Claudette Colbert, Charles Boyer. Faith had heard that Bob Hope, the emcee, was said to be trying to muster a Christmas show for servicemen overseas. The very chic Olivia de Havilland was so unlike the simpering Melanie in *Gone With the Wind* that Faith had to look twice.

Celebrities milled about having their pictures taken with fans, personally selling bonds, collecting money. Newspaper reporters threatened to jam up the proceedings at Kay and Faith's booth when Cary Grant came by. He gently nudged one of them aside, explaining that he was there to do his part for the war effort, not for publicity's sake.

"Isn't he absolutely the most gorgeous thing you've ever seen?" said the other young girl who was helping in the booth. Her voice was breathless as she added, "Look at that adorable dimple in his chin. I wish I were one of those little dots on his tie."

Faith and Kay laughed, but privately Faith was finding it a little difficult to control her excitement. Cary Grant's pin-striped suit fit his shoulders as though he'd been poured into it. The tie in question was undoubtedly silk and knotted to perfection underneath the points of his white shirt.

He caught her eye at that moment and said something in an aside to Claudette Colbert. They came over to the booth. "How are the sales going?" asked Miss Colbert.

Before Faith could answer, the reporter who was dogging their heels interrupted. "Can we have a picture of you and this lady, Mr. Grant?" he said, nodding at Faith.

"I would be charmed," said the star in his famous drawl. He smiled down at her. "What is your name, my dear?"

Faith considered herself a woman of the world—she'd met famous people before without embarrassing herself—but she couldn't help but feel the pull of his magnetism. "I'm Faith Parker, Mr. Grant," she said with a sigh. They shook hands.

The cameraman missed the shot. "Would you please shake her hand again?" he asked.

"Why don't I just hold it?" asked Cary Grant, smoothly. His fingers were warm around hers.

"Because she's my date for tonight," came a voice from behind her. Faith turned to see Cody standing there, resplendent in his uniform. His smile seemed to drift off-center. He introduced himself to the movie star, who pretended to be gracious in defeat, and the cameraman got a picture of all of them.

"Let's get out of here," mumbled Cody.

Faith hid a smile.

Chapter 17

Sunday, June 28, 1942

This morning Kay had to practically squeeze her way into the Presbyterian church, it was so crowded. Last week it had been the same. The war seemed to have brought on an upsurge in religion as well as patriotism. Despite the open windows and overhead fans the sanctuary was stifling, and she was glad when the service was over.

The minister said good-bye to them at the door. Outside Kay and the children paused at the top of the steps, moving to one side to let the flow of people pass them.

The church sat on the edge of a hill, the entrance atop a long, broad set of granite steps, lined with blooming tulip trees leading up from the sidewalk. From almost anywhere in Seattle you could see water, but here, today, from the threshold of the venerable building the view was especially beautiful. The air was clear; the sky, a brilliant azure. People were dressed in their Sunday best. If the hats were slightly out of style, if their shoes were beginning to show wear, no one cared. They were full of spirit and hope.

Billy laughed aloud—for no apparent reason—he just laughed. The sound was beautiful.

Kay smiled at him in full understanding. The sun shone brightly, warming the tops of their heads, and the clean scent of the breeze from the sound added further optimism to the day.

"There have to be days like this, or human beings couldn't survive, could they?"

Kay turned. The minister had followed them out. He stood with his hands folded at his back, his head lifted, as though

189

scenting the complexion of the day. His black robe whipped around his legs with a sudden gust of wind.

"No, Reverend. I don't think we could."

Though some stragglers were still inside, most of the worshippers and their chatter had moved down to the sidewalk; some of the people walked toward the bus lines, some toward their homes, and, the more fortunate, toward their cars. Quiet seemed to settle on the scene like a benediction.

Then from the serenity—Kay looked around to pinpoint the source—a song, a clear voice, a wisp of melody reached their ears.

"Is that music coming from heaven, Mama?" asked Billy.

Kay nearly answered yes. Indeed, it seemed so.

The minister looked puzzled. "That's the Baptist church but I've never heard that voice before."

He pointed. Two blocks away, from another, smaller church— Kay remembered passing it—rose the contralto, as clear as the air, soaring like the birds above, as pure as peace and joy, as majestical and powerful as the words and the music of the song she sang:

"Lead on, O King Eternal, till sin'd fierce war shall cease.
And Holiness shall whisper the sweet Amen of peace. . . ."

"She does sound like an angel, doesn't she?" said the minister.

Millie had been listening, her head cocked to one side, an intent look on her face. Suddenly she smiled. "That's Mrs. Bingham!"

"Sydney Bingham?" asked Kay in surprise.

"You know her?" the minister inquired of Millie.

"Yes, sir. She lives in the same hotel where we live. She plays the piano in the lobby for us sometimes and my Auntie Faith told me that she sings for the boys at the hospital, too." Millie turned to her mother. "She used to be a nightclub singer, you know."

"No, I didn't know," said Kay weakly, shooting a glance at the minister.

He was one of the leaders in the campaign to close down the "fleshpots," the area of First Avenue from Pioneer Square to Stewart that was the roughest in the city. Bars, dance halls, sleazy hotels, and brothels abounded; the area was notorious. Seattle's leaders were pushing for alternatives, like the USO and service canteens, to take up the slack. He'd preached this morning, encouraging his parishioners to invite young servicemen to their homes for a home-cooked meal or an occasional weekend.

"Nightclub singer?"

Millie realized what she'd said. She blushed. "She *used* to be one."

The man stroked his chin, frowning thoughtfully, then shrugged. "I just wish she were Presbyterian," he said wryly.

"Mrs. Parker."

Kay turned at the sound of her name. "Mrs. Evans, how nice to see you."

Mrs. Evans was about her age, Kay judged. Pretty but harassed. "Mrs. Parker, have you thought any more about taking the job we offered you?"

"Well, as a matter of fact—"

"Please, Mrs. Parker. We need someone with your talents. The General Insurance Company is planning to donate the Leary Mansion to the chapter. It is a wonderful offer. We will be able to accomplish so many things that we have only dreamed of until now. But we must have someone there to supervise."

"Thank you, Mrs. Evans. I'm very flattered. I've decided to accept. But I have some business that I have to take care of first." And I don't want to start to work until my husband's ship leaves, she added to herself. "Would the middle of July be soon enough?"

Mrs. Evans was clearly disappointed. "Well, I suppose so."

"If you find someone else before then, please—"

"Oh, no. The middle of July will be fine," said the woman.

When Kay and the children arrived back at the hotel, they went upstairs to change clothes. Kay was looking in the cabinet under the hot plate trying to decide what to have for lunch when Billy announced that Maurice was serving cherry pie in the dining room today.

"The dining room it is, then."

Millie approached quietly to stand beside them. "Mama, after lunch can I go to the picture show? *Miss Annie Rooney* is on."

"I want to go, too," Billy chimed in.

"Oh, Mama, no!" groaned Millie. "I was going with Jeanne and Grace." She turned on her brother. "You wouldn't like the movie anyway. It's Shirley Temple."

"I like her all right," he protested.

"She gets kissed," Millie countered.

"Kissed. Yuk."

"See. I told you so."

Kay laughed. Funny she hadn't noticed before, Millie was more—like herself nowadays, still quiet but provokable, thank goodness. She was grateful to Faith for the improvement. "Okay," she said.

"We're having lunch in the dining room," she announced a few minutes later when Faith came in from the hall. She had skipped church and her arms were full of freshly laundered clothes.

She suspected her sister-in-law had done the laundry chore to appease her conscience for not attending church with them. Before the war Kay hadn't been much of a churchgoer, either. But with all the bargains she continued to strike with God, she thought He might consider her attendance a condition.

Kay wondered in passing about the shadow she had noticed in Faith's eyes this morning. Faith had gone out with Cody and come in very late last night. However, she was a grown woman now, old enough to make her own choices. The thought reminded Kay of Sydney Bingham and the beautiful music. Perhaps she had misjudged the girl. Of course, the fact that she sang in church didn't make her a saint any more than Kay's presence in a place of worship made her one.

Later when they'd finished eating, they returned to the room rather than linger in the lobby. Millie had left with her friends for the movie and Billy went off to play with his model planes. Kay and Faith sat down to talk.

"When would you start to work?" Faith asked, when Kay told her she had decided to accept the job offer.

"I won't have to be there full-time until Bill leaves. I hated to put them off, they're so short-staffed. Believe it or not, it will be very much the same duties as I have here—"

"Uh-oh," Faith interrupted, laughing. "Maybe you'd better think about this some more."

"But at the Red Cross I'll have an assistant and a secretary."

"Are you nervous?"

"God, yes. I'm scared to death." She thought for a minute. "The job title is Director of Home Service," she explained. "You know what the Home Service Department does: information and communication between servicemen and their families, reporting, claims, and the family help—financial aid, consultations, referrals."

"Sounds like a big job," said Faith slowly. Then she grinned. "But you'll have a secretary." She quoted a statement Billy had made during lunch. "She can do all the real work."

Kay was already thinking ahead. "The business of the hotel worries me, though. My recommendation to Captain Conway that he bring someone in from outside has been overridden." She sighed heavily and shook her head. "I'm afraid he's going to appoint Valerie to the job."

Faith groaned and rolled her eyes. "Fascism rears its ugly head at the Elysium."

"I know. The woman is efficient, I have to give her that. He's going by her proven ability. And, I suspect, a phone call from her father-in-law.

"None of us wants to see this experiment fail. Charles Wagner has more or less abdicated any responsibility. Valerie might not be the most likable person in the place, but she's certainly competent to take both my place and his."

"Maybe she'll stay so busy she won't have time to manage other people's business."

Kay agreed but she didn't respond to the quip. She had something more important on her mind. "Another thing, I don't want the children to suffer for my decision. The Red Cross has made me a very flexible offer. I can set my own hours as long as everything is accomplished that needs to be. They were very flattering."

"They know when they're on to a good thing," Faith interjected.

"Will you help me out with the kids when you can, Faith?"

"Between us we can see that they're taken care of. And I think you'll be pleased with the Y." Faith's eyes dropped to her lap. "But I'd have hoped you knew without asking that I'd help."

Kay touched Faith's hand affectionately. "I did know," she said softly.

Faith returned her smile with an ironic grin. "Isn't it a shame that it took a war for us to learn to get along?" On impulse she got up from her chair and came over to hug her sister-in-law. "I'm happy for you, Kay." She hesitated. "Did you talk to Bill about taking the job?"

"He was against it at first, which is not so unusual, I guess. But then he changed his mind. He said I have to do what's right for me."

"I'm proud of big brother. Maybe he's finally stepping into the twentieth century."

* * *

Vance had come walking in at noon, surprising Sydney.

"I only have a few hours, but I thought I'd like to spend them with you," he said simply.

She was touched. "Vance," she said, going into his arms. She had never been much for showing her emotions openly, but it was getting easier and easier to greet him this way. "I'm glad you came," she said.

"So? What shall we do?" he asked, drawing back to look at her.

"Do? Why do we have to do anything?"

"Come on, Sydney. Shall we take in a movie? Or go out to eat?"

He was too hearty; his smile was a dash too snappy. "Vance, why can't we just stay here?" she asked. "Is something wrong?"

He studied her, the smile slowly fading. "I don't want you to be bored, honey," he stated earnestly. "I know you stay here by yourself a lot. I thought—"

She planted her fists on her hips and rounded on him. "Vance Bingham! Do you mean all this chasing around we do every time you get a pass is because you thought I was *bored*?"

He looked sheepish. She had to laugh. "I'll let you know when I'm bored, okay? When do you have to be back?"

"Seven."

"Good. I'd like to stay in, scramble eggs for supper and read or listen to the radio." She grinned and shot him a look out of the corner of her eye. "I may even beat you at checkers," she threatened.

"That'll be the day," he chortled.

Later Vance was reading the *Seattle Post-Intelligencer*, while she washed their few dishes in the bathroom sink. "Did you say you were thinking about taking a job in one of the defense plants, honey? Here's a notice about the next training class."

Sydney came back in the room, drying her hands on a towel. She came up beside his chair and read over his shoulder. "That class begins tomorrow. I don't want to start until after you leave."

He closed the paper and pulled her down on his lap. He held her for a long time. She was content, there in his arms.

Finally he spoke. "You don't know when there will be another class. You go tomorrow."

Faith anchored a comb into her hair to hold it away from her face and reached for her lipstick. The color was not exactly right for what she was wearing but it was her favorite, and the only one she had. It was getting low, she noted, as she twisted the tube to its furthest extension. She'd have to start looking for another. Or write to Glo in New York. Maybe she could find one there. Lipstick was another of the little luxuries that women were learning to do without. She wondered what they used the oils for in lipsticks. After this war is over, I'm going to have a dozen lipsticks, each one a different color, one to match each outfit.

She reconsidered. Lipsticks didn't *come* in that many colors. There were a lot of other things she used to take for granted that were either scarce or had disappeared from the shelves altogether.

One of them was elastic. Bras made with elastic backs and girdles were almost nonexistent. Leg makeup substituted for nylon stockings. Girdles were no loss as far as Faith was concerned—she'd always hated them, but a bra was a necessity. No decent woman would go without.

Last week she'd seen elastic among the items for sale on a street corner not far from the hotel. The man had spread his wares on a blanket. A black market had sprung to life in Seattle. It made her angry; she refused to buy anything from the people who accosted her on street corners, but she had to admit she was tempted by the elastic. Fortunately for her conscience the man had scooped it all up and whisked it away as a policeman came walking along. The police were trying to clamp down on the sellers but met with little success.

"Auntie Faith! Cody's here!"

"I'll be right out," she said through the closed door. She replaced her few cosmetics in the zippered bag and smiled toward her reflection in the mirror over the bathroom sink. With a finger she wiped a touch of lipstick off her tooth.

Kay was entering the bedroom when she came out. "I forgot to give you yesterday's mail," she said, dropping a bundle of letters on Faith's bed. "I think they're all from your soldiers and sailors."

Faith glanced down, hesitating.

Kay read her hesitation correctly. "Bill and Cody are replaying the Battle of Midway. You have a few minutes before victory is declared," she said, smiling brightly as she left the room.

Faith sat on the edge of the bed and picked up the letters, staring without seeing them. Kay and the children were delighted that she was having a second date with the man they liked so much. She let her hands fall to her lap. Maybe she shouldn't have accepted.

But last night with Cody had been fun. Secretly she had been as pleased as she was surprised by the dash of jealousy he'd shown when Cary Grant had posed for a picture with her. It had added spice to the evening. When they left the rally they'd had supper at a little, out-of-the-way place and talked long into the night.

Faith had always considered the phrase "a good personality" a shallow way to characterize someone, but she found it to be true when applied to Cody. He was serious when appropriate, but he also had a deep sense of humor and a quick mind. She'd not gotten back to the hotel until after three.

They talked about the war, as everyone did, and themselves. He told her about his father, who struggled to earn a living on a small Texas farm. He would never go back there, he declared. She told him of her ambition to be a fashion designer and how frivolous that ambition seemed now. He argued that bringing a greater degree of beauty to the world was not frivolous at all.

He had invited her to go for a drive. At some cost, he'd hired someone to drive his car to Seattle from Texas. Gas was another scarce commodity, already rationed on the East Coast. And all the new cars were going to the military. But Cody had told her that he'd feel like a man without a soul if he didn't have his car. She'd wavered over her answer—he was going too fast for her— but he would be returning to base the next night . . . tonight. He had no idea when he'd get leave again. So she'd finally said yes.

She sighed and riffled through the letters in her hand. There was one from John Harrison. She smiled as she unfolded the flimsy V-mail paper that made an envelope She smiled more broadly at the heavily blacked-out phrases that the censor obviously thought she shouldn't see. John would have to learn discretion. It was hard to believe that some faceless person in an office somewhere actually read each letter from overseas.

She selected another, one with an unfamiliar address. It was a letter from the mother of one of the servicemen she corresponded with. "I know that Kevin would have wanted you to know . . ." the letter began. Her hand shook. The words blurred before her eyes.

Kevin was only a name to Faith. A name from the newspaper in Saratoga Springs, a boy, one from among many who'd written to the paper asking for letters from home. She and Glo had thought it would be fun to write to boys in the service.

When she quit school to take part in the war effort she'd done it partly because she didn't want to miss anything. Dear God, how could she have been so selfish, so naive? Another thought struck her. If Kevin hadn't mentioned her to his mother, she would never have known of his death. The letters would simply have stopped coming.

Cody had the top down on his convertible. The night was clear, with the moon and a thousand stars set in a canopy of velvet over their heads. The road was straight; he drove fast. But Faith felt no fear. He was fully in control of the vehicle. The wind rushed through her hair, wrecking her attempts to hold it to some semblance of order. She gave up and rested her head against the seatback. Maybe it would blow some of the chaos out of her brain.

Cody glanced across at her. "I'm sorry. I should have told you to bring a scarf." He raised his voice to be heard over the rush of air.

She had been able to bank her emotions in front of her family, but she was subdued. Now she turned her head to look across at Cody, so full of life and energy. Dear God, don't let anything happen to him. "Don't worry about it. The breeze feels good," she said, and forced a smile. "Where are we going?"

"A buddy in the BOQ told me about this park on one of the hills around here." Cody had moved into the Bachelor Officer's Quarters after a futile search for a room in downtown Seattle.

He slowed, turned left, and guided the car along twisting, climbing roads through a residential section. "It should be . . ." He leaned forward over the steering wheel to peer out. The headlights, taped over because of the blackout, provided almost no illumination, but the moon was bright enough to see the small parking area.

He got out of the car and came around to open her door. They climbed the path hand in hand. Faith was very grateful for his hand, fingers curled warmly around hers.

"It's called Volunteer Park," he explained as they came out of the trees.

Faith caught her breath. To their right was a huge, impressive building, its architecture modern in the extreme. "That's the art museum," he told her. But it was to the left that she was drawn. A large reservoir clung to the side of the mountain and beyond it the city was laid out below them, dark and mysterious in the moonlight. It might have been uninhabited. They walked that way, passing several other couples murmuring in the shadows, seemingly oblivious.

Faith couldn't help the shudder that ran through her.

"Are you cold?" asked Cody. He started to take off his uniform jacket.

She stopped him with a hand on his arm. "It's cooler than in the city but, no, I'm not cold. It's just . . ." She was at a loss for words. She didn't often share deep feelings. Things that touched her emotionally were kept buried, but tonight she was visibly upset and unable to hide it.

"What's the matter, baby?" he asked, concerned. "You're very quiet."

"Look down there, Cody. What do you see?" she demanded, her shaky voice rising.

He followed the direction of her gesture, was silent for a moment. Then he put an arm across her shoulders and drew her closer. "I see a city that looks dead."

He did understand, she thought thankfully. He was tall and she had to tilt her head back to study his face. His profile was outlined in silver by the moonlight. There was strength there.

"But beneath the darkness I can see a city, a country that is very much alive, Faith. In all those darkened buildings are people who are working, sleeping, laughing, crying, making love."

His eyes met hers on the last words. She looked away.

"Something has happened."

"Yes." She threw her head back, blinking rapidly at the stars. "I heard that a boy I write to—wrote to—is dead."

"And this is the first time that's happened to you," he guessed correctly.

She nodded. "I never even met him, Cody. I got his name from a newspaper." She spoke in rapid sentences, swallowing often. "He was eighteen years old. His mother couldn't be sure, but she thought it happened off the coast of Italy. Sometimes I forget there is another war on that side of the world." She turned her face into his coat, sobbing once. His arms tightened around her. "How many boys do we have, Cody? How many to send away? Will we run out of boys before the war is over?" She bit off another question: Will you be coming back?

Cody stroked her back firmly. She felt his lips on her brow. He didn't even try to answer. There was no answer.

He held her until her shaking had stopped and she released a shuddering sigh. "I'm sorry," she said. She pulled away and groped around in her pocket for a handkerchief. "Girls are not supposed to blubber all over their dates. It isn't patriotic."

His hand cupped her chin. He wasn't gentle as he raised her face to his. His expression was grim. "I don't give a damn about what a girl is supposed to do or not supposed to do. You just shared an honest feeling with me, Faith, and I thank you for it." He raked through her hair with his other hand to hold her head steady as his head blotted out the stars. "Believe me, that means a hell of a lot more to a man than a lot of flag waving."

She went on tiptoe to meet his lips. Like the couples they had passed she was oblivious to anyone else except the man who held her in his strong arms. The kiss seemed to go on forever. Finally he broke away, laughing unsteadily at her dazed expression. He gave her a hug that was more affectionate than lover-like.

"Come on, baby, let's climb the observation tower. I need to work off some of this . . . energy."

It seemed like they climbed forever. She was breathless by the time they reached the top. He had to pull her bodily the last few steps. But the view was worth it. He wrapped her in his arms from behind and turned her slowly in a full circle.

They were quiet for a time. Faith was comforted by his presence and the security she felt in his arms. "This is more beautiful than anything in Texas," he said at last.

"That's high praise indeed from a Texan."

"I really like this area of the country. I might want to settle here someday."

"What *do* you want to do after the war, Cody? Are you going to stay in the service?"

"I'm not sure. I may. Or I may go to work for one of the airplane companies. I have an engineering degree. Whatever I do I want to be a part of the new age in aviation. I want to fly jets."

She'd heard all about jets from Bill and she thought the whole idea was insane. She told him so.

He pulled down his chin and eyed at her strangely.

"Bill compares them to a balloon when you blow it up and let it go. What happens when the balloon runs out of air?" she demanded. "It falls on the floor, that's what."

Cody threw back his head and laughed in pure enjoyment. The sound scattered over the scene below them and echoed from the hills across the valley. He had a wonderful laugh, she thought; even when his laughter was directed at her, she liked it.

When he sobered, he went on to explain, "That's what the jet engines are for, baby. They keep pushing the air through the turbines."

"Well, I still think it's an insane idea."

"Some people thought flying itself was insane. One day, Faith, we'll fly faster than the speed of sound, one day we'll fly to the moon."

A dreamer, that's what he was. But a nice one.

On the way back to the hotel he asked, with studied casualness, "You said you write to men?"

"Servicemen," she supplied the correction smoothly.

He reached over into her lap and took her hand. "Have you begun any correspondence with anyone since you've been in Seattle?"

"Yes, one boy. I met him on the train from Chicago." She looked down at their clasped fingers. "He's very young, too."

"Will you write to me?"

"Of course," she said, surprised he had to ask.

Chapter 18

Monday, June 29, 1942

Valerie sat in her office off the coffee shop and worked on her books while she sipped a cup of coffee that she had unobtrusively laced with brandy. Only two more weeks and Kay Parker would be out; she would be in charge. Her smile was filled with satisfaction as she tossed her pencil aside and sent her swivel chair into an arc with her toe. She wasn't supposed to know that the final decision had been made but—Suddenly her attention was caught by the sight of Sydney Bingham leaving the coffee shop, all dressed up and alone.

Her lips pursed and she frowned. She had given the woman time off to be with her husband, not to flit around by herself. She got up, intending to waylay Sydney for an explanation, but she was stopped by the sound of breaking crockery. Her icy gaze swung to the source of the sound. One of the new girls— she sighed.

Billy ran into the lobby of the hotel. He had been outside conferring with the junkman. "Mom, Mr. Meyers told me—"

Kay was discussing a plumbing problem that had developed on the fourth floor with the man who had come to solve it. "Later, honey," she said.

Anxious to share his news he looked around. In the far corner of the reading room his sister and her friend were playing with the Ouija board. "Hey, Millie, guess what. Mr. Meyers wants garden hoses to send to the gas mask people. He doesn't even care if they've got holes in them!"

She whirled on him in exasperation. "Billy, I'm trying to concentrate. Now, get out of here."

He stuck out his tongue.

"Billy," she warned.

"No one really believes all that Ouija stuff anyway," he muttered as he wandered away.

Faith watched the small scene play out with an indulgent smile. Billy was always on hand for the man's weekly visit and gave them a rundown of the interesting stuff he saw piled on the truck—old bottles, cans, rags, anything metal—a skate, a sled, a washtub. Her sympathy aroused, she was about to call him when she was stopped by the sound of her name.

It was Sydney.

The redhead was dressed in trim slacks and a tailored shirt. "Guess where I'm going?"

Faith smiled and glanced at the clock over the front desk. She came around the counter to join her friend. "It's awfully early to be going anywhere."

"You're right. Lordy, I can't believe I used to sleep till noon. Anyway, I'm going to apply for the training class for factory workers out at Boeing."

Faith knew Sydney wanted a job, but she was shocked at the idea of the glamorous redhead as a welder or riveter. "A factory worker?" she said faintly. "Sydney are you sure—"

"Sydney, I want to talk to you."

Both women turned at the sound of Valerie's voice. "Yes, Valerie?" Sydney responded guardedly.

"I understood that you wanted time off to be with your husband. Where is he?"

"He's on duty this morning."

"Then you're free to help out right now and I need you. There's a new girl who's made a mess in the kitchen—"

"I can't right now. I'm—"

Valerie's eyes narrowed. "Of course, you can," she interrupted, then turned away. "Right now," she repeated pointedly.

"Oh, for heaven's sake, Valerie," Faith snapped. "Sydney's on her way to apply for a job. You're not the queen around here, so quit treating us like your subjects."

Her words halted Valerie in her tracks. She whirled to confront Faith. "And you shouldn't even *be* in this hotel," she spat. "You're only tolerated because of your brother." She flounced off.

"Whew! I'm afraid you've made yourself an enemy," Sydney drawled.

"I can't imagine anyone I'd rather be enemies with. Can you believe that woman?" She started to share the unhappy news she'd had from Kay, that Valerie would soon be in charge of the hotel, but she wasn't sure it was supposed to be known.

Sydney spoke again. "I wanted to tell you that I'll be back in time for our shift at the hospital tonight. Will you wait for me?"

"Sure, I'll wait," Faith said.

She went back to the desk and her thoughts returned to where they'd been before Valerie interrupted. Sydney—working in a factory? Dear God, she thought as she watched the tall redhead stride through the doors.

We're trying to fight this war by sending our young men—our boys—overseas to do battle far from home, and by collecting old rubber hoses and washtubs to make our weapons and ammunition, and by consigning women to do men's jobs. Is there the least likelihood at all of winning under such conditions? God, do we have a prayer? She wanted to cry.

Sydney nervously climbed aboard the crowded bus and found a seat near the front. She'd filled out the necessary forms at the downtown office and had been accepted for training by the Boeing Aircraft Company, but she had a lot of misgivings.

She hadn't been in any kind of school in so long, what if she failed? And Vance was leaving Saturday. If he got time off during the week she was going to spend it with him even if she got fired before she began.

An older woman greeted her cheerfully from the adjoining seat. "Hello, I'm Maurie O'Conner."

"I'm Sydney Bingham," Sydney responded with a friendly smile. She was surprised; the advertisement for women to work for the Boeing Aircraft Company hadn't specified an age limit, but Maurie O'Conner must be in her fifties, at least, unlike anybody's idea of an assembly-line worker. Gray curls framed a round face scored with fine lines. Her eyes were a trusting blue. A tidy grandmotherly type, she smelled of lavender and the starch in her neatly pressed cotton dress.

"Isn't this wonderful? I've been wanting to get into the war effort doing something really important, ever since Pearl Harbor." She made a face and gave a small snort. "But they kept telling me I was too old. That they had no place for a retired schoolteacher.

"Finally I told them that our country was in a jam and they needed me even if they didn't know it. I guess they're scraping the bottom of the barrel, but I don't care as long as I have the job.''

Sydney revised her estimate of the woman's age, but Maurie was plump and radiant in her anticipation. Sydney couldn't help smiling with her.

The atmosphere on the bus crackled with anticipation and suspense. The women's voices were restrained, slightly anxious.

''You're not the bottom of the barrel.'' I'm further down than you are; I didn't even finish high school, she added silently to herself.

''If I am, I won't be for long. I've got four boys fighting in the South Pacific and I want to do everything I can to help bring them back quickly.''

''Four! Well, with four sons fighting, Mrs. O'Conner, you sure have more reason to do a good job than anybody else.''

''Call me Maurie, please. And what about you, dear? Are you waiting for someone special?''

''My husband. He's going on a ship.'' Sydney clamped her lips shut on the word. She must learn not to respond so freely to a friendly inquiry. She had just given away secret information.

Maurie patted her hands where they lay folded in her lap. ''That's right. Never mention a name or a place. You don't know what ears may be listening or eyes watching.'' She glanced around. ''I heard that the spies are learning lip-reading from deaf people. They put plugs in their ears and are not allowed to speak out loud until they pass a test. So tell me something about yourself. What part of the South are you from?''

''Mississippi originally and then New Orleans.'' She glanced out of the window to see that they had left the congested part of the city behind. She didn't want to think about where she was from, just where she was going.

''Ah, New Orleans. I've never been there but I've heard about it.'' Her tone was teasing. ''Is the French Quarter as wicked as they say.''

Sydney forced a laugh. ''Every bit as wicked.'' She was surprised at how easily she answered. The pain of the past was fading. ''And what about you? Are you from Seattle?'' Her question was a legitimate one. Almost everyone here was from somewhere else.

''Born and raised. I'm one of the few natives. Look at that.''

They had stopped at the gate to the huge facility. A woman dressed in a blue-gray gabardine uniform boarded the bus. She worked her way slowly down the aisle checking each purse, examining each face until Sydney was sure she could identify any one of the women in a dark alley from fifty paces. When she reached their row, Sydney held out her open purse, offering a tentative smile that was answered with a cold glare.

After a brief word with the driver the uniformed guard left the bus. She signaled for the driver to pass through the gate. They drove further, through narrow streets lined with innocuous buildings painted bland colors, which could have been used for anything from warehouse space to office space. Nothing here gave the appearance of being a place where they manufactured or assembled airplanes.

Finally the bus ground to a halt in front of an old red building, which resembled an oversized schoolhouse. The driver opened the door and spoke over the whisper of speculation. "Please wait in the vestibule, ladies. Your supervisor will be with you shortly."

The women milled about quietly, waiting. Those who had come prepared were dressed in slacks, but the majority, like Maurie, wore dresses for this first day. Sydney presumed that would change. From what she understood the work would involve climbing up on airplane wings, crawling through the fusilage, and a dress certainly wouldn't work for that.

"Good morning, ladies." The supervisor was a sour-faced, pudgy man in his mid-forties. He was dressed in wrinkled brown trousers and a matching suit vest. He wore his sleeves in fat little sausagelike rolls around his elbows.

Sydney didn't like the almost insulting way he stretched out the sound of the word "ladies."

"My name is Mr. Nicholson." He took his time looking them over, then his sparse brows tried to curl together over his eyes in what she presumed was supposed to be an intimidating frown. Instead it made his eyes look crossed behind the narrow, wire-rimmed glasses. "Would you step in here, please?" He didn't bother to hide the sarcasm as he crossed to open a side door with exaggerated politeness. Sydney would be willing to bet it was the last polite gesture they would get from the man.

They obligingly filed past him, a few giving him uncertain glances. They had been drawn here by various motives, some out of patriotism, some out of need, some because the money was a whole lot better than slinging hash in some diner downtown. But there were some who looked as if they were having second thoughts.

There were chairs in the room they entered, but Mr. Nicholson didn't invite them to sit. He took a stance on a platform at one end of the room, and they all turned toward him.

He put his hands on his ample hips and surveyed them like a lord from on high looking over his peasant labor. "The first thing I must ask you, ladies"—again he drew out the word—"is: Are you sure you want to be here? This isn't going to be easy work." He paused for a moment, giving them an opportunity to reply. There was no response.

"Very well." He sighed and explained about security passes and rules. "I must warn you, there won't be regular opportunities to keep your makeup fixed. Your nails will have to be kept short and you can't wear polish. Your hair will have to be bound up in some way or cut off like a man's. High heels are out. You will wear slacks or coveralls on the job. You'll be on time for the bus, which will pick you up in town each morning at seven. If you're late, don't bother to pick up your severance pay. If there's anything coming, it will be mailed to you."

Then, leaving them with the impression that they had wasted enough of his important time, he assigned Mr. Smith to take them on a tour of the facilities where they'd be working. Mr. Smith turned out to be a young, pale-faced man who'd been standing unnoticed by the door.

They started to move as a group. Nicholson halted them with an upraised hand. "I'm not quite finished. Before you go, I'll ask again. Is there anyone who would like to leave now?" He paused. Again there was no response. "We won't make allowances for the fact that you're the 'weaker sex.' If you can't keep up or do your part, you're out."

Maurie stirred beside Sydney. She saw that the older woman was clutching her purse tightly in two hands before her. Though her face was calm, her knuckles were white.

Suddenly the man's attitude made Sydney mad. He was probably the one who'd suggested they were scraping the bottom of the barrel. What right had he to scare the pants off an old woman who just wanted to contribute to the war effort?

Sydney fought her anger; it wouldn't do to blow up on the first day of her job—or the training for her job. Besides he wasn't worth it.

Maurie O'Conner had already given a lot, four sons, to the defense of her country, more than this pompous SOB who was standing before them with a derisive sneer on his lips. He was willing to write off any contribution they might be able to make just because they were females and he was a bigoted old windbag.

Nicholson smiled, revealing small teeth. "I understand that women have to pee more than men."

Sydney felt Maurie flinch at the crude comment. Several of the other women shifted uncomfortably.

"Arrangements have been made for you to have two extra breaks during an eight-hour shift, but you'd better not waste time. I'll push you hard. Hard," Nicholson went on. He thrust his fingers into the armholes of his vest and reared back contemptuously on his heels. "You may as well know this about me. I don't approve of women doing men's work."

No damn joke, thought Sydney.

Another voice interrupted his tirade. "Fortunately for the success of the war effort, your superiors don't feel that way, Mr. Nicholson. Now, can we cut the crap and get started? We've got boys waiting for airplanes."

Astonished, Sydney jerked her head around to stare at her companion. Maurie's voice had been as soft and smooth as sweet cream and now her lips curved in an innocent, grandmotherly smile. Sydney swallowed a hoot of delight. Then she heard a smattering of applause.

Before it could grow into a full-fledged tribute, however, Nicholson spoke again. Sydney had to give the old goat credit for aplomb in the face of adversity. "Indeed, we have. Now, our Mr. Smith will take you to the training area."

Kay put her head out the door and spoke to Edna McCoy. "Edna, would you ask Mrs. Adair and Mrs. Cabot to join us please? And Mr. Wagner, too." If you can find him, she added to herself.

"I'm sorry you don't agree with my choice, Kay," said the officer who sat beside her desk. His shoulders, his voice, his whole demeanor, were stiff.

"It's your decision, Captain," she said mildly. Inside she was churning with anger. She had worked hard to set up this experiment in accord with his wishes; and now he had carelessly dismissed her recommendations.

Valerie entered, a look of triumph on her beautiful face. Patsy followed, and they both sat down.

At least she had accomplished something, thought Kay as she performed the introductions. Captain Conway had finally consented to an assistant to the manager. With Charles almost out of the picture, Valerie would need help.

An hour later she showed everyone out of her office and collapsed back into her chair. Her responsibility for the hotel was almost finished. The captain had made his announcement. Valerie and Patsy would begin working with her immediately to learn the organization and schedule of the hotel.

Charles was indifferent during the meeting, a fact that was not lost on the captain. And he was extremely impressed by the senator's daughter-in-law. Of course, the fact that the senator was a member of the Armed Forces Committee helped.

Kay laughed. She had actually done it!

Sydney and Maurie boarded the bus and sank gratefully into their seats. The day had been spent gathering a confusing blur of information. They had broken for a quick lunch in the employee's cafeteria. Then back to a classroom for more instruction.

Sydney glanced over at her friend. At the sight that greeted her eyes, she wanted to laugh; but she was too tired.

Maurie caught her smile. "What?" she asked.

"I was just thinking about the contrast between the neat, grandmotherly person I sat beside this morning and the disheveled woman beside me now. Do I look as tired as you do?"

Maurie studied her. "Probably not." She put a hand to her curls, then let it drop. "I don't care. All I want to do is get home and soak my feet. We must have walked miles today."

"We'll walk more. Especially if we're chosen for the secret job." They had taken additional tests, filled out more forms, the explanation being that certain ones of them would be assigned to a special crew.

When the bus reached the city they parted at the bus stop. "I'll see you tomorrow," said Sydney. "Save me a seat."

As Sydney trudged up the hill toward the hotel, she thought about the day and the new friend she'd made. Maurie was an exceptional woman. She had four sons in the service. Sydney shook her head at the idea of sending her entire family off to war. The thought made her pause. Wasn't she doing the same thing? Vance was, for all purposes, her entire family.

Sydney drew her cape tighter around her shoulders. "I hate this rain. My hair kinks up." She and Faith walked along the streets from the hospital toward the hotel.

"Kay's not going to be happy about us walking home. I promised we'd take a taxi."

"You can't take what isn't there," said Sydney offhandedly. "Did Cody call you today?" Faith gave a happy little skip that brought a smile to Sydney's lips.

"Yes, yes, he did. Oh, Sydney, I really like him."

Sydney resigned herself to a recitation of Cody Bristol's wonderful qualities. Occasionally a wave of sound—music or laughter or something more ominous like the crunching exchange of blows—would emerge from one of the nearby buildings, but the girls barely noticed.

With shifts running round the clock at the plants and military men on passes, most night spots as well as all the movie theaters stayed open twenty-four hours a day.

They had gone only a few blocks when suddenly Sydney became aware of muttered voices and clumsy movement from the shadows ahead in the next block. Her head came up with a jerk. "Shit," she said, cutting off Faith's chatter.

"Sydney Bingham!" Faith admonished with a giggle. There was no moon tonight. The sky was overcast and occasionally the clouds leaked a bit. All other light was either extinguished or shielded by the heavy blackout measures.

Sydney had been in some precarious situations and she definitely wasn't a scaredy-cat, but she'd always had a healthy respect for caution. This area of the city, while not the worst section, was peppered with cheap bars and cheaper nightclubs and drew some of the rowdier types. The streets were fairly deserted; everybody was inside having fun.

"They're just drunks. Don't be afraid, Faith."

"I'm not afraid," Faith informed her.

Sydney grimaced. "We'll keep walking naturally. Don't run unless they make a move we can't handle. Then run like hell."

The voices from the shadows, now identifiable as male, had amplified a couple of decibels. The sounds were harsh and loud and the language, crude.

Sydney heard curses, saw someone stagger and fall. Laughter greeted his misfortune. One of the men had turned to look at them. He said something to his companions.

"I've changed my mind. We'll turn at the corner." The girls continued to walk at the same speed while they were in the light, but when they rounded the building they moved faster. Sydney's legs were longer and could have eaten up the distance, but she kept pace with Faith. She glanced over her shoulder and was slightly relieved when she saw that they hadn't been followed. They weren't out of danger yet, though.

They cut back on the next street to travel a parallel route. "I figure we should keep on this street for at least three blocks," she said.

Suddenly she realized that the noise coming from the younger woman wasn't a whimper of fear—she wondered why she ever thought it was. It was a muffled giggle.

"There's nothing funny here," snapped Sydney.

"I know," gasped Faith, trying very hard to suppress the laugh that threatened to escape. "Let me ask you something. Did my sister-in-law ask you to look out for me?"

Kay had been concerned about them being out after dark, but she hadn't come right out and asked. "She said it would be safer if we took a taxi home, but how were we to know they are as scarce as hen's teeth at this time of night?"

Faith shook her head. "She thinks she's being so protective. But she and Bill never worried about me when I was visiting my roommate Gloria in New York City. If you think New Orleans is bad, you ought to meet the cream of New York society. I learned very quickly to take care of myself."

"Fending off a Park Avenue drunk is a little different from handling a plastered dockworker," Sydney answered absently. She decided their evasive action had been successful. "Okay, I think it's safe now." They turned back toward their original route.

"A drunk is a drunk," Faith argued.

"Not by any stretch of the imagination. If you have a date when you're visiting your friend and the date gets too enthusiastic, he still knows that they know who you're out with. If he doesn't bring you back the police also know where to begin looking. That demands a sensible amount of caution and responsibility from him. But if you're on your own in a city, no one knows except you. And you're so tiny; I'll bet you've never had any training in taking care of yourself, either, have you?"

"Now you sound like Kay. No, but I can reason with a substandard jackass."

"Don't count on it. A jackass is an animal, remember."

"A dumb animal," Faith said as they approached the corner.

"For pete's sake, Faith, don't let's argue about it. I just want to get home."

Without warning, as they rounded the building, a large shape loomed in their path. Sydney gasped aloud; Faith's hand flew up to cover her heart.

"Well, well," came a slurred voice from out of the darkness. "Were you trying to dodge us back there, ladies? That ain't very friendly."

Sydney could almost feel the confidence drain from Faith. She, too, felt apprehensive, but instead of keeping quiet, she stepped forward. "Evenin' boys," she said. "Whatcha up to?"

The large shape had been joined by three others. Now that they were closer she could distinguish the men's features. They were looking at her, their interest caught. Faith took a step that brought her side-by-side with Sydney.

"Where you from, honey?"

A southern accent! And it came out reasonably sober. If she were lucky, the fact that the man was southern might help to even the odds somewhat. "I'm from McNeill, Mississippi. Where're you from?"

"Etowah, Tennessee," the man answered, putting the accent on the first syllable of the name of the state. This was a country boy. "Where you girls goin'?"

To her dismay Sydney noticed that Faith was getting her courage back. She was about to take part in the exchange, when all Sydney wanted her to do was stay quiet. She could handle this better alone.

"We're on our way home," said Faith. "We've been doing volunteer work at the hospital."

Sydney almost groaned aloud. She reached for the younger girl's hand and squeezed her fingers.

"Regular little Florence Nightingales, ain't we?" said another voice, this one heavy with sarcasm and thicker with drink than the others.

Faith wisely kept silent.

"So you been holdin' hands with the little soldier boys. You get to wear a uniform, too? Lemme see your uniform." The first man, the biggest one, reached out and pulled Sydney's rain-cape open. She tried not to flinch as his red eyes took in her shape. "Well, you don't have any medals on your uniform but you do fill it out nice. Should I salute ya?"

"Leave her alone," said Faith. She took another step forward but the drunkest man, the one who had called them Florence Nightingales, grabbed her left arm.

"You got a uniform on, too, honey?" He reached for the belt of her raincoat.

She struggled, but it wasn't much use. "Let me go, this instant!" she commanded.

The man laughed, and it was not a pleasant sound. "Boys, if my ear don't mistake me, we got one of the la-ti-dah upper crust, here."

Faith swung her purse. And missed. "Take your filthy hands off me."

The man had her coat open now. "Filthy?" He grabbed a handful of her hair and gave a yank. She cried out.

"You think I'm filthy?" he snarled. With his other hand he squeezed her breast. "Not good enough for you, huh? You prob'ly got a fancy boyfriend, a lawyer maybe, or a banker, to get in your pants? Maybe I oughta take you down a peg, girlie. Maybe the boyfriend wouldn't like you so much if you was messed up a bit."

Sydney's voice cut off any response. "Boys," she said cajolingly, frantic to hide the desperation she felt. "This one's fresh from the schoolroom. You don't want a baby, do you? Why not wait for some real women."

"I don't see any reason to wait," said another man who until now had been silent. "We came out looking for girls and here are two."

Sydney tried another tack. "Boys, our dogs are tired tonight. We wouldn't be much fun."

The big man pulled at her arm, bringing her closer. "You'd be fun if I told you to be fun, now, wouldn't you, missy," he said, the threat menacing in his voice.

His breath was foul with cheap whiskey and his manner was designed to terrorize to the point of acquiescence. He ran a hand down her arm and around to fondle her butt. But the move didn't anger her as much as the glimpse she had from the corner of her eye. The man who held Faith was pulling back on her hair, trying to kiss her while he still mauled her breast.

"She's just a child," Sydney protested, unable to hide her fear any longer. "Please, stop him," she said to the Southerner.

The man from Tennessee glanced over and shrugged, unconcerned. "I never seen tits like that on no child."

Sydney knew she had only one chance. She leaned into the man who held her, hoping to throw him off balance for just the second she needed. As she'd hoped, he relaxed and Sydney suddenly erupted with all the strength she could generate. Her knee caught the big man squarely in the crotch. She felt the sensitive tissue give way under the impact. He howled and, releasing her, fell to his knees, holding himself.

Sydney whirled on the second man. "Get your dirty hands off her, you goddamned son of a bitch," she muttered in a low voice. She knew that if she screamed and cried the two unoccupied men would have taken pleasure in subduing her, but the controlled tone along with the fury in her gaze was enough to make them pause.

"You!" She pointed to the man from Tennessee. "Your mama would have your balls for breakfast if she saw you acting like this."

It was a calculated gamble and it worked. The Southerner, who hadn't seemed to have much appetite for the foray anyway, backed off, grabbing the arm of the man who threatened Faith. "Let's get out of here before the cops show up."

They helped the big man to his feet and dragged him, groaning and cursing, down the sidewalk. The fourth man, seeing that he was the only one left, shrugged and took off after them.

When they were gone Sydney crossed her arms over her stomach in a protective gesture—she was shaking like a leaf in a windstorm—and let her head fall forward.

Faith sagged against the wall of the building. "Oh, God," she whispered.

Sydney looked at her friend from under a worried frown. "Are you all right, Faith?" she asked.

Faith shook her head, then nodded. "Yes. I'm all right. Are you?" she said between shallow breaths.

"More or less. Let's go."

If either of them had had the energy they would have run; but, drained as they were, they walked very fast indeed. They'd almost reached the hotel when Faith stopped Sydney with a touch on her arm. "Thank you, Sydney," she said quietly.

"There's nothing to thank me for. We were lucky." She managed a weak smile and patted the hand on her arm. "Next time, though, if we can't get a cab we spend the night at the hospital. Okay?"

"On the floor if necessary," Faith agreed, meeting her smile with obvious relief.

Sydney started toward the hotel entrance. Faith stopped her again. "Had you planned on telling anyone about this?"

Sydney scratched absently behind her ear. A month ago she wouldn't have had to think. She would have kept the experience to herself, figuring that someone, someday, would catch up to those creeps. Not her problem, she would have thought. There was no way she'd have become involved.

When she finally answered, she surprised herself. ''I guess we should report it to someone. We're both safe but the next girls to walk that way might not be so lucky.'' She laughed inside, wondering when the hell she'd become so high-minded.

''You're right,'' Faith said as she pulled aside the blackout curtain and motioned for Sydney to precede her. When the curtain fell closed behind them they entered the lobby.

A sleepy Edna McCoy looked up at their arrival and waved. Sydney crossed to the telephone on the desk. ''Edna, will you get me the police, please?''

''The police? What happened?'' said Edna, instantly and fully awake.

''We had a run-in with some drunks,'' Faith explained briefly. She met Sydney's eyes. ''I suppose Kay will have to know, too. I just hope she won't tell Bill.''

''She won't if you ask her not to.''

The two policemen arrived shortly and began to question them, taking careful note of their descriptions.

Kay came downstairs during their questioning. Faith shot an accusing glance at Edna.

The policemen were nice, and patient, and concerned but they didn't hold out much hope of finding the men. They explained that Seattle was dealing as best it could with the crime wave that had accompanied the phenomenal tide of growth in the city. A certain free-wheeling, pioneer spirit still lived here, one that tended to overlook the off-duty antics of hard-drinking, hard-working, hard-living men. The authorities were just beginning to realize that the tide had also washed up the dregs, a lot of people with questionable backgrounds, people who couldn't hold jobs elsewhere, and people whose morals weren't that pure to begin with. They continued to arrive from all over the country to take advantage of the high paychecks. Few were turned away because the need was so extreme.

Prevention took manpower though, and that was at a premium. The crime rate continued to rise.

''The men are probably sleeping it off in some alley by now, but we'll take a look in the area,'' said the older of the two policemen, a lieutenant. He closed his small notebook and they prepared to leave.

''Don't you have some—those pictures, what do they call them—mug shots we could look at?'' asked Faith.

The lieutenant took off his black-billed hat and smoothed back his hair with a tired gesture before settling it again on his head. "Ma'am, with all the people coming and going in Seattle, we barely have time to book them. I appreciate your offer to try to identify these men, but the mug shots we have are three years old. If we pick up anyone who resembles the descriptions you've given us, we'll call you then."

They left, one of them muttering something under his breath about the Lone Ranger.

Chapter 19

Saturday, July 4, 1942

Vance rolled to his back, pulling the sheet taut across his thighs. He levered himself on his elbows and looked around with sleepy eyes. His jaw was dark with beard, his hair tousled.

Sydney smiled over the rim of her mug and wondered why she hadn't thought this man was good-looking.

"Coffee?" she asked, recalling the first morning of their marriage, and the coffee they had shared in her small room at Mrs. Deveraux's house. She filled a mug for him and set it on the table beside the bed.

He was remembering, too. She could tell from his reminiscent smile. He piled both pillows behind him and sat up. "Why didn't you wake me?"

"I thought I'd let you sleep as long as you could. But it's late." She indicated the clock. He frowned and she laughed unsteadily. "You'd better get up now. I'll finish your packing while you shower." Last night he had divided the things he was taking from the things he was leaving.

Vance caught her hand and urged her to sit on the edge of the bed beside him. They looked at each other, and then she laid her head on his shoulder and he gathered her close.

"You haven't even left yet and already I'm upset over how long it will be before I see you again," she said softly.

"I'll be back in Seattle in a few months, honey."

She didn't want him to leave at all, damn it. There was nothing to say, no words to ease the pain of parting. In the relatively brief time they'd spent together, their relationship had undergone a radical change. Her feelings were no longer tenuous or remote as they'd been when she said good-bye the morning after their wedding. She knew him now as well as she had ever known anyone, knew him as clever, caring, compassionate. She knew him as a man she could trust and love for the rest of her life.

What a fool she'd been that first day in Seattle when she'd been so wary of this man.

She touched his face and heard the steady beat of his heart under her cheek. Her eyes filled but she blinked back the moisture. All she could do was behave, on the surface, the same way she behaved every other morning.

But this wasn't like any other morning. Today her husband would board a ship bound for a war from which he might never return. She couldn't dwell on it or she would cry. Instead she pulled out of his arms, smiled at him as though he were going on a pleasure cruise for the day, and warned, "You're going to be late."

Sydney was wearing a navy blue slim skirt and a matching blouse in a linen-rayon combination. Over it she had on a white collarless bolero with navy braid frogs. Her hair was arranged in a neat twist under a wheat-straw sailor style hat with a red band at the crown. She never wore red because of her coloring, but today she wanted to broadcast her patriotism. Vance's emphatic compliments had been worth the time she'd spent choosing.

The destroyer was docked at Pier Four. The ship's gray hull was blurred by the morning mist that rose from the surrounding waters. It had been moved across to the Seattle side of the sound two days earlier to take on supplies.

She had seen ships coming and going in the sound but this was the closest she'd ever been to the beehive of activity that surrounded a departure. She was awed by the huge guns mounted on platforms, by the acrid smell of fresh paint, by the energy of the men working in, on, and around the giant. They looked like the tiny black soldiers that swarmed on a Mississippi anthill.

Her footsteps slowed as she and Vance approached the waist-high barrier that kept unwanted visitors away from the gangplank. She knew that a destroyer wasn't one of the largest ships in the navy but seen from up close like this it was an enormous, reassuring sight.

Vance spoke to the seaman at the barrier. He consulted his clipboard and nodded. "You have an hour, Chief," she heard him say. "All civilians ashore at 0800." He showed her the noncoms' wardroom, the sleeping accommodations and the bridge. Every nook and cranny was utilized even in a ship this large. All the while he kept a tight hold on her hand.

Sydney wished she'd picked more sensible shoes but she wanted to look pretty for Vance this morning. She wanted the memory he took away with him to be of her at the best she could be. It seemed to her they'd walked <u>miles</u> and miles of corridors, climbed ladders to the stars, by the time they returned to the gangplank. Below them on the dock a large crowd had gathered. A steady flow of young men boarded the ship, fresh faced, enthusiastic, yet with eyes that were shadowed with disquiet as they turned to give a last wave, a last smile to those below. Out of the crowd appeared another face, a familiar one.

"Lieutenant Adair?" Vance's tone held no note of surprise as the officer approached them. Vance saluted, was saluted back, then shook Jordan's outstretched hand.

"Chief Bingham. I wanted to come and see you off," said Jordan carefully. He obviously hadn't expected Sydney to be here.

If Sydney hadn't been so astonished she would have laughed. His presence must be related to Vance's device. But the idea of an officer coming to see off a lowly chief petty officer would have been amusing if only it wasn't Jordan.

She turned to Vance. "I suppose I'd better go ashore. The man at the gangplank said one hour."

"Sir?" said Vance. "Will you excuse me for a minute while I see my wife ashore?"

"Of course, Chief." He touched the bill of his hat. "Mrs. Bingham."

At the hotel they were Vance and Jordan and Sydney, but on navy territory, protocol was to be observed. "Good-bye, Lieutenant."

Vance accompanied her, against the stream, back to the barrier.

And it was time to say good-bye.

The Marine Band at dockside was playing rousing patriotic marches. Women and children, some weeping and distressed, some smiling stoically and waving, lined up, pressing against the obstacle. A few older couples, parents maybe, stood aside, their damp eyes yearning toward the ship.

Sydney felt a solid lump of fear and sorrow in her own throat and tried to swallow it, but it wouldn't go down. "Write when you can," she said, her voice husky as it emerged over the lump.

He took her hand and led her to a corner away from the crowd. "You, too."

"Every day," she promised. He kissed her and held her for another brief minute, tightly, so tightly that she couldn't breathe, but she wouldn't have dreamed of protesting.

He framed her face in his callused hands, drinking in the sight of her for one last time. She managed a smile for him. "Oh, Vance—"

"Don't hang around, Red," he said and then he was gone.

She kept her gaze on him as he made his way through the noisy crowd, as he stopped for a brief word with the seaman holding the clipboard, and up the gangplank. Suddenly she had to follow. Pushing through the people, murmuring her apologies, she finally reached the barrier and stood staring up at the ship.

Neither of them had ever said, I love you.

"Vance," she whispered. She wanted to say the words, she wanted to thank him for all he'd done, for his love and support—but it was too late. Vance had reached the top of the gangplank. He didn't look back.

Vance joined Jordan Adair where he'd left him. "Lieutenant? What's up?"

Jordan motioned Vance aside. "Nothing really. I just wanted to wish you luck when the tests start," he said in a quiet undertone.

"Thanks. I don't mind telling you I hope the damn thing works."

"Well, we know it works on ships. Is there anything else I can do from this end? We have the small facility east of Seattle all set to begin production as soon as the tests are finished and you return with the diagrams of the system."

"Sounds like you're on top of everything." Vance's voice ended on a hesitant note.

"Something else worrying you?" asked Jordan.

The chief furrowed his brow as though he were trying to make a decision. Finally he looked Jordan in the eye and said, "Yeah, something personal. You know, Lieutenant, Sydney isn't as independent as she'd have everyone believe. I'd like to know she had someone she could count on if she needed anything." Through the whole statement, Vance's gaze had not once faltered from Jordan's. "Since you and she knew each other in New Orleans . . . ." He let his voice trail off and shrugged.

Jordan kept his face expressionless but he nodded. *You don't know what you're asking of me.* "I'll keep an eye on her, Vance."

The ship's horn blew. Vance held out his hand and smiled. "Thanks."

Jordan returned the handshake firmly, thinking how much he liked and admired this man. He had no right to feel jealous; he'd had his chance with Sydney Jackson and he'd squandered it. Although the image of them together would probably always haunt him, he was glad she had found someone as fine as Vance Bingham.

Sydney stared at the ship, unaware of time passing. The engine's loud rumbling finally intruded upon her reverie. The gangplank was raised, and now the last umbilical to the shore was dropped. A hush fell over the crowd. A few people had drifted away but the majority clung to their positions at the rail as though their wishes alone, like strong intangible cables, could tether the ship to the dock.

But slowly, so slowly that it seemed not to move at all until you saw the distance widen to the shore, the monstrous floating colony of Americans moved away from home shores, bound for war.

A shout erupted from the barrier, as though the people there had become one person, and they wouldn't let their men leave with memories of melancholy. Suddenly they were laughing and waving, shouting, though they couldn't possibly have been heard.

Sydney was frantic to see Vance one last time. But in the mass of uniforms that lined the rail of the ship, she had no idea which one he was. Still she held her hat and waved and shouted, too, heedless of the tears that streamed down her face.

A woman next to her had a pair of binoculars on a strap around her neck. She tapped Sydney's shoulder and pointed. "Would you . . . ?" she mouthed.

Sydney returned the woman's smile and nodded her thanks. It took only a moment to focus and without warning the blur of faces aboard the ship sprang to full-blown individuals. They looked so young. Occasionally, as she scanned the deck, she would come upon a face with maturity, but mostly they looked like children.

She almost missed him. There were so many faces. Her gaze slid by and stopped, backed up. She gasped as she recognized Nate Bell. And he was staring at her!

Chapter 20

It couldn't be!

What in God's hell was Nate Bell doing on that ship?

For a moment as she stared at him Sydney thought he was staring back, that he could actually see her, but then she realized he was too far away.

Sick with apprehension, she thrust the binoculars into the startled woman's hands and ran, pushing her way through the crowd. She didn't stop until she reached the shadow of a warehouse where she collapsed, shaking, against the wall. Her heart pounded with shock and dread as the possibilities and consequences of what she'd seen raced through her head. What was Nate doing, in uniform, on the same ship with Vance and his secret device?

Damn it, why did this have to happen to her? She was probably the only one in the whole city who knew what Nate Bell was, who knew that he spoke German fluently and was a nightclub owner, not a sailor.

She worried her lip as she played with the idea that perhaps he had joined the navy, then dismissed it immediately. Nate Bell wouldn't take orders from anyone. Not Nate. Not as she'd last seen him in New Orleans just a little over a month ago.

Not as she had known him years ago.

Her stomach turned as she recalled that painful time. The New Orleans of the thirties was a place for sin to thrive. Dope, sex, money, were only three of the things that could be had with little or no effort. Clyde Cook's was one of the cleaner spots, but it was certainly not lily white.

Sydney had been in New Orleans for three years. She was barely nineteen years old when she first met Nathaniel Bell.

"Hey, Clyde! Introduce me," the handsome newcomer to the club had ordered after the first set.

Clyde was reluctant but he complied. "Sydney Jackson. Mr. Nathaniel Bell," he said, his deep voice resonating like thunder.

"How do you do, Mr. Bell?" Sydney wondered as she acknowledged the introduction. Clyde only used that voice when he was wrought up about something.

Clyde said with not a little irony, "Mr. Bell is an important man in New Orleans. He owns the Sunset Club down the street and, from what I hear, several politicians, too."

Nate Bell shot him a look of mild dislike. "How do you do, Miss Jackson? May I buy you a drink?"

Over the next few weeks Nate Bell came back occasionally, making it perfectly clear that she was the reason.

Nate had the bluest eyes, the blondest hair, and wore the most beautiful clothes she'd ever seen on a man. He went to the barber shop every morning for a shave and a trim, and he always smelled of burberry. Once a week he had a manicure. His fingernails were shiny and white at the ends.

Sydney was mesmerized, like one of Mama's chickens when you drew an imaginary line in the dirt in front of its beak. She had never known such a *clean* man.

Clyde was right about one thing: he was an important man. He knew everyone in New Orleans who mattered, all the politicians, all the landowners. He took her to dinner, treating her with affection and respect. His manners were impeccable and he never made a move. Finally he offered her a job at the Sunset Dinner Club a few blocks down on Bourbon Street. "The Sunset has class, real class," he told her. "A master of ceremonies, your own dressing room—you'll be stepping up."

She was awed by the size and elegance of the place when he took her to see it. Red velvet drapes and upholstery, gilded brass and polished mahogany, a real stage, and a dressing room with her name already painted on the door. She could hardly believe her luck. The salary he quoted wasn't much more than she was making at Clyde's, but he offered to buy her clothes as well.

Rather he offered to send Dennis with her to buy her clothes. Dennis was Nate's friend and lover, also blond and beautiful. They made a startling couple. She was both relieved and apprehensive when she found out about Dennis, relieved that Nate wouldn't expect more for his money than her singing ability, but apprehensive because she'd never known a fairy personally before.

She knew about them—you couldn't work in the French Quarter for a week and not learn about fairies and pimps and transvestites and many other things that were foreign to a farm girl from southern Mississippi—but she wasn't quite sure how to carry on a conversation with him. She needn't have worried; Dennis was as kind and talkative as he was handsome.

Clyde Cook and the rest of her friends in the band didn't like Nate, and they didn't trust him. They calculated that he was egotistical and selfish and said there was something almost too perfect, too precise about him. They called him a peacock, which was surprising to Sydney when she considered what they usually wore.

They tried to tell her that the Sunset had a bad reputation. They tried to tell her that New Orleans was a fickle town. In clubs like that, they said, people who come to hear a singer tonight might prefer a dancer next week, or a pianist who was different, and they warned that Nathaniel Bell would drop her like a hot potato if her popularity began to fade.

She ignored their warnings, thinking that, good friends as they were, they were also just a little bit envious.

And they never did tell her what she really *needed* to know; she had to discover for herself that she had enough talent to feed her dreams but not quite enough to become a star.

The one exception to the cautionary advice was Bobby Dick's. He let her know he would be happy to see the last of her. She didn't reveal that he was one of the reasons she was leaving.

She had been singing at the Sunset Club for almost three months when the ax fell. One night there were fewer people than there had been the night before. And fewer the next night, and fewer the next. When she finally woke up to what was happening, fear struck like lightning. The next night she tried harder, too hard, and thus lost the very essence of her appeal, that sort of "I don't give a damn" style that was her trademark.

She went to Nate and offered to quit. He admitted the truth that she'd already seen. She wasn't drawing the crowds anymore. But she could help him in other ways. He had customers, special customers, who liked feminine companionship when they were in town.

Sydney laughed at his suggestion, refusing to get angry. She'd met a lot of Nate's friends. She'd had dinner with them and, she knew, some of them would have liked a sexual relationship as well.

Sydney had avoided that pitfall, though she suspected the

other girls who worked at the club hadn't been so particular. She dated—when she dated—people she chose herself. She was certainly no angel, but she had her own standards and acting the whore for Nate Bell didn't fit into them. She didn't realize though, until much too late, that she would be classed as one, "tarred with the same brush" as her daddy would have said, without justification.

"Think it over," Nate had suggested.

"Nate, I don't have to think it over. I've seen too many girls brought down by this town. And it isn't going to happen to me."

A few days later she agreed to have late supper with Fred Bailey, a man she'd been out with before. But that night, Fred was like a different person and she knew immediately that Nate had proclaimed open season on Sydney Jackson. It had taken all her strength to fight him off. She had arrived home covered with bruises, her dress ripped beyond repair or modesty. Sobbing and shaking she had crept upstairs to her room, relieved that Mrs. Deveraux had been in bed.

The next morning she had arrived at the club to find that her name had been painted over on the door to her dressing room. Her things—clothes, makeup, snapshots, trinkets, everything— had been dumped into a cardboard box and left in the hall. That was okay; she was leaving anyway.

She should be grateful, for the malicious maneuver stirred her temper to compete with her shame and humiliation and strengthened her backbone. She managed to retain a certain composure until she went to Nate's office to demand her previous two weeks' salary.

His secretary explained coolly that her last paycheck would be used to reimburse the club for her costumes. She also told Sydney that Nate wasn't in, which was a blatant lie.

The door to his office hadn't been closed securely. Sydney could hear him and his friend, the baron, talking. She didn't hear the words, only the voices; the strange cadence of Nate's speech didn't register at first.

She burst through the door to confront them, figuring both the insulting way Nate had chosen to dispose of her, plus her red hair, gave her a damned good excuse. But she wasn't half as angry as she would be.

The baron muttered something and left quickly.

Ignoring her outburst, Nate remained behind his enormous desk. He calmly clipped the end of a cheroot, lit it, and offered to fix her up with another one of his customers for a percentage of the fee.

"Of course you'll have to learn technique, so the clients won't get bored."

Sydney stared blankly at him while he elaborated in disgusting, repulsive detail. At first she was stunned to hear such language from that beautiful mouth.

"You might as well, you know," he concluded. "Everyone in the Quarter thinks it of you in any case."

"That's not true!" Then, storming around the desk, she slapped him as hard as she could, drawing blood from the perfect, clean-shaven cheek with her long nails.

Nate stared at her for an endless, awful moment, then he went crazy. He caught her arm and twisted it viciously behind her back. A knife appeared in his other hand as though it had sprouted there.

Immediately fear replaced Sydney's anger. She would have run had she not been caught between the desk and his surprisingly strong body. He bent her backward across the desk and his knees battered her stomach. The cold flat edge of the knife pressed into her neck with the sharp tip just below her ear.

Unable to speak she held her breath and waited for the worst. A sadistic smile curved his lips as he shifted the knife. She felt no pain, but she did feel the blood, warm and dripping, on her neck, her chest.

He spoke in a low, savage voice; the filthiest, most abusive language she'd ever heard was interspersed with strange words in a strange tone, in the language that hadn't registered a few minutes ago. Her ear was educated to sounds.

Suddenly she knew—from listening to the radio, from the descriptions of Hitler's "superior race," from the gutteral quality of his voice, she knew. "You're German!" she gasped.

The physical fear was transformed to a deep psychological terror. Nate was the personification of all the fearful stories coming out of Europe, and he had her in his grasp.

He hesitated for a minute and she knew he wanted to kill her. Something held him back, however. Wrenching her arm tighter, he drew her up until their noses were almost touching. Up close his breath stank from the vitriol of his rage and frustration. Slowly, using the flat side of the knife, he painted her face with her own blood. "You keep your mouth shut, you bitch, or I'll find you again someday and finish this."

He released her. Sickened, she stumbled to the door and fled.

She fled from Nate, the French Quarter, and jazz. The only regret she felt was for the music. She found a job waiting the counter at the Toddle House where she spent her days dishing out waffles, scrambled eggs, toast, sausage, and grits.

The grapevine worked particularly well in New Orleans. Oddly it was Bobby Dick who came for her when he discovered that she was no longer singing at the Sunset. He admitted that his conscience hurt. He felt guilty about the whole affair and urged her to come back to Clyde Cook's.

Sydney was touched by his unexpected concern; he didn't have to be so kind. She had walked out on them. She tried to explain—she knew they'd heard the stories—but Bobby Dick wouldn't listen to it. He said that if you were black you learned early to keep your nose out of things that didn't apply to you. A lesson anybody could learn, she concluded.

She offered to sing two nights a week. He said Clyde and the boys wanted her five nights, and they compromised on three. On those nights Sydney didn't linger in the Quarter. She went straight to the club and straight back to the Victorian house on the Esplanade; not because she disapproved of the place, but because she'd had the bejesus scared out of her.

She had only a small bout with her conscience and decided to keep the information about Nate's nationality to herself. It was 1938. The United States, her country, wasn't at war with Germany. Most of the stories she heard said it wouldn't ever be.

It would take a long time and a lot of effort for her to live down the reputation she'd earned by her ambition and naïveté, but she vowed never to make another mistake over a man. Then along came Jordan Adair.

The name brought Sydney back to the present with a jolt. She straightened from her slumped position against the wall of the warehouse. She could still hear the faint notes of "Anchors Aweigh." Her nausea rose again at the thought of what she was about to do. Her mind raced over the consequences. But there was no alternative. She had to find Jordan either as he left the area or later back at the hotel, to tell him about Nate.

As she edged toward the passage leading from the docks to the street, she thought back to the day she'd left New Orleans, the questions Nate hadn't quite come right out and asked, the information he'd had about her marriage, about her husband, the implied threat when he'd told of the visit from the navy's investigator.

She had been so eager to escape his company that she hadn't

thought carefully about the encounter. She realized now that the questions had been more prodding than personal. He was trying to gain information about Vance, not her.

Why hadn't she gone to someone years ago, when she'd first realized the man was German himself, and a friend of the baron, as well as being a sadist? Now here he was wearing a uniform that, as far as she knew, he had no right to wear. He was aboard a ship he had no right to be on, the ship that her husband and his valuable device were also on.

There was no way now to escape her duty. She had to tell someone—Jordan. Dear Lord, she hoped she was wrong. Maybe she was seeing phantoms where none existed. Nevertheless, she couldn't take the chance. No matter what it cost her personally she had to tell the truth—even if it meant losing Vance.

Chapter 21

Jordan's tall figure appeared at the edge of the departing crowd.

Sydney started a path through the people that would intersect with his. "Excuse me. Pardon me," she murmured as she pushed her way. People ignored her.

"Jordan!" she called when he drew even. "Jordan, over here!"

Jordan met her eyes across the head of a young woman with a baby on her hip. Sydney reached out above the girl's head and he took her hand to pull her to his side. In an involuntary action he glanced back toward the ship, but even if Vance had been watching it was too late to tell.

"I've got to talk to you," she said, loudly enough to be heard over the noise of the crowd.

He studied her for a moment. Then, perhaps seeing the turbulence in her expression, he nodded.

"Alone," she added.

Jordan looked around. "Then we'll have to get out of here," he said from behind a tight smile. He didn't look forward to an encounter with Sydney. He'd just come to grips with his own feelings about Sydney and Vance together.

The coffee shop near the pier was deserted. Jordan ordered for both of them and when the two mugs of coffee arrived and the waitress moved away, he asked, "What's up?"

Sydney dawdled over the sugar and cream and stirred for a long time, searching for the right words. Maybe she wouldn't have to tell it all. Maybe she could convince him without revealing everything. The thought brought back a sudden pang of guilt. When she'd found out he was married, she'd accused him of being a liar. He'd accepted the accusation but had said it was a lie of omission. Hadn't she done the same thing?

"Jordan, there was a man on that ship who had no business being there."

"Sydney, what are you talking about?" he inquired patiently.

"Do you remember a man called Nathaniel Bell from New Orleans?"

He frowned slightly. "The nightclub owner?" He'd met him once—an official function of some kind. Didn't like the fellow particularly. There was something shady about his club. . . .

"Yes. I saw Nate Bell standing by the rail on Vance's ship. We've got to tell somebody."

"Nate Bell?" He hesitated. "Are you sure you're not mistaken?"

Sydney was grateful for Jordan's memory. At least she didn't have to explain to him who Nate was. But she wondered at the hesitation. Did Jordan know more about Nate than that he was a nightclub owner? "Yes. I'm very sure." She couldn't control the shudder at the very thought of the man.

Jordan didn't seem to notice her reaction, but he considered for a minute. "I saw him, once at least, while I was there. Tall man, very blond, always neatly dressed?" he asked slowly and thoughtfully.

"Yes, that's him."

"What would he be doing here?"

"I have no idea. Jordan, Nate Bell isn't a sailor but he had on a sailor's uniform. He was on that ship."

"You must be wrong, Sydney."

"I'm *not* wrong, Jordan," she stated positively. "And there's something else." She inhaled a deep breath. "I think Nate Bell is a German."

Jordan smiled for the first time. She said the word as though she were proclaiming Nate Bell to be the devil. "Sydney, there are a lot of Germans in America. My own mother's grandmother was German. That doesn't make me a traitor," he told her indulgently.

"Don't patronize me, Jordan. I know that man. I know what he's capable of doing. I mean it. I—" She paused, then plunged on. "—worked for him for a while."

"You worked for Nate Bell?" Jordan asked disbelievingly. He had remembered what it was about Bell's club. The Sunset— that was it—had been declared off-limits to all military personnel after an investigation into drugs and prostitution. In New Orleans a club had to be pretty rough to be off-limits. His gaze fixed on Sydney. It was hard to conceive of her working for the man.

Sydney's heart sank. He *had* heard of the Sunset Dinner Club's reputation. "For a short time," she answered hurriedly. "Look, Jordan. My husband is on that ship doing some work that is a mystery to me but he's suggested that it is of great importance. Now I see a man on board who may be a German and a spy. Someone with the authority to investigate has to know about this and if you won't help me I'll have to find someone who will." She picked up her purse and started to stand.

Jordan stopped her with a hand on her arm. "Hold on," he said. "I didn't say I wouldn't help you. But let's think for a minute."

"The ship has to be stopped and searched. Or you can call Washington."

"Sydney, you don't just stop and search a ship that's on its way to battle. But I'll see what I can do."

When she opened her mouth to protest further, he held up his hand in a placating gesture. "I can call Washington if I have to, but Sydney, let's try to handle this rationally. Bill Parker might have some ideas. Let's go." He threw a bill on the table and stood.

A navy car had been waiting for Jordan. The driver deposited them back at the hotel a few minutes later. Naturally Valerie was standing at the curb waiting to cross. "Oh, God, your wife," said Sydney with disgust. "She'll love this."

"What the hell do you mean by that?" he demanded.

"Nothing. Forget it," said Sydney as she climbed out of the car. She saw the shock on Val's face quickly replaced by icy composure.

"Jordan?" said Valerie, looking from one of them to the other.

"Sorry, sweetheart." Jordan gave her an absent kiss. "I'm really in a hurry. Have you seen Bill Parker?"

"He was in the coffee shop a few minutes ago."

Jordan headed for the door. When Sydney would have followed, Valerie stepped in her path, blocking the way. "What's going on here? What were you doing with my husband?" she challenged.

Sydney looked at the pinched muscles around the woman's mouth. Suddenly she felt an overwhelming pity. Valerie was a thoroughly unhappy person, trying to play more than one part. She restrained her impatience and spoke softly. "Vance left this morning. Lieutenant Adair had come to say good-bye and we shared a car on the way back here.'' What more could she say? The device was a military secret. Vance had warned her not to discuss it with anyone. "Now there's a matter to be taken care of. That's all.''

"What kind of matter?'' snapped Valerie.

Pity or not there was no way she was going to explain her personal affairs to this woman. She might have to reveal more than she wanted to the navy, to Bill and Jordan, but not to Valerie Adair. "Nothing that concerns you, Valerie,'' she said finally. She ignored Valerie's dagger look, stepping around her into the hotel.

Inside Jordan had reentered the lobby with Bill in tow. "Let's go up to my room,'' said the commander.

When they were settled in the room, Bill took the initiative. "Jordan gave me a sketchy picture but let's go over this again. We have to be careful, but I don't want to go to intelligence until we're totally sure we have something for them.''

"I'm sure,'' said Sydney.

"And the more I think about it the more I think she's right. It bears investigation,'' added Jordan.

Sydney threw him a grateful look.

"Okay, let's hear it again.''

Bill's mind grew cold with dread as he listened to Sydney tell the story clearly and without excess emotion. As he listened he felt a surge of sympathy for the woman who was obviously revealing more than she wanted either of them to know. Her hands rested quietly in her lap, too quietly. He mentally saluted her courage as well. He knew that life hadn't been easy for her here.

He rose and began to pace. Where should they go with this? Not through normal channels, that was sure. Most likely, if Bell was on that ship, channels had been breached. Filing a report with the intelligence department would bring an investigation that would open up all kinds of questions. The fewer people who knew about the device, the better chance they had of running a successful test.

The fight for the Pacific was beginning to turn around now, but one of the crucial problems remaining was the free use of communications. With the big battles still to be fought, secrecy was top priority for the Vocat.

Finally he halted his pacing and faced Jordan. "You're the one who has all the connections,'' he said accusingly.

Jordan smiled, then he chuckled. "But you outrank me, Commander. Shall we flip a coin?"

In the end it was Jordan who went to make the phone call. When he came back he advised them that he and Sydney were due at the Federal Building at once.

The interrogation went on for hours.

"How do you know this man is German, Mrs. Bingham?"

Admiral Murray Cleveland was a tall man with strict bearing. He would have been intimidating in a bathing suit, thought Sydney; in his uniform, with his grim visage, he was frightening.

She had wondered why she rated such an exalted figure, and after a while she asked. The man avoided her eyes and muttered something about just being in town.

"Admiral, I told you. I don't *know* for certain that Nathaniel Bell is German. When I was younger I worked for him for a brief time and I once heard him speak the language. He was talking to a Baron Edgar Spiegel von—I can't remember all the name."

"Baron Edgar Spiegel von und zu Peckelsheim," he supplied.

"That's it! This was in 1938, before the war. I didn't particularly admire Nate for speaking German or for having a friend that was German but it wasn't against the law as far as I knew. When I inadvertently revealed my knowledge, he threatened me. Later I heard the baron was kicked out of America."

"He was asked to leave last year."

"I don't know why I never told anyone." She brushed her hair back with both hands, the sleek style that she'd arranged so carefully for Vance's farewell long since destroyed. "I was afraid, a coward, I admit that. I feel horribly guilty, especially since I saw Nate just before I left New Orleans and thought about telling someone. But I do know that the man is not in the navy, so what was he doing on the ship in a uniform?"

The admiral's lips thinned in an unpleasant way and his eyes grew colder, if that was possible. "That is what we are going to find out, Mrs. Bingham. Now, let's get back to the work you did for him. When was this again?"

Sydney sighed heavily and repeated her story yet again. She was so tired. And he was determined not to let up on her for a minute. He also seemed convinced that she was some kind of spy as well. He kept going over and over the questions about her relationship with Vance—when they had met, how Nate had known she was going to be in Seattle, had Vance met Nate.

"To my knowledge they never met," she answered again.

"But can you be certain?" he persisted.

"No," she admitted slowly.

"You work at Boeing?"

He threw that in every so often to keep her on her toes, she supposed. "I'm in their training program."

"You also work at the hospital and the Elysium?"

"As a volunteer," she repeated. Again.

"You don't have anything to do with an air-raid advisory service operating in this area?"

"What?" Her eyes widened in surprise at the new tack.

"You didn't try to arrange a meeting so your former boyfriend could question your husband?"

She kept a strong leash on her temper. "He wasn't my boyfriend, he was my employer. And only for a few months. What is an air-raid advisory?"

"Let's get back to the subject of the threat, Mrs. Bingham. You claim Nate Bell threatened you."

"At the time I worked for him, yes. When I saw him again after my marriage, his threat was more subtle, like a reminder. He said that a navy investigator had come to see him. I didn't know until after my marriage that I'd even been investigated. I remember thinking that whoever did it did a piss-poor job if they didn't find out about him."

"Why did he fire you?"

She caught her breath and raised her chin. "I left Nate's employ because he expected things of me that I wasn't prepared to give and because he hired someone to take my place as an entertainer. He was a violent man and I was afraid of him." She touched her neck where the gold chain and piano had been ripped away. She had explained about the incident earlier, and thanked her lucky stars that Vance had been too preoccupied with his device to notice the necklace was missing. "Besides, he had powerful friends in New Orleans." Oh, God, if Vance found out about all this, she would lose him. He'd think she was a—

"But later, when we *did* go to war with Germany, why didn't you tell someone then?"

"He still had a lot of powerful friends. I learned a long time ago to keep my mouth shut when dealing with those people."

Admiral Cleveland made a note on the pad before him. "You

may go, Mrs. Bingham, but rest assured, we know where to find you should the need arise.''

Sydney blinked, surprised at his sudden dismissal, but she didn't waste any time in getting out of there.

Jordan was waiting.

His expression was unreadable, but Sydney didn't have the urge to try anyhow. All she wanted to do was to get back to her room, into a hot tub, and then to bed. The questioning had gone on for the better part of eight hours. She was exhausted. They traveled to the hotel in silence.

He parked the car and came around the hood to open her door.

''Thanks for the ride,'' she said.

''You're welcome.''

As they reached the door she stopped, looking at him. ''Tell me, Jordan, why didn't they question you? You knew Nate in New Orleans.''

''They did. In another room. I finished not long before you came out.''

''Oh. Then being the son of a senator didn't help.''

''Not a bit.''

Bill Parker had been watching for them. As soon as they entered the lobby he stood up and led the way to Kay's small office behind the front desk. Sydney followed along. She didn't intend to be left out.

The office was empty. Bill closed the door behind them. ''I just talked to Kay,'' he said. ''She was contacted by some fake advisory service but she put them off with the excuse that she'll soon be quitting as manager. However, she kept the address. Admiral Cleveland had someone check it out. It's an abandoned storage building down near the waterfront. Hasn't been used for years.''

Sydney's brow furrowed. ''The admiral asked me something about an advisory service,'' she said. ''I didn't know what he was talking about.''

Jordan explained. ''Admiral Cleveland is with Naval Intelligence. He had been sent out here to investigate reports of a scheme by German nationals to gain valuable wartime information about our cities. When I called a contact in intelligence with this story involving a possible German connection to one of our ships, he was handed the case.''

''How does this advisory service work?'' she asked.

''It's pretty slick really. They offer a free service for setting

up air-raid shelters and charge a nominal fee to put up direc-
tional signs. Then they evaluate the structures, entrances and
exits, blueprints, locations of power plants, and heating equipment as possible targets for sabotage.''

"That *is* slick," said Sydney softly. "Who would ever suspect? And they think Nate may be involved?"

Bill supplied the next. "They don't know. It's possible but it
will take a while to follow up. You've certainly given them a
valuable lead by identifying him as a friend of the baron, who
may have had a hand in setting up the operation, identifying
potential German sympathizers. This advisory group was operating on all three coasts. The admiral has stopped their activities in the East, on the Gulf Coast, and in California. This area
is his last objective.''

"Weren't we lucky that he happened to be here?" she said
caustically. "That man is a real . . ." She shrugged.

Kay came in. "Oh, sorry," she said, starting to back out.

"We're finished, honey. You can have your office back."

Sydney had more questions for Jordan. He anticipated one of
them. "I'm flying to Hawaii with Bill to identify Nate Bell," he
told her as they left the office. "We'll be there when Vance's
ship docks.''

"What about before that? What if Nate gets to Vance
himself?" Her voice shook.

Jordan shoved his hands into the pockets of his trousers and
looked down into the wide green eyes. "The admiral talked to
the captain of the destroyer. Security around Vance has been
tightened," he said reassuringly.

At first he'd been dismayed by her admission that she'd worked
for Bell. The man was slime. But, knowing Sydney as he did,
he was well aware that she was a good woman, with strong
convictions. She might make mistakes but she wouldn't let herself be used by someone like Nate Bell. He laughed to himself.
He'd be willing to bet she had put the man in his place. "Sydney,
it took a lot of courage for you to do what you did today.''

At his gentle tone her chin came up. "I didn't—"

"I never thought you did," he said.

Sydney gave a tired sigh. She nodded and left him standing
there as she headed for the stairs.

"Wait." He caught up with her at the foot of the steps. "I'll
walk up with you.''

She was cautious. "All right. If you're going to Hawaii will
you take a letter to Vance?"

"Sure. But be careful what you say."

Her glare stabbed him. "I don't have to be reminded, Jordan."

"Sorry," he said.

She watched his mouth curve in a rueful grin, then a genuine smile, softening some of the lines around his eyes. The expression was one that was a part of the Jordan she'd known in New Orleans, but one she had not seen on his face since she arrived in Seattle. She almost smiled back.

"Try not to worry too much," he said as they passed the second floor and continued the climb.

"Are you nuts? Of course I'm worried."

He took a long breath and let it out. "I promised Vance I'd look out for you."

"You did what?" She stopped, hanging onto the banister. He'd taken a couple of steps beyond her so she had to lean back to meet his eyes. Surely she'd misunderstood.

He gave a laugh that now held no trace of humor. His expression had reverted to one of strict control. "Yeah, isn't that a hoot? I'm probably the only man of your acquaintance that you wouldn't trust with the crumbs from your plate."

If he expected her to contradict that judgment he was going to be sadly disappointed. "Not the only one, Jordan." She started climbing again and passed him. "There's Nate Bell."

Chapter 22

Tuesday, July 7, 1942

The whales and the giant sea turtles played off the eastern coast of the big island of Hawaii, unconcerned with war or the men flying above them at ten thousand feet. The sight of the animals, the beauty of the clear, pure-blue water and the twin volcanoes that rose to the right of the plane were lost on Bill Parker.

Last night in Seattle Bill and Jordan had boarded a naval air transport plane, for the trip to Oahu. They had flown over—and been silenced by—the evidence of the devastation still remaining at Pearl Harbor. Across the water, Ford Island, where so many planes were destroyed before they could get off the ground, still bore signs of the ravaging the base had taken. The hull of the lifeless *Arizona* was visible.

He was thinking of Kay and the children, and the little time he had left with them. He hated to sacrifice even a day, but he was going to be in charge of testing the Vocat. He needed to be here, to see for himself the device was secure. Fortunately his part in the preparations for the *Shiloh*'s sailing had been almost complete. He could safely leave Cody in charge of the few remaining tasks.

Bill hated to fly in a plane he wasn't piloting. But he'd accepted the invitation of Ensign White to join him in the cockpit.

"I saw some films of you testing the F4F, Commander. You're some pilot, sir."

"Thanks, Jere. Where are you from?" It was the standard opening in any conversation between sailors during wartime. It was also a reminder that there was a home, somewhere, and someday they'd return there.

Jere grinned and drawled, "From Cartersville, Georgia, sir. That's in the north Georgia mountains."

"How do you like your duty?" This was a Utility Flight Unit, an interisland flight taking them from Honolulu to Hilo.

It occurred to Bill that planes like this one, which kept the supply lines moving, were as much a part of war as victory in battle. This group hauled anything that had to be moved, from mail, to equipment, to food. Bill was grateful to the young Southerner for holding the flight for them because the UFU took a lot of pride in meeting their schedules.

"I like it pretty well, Commander," answered Jere.

Bill had to remind himself of the question.

"Sometimes it gets a little boring," the ensign continued, "but you can't beat the atmosphere. And every now and then something breaks the monotony."

"Sounds like there's a story there." Bill was impatient to get to his destination, but he couldn't make the plane fly any faster so he settled back to listen.

"Yes, sir. The other day my buddy and I were flying this same run from Honolulu to Hilo. Along about the time we were flying over Molokai we heard this crazy jibberish on the radio. We couldn't make out any of it except the coordinates. We knew it wasn't Japanese, but we didn't know what 'n hell it was. And the coordinates were too close for comfort, so we radioed ahead.

"Well, sir, when we landed we were met by Naval Intelligence and hustled off to a deserted hangar to be questioned. Turns out, some marines had come up with a way to fool the Japs. They had some Navaho Indians on board to speak their language over the radio." He laughed. "Not many people around here speak Navaho. It fooled us all right and if there were any Japs listening I guess it fooled them, too. Maybe we ought to teach all our pilots to speak Navaho. Then we wouldn't broadcast our positions so clearly."

Bill shared his amusement. He was something of a storyteller himself, and he launched into a tale. Underneath the good-natured byplay he was wishing he could explain to the young man why he was here. If the testing went well on Vance's radio device, they wouldn't have to worry about learning to speak Navaho.

"You look troubled, Commander."

The boy was sharp. Bill avoided answering directly. "I'm not used to flying with someone else," he conceded.

"I know what you mean. Would you like to take the controls for a while?"

Bill was tempted but he refrained. "No thanks, Jere. I think I'll see what's going on in the back." He climbed over the cargo and joined Jordan. They sat with their backs to the fuselage and Bill propped his feet on a big mail sack. There wasn't any other place for them. They spent the remaining flight time discussing the problems that lay before them. They would be waiting at the dock when the ship came in.

The captain of the ship had been given a full report, with a description of Nathaniel Bell, including Sydney's addition of the scar on his face, by Naval Intelligence. He had been ordered not to do anything to spook the man. He'd argued back. The description could fit a hundred of the men aboard his ship. The only thing that distinguished Nate was his obsession with cleanliness and the scar, which Sydney admitted was small. So there was no alternative but to fly Jordan Adair out to Hawaii, too. Jordan and Sydney were the only two people involved who had actually seen the man.

Bill was sorry when he heard that the intelligence people had been so rough on Sydney. After all she hadn't been forced to come forward. It had been tough on her to admit her involvement. Jordan had been quiet that day in Bill's room but he had kept his eyes on her while she told her story. In the light of that rather intense scrutiny Bill had an idea that those two had once meant something to each other. It was an interesting thought. In his judgment Valerie Adair was a lovely ice maiden, the exact opposite of the warm and sensual Sydney. He really couldn't blame the senator's son.

Jere made a smooth landing. Bill and Jordan said good-bye to the young pilot and walked over to the pier, just a few hundred yards from the field. With the intelligence agent who met them, they scouted for a place that would give them a clear view of the gangplank and yet offer concealment. Nate Bell could logically be expected to have a cohort standing by when the ship docked.

The last thing they wanted was for him to receive a signal that would alert him to their presence. Now all they had to do was wait.

But Nathaniel Bell never materialized.

Jordan kept a leash on his temper; Bill cursed liberally. "The mission is over before it even started," he ranted.

No one could explain how it had happened—unless he jumped overboard—but Nate Bell had simply disappeared.

What was worse, someone had taken some of Vance's supplies, most importantly, several rolls of copper wire without which Vocat could not be installed. That person was almost surely Bell.

Probably forewarned by the doubled security on Vance's workroom, the thief had instead broken into the area where the supplies were packed. They were clearly marked with Vance's initials. Vance's theory was that the extra security had tipped the man off in the first place. He'd wanted to use the device as bait but the captain of the destroyer had vetoed that idea. And now there wasn't a scrap of copper wire on the ship. Copper was high on the list of critical war matériel and replacing it wouldn't be easy.

"Commander?" Jere White caught Bill's attention and Bill lifted an arm in greeting. "Are you going back to Honolulu with us, Commander?" he asked when Bill joined him.

"We may as well," said Bill. He was tired and discouraged. "Just let me have a word with the man who met us and we'll be ready, Jere."

"I heard from scuttlebutt that you need copper wire, sir," the ensign said in a low voice. "I may know where I could get hold of some."

Bill's head spun. "Where?"

"Well, sir, I wouldn't want you to ask any questions—sir."

Bill eyed the young man speculatively and nodded. "If you can find copper wire, Jere, I'll not only ask no questions, I'll even pay for the damned stuff. Come on, I'll introduce you to the chief."

They approached Vance, who was as worried as Bill. "Vance, this is Jere White. He flies transport around the islands. He may know where to get you some replacement supplies."

Vance turned his intense gaze on the ensign. "Sir, if you can do that I'll be in your debt."

"I'll have them here by tomorrow morning. Maybe someday you'll explain what's going on," he added rather longingly. "I have a hunch it'll make a hell of a story."

Bill laughed, feeling better already and clapped the young man's shoulder. "We owe him the story, Vance."

Vance nodded his head, visibly relieved. "Indeed we do."

Jordan had come up while they were talking and got the jist

of their renewed optimism. "It looks like you're in business again," he said to Vance.

"I'm just sorry we didn't have any luck catching that bastard. I was really surprised when we got your radio message. Sydney—"

"Good God, I almost forgot." Jordan took Sydney's letter out of his pocket.

Vance took the letter, stared down at it with a smile of quiet satisfaction that sent a stab of jealousy through Jordan. The thrust was quickly replaced by sadness.

"Thanks, Lieutenant," Vance said, stowing the letter in his own pocket. "Anyway, I'd heard of the man. Sydney told me that she'd worked in his club, and I know she doesn't like him, but I never had any idea he was a German."

Neither Jordan nor Bill had gone into great detail about the reasons for their arrival. Vance had looked worried and had questioned his wife's safety; but when Jordan reassured him, his worry turned to pride.

"She's quite a woman. Imagine her noticing that one man out of all the others on this ship and realizing that he had no business being there."

Jordan and Bill hadn't mentioned the grilling Sydney had gone through at the hands of Naval Intelligence, either.

"We'll get Nate Bell," said Jordan grimly. "Somehow, we'll get him."

They landed on the runway at Sand Point at nine A.M. the next morning. Both had reports to make first, but then they were going back to the hotel. Neither had slept. "I'll get us a ride. What time will you be ready to go?" Bill asked.

Jordan glanced at his watch. "A couple of hours?"

"Fine. I'll meet you at the admin building."

Bill had changed his opinion of the senator's son on this trip. He discovered that he liked Jordan Adair and admired him. The strict control he seemed to wear like a hat, was not, as Bill had first assumed, patronization or arrogance. He used it rather as protection against being judged as his father's son. As the son of a navy captain and World War I hero, Bill could relate to that. He had chosen to divorce himself from his father's legacy, too. Instead of battleships he'd gone in for planes.

When they met two hours later in the admin building Bill was shocked to learn how Jordan Adair had spent the time—he had volunteered for duty aboard the carrier, leaving Sunday. "I think you should reconsider, Jordan," he said. "Hell, you've got a job to do here at home, a job you can be proud of. Why the hell would you want to sail into a battle zone?"

Jordan responded, "I can't do anything more here until the tests are complete. Besides, a carrier the size of the *Shiloh* is like a small city. The boys who go to war need legal advice just like anyone else."

"Hell, I know that. One of the boys in my squadron got taken by a greedy ex-wife last winter. It would have been worse if there hadn't been a legal officer aboard. But the *Shiloh* has one anyway."

"It's a big ship. It can use two."

"Why you?"

"I don't know if I can explain, Bill," Jordan said. He seated his hat firmly on his head. "I just know that I need to do this."

Bill sighed. "You don't have to explain to another sailor." He was silent for a minute, then he asked, "How does your wife feel about it?"

"She doesn't know yet. I'll tell her today."

"She won't like it. Hell, what woman would?"

Valerie had decided to ignore Jordan's association with Sydney Bingham. She'd asked once, when he finally came in that night she'd seen them together, and he cut her off impatiently. She wouldn't degrade herself by asking again. But when Jordan returned from Hawaii and dropped his latest bombshell—well, to say that Valerie was furious was an understatement.

"How can you do this to me?" she railed, using anger, tears, pleas. "Jordan, please. I came out here with you. I've done everything you want me to do. Please, *please* don't go on that ship."

But Jordan refused to be swayed. Something had happened to him, something inexplicable. He wasn't even sure when his determination had solidified. He didn't know why, but he knew, beyond understanding, that he had to be on that ship when it sailed. And if he had to use his father's influence or that of Senator Truman, he would do it.

Now he had other things on his mind. He had to see Sydney. He and Bill had reported briefly by telephone to Admiral Cleveland, who had returned to Washington. The admiral had not been pleased with the failure of their mission. The manhunt in Hawaii had begun immediately and was now being implemented by military intelligence in every airport and harbor on the West Coast. But Cleveland had been blunt about their chances of catching the man known as Nate Bell.

"I'm certain now that the name is an alias. I've been in touch with the authorities in New Orleans. They didn't want to say much—I gather some of them were closely involved with him, as Mrs. Bingham said. He closed his club a few weeks ago and simply dropped out of sight.

"If Nate Bell wanted to lose himself it would be a snap, especially with the help of a group that could think up something like the advisory scam, or the Bunds," he said, referring to the organized Nazi believers, who operated openly before the war and now had gone underground. "He'll either be smuggled back to Germany or he'll change his appearance and surface somewhere else. Our only defense against spies like this is the FBI and other intelligence agencies.

"I'm putting a surveillance on Mrs. Bingham," he had added grimly just before he hung up.

Bill and Jordan had looked at each other. "For her protection or because he suspects her? Which do you think?" asked Bill.

Jordan said very coolly, very deliberately, "I know that girl as well as anyone. If he suspects her of deception, he's dead wrong."

After he had spoken to Valerie, Jordan went to find Sydney to reassure her about Vance's safety. The young McCoy girl told him she was at her training class and would be back about five. "If she doesn't go straight to the hospital," Edna added. "She's there several times a week."

Jordan shook his head in wonder at the number of hours a week American women were putting in. He left a note in her box.

"What the hell do you mean you *lost* Nathaniel Bell?" Sydney demanded hotly.

She had just returned from the hospital. They were in her room.

Jordan ignored her outburst and went on, "Evidently he went overboard before the ship reached Hilo. Admiral Cleveland wanted you to know in case he makes his way back here. He says he'll have changed his appearance. Notify someone if you have any suspicions at all."

She couldn't sit still. She roamed restlessly from the door to the window. "Admiral Cleveland," she sneered. "Do you know that bastard almost lost me my job? I had to answer a thousand questions for him and a thousand more for my boss at the plant. He's been talking to the people in the hotel about me, too.''

Jordan rubbed his chin and the lawyer in him tried to see the admiral's side. If it had been anyone other than Sydney, whom he knew wasn't capable of betrayal, he would have been suspicious, too. She could be pretty damned headstrong at times, and the admiral had a job to do. He had to make a try at calming her down. ''Honey—''

The word froze them both.

''God, Sydney, I'm sorry,'' he whispered.

Sydney seemed to cave in before his eyes, but she recovered quickly. She fixed him with a stare, daring him to mention the slip of the tongue.

''Nate Bell won't come here, Jordan. He has no business here anymore. He's gone, loose somewhere in this country, and we'll never know what happened to him.''

Jordan didn't argue with her. He had an uncomfortable feeling that she was exactly right.

''Has Vance's ship left Hawaii yet?''

Jordan opened his mouth to ask her what she was talking about. Then he remembered that she didn't know of the plan to transfer Vance to the *Shiloh*. ''Yes, the destroyer has left Hawaii.''

''Good. At least Vance is out of his reach.''

Chapter 23

Saturday, July 11, 1942

Faith sat on the high stool beside the cash register. "Are you working at the hospital tonight, Sydney?" she asked as she gave the redhead back her change.

She and Sydney often worked at night on the weekends when neither of them had to get up early to go to work. Night duty was the most peaceful and therefore, if the volunteers were willing, they often took two shifts, napping on a couch in the nurses' lounge.

Sydney read the appeal in her friend's eyes, almost as though Faith were afraid she was going to say no. Sydney wondered why. "Yes. I'm leaving at ten. Do you want to walk over together?"

Faith shook her head. A pink blush stained her cheeks. "I swapped with Mary Anne so I wouldn't have to go in tonight. Cody reports to the ship tomorrow. By the way, he's waiting in the lobby. He wants to ask if he can spend the night in your room."

She didn't have to explain further. Her red face said it all for her. Sydney and Faith had had this discussion before, or one very nearly like it. Sydney cursed her wayward tongue, remembering her own suggestions.

"What would you do if you wanted to be alone with your boyfriend?" Faith had asked earlier this week when they were walking home from the hospital. Sydney had supposed Faith was asking on behalf of Louise Cass, who was in love with an army air force second lieutenant, and whom they had just been discussing. Louise lived at home with a father and mother who thought that the young people of today had morals only one step

246

above the devil's. They brought Louise to the hospital each night she worked and waited for her when the shift was over. Sydney often wondered where they got the gas.

"I'd find a way," Sydney had answered, laughing. "I'd probably bribe the clerk at the Olympia."

Faith had been self-conscious when she protested, "She couldn't go to a hotel. What if someone recognized her?"

"Then I'd find a good friend who was going to be working and ask to use her room," she'd answered casually, forgetting the conversation as soon as it was over.

Now the supposedly hypothetical question wasn't hypothetical at all. A line for the cash register was forming behind her. She had to move on. Clearly Faith was going to let Cody be the one to ask for the use of her room, but she couldn't answer him until she knew how strongly Faith felt. Faith played the part of the sophisticate but Sydney had soon realized that in reality, she was still an ingenue about a lot of things. Many girls did this just before their boyfriends shipped out, but Sydney didn't want her friend to be pressured into something she wasn't sure about.

She looked directly into Faith's eyes. There was apprehension there. "Are you absolutely certain this is what you want?" she asked deliberately.

The blush on Faith's cheeks turned to crimson, but the expression in her eyes softened in appeal. Apprehension became certainty. She might be wary, but she sincerely wanted to spend the night with Cody. "I'm positive."

Sydney sighed, hoping she was doing the right thing. Kay Parker would kill her if she ever found out. Kay had never quite approved of her. She'd not been rude, but she'd not been warm and approachable, either, until after the incident when Sydney and Faith had been accosted by the dockworkers. Since then Sydney had felt that in Kay she had a good friend. "Okay," she said finally over her own misgivings.

Faith watched Sydney leave with a mixture of relief and consternation. She hadn't told Kay and Bill that she wouldn't be on duty at the hospital tonight, so there would be no questions asked there. She glanced at her watch. Another half hour and she could join Cody. She grew warm and weak at the thought.

She hated the deception, but there was no way around it as long as she was living with Kay and Bill. They wouldn't be hurt though; they wouldn't be hurt because they would never know. She herself would certainly never tell them and Sydney, she knew, would keep her own counsel.

Cody was shipping out; she didn't know when—if ever—she would see him again. So why did she feel so scared? True, they had known each other for only three weeks, but their romance had flourished rapidly. She'd found tenderness in him as well as passion and longing. She had actually decided long before tonight that she wanted to make love with him.

Cody wasn't going to suddenly turn into an ogre when they reached Sydney's room. He would be smooth about the whole thing. They would go out to dinner, maybe dance a bit. She loved to dance with him. The only difference was that tonight, instead of dropping her off at the hospital or, when she wasn't working there, turning off the stairs at the second floor, they would continue up the steps to the fifth.

Privacy was the scarcest commodity of all in wartime. Tonight they would luxuriate in privacy for the brief time they had. They could talk without watching every word in case someone should overhear. They could touch each other freely, lovingly. She resolved to give Cody some potent memories to take with him when he left tomorrow.

She laughed at herself; she had fallen right into the trap she'd sworn to avoid. Now, with Cody, she didn't think of it as a trap at all, or if it was, it was a silky, soft trap and she was walking into it with her eyes wide open, eagerly.

Cody was waiting for Faith when she left the coffee shop, looking very serious. Dear God, had Sydney changed her mind about letting them use her room?

"Hi," she said, her question in her eyes.

A small smile curved his lips as he looked down at her. "Hi, yourself. Are you ready to go?"

"Just let me run upstairs and comb my hair. I'll be right back." She hurried. She thought she'd read the answer in his face but she wanted to hear the words.

When they were on the street she slipped her hand into his. His fingers were warm. "Well?" she asked. "Did you see Sydney?"

In answer he held up the key.

She laughed, delighted.

It was barely six A.M. when Valerie locked her room behind her. Jordan slept on. She could probably have designated someone to take her place this morning since Jordan had decided, like some emotionally guided patriot from the eighteenth century, that he was obligated to go off to war.

She, however, refused to think about, or make a big occasion, over his departure. She had told him as much last night when he'd wanted to talk to her about it. She would carry on, she informed him, as she had always done, and pretend he was simply traveling for the government again. Besides, now that she was to be the new manager of this hotel, she was going to be very busy.

She was passing the alcove when the telephone rang. She backed up a step to answer. "Fifth floor," she said.

"Room 503, please. Abby Edwards. This is her husband."

"Just a minute." Valerie laid down the phone and hurried to the room at the end of the hall. She tried to knock quietly so as not to disturb anyone else.

"Hi, Mrs. Adair," said a sleepy-headed Abby around the edge of the door.

"Telephone, Abby. It's your husband."

"Thanks!" The head disappeared for an instant and reappeared. Abby was pulling on her robe as she emerged. She had one slipper in her hand and half hopped down the hall as she tried to put on the other.

Valerie stood forgotten by the open door of room 503. She watched the girl rush toward the alcove. Then a flash of movement at the far end of the hall caught her eye. It was Faith Parker. Valerie frowned, wondering what she was doing on this floor. The girl gave the hall a cursory glance—any more and she would have identified Valerie even at this distance—and vanished once more.

Valerie stepped through the door that Abby had left ajar, taking herself out of the line of vision. She waited for a heartbeat, then peered around the edge of the door. Faith had been joined by another, also easily recognizable figure. Cody Bristol. They disappeared into the stairwell.

Valerie emerged from the room and walked determinedly toward the other end of the hall. When she came level with the door from which Cody and Faith had appeared a small smile curved her lips. The room number was 502.

Sydney Bingham's room. She knocked quietly. When there was no answer her smile grew, relishing how Kay Parker would react to this bit of news.

Bill couldn't explain the feeling of foreboding he woke up to this morning. He took a long look in the mirror as he shaved but found no answer there. His dog tags clinked lightly as he bent to rinse his face. He thought about the feeling while he showered but put it out of his mind as he dried with the meager towel, put on his underwear, and returned to the bedroom.

Kay had left his uniform laid out on the bed. Like wives of the warriors of old, laying out their husband's armor before they went to battle, he thought whimsically as he gazed at the neat arrangement of his clothes. Pretty flimsy armor.

The room was too quiet, no sound at all except for the soft murmur of the radio. He hummed along with the song. Kay must have taken the kids to the coffee shop for breakfast while he was in the shower. He pulled on the pants but left them unzipped while he reached for his undershirt. Kay had already affixed the commander's shoulder boards with their three stripes to the white tunic; the wings, the rainbow of ribbons, were the exact measured distance from the top of the pocket. The military creases in the starched white duck were perfectly aligned.

With a melancholy smile he remembered the first time Kay had tried to iron a uniform the way the navy required. They'd been living in a Quonset hut on the edge of the Hawaiian sugarcane fields; Barber's Point was a far cry from Pearl Harbor and a long dusty drive to Honolulu. She'd been so serious, trying so hard. She'd mangled the damn thing in no time and so, amused, he'd stepped in to show her how. By the time he'd finished, the shirt was a total ruin and it was her turn to laugh at him. They'd finally started over and managed a semblance of success, but he'd had his uniforms laundered out after that.

He sat on the edge of the bed to don his socks. The white shoes were arranged parallel, ready to step into. Billy had polished them last night, working as soberly, as industriously, as the shoe-shine boy in the train station. He slid his feet into them and jerked the laces tight before tying a strangling bow.

Damn it, he couldn't shake the sense of foreboding. Owed partly to the imminent ordeal of leave-taking, it was a fear that this might be the last time he'd spend with all his loved ones around him.

The emotion wasn't completely unfamiliar. He had it every time he left his family for an extended period. He'd had it before he left to join the carrier the first tour of duty. Hell, everyone had it. He'd always wished he could just walk out when the time came to go.

Slapping his thighs, he stood and reached for his belt. He threaded the woven white strip through the loops at his waist and fastened the gleaming buckle. Millie had polished the buckle and the buttons down the front of the tunic using, to his surprise, Worcestershire sauce. She told him she'd read about it in a magazine. He laughed to himself, but he was careful not to leave fingerprints on the bright surface.

His children—he loved them so much.

They had also prepared a "going away" kit. There had been an article in *Yank*, an army magazine—heaven knew where they got it—about items that would be of value in the South Pacific. Technically they weren't supposed to know where he was going, but it wasn't very hard for them to figure it out. They had convinced Faith to sew a roomy drawstring bag for them to fill. In it they had stowed a metal shaving mirror, a flashlight, a pair of rubber-soled sneakers, extra socks, a bottle of anti-mosquito dope—oil of citronella from the smell—and most surprisingly, a hunting knife in a well-worn leather sheath. He wondered aloud where they'd found such a scarce item. Millie announced that the knife was a contribution from their grandfather in Nebraska.

Kay's dad. The man who had never quite forgiven him for taking his only daughter away. He tightened the string on the bag and put it beside the orders he'd picked up last week from the big red-brick building downtown.

Bill had his superstitions. Every military man had them. He didn't discuss his job with his family. He didn't voice his reservations about his own mortality for fear they would come true.

He glanced at the dresser where he'd emptied his pockets last night. He always took along his talismans when he flew. One of them was a St. Christopher medal that Kay had given him the first time he'd left her after they were married. The other was his father's watch.

Painted by the sunlight, the watch gleamed and the medal rested in its puddle of gold chain. A fold of bills, a handful of change. A wallet, slimmer than it had been. He had reluctantly removed the pictures of his wife and kids. If he was captured he knew the Japanese would use the likenesses of his loved ones to try to break him. He didn't want some dirty little Jap with his hands on Kay's picture, calling her a whore, or worse. So, stowed in his seabag, he had a five-by-seven studio portrait of the three to leave in his cabin on the ship.

With a silent curse, he bent slightly at the waist and swept the tunic off the bed with an impatient swipe. He fastened the buttons and the hooks on the high stiff collar and turned to the mirror to check the uniform. His eyes were drawn again to the dresser top.

"Oh, give me something to remember you by, when you are far away from me," the radio sang softly from the bedside table. He pocketed his change, the bills, and his wallet. He picked up the medal and the watch and held them in his palm, looking down at them. He always took these things with him. "Some little something. . ." Bill turned on his heel and entered the kids' bedroom.

Faith was asleep, dead to the world. He looked down at his little sister for a long minute. Then he walked silently to the other beds, leaving his St. Christopher medal on Millie's pillow, his father's watch on Billy's. Just in case he didn't come back this time, he wanted his children to have these two things. To remember him by.

When Bill joined his family in the coffee shop a few minutes later, he greeted them pleasantly. Key lifted her face for his kiss, a determined smile frozen on her own face. The big day had arrived.

Bill ordered a huge breakfast and ate heartily. When Kay joked about his appetite he laughed. He teased the children and smiled his gorgeous smile at the waitress.

Kay knew that her husband was as restless inside as she was. She knew him so well, it was all a facade. They both hated the moments before the good-byes were said. They pressed in on you, no matter how hard you tried to stretch them. On departure days she considered her duty done if she kept the tears at bay until she was alone in bed.

Bill had insisted they not come to the ship with him today. The kids were disappointed and had pleaded with him to change his mind. But she was unreservedly relieved when he stuck to his guns. They had said good-bye so many times since their marriage. Once she'd tried to count up but it became too depressing so she'd quit.

To appease the kids he'd proposed a midmorning trip to the ice cream parlor. He had to be at the dock at noon. Finally he drained the last swallow from his coffee cup and set it back in the saucer. His eyes met hers. "Do you want to go with us?"

Kay smiled, trying to hide the sadness that threatened to overwhelm her. "No. You go ahead. Have fun."

An hour later Kay answered the door to find Valerie standing there. "Are you alone?" she asked.

Kay wondered at Valerie's quiet, almost conspiratorial air.

Most wives—most regular navy wives—wouldn't intrude for anything on the day the man's ship was to leave. It was another of the unwritten rules.

As a matter of fact what was Valerie doing here? Kay knew that Jordan Adair had put in for duty on the *Shiloh* at the last minute and that Valerie was furious about it. His strange request was the talk of the hotel. Did this have something to do with the ship?

"Yes, I'm alone. Faith's still asleep. Bill and the children just left," she said.

"I know. I saw them downstairs. May I speak to you in private?"

"Certainly. Come in." Kay stepped aside. "I heard that Jordan was leaving on the *Shiloh*, too. Would you like some coffee?"

Valerie's face closed. "Yes, Jordan is leaving and no, I can't stay. Something has come up that I thought you would want to know about."

So it wasn't anything to do with the ship, thought Kay. "Please, sit down," she offered.

"I was unsure about telling you this," Valerie began, settling into the easy chair Kay indicated and crossing her legs. She laughed lightly—and, Kay suspected, insincerely. "But then I decided if I were in the same situation I would want to know, no matter how unpleasant the information might be."

Another way of saying "this is for your own good." Kay nodded, careful to keep her expression noncommittal.

"This morning about six o'clock I saw your sister-in-law coming out of Sydney's room with Cody Bristol."

Kay was puzzled for a minute, until the significance of what she was hearing finally registered. "Faith?" she said weakly.

"Yes, Faith."

"Maybe Sydney—"

"Sydney wasn't there. She was at the hospital all night. I checked."

Kay struggled to gather her scattered faculties. Oh, God. What if Bill found out? He would be livid. "Valerie, I would appreciate it if you wouldn't mention this to anyone else."

Valerie looked offended. "Of course, I wouldn't. I only mentioned it to you because you are responsible for the girl."

Kay was grateful for the bit of steel that suddenly strengthened her backbone. She would not give Valerie the satisfaction of knowing she was upset. "Faith is twenty-one years old. As of her last birthday she is responsible for herself. I just don't like the idea of her as the object of the gossip that seems to travel like wildfire through this hotel.''

''Well, no one will hear it from me. You can be sure of that,'' Valerie responded huffily. ''But I doubt that I'm the only one who knows, unless the two of them picked the lock of Sydney Bingham's room.''

Sydney. Kay's heart suddenly felt as though it had been pierced by the hot, hurtful sting of betrayal—by Faith, and by Cody, and most of all by Sydney. She had even begun to like the southern girl. ''I'll speak to them myself,'' she said.

''This war is becoming dangerous on more than one front. It's going to be responsible for the gradual disintegration of young people's morals.''

Silently Kay agreed, but she hated people who preached without benefit of a divinity degree. She tuned out the rest of the discourse and finally Valerie left wearing a rather unpleasant, self-satisfied smirk that Kay would have liked to wipe from the beautiful face.

She crossed to the door of the adjoining room. She put her hand on the knob but, all of a sudden, it was heavy in her hand, so heavy that she couldn't turn it for a minute. She laid her forehead against the frame. Damn it! She didn't *need* this, not today!

The painted wood was cool and soothing against her warm brow. Her thoughts were distressing and so haphazard and random that they tumbled, disorganized, over each other.

What if Bill found out? He trusted her to take care of things on the home front. She had let him down dreadfully. What she'd told Valerie was true; Faith was twenty-one years old. But Kay was responsible for her as long as she was living with them.

What if Faith was pregnant? Cody was leaving today. What if she discovered such a condition two months from now when the carrier was in the middle of the South Pacific? Where would she be then? Alone, with an illegitimate child to raise. Cody clearly felt something for Faith. Why couldn't they get married before the carrier left? Was that impossible? Of course it was, obviously. And then: was it really so bad, what they had done? After all, Cody might not come back.

Slowly Kay opened the door. Faith was asleep; she was curled underneath the blanket and her eyes were shut. Kay sighed and closed the door again.

Kay was waiting when, a half hour later, she heard movement in the adjoining room.

Faith came out, dressed in her robe and rubbing sleep from her eyes. "Hi. Is there coffee?"

"Yes. Help yourself. Then I'd like to talk to you."

Kay's manner was definitely chilly this morning. Faith felt her stomach sink to her feet. Kay knew. "May I dress first?" she asked, filling a cup from the pot and hoping to delay the inevitable.

"Yes."

Faith took her coffee back into the other room. She put her dread of the confrontation out of her mind and dressed slowly, wanting to relive last night, to savor the wonderful memory, the sensual feast, of Cody's lovemaking. He was forceful, all man, but as tender and careful with her as she had known he'd be. Neither of them had slept during the night; they were unwilling to sacrifice even a moment of their time together to insensibility.

Finally she was dressed. There was no point in delaying any longer. Absently she smoothed the covers on her bed and was about to leave when her eye was caught by the reflection of sunlight on metal. She caught her breath and moved quickly to stand between the children's beds.

On Millie's pillow lay Bill's St. Christopher medal, his good-luck piece; she recognized it immediately. And on Billy's bed was their grandfather's gold watch. Bill always carried it. Faith didn't know what made her do it, but she scooped up both and hid them away in the top drawer of her chest.

She opened the door between their rooms and, when she saw the expression on Kay's face, all other thoughts flew out of her head. She'd learned to love her sister-in-law, but there were some things about her she still didn't like. "Okay, Kay, I'm ready."

"Ready?"

Faith sighed. "Yes. I can see from your expression that something is wrong. I'm afraid I know what it is. Who saw us?"

"Valerie."

"Oh, God. Of all people."

"You don't seem too upset."

Faith paused a minute to order her thoughts. "I'm upset that my actions have upset you," she said quietly. "I'm not upset about what I did—" She paused. "—except to the extent that I'd sworn not to get caught up in the war hysteria. But I do love Cody." She sighed. "Are you going to tell Bill?"

"No. I won't put that burden on him, not hours before he leaves. To put things on a purely practical level, what if you're pregnant, Faith?"

Faith took an involuntary step back. Then she turned and crossed to the window. "Is that all you care about? The consequences?"

"I'm worried about them."

"So it's okay to do anything you want to do as long as you don't get caught?"

"I didn't say that," Kay responded immediately. "But I do think you should give some thought to marriage."

Faith spun on her heel. "Marriage? The ship leaves this afternoon. Are you crazy?"

She regretted the accusation as soon as it left her lips. Kay visibly stiffened. "I don't think I am. It's a logical suggestion under the circumstances."

Faith gave a short harsh laugh. "Aside from the fact that my brother might raise a few pointed questions about a hurry-up ceremony, can you imagine how a man like Cody would react to that kind of reasoning?" she asked sarcastically.

"The *Shiloh* is about to leave for God knows how long. What if you find out you're going to have a baby with no husband?"

There was a desperation in Kay's voice that Faith didn't like. Her own anger was building and she knew she had to get out of here or it would erupt. She might say things she would regret even more. She had to stay calm, to make Kay understand and then escape.

"Kay," she said, trying to be gentle. "Cody would decide right off the bat that I'd tricked him into marriage. He's too free-wheeling not to resent that kind of trap. We wouldn't have a chance of making a marriage like that work. No, Kay. Cody took precautions; but, even if he hadn't, even if something went wrong and I find out two months from now that I am pregnant, I couldn't do that to him. If we ever get married it will be because he has made the conscious decision to settle down."

She noticed suddenly that Kay's face had turned whiter than it had been when this conversation started. "I'm sorry if I've disappointed you, Kay. I don't know what more to say."

"It isn't only you who's disappointed me. It's Cody. I've known him for years. The children love him." Her voice turned decidedly bitter. "And Sydney Bingham."

"Sydney didn't know," Faith said quickly. "She agreed to

let Cody use her room so he wouldn't have to leave early to go back to the BOQ. My staying with him was my own decision.''

A knock on the door splintered the tension in the air—to the relief of both women. Kay crossed to open it.

Edna McCoy stood on the threshold. Her eyes sought Faith. ''I'm sorry to bother you, Miss Parker, but you said you'd watch the switchboard for a little while this morning.''

''Yes, Edna. I'm sorry I forgot. I'll come down with you now.'' She glanced back over her shoulder as she left the room. ''Kay?''

Kay waved her away. ''Go ahead. I'll see you downstairs later.''

When she was alone Kay took a long breath and let it out slowly. Her shoulders bowed under the weight of this knowledge. Why the hell hadn't Valerie kept it to herself? She sank down on the bed, folding her arms across her body. She felt as though a very heavy boulder had fallen on her chest.

Faith could not have known that she'd chosen the one argument guaranteed to leave Kay wounded and without a come-back. Free-wheeling was a good word to describe Bill Parker, too, as he was thirteen years ago. Glamorous, dynamic, intriguing—all the things that enchanted a Nebraska farm girl. She had been too reserved and rather bookish that summer when she visited her college friend in Corpus Christi, Texas.

Charlotte had decided that Kay should experiment with cosmetics and wear her hair up for the dance at the Officers' Club. The results were astonishing, if a little uncomfortable.

She hadn't been in the room for five minutes when Charlotte's father, the commander of a bomber squadron, introduced her to Bill Parker, who, he explained, was a test pilot. Kay didn't give a hoot what he was, he just happened to be the handsomest man she had ever encountered. She was thrilled when he asked her to dance.

Having grown up in a houseful of men, Kay wasn't hard-pressed to find a topic for conversation during their first dance. So the exchange between them was lively. And the liveliness seemed to feed on itself. The wittier she was, the cleverer she became. They laughed together, danced together all evening, and talked—incessantly and rapidly. There was so much to say and so little time for them to say it. He asked to see her the next day.

Kay knew she was in love before her head finally found the pillow in the wee hours of the morning.

God help her, Bill had taken her ebullience for sophistication. She was a guest in someone else's home, but they had been together as often as possible. Two weeks later, when it was time for her to go home, she had been despondent. He promised to write and come to Nebraska on his next leave. Of course, by the time he'd arrived she'd known she was pregnant.

She felt all her old insecurities well up in her. Tears dripped onto her forearm. She sniffed and wiped at them with her fingers. Faith had unwittingly put a name to Kay's most dreaded fear. Bill had never said so, but in the back of her mind, she'd always felt that he thought she'd trapped him into marriage.

For more than twelve years Bill had been a loving husband and father. But that question would always be there, deep within her heart, to torture her. Would Bill Parker ever have proposed; would he have married her if she hadn't been pregnant?

The telephone began to ring, its shrill bell muted through the door. She grabbed a Kleenex and blew her nose, waiting for someone else to pick up, but the hall was unnaturally quiet. At last, she rose and went to answer.

PART THREE

As we go to press no bombs have been dropped on our mainland, but the president considers air raids highly probable, and we should be prepared. . . . Keep radio on for raid news. . . . If you can't reach safe shelter in time, lie flat, face down, protecting back of neck with hands. . . . Turn off all gas jets but pilot light; leave main electric switches, gas and water valves alone. . . . Unless on duty, stay indoors.

Ladies' Home Journal, July, 1942

Chapter 24

Sydney's work at Boeing Aircraft began in earnest after a short period of training. She welcomed the hours she spent there and at the hospital, hours to be used up by something other than loneliness. She missed Vance so very much.

Soon she lost the spooky feeling she'd experienced when she first walked into the surrealistic atmosphere of the cavernous assembly plant. The sounds of chattering rivet guns and screaming power tools became appropriate background music for the job. To their surprise she and Maurie were both chosen for the secret project, which, they found out, was the building of a long-range bomber. Boeing had been producing the B-17, called the Flying Fortress, since 1936. This one was numbered B-29 and was called the Superfortress. It was exciting and flattering to be chosen to participate in the project.

She and her fellow workers watched the daily progress as the Army Corps of Engineers began to build, out of chicken wire and canvas, feathers and spun glass, a village over the rooftops of the Seattle plants. Houses, trees up to twelve feet tall, a corner service station, a store, greenhouses, garages, and roads, the twenty-six acre site was constructed to resemble, from the air, a small town. Who, they reasoned, would bomb a small town?

Street signs bearing names like Synthetic Street and Burlap Boulevard were erected. There was even a real cow, eating real grass. There were also two buildings that were genuine; they housed antiaircraft gun crews.

The days stretched into weeks, a month. Sydney reminded herself of Vance's warning: this was only the beginning of a war that could go on for years. The mail from the Pacific was scant, almost nonexistent, and the anguish of living day-to-day, not knowing anything, added to the tension. The other mail she received—from Mrs. Deveraux, Clyde and the boys, and from Bobby Dick—lifted her spirits.

For Kay the days following the departure of the *Shiloh* passed slowly, like the footsteps of a giant struggling to be free of quicksand. But her job soon began to occupy more and more of her time.

She had no regrets when the hotel, which had been home for the families of a lot of men assigned to the ship, underwent a change. The carrier would be at sea for months, so some of the wives decided to return to their homes in other parts of the country, to be near their families. Theirs were replaced by new faces. To no one's regret, Charles Wagner moved to San Francisco. Valerie and Patsy, working together, were doing a good job. So many girls were working at full-time jobs that, to supplement the volunteer hours, they had hired a number of paid workers.

Maurice had even learned to get along with Valerie, the result, Kay thought, of a long-dormant snobbery brought to bloom by Valerie's name-dropping.

The strain between Kay and Faith eased with the passage of time, but Kay still found it difficult to relax around Sydney. Finally, one morning in late August, Kay was confronted by her sister-in-law. School was again in session, and they had walked with the children to the bus stop. Before they separated to go to their respective jobs Faith plunged in. "I've invited Sydney to have supper with us tonight. Don't worry about the meal. I'll shop on my way home."

Kay didn't reply.

"Sydney is my friend," Faith went on doggedly. She was determined to end Kay's hostility toward her friend. "None of this was her fault. I don't like to have to watch every word I say, Kay."

"I'm sorry if I've seemed overly sensitive," responded Kay. "I'd be happy to have Sydney for supper."

She didn't sound happy, thought Faith, sighing, but she did sound resigned. It was a beginning.

Faith finally caught up with Sydney, sifting through her mail in the lobby after work. She juggled the bag of groceries she was carrying. "Anything interesting? Did you get a letter from Vance?" she asked, peering around Sydney's arm.

Sydney laughed and hit the top of her friend's head playfully

with an envelope. "No, Miss Nosy Parker, I did not." She'd
heard from him last week but nothing since. "I did get a letter
from one of the boys in the band I used to sing with. Do you
remember the fellow who was going to flight school in Alabama?"

"The Negro? Yes, I do."

"Well, he's somewhere in the Mediterranean." She chuckled
with satisfaction. "The army air force formed a squadron of all
black men and the Germans are superstitious toward them;
they're calling them the Black Birdmen." Sydney hesitated. "I
sure hope Bobby Dick's okay," she added in a low voice.

"I hope they're all okay," said Faith, recalling the day she'd
gotten a letter from Kevin's mother telling her that he had been
killed. She also remembered how considerate Cody had been
when she told him that night in Volunteer Park. Since then she
had erased the names of two more boys from her address book.

Sydney interrupted her thoughts. "Did you hear from Cody
today?"

"No." Faith shook off her mood. "By the way, you're having
supper with us."

Sydney held up her hand in objection. "Ah—now wait a minute, Faith."

"No argument."

Sydney studied her friend carefully. Finally she shrugged and
her mouth flattened in a grimace. "If we're all miserable, it's
on your head."

Faith glanced at her watch and got a firmer grip on the bag
she was carrying. "Half an hour. I'm cooking."

Sydney groaned. "You should have warned me about that
first!" Faith laughed.

That night after supper the two younger women faced Kay
with a request. "We want you to put on your Swami hat and tell
us where you think our men are."

Kay turned to the map. She mused for a minute. "There was
a communiqué last week that a large-scale air and naval battle
was about to be waged in the area around the Solomon Islands."
All their gazes were drawn to the map. Kay pointed to a few
large land masses that were surrounded by hundreds of tiny
islands.

Faith pictured the jungle scenes that she'd seen in the newsreels—hot, steamy climate, men slogging through mud and
fighting insects and disease. Thank God, Cody and Bill were
flying above that, in the cool, blue sky.

"The position of the islands is critical to the sea lanes and very close to Australia," Kay went on. "It will take months, perhaps years, and hundreds of thousands of men, to clear out all of them. They will have to go step by step, island by island. I think that if our men aren't already there, they are on their way."

Chapter 25

Tuesday, September 15th, 1942

Kay sat bolt upright in her bed, her body drenched in sweat and her breath coming in gasps. When she realized that it had only been a nightmare she fell back again.

The Klaxon screamed and Bill's feet hit the floor. "All hands to battle stations," came the call. He was reaching for his pants before his gritty eyes were fully open. The four-man test group had landed only an hour before. The men were exhausted after eighteen hours on duty, and he prayed this was a false alarm.

The zipper in his flight suit jammed, and he cursed as he shoved his feet into his boots, working the metal tab furiously. The gangway was crowded with men.

"They were refueling when they spotted the incoming planes," said Cody from behind him. "We're being attacked!"

"Shit. Come on. I just hope they were finished with our four. We've got to save those planes." At that moment the floor beneath their feet vibrated like an angry giant awakened from a deep sleep. The ship gave a surge, then the familiar sounds of the huge vessel, normally calm and reassuring, became like a beast crying out for help. Cody picked himself up off the floor and Bill grabbed for the ladder.

The main deck was enveloped in black smoke. The two pilots gagged on the fumes.

"We've got to get these planes in the air," Bill shouted to a signalman.

The man nodded, pointing. A breath of wind cleared the deck for a minute, giving Bill an unrestricted view of the damage. Men were working frantically to put out the fire. Water hoses snaked from the sea to pumps and were aimed at a huge hole in the side of the superstructure.

So far the fire seemed to be contained on the port side. But with all the fuel spilled it would spread quickly across the deck. He raced for his plane. The mechanics were pulling the chocks away before he had his headset on. He glanced back to see that Cody was right behind him, ready to be hurled from the pitching and heeling platform as soon they were rolled into place. He revved the engines to maximum power and got the go-ahead from the signalman. He eased back on the throttle just before his plane reached the edge of the deck. As his wheels left the ship it took a dip, and he felt his stomach hit his throat. His hands fought the stick, jerking it back into his belly, and he was airborne.

He banked to the right. A Japanese torpedo plane was disappearing behind the column of smoke. He hurled his plane in pursuit. If he could get off a shot before—

But he was too late. He saw the torpedo erupt from the plane, hit the water, and swim, tracking a deadly wake. It looked almost silly, like a small mosquito about to land on the hide of an elephant. But when it bit into the metal hull of its host, the destruction was in devastating contrast to the size of the weapon. The air throbbed with the tremor from the explosion.

He spotted two more torpedo planes, escorted by a dozen fighters. He could see the explosions, feel the vibrations, from the big guns of other ships in the American convoy but he couldn't hear them.

The radio crackled in his ear, the voices of his men clear to him but inaudible to his enemy, thanks to the device perfected by Vance Bingham.

Fury surged through him as he saw one of his group, perched on the deck of the *Shiloh*, propellers reeling ready for takeoff, receive a wing hit, spin, and fall tailfirst into the sea. It was Jersey.

"Parker! Parker! Zeke at eleven o'clock! Eleven o'clock!" Mason's voice! He thanked God that three of the four test planes had made it into the air.

"I've got his ass," said Bill, grimly maneuvering his Wildcat to avoid the oncoming Zeke. The four 50-caliber machine guns spat and the Japanese plane wobbled for a minute before going to the deck, flying just above the tips of the waves in an attempt to escape. It was trailing white smoke. He left it; it wouldn't get far.

"Does anybody have a fix on the bastard that laid the egg?" Bill said into the microphone.

"Where else? Into the setting sun."

Bill banked into a turn, surveying their position. "Yeah, and I'll bet you ten to one the nest is just over the horizon." The glare from the great orange ball stung his eyes. He reached for his dark glasses. "Cody, you want to go see?"

"What do you think? Besides, there doesn't seem to be much to go home to, does there?"

Below and off to the left Bill could see clearly that the *Shiloh* was burning badly, sending monumental columns of black smoke toward the sky. The faces of Bingham and Adair flashed before his eyes. They were down there somewhere.

A couple of fighters and three torpedo planes had taken off now, and they were following the same path Bill had decided upon. "Come with me then. You, too, Mason. Approach from the north. Cody and I are going straight in to clear a path." The other fighters, the regular squadron, were lifting off the crippled ship as quickly as possible now. It was burning fast. Some of the planes wouldn't make it in time, but it looked like a majority might.

"Let's go," said Bill grimly, determination in his voice. He fixed his eyes on the tail of a fighter. His fingers closed on the red trigger mechanism, causing the stick to shiver under his hand.

"You got him!" shouted Cody.

Bill was about to reply when he felt the hand of a giant clasp his plane and shake it. He was hit! He grappled with the stick as he reasoned coolly what had happened. A second Zeke had come up beneath his belly. He cursed but felt the satisfaction of seeing his target plunge into the sea. The furious wind whistled through a jagged hole in the starboard side of the cockpit, whipping the smoke into his eyes.

"Commander Parker! Come in!" shouted Cody. "Damn you, Bill!"

Bill could hear Cody's voice and he opened his mouth to reply. But the smoke choked him; he coughed but couldn't speak. He was losing altitude rapidly. His right leg was numb and didn't respond to his brain's command to the rudder. He glanced down to see a shard of the fuselage protruding from his flesh. He pulled it free and then realized his mistake as blood gushed out to drench his hand.

Another burst of gunfire made him forget all about his wound.

The Wildcat was losing power rapidly, the engine coughed. One more chance! God, give me one more chance. The Zeke had emerged from the blanket of smoke at two o'clock. Using his good leg, he managed to bank his crippled plane to the right, and opened up his cannon. A burst of gunfire found the wingtip, and he watched with elation as the plane tumbled end over end. But the pilot managed to regain control. He turned back.

Bill opened fire again, spilling his remaining ammunition into the sky around the Zeke. At that moment his engine gave its last gasp and feathered, the nose propeller lazily giving its last turns. He fought the wind currents, trying to keep the plane level while searching the horizon for a place to glide the plane in. There was no land in sight. When he ditched he would be on his own in the middle of the sea.

There wouldn't be time for the rest of his crew to search for him. They had to find a place to put down; they had to save these planes with their vital instruments. The Zeke took another pass, but apparently decided not to waste his ammunition. He could see that Bill was done for. And Bill saw that his last fire-burst had hit the Zeke's fuel tanks. Smoke trailed out behind the plane. "I got you, you son of a bitch!"

"Bill! Commander! Come in!" He saw Cody's plane come around to starboard. He heard the sharply indrawn breath through his earphones, the whisper, "Dear God," when Cody saw the damage.

Though he was losing blood with every heartbeat he summoned the strength to ask about his men. "Give me a status report, Cody."

"We lost Jersey. Mason and I are okay. I count four Zekes, including two for you."

Saddened by the loss of one of his best men, Bill nevertheless nodded his satisfaction over enemy losses. "I'm going down. Get these planes back to the vicinity of the carrier, Cody. Somebody will be in contact and can tell you where to land. I hope."

His voice was weak, his entire body seemed to be melting away, and the plane was rapidly losing altitude. His wings were just above the waves now. It wasn't an unpleasant feeling, this sense of skimming the water. A mental picture of Kay standing on the deck of the ferry comforted him. He was glad he'd written the letter to her.

"I won't leave you! Hang on, Bill!"

With a last superhuman effort Bill put the grit of command into his voice. "I've got a hole in my starboard side big enough to drive your fist through. Get your planes back into radio contact with the carrier. Now! That's an order, Ensign!'' He reached over to turn off his radio. The absence of static, the sudden quiet, was soothing. He glanced over to see that Cody was still flying on his wing. The boy's anguish was clearly visible. He motioned with his hand toward the blue sky, its perfection now scarred with dense black smoke. ''Get out of here,'' he mouthed. Cody hesitated for a minute before giving him a grim nod and a thumbs-up sign. The younger man peeled off.

He was alone now.

God, his leg hurt. He could feel his life's blood draining out of him. He grasped his thigh in an attempt to stem the flow and his fingers came away sticky.

One more try. He grasped the stick with both hands and pulled back. The nose came up, then the belly touched the sea. The plane jumped, sending up a spray from its tail, and slowed. Its wings touched water and it finally settled comfortably onto the waves, like a wounded silver bird. The plane would rock this way for a while, gradually taking on water, until the weight of the water added to the weight of the aircraft would send it sinking to the depths.

Wildcat, we gave 'em a helluva fight, Bill thought as oblivion overcame him.

Cody watched over his shoulder, saw the plane kiss the surface of the sea. His heart jumped as the nose lifted, only to sink again when the plume of water obliterated the body of the plane from his sight. ''Bill!''

Across the curve of the horizon he saw something else, which did him more good. The Zeke had exploded on impact, scattering parts of plane and pilot over the ocean.

Goddamn the little Jap bastard! A fiery death was too good for him. Goddamned bastard. Cody was oblivious to the tears streaming down his face. Bill Parker was his friend, his mentor. Bill knew more about these planes than the men who designed them, more than the people who built them because Bill Parker was a part of the plane; he was its soul.

''Cody! Come in, Cody. We're running on fumes, man!''

Cody could hear the tears in Mason's voice. He knew how the other man felt. He would like to bury his face in his arms and bawl. He hadn't felt like crying in a long time. Hadn't actually done it since his dog died when he was ten. Texas men didn't cry. If your horse threw you, if you broke your arm while playing football, if your best girl found someone else—you didn't cry. You gritted your teeth and took it like a man, like a Texan.

"Cody!" The tears were turning into panic.

"Yeah, let's find a place to set the birds down."

When the remnants of the group got back to the ship they knew immediately they were going to have to find another place to land, and soon. The *Shiloh* was listing badly. Men swarmed over the sides and other ships, a destroyer, an escort, circled to pluck the crew from the ocean. He radioed the escort. They gave him a fix on an island toward the southeast.

They flew low to conserve fuel. When the island appeared over the horizon Cody breathed a sigh of relief. Both his and Mason's planes made it to the beach to land without further mishap. He saw a torpedo plane from the carrier go in the drink. But the pilot put it down close enough to swim to shore.

They would be picked up—sooner or later.

Chapter 26

Monday, October 26, 1942

Sydney pushed through the doors into the lobby. Though it was midnight the room, as usual, was stirring with people and talk. Uniforms, though fewer of them than before, mingled with fall dresses, sweaters and skirts.

The children were all in bed by this time of night but it seemed that the adults were ready and eager to fill the void left by the loss of their bright noise. Soft laughter from one corner, where a couple sat cuddled on the arm of an overstuffed chair. Someone had brought down a record player and the strains of a romantic ballad played in the background.

Giggles overlaid the deeper tones of masculine laughter in another corner, where a group of couples had gathered, probably telling jokes about the little slant-eyes or the Hun. Jokes about the enemy were common, as though reducing them to an object of fun diminished both their importance and the threat they represented.

There was an island of deadly quiet in yet another corner, where three women labored earnestly over the Ouija board.

Sydney was grateful for the warmth, the noise. For some reason she had been feeling lonely all day. Even in the midst of hundreds of her coworkers at the plant, and even in the hospital, surrounded by desperate boys who needed her attention, she'd felt terribly lonely. The weekends were the worst and next was Mondays. She should head directly for bed. Five-thirty came awfully early. But she hesitated. The mere thought of entering her room at this particular moment sent a wave of claustrophobia through her.

Instead she headed for the coffee shop. One cup of that obnoxious brew and a last cigarette and she would go to bed.

Connie was working tonight. "Hi, Sydney," she piped as Sydney took a stool at the low counter. "Coffee?"

"Please," answered Sydney. "If it's still drinkable."

"I just made some fresh. I've really been busy in here tonight."

Sydney took off her sweater and dropped it on the next stool. "Damn. I got a spot on my uniform." With a fingernail she scraped at the place on the skirt of the striped pinafore.

"Faith was looking for you a little while ago. Did you see her as you came in?"

Sydney took a sip of the coffee when it was placed in front of her. Maybe Faith had finally gotten a letter from Cody. She hadn't heard from Vance in well over a month but the slow mail delivery was nothing new. She'd probably get a stack of letters all at once. "No, I didn't see her." She glanced at her watch. "She's probably in bed by now. Do you know what she wanted?"

"She didn't say. I suppose it will keep until tomorrow. She did seem kind of upset, though."

Connie, one of the girls who had been hired from outside the hotel, was not known for her perception. If she had noticed Faith was upset something must be wrong—really wrong. Sydney pulled a handful of change from her purse. "I'd better go find her."

Sydney checked the lobby first. Then she hurried up the stairs to the second floor. First she paused at the door to the Parkers' room. At this late hour she certainly didn't want to disturb Kay or the children. Especially since Kay hadn't been too friendly to her lately despite Faith's attempts. She took a deep breath and put her ear to the door. The sound of muted voices seeped through.

She thought briefly of going to her room and seeing Faith tomorrow.

But she straightened her tired shoulders and knocked softly. The conversation from within stopped.

Faith opened the door. Her lovely blue eyes were red-rimmed and swollen.

Sydney felt her heart contract. Faith didn't cry—something dreadful must have happened. The room was dim, lit by one small lamp. Beyond Faith's shoulder, Kay sat propped against the headboard of the bed.

She seemed shocked by Sydney's presence. "Sydney!" she blurted as Faith stepped back.

Unsure of her welcome, Sydney remained at the threshold. "Connie said you were looking for me, Faith. What's happened?"

Kay recovered first. She slid off the bed. "Come in, Sydney. Have a seat." She pointed to a chair and Sydney obeyed without thinking, as though she had been doing what this woman told her to do all her life.

Suddenly Sydney had a thought. Maybe it wasn't the carrier after all. Maybe it was something else. Maybe Faith was pregnant. Maybe one of the children was sick. But the thought was short-lived. Kay answered her unspoken question without further delay.

"The *Shiloh* was attacked and sunk on September 15."

Speechless for a moment, Sydney finally found her voice. "September fifteenth? Good Lord, that was six weeks ago. Oh, Kay, I'm so sorry."

Kay nodded, a trace of the bitterness she felt reflected in her eyes. "I can't believe they didn't let us know anything before this. The news is still rather muddled, I'm afraid. We're not sure. . . ." Her head dropped; her voice trailed off, then she straightened, her voice gained strength. "They were refueling the planes when the attack came. There was a fire." She shoved her fingers into her hair and squeezed her head. "Oh, God, fuel must have been everywhere. They were forced to abandon ship. Most of the crew were saved but some of the men were scattered, were picked up by other ships in the area or landed their planes on islands." Again she spread her hands, helplessly. "There are only a few names of men known to be—to have been killed."

Sydney leaned forward to the edge of the chair, linking her fingers together to have something to hold onto. "Is Bill all right?" she asked softly.

"We don't know for sure. The planes on deck were launched immediately. Some were already in the air. A navy chaplain came by. He promised more news about the pilots. Everything is really confused. But Sydney . . ."

Sydney's gaze went to Faith. She couldn't voice the question, not here in front of Kay. But she had to know. "Cody?" She couldn't speak the name that was really on her lips.

Faith came over to kneel at Sydney's feet. She reached for her hand. "We don't know for sure about all the men," she said. "Nothing about Bill or Cody. Just a few names have been released."

Sydney knew a horrible dread. She was married to another man, but a feeling for Jordan Adair would always live in her heart and she didn't want to hear that he was dead.

Just then a knock sounded, shattering the uncanny stillness, startling them all. Instant relief was broadcast from Faith and Kay like a charge of electricity. Faith jumped up and went to the door.

The young uniformed officer was speaking before he was in the room. His voice was high and childish. Although his hat was tucked neatly and correctly beneath his arm, he wore the harassed air of a man out of his element. He spoke to Faith as though he knew her. "I missed her at the hospital. Has she come back . . . ?" His voice trailed off as he spied Sydney. He looked to Faith for confirmation.

"Lieutenant Hudson, this is Mrs. Bingham."

Sydney saw the small cross on his collar. A chaplain? Looking for her? Slowly she rose and turned to face the young man fully, knowing now that she was going to hear something unbearable. "Yes, I'm Mrs. Bingham," she said.

The man had regained his composure. "I'm Lieutenant Hudson. I wonder if I might have a word with you in private."

"For Christ's sake, Lieutenant. We're her friends. We've already told her about the carrier," blurted Kay harshly, stunning them all.

The young man nodded. When he swallowed, his Adam's apple bobbed in his throat. "It is my unpleasant duty to inform you that your husband, Chief Petty Officer Vance Bingham, was killed in the line of duty when the carrier, *Shiloh*, was attacked."

The supercilious bastard was a comical sight. Sydney laughed aloud, and the young man's eyes widened in a stare of absolute panic. "You're mistaken, Lieutenant. My husband wasn't even on that carrier. He's aboard a destroyer."

Suddenly the young man's features softened. His sympathy rose visibly to soften his eyes, dimming their dutiful expression into something more appealing. "Mrs. Bingham, the chief was on board the *Shiloh*. I'm sorry you had to find out like this."

"No. Tell him," Sydney said, hysteria in her voice. She looked at Faith, who avoided her gaze. Then she swiveled her head toward Kay. The silence in the room was palpable, heavy, and it threatened to suffocate her. This had to be straightened out and quickly, so she could breathe again. It couldn't be—but she read the belief of this ridiculous story in the faces of the other two women.

Her features hardened into a mask. She had to get out of here, had to think about this information, not that she believed it for a minute. It had to be another chief mistakenly identified as Vance. She'd heard of that happening before and she'd always thought what a cruel mistake it was. The navy should be absolutely sure before they handed out emotionally damaging gossip as fact.

Sydney wasn't aware that Kay had moved until she felt the older woman's arm across her shoulders. It was the ultimate weight, and she couldn't bear it. She shrugged off the arm and fixed the young man with an angry glare. "I'm going to bed. Tomorrow, when you discover your mistake, I'll expect you to come back and apologize, Lieutenant."

Kay spoke. "Vance was on the carrier, Sydney. You have to face that."

"Why are you saying such a thing? You don't know! If anyone knew it would be me, his wife! You can't be sure. He was on the destroyer! I went to the dock myself. I saw the ship."

Kay took her hand—she fought the pressure for a minute then gave in—and led her back to the chair. "Lieutenant, thank you. If you'll leave us alone now . . ."

"Ma'am? I'm supposed to stay for a while to see that she's all right."

"We'll handle it from here. Good night, Lieutenant," said Kay firmly, showing him to the door.

The young minister wavered between his duty and his unwillingness to argue further with the tone of command in Kay's voice. At last he left.

Faith resumed her place on the floor at Sydney's feet; she grasped Sydney's cold hand. Sydney turned her fingers to grip tightly. "Faith, you know better than this. It's cruel. It's barbaric for them to make such a horrible mistake!"

Faith's explanation was brisk. "It isn't a mistake, Sydney. The chaplain was here an hour ago and he gave us the details before he left to look for you. Evidently Vance left the destroyer in Hawaii. The *Shiloh* picked him up there."

"No."

"They have a positive identification," Faith went on as though Sydney hadn't spoken. "Jordan was injured trying to save him."

The flat, no-nonsense tone finally pierced the wall of denial

with which Sydney had surrounded herself. She searched Faith's
eyes and saw a strength and friendship there that she knew she
could call upon if she needed it. But she didn't.

She didn't need anyone else's help; she hadn't needed anyone
since her mother died and she certainly wouldn't accept pity.
She could depend only on herself. And now she had to get away
from them, to regroup, to find her own strength in solitude.

She still wasn't absolutely sure the navy hadn't been mistaken
about Vance, but she'd think about him in her own room. And
about Jordan. "Was Jordan injured seriously?" she asked, unable to leave the question unasked. She might as well know it
all now, before she went into hiding.

"We don't know," answered Kay.

"I'll see you in the morning," she said, rising. Deliberately
she picked up her purse and sweater and looked around to see
if there was anything else she needed to collect. There wasn't.
"Good night."

Faith was still on her knees. "Sydney, don't you want me to
go with you?"

"No, thank you. I'd rather be alone. Bill and Cody . . . I
hope the news is good."

The door closed behind her. Faith and Kay were quiet for a
while. There was nothing to say.

Finally Faith dragged herself to her feet. She crossed to pick
up the coffeepot and rattled it. "There's enough for two cups, I
think. Do you want some?"

Kay shook her head. "If I was right about them being on their
way to the Solomons," she said almost distractedly, "then there
is a good chance that Bill and Cody are okay. There are thousands of tiny islands in the South Pacific. They could have landed
almost anywhere."

Sydney's room was a haven. Why in the world had she ever
dreaded coming back to it? This was where she and Vance had
lain together. This was where they'd made love, where they'd
whispered in the dark afterward. Where he'd beaten her at
checkers.

She felt his presence. The kindest man, the finest man she'd
ever known. She'd betrayed him. Oh, not physically, but emotionally. Why hadn't she told him she loved him? She'd written
of her love in the letters she'd sent, every day since he left, but
why hadn't she said them out loud to him? Easy words to say.
And she would have meant them. He'd been sure of her loyalty—

that was one consolation—but she'd let him go off to a barren ocean without the certain knowledge ever being voiced. Would it have made a difference? Would he have struggled harder at the moment of death?

Jordan had tried to save him. Jordan, of all people. Jordan, the man of honor. Jordan had tried to atone in an unrelated way for his long-ago lapse; he had tried to save Vance for her. Oh God, thank you, Jordan. Thank you for trying.

The back of her throat burned with the metallic taste of tears. She continued to evade total acknowledgment of the unbelievable reality. She released a bark of harsh, wry laughter but swallowed the tears. She wasn't ready to cry.

She went through her nightly ritual by rote. She washed her face and brushed her teeth, turned down the steam-heated radiator, checked the alarm—set for five-thirty as usual. She turned off the light and opened the blackout shade and the window, leaning out, letting the soft kiss of rain fall on her face, letting the moisture-laden air fill her lungs. And when she was in bed, with the covers pulled up to her chin, she stared dry-eyed at the mysterious patterns on the ceiling.

Chapter 27

When the alarm went off Sydney rose quickly, grateful to be out of bed. She tidied the room, dressed, and was downstairs by six-fifteen. The coffee shop was crowded.

Patsy was on duty at the register this morning. She caught Sydney's eye. "Tonight's your night to wait tables," she said. "Did you remember?"

Sydney nodded and sat down at the counter. The scuttlebutt usually spread more quickly. Patsy didn't like her much; that had been clear from the day they arrived in Seattle on the same train. She always spoke as few words to her as possible. But even Patsy would have shown more concern had she heard of Vance's fate.

Sydney ordered her usual toast and coffee, but when it was placed before her she couldn't eat. She sipped the coffee and smoked, and the same thoughts she'd had all night ran through her head. Thoughts of denial and anger and fear. Fear of the future. Damn you, Vance, for marrying me, for bringing me out here, and then for abandoning me.

She didn't realize how long she had sat there until she looked at her watch. She would have to step on it if she was going to make the bus. It never occurred to her that she could miss work, that she could stay in her room today.

As usual Maurie had saved her a seat, but after a word of greeting the older woman must have surmised that something was wrong.

One of the other girls started a song:

Hickory dickory dock,
I'm off to punch the clock.
The clock strikes one,

I've barely begun,
Hickory dickory dock.

Other voices joined in the clever little ditty written by one of
the girls in assembly. Soon the bus rocked with energy.

Hickory dickory dive,
I have to work 'til five.
My dogs'll howl,
My stomach'll growl,
To remind me I'm alive.

Hickory dickory dee,
We work for victor-y.
Though we get dirty,
Our planes are sturdy,
They bomb the en-em-y.

Sydney was grateful for Maurie's silence. Maybe at lunch she
would explain to her friend. But for now she could not speak
the words, as though saying the horrible news out loud would
make it true. And conversely, keeping silent would make it a
lie. Maurie clearly sensed something, however, for Sydney often
caught the concern in her look before she hid it with an offhand
remark.

Remarkably the day passed quickly. Sydney returned to the
hotel, donned the hated hair net, and reported to the coffee shop.
When she finally escaped to her room at ten o'clock, she was
asleep before her head hit the pillow.

Sydney existed that way until Wednesday—eating, sleeping
when she could, when she was so exhausted that her body demanded it, and working. Kay and Faith checked on her each
evening but their kindness became an unbearable intrusion.
When she didn't come down to the dining room or coffee shop
for dinner, Faith would knock on the door to see if she'd eaten
in her room. Over her protests that she wasn't hungry, the
younger woman would bring her food, sitting with her, forcing
her to eat.

On Wednesday as she was leaving the plant she noticed a man
waiting beside the gate near the bus. He was dressed in civilian
clothes but had the bearing of a military man. He approached
her. "Mrs. Bingham?"

"Yes?"

"Do you remember me?"

Dear God, how could she ever forget this man? The sight of Admiral Cleveland brought home the truth as nothing else had. "Yes."

"I have a car. May I give you a lift to your hotel?"

Her coworkers were leaving the building in a stream, which separated, then remerged, as though they were a minor obstruction. A few looked on curiously as they passed. Maurie lingered nearby. Sydney shot her a look, then returned her attention to the man. "Thank you, no, I'm with a friend."

"I'd be happy to give her a ride as well."

"I doubt that she'd want to ride with you any more than I do. Why aren't you in uniform, Admiral?"

He reached into his breast pocket for his wallet and opened it, taking out an identification folder. "I have a new job now."

Sydney studied the folder he held out to her. Studied it carefully. Office of the Coordinator of War Information. She had no idea what it meant and didn't really care. She returned the folder to him.

"Admiral Cleveland," she acknowledged wearily, "what do you want from me?"

"May we talk in the car?" He turned to Maurie. "Would you like to join us?"

"No, thank you," said Maurie after a glance at Sydney. "I have to stop at the market on the way home. I'll take the bus."

He nodded. Then he held out his hand in a courtly gesture to indicate that Sydney should precede him to the dark sedan at the curb. When she was settled in the backseat, he waved the driver on and came right to the point. "Mrs. Bingham, I'm sincerely very sorry for your loss. I'm here to go through any papers your husband might have left with you."

She met his chilly gaze. "With or without my permission?"

"With it, I hope."

Sydney didn't think she stood a chance in hell of winning a battle with this man, but, unexpectedly, she found that she wanted to give it a try. After all the intelligence types had put her through, it was constitutionally impossible for her to hand over everything of Vance's without question. "I'll write to my husband's lawyer," she said.

"Mrs. Bingham, it's your patriotic duty to—" he began.

Her head whipped around; she pinned him with her green gaze. "Don't give me that patriotic duty shit, Admiral," she said through clenched teeth. "It was my duty to work for the war effort and yet you almost lost me my job. You questioned my friends and fellow workers. You made my employer suspicious, you threatened my marriage, and your navy let my husband—'' She broke off.

He leaned back in his corner of the car and let the silence stretch for a long time. As they entered the city and neared the hotel he finally spoke again. "We could get the prototypes from New Orleans, but those were designed for surface vessels. When the ship went down, all of the plans for the conversion of the device to aircraft use, all his notes, everything went with it. Let me ask you something, Mrs. Bingham. How's the security at the hotel?''

She shrugged. "We have at least two people in the lobby at all times. They have a direct line to the police station.''

"That wouldn't stop a really smart thief. What if someone broke into your room and stole your husband's notes? Would you consider that patriotic? For the enemy to get their hands on a device that has proved as successful as the Vocat?''

"The what?''

"Your husband's radio device. That's what we call it. Any fifth columnist could walk in there, go up the stairs, and pick the lock on your door. It is criminally negligent for you to have those notes in a room where a bobby pin could probably open the door,'' he admonished. "If you don't have a sense of responsibility, the navy does. The notes will be safer in our hands.''

"I thought you were out of the navy. Office of the Coordinator of War Information, wasn't that what I read? Fancy name for a dirty job, isn't it, Admiral?''

He acknowledged the thrust with a nod of his head and corrected his previous statement. "In the hands of the federal government.''

"I'll ask my husband's lawyer,'' she repeated.

"Mrs. Bingham, your lawyer has been instructed not to interfere with this.''

"Oh, really?'' she said sarcastically. Then she thought for a minute. "And I suppose the patent office has no record of any of my husband's inventions ever being registered.''

He was quiet, which gave her the answer. She thought for a minute. What he'd said about Vance's notes being stolen had made her stop and consider. "The testing was a success?'' she asked quietly after another minute.

"Yes, it was. We were able to save two of the devices. We can reproduce them, given time."

"Vance said there wasn't much time."

"That's what I've been trying to tell you!" he said impatiently. He took in a long breath in a visible attempt to calm his temper. "We have the materials, we have a plant lined up, ready to go into production; but we don't have the completed plans. If he left notes with you, Mrs. Bingham, we may save some of that time."

The car drew up to the entrance to the hotel. She reached for the door handle, but he stopped her with a hand on her arm. His fingers were like steel; his eyes were the color of thunderclouds. "And you will be a very wealthy woman," he finished coldly.

She felt the grief hit her in a wave. The guilt followed, threatening to drown her. "You really are a bastard, Admiral," she whispered. Her voice was harsh when she spoke again. "Come with me."

She led him inside and ignored him when he would have headed for the stairs. His double take was almost comical when he realized she wasn't headed in that direction. She knocked on a door behind the registration desk and opened it without waiting for a response. He joined her in time to hear her ask, "Valerie, I have some things in the safe that I'd like to get out and present to this gentleman. Will you open it please?"

It gave her a great deal of pleasure to thrust the notebooks into his hands and say, "I'm not a dummy, Admiral Cleveland." She thought Vance would have laughed.

Kay and Faith met in the lobby. Their first greetings to each other, as always, were tense. "Have you heard anything?" "No, have you?" They knew from reports that both Bill and Cody had gotten their planes off the ship. But that was all; further information was sketchy and slow in coming. She and Kay had made a pact—to stay busy and not to dwell on the worst—until they had definite facts. But it was hard. So very hard.

Faith hugged the children and they went upstairs to change into play clothes. "You're home early for a change," she said to Kay.

"Yes, thank goodness," Kay answered with a smile. "The kids had almost forgotten who I was. I thought we'd have dinner together. Can't you join us?"

"I'm sorry," said Faith. "We're shorthanded; I promised

I'd be back in time to help with dinner.'' She laughed without humor. "Sometimes I feel as though I should move my clothes."

Kay shook her head ruefully. Faith worked mornings in the office of the hospital and evenings as a volunteer on the wards. Her afternoons, when she wasn't teaching a sewing class at the Y or selling war bonds and stamps at various places around the city, were the only free time she had. And during those times, like all the rest of them, she was nervy, jumping at the sound of the telephone or a knock at the door. She had lost weight that she didn't have to lose.

"Maybe this weekend?" Kay said.

"Definitely," said Faith as she waved good-bye.

Kay was hailed by Valerie before she made it to the stairs.

"Kay, may I have a word with you?"

"Certainly, Valerie. How is Jordan? Have you heard from him?" she asked.

Valerie's brow wrinkled in a worried frown. "I had a letter a few days ago, written by a nurse. They keep assuring me he's all right."

"And the hotel? Everything seems to be going well."

"Yes, since I got a few things reorganized, I've had no problems." Valerie realized what she'd said. "I didn't mean—"

"Of course, you didn't," interrupted Kay. She wanted to get this conversation over with as quickly as possible. She wanted to get upstairs, out of her uniform, and into something comfortable. She wanted to talk to her children. "What can I do for you?"

"It's about Sydney. I thought it might be best coming from you. We have a long waiting list, as you know. And now that Vance is . . ."

"Dead," Kay supplied quietly.

Valerie's chin came up. "She must find another place to live as soon as possible."

And you don't want the unpleasant assignment of telling her so. Kay dreaded to be the one, but better she than Valerie. If Faith got home early enough she could help soften the blow by her presence.

"I'll tell her." She glanced at her watch. "She probably isn't home from work yet. Will after dinner be soon enough?"

"That will be fine," said Valerie.

As Kay started up the stairs she heard Edna call Valerie to the telephone. "She says it's important, Mrs. Adair."

* * *

Faith hurried up the street toward the hospital. As she entered through the double doors, she was stopped by the ward nurse going off duty. "Faith, you live at the Elysium, don't you?"

"Yes, with my brother's family. Why? Has something happened?"

"They've brought in a Lieutenant Adair off the hospital ship from Honolulu. He's in pretty bad shape. We've notified his wife that he's here. I thought someone who knows her ought to be with her when she sees him. Do you mind?"

She had to bite back a protest. Valerie, of all people . . . but "pretty bad shape" wasn't the news they'd all heard. "Of course I don't mind. What room is he in?"

"He has a private room. 206."

"I'll go right up. Can you tell me—how bad is it?"

"It's very bad indeed. They had to amputate his left leg. The burns along that side of his body and face are extensive."

"Oh, God." The news was like a blow. And one Valerie wouldn't be prepared for, either.

"He really looks bad," the nurse added. "So prepare yourself and please, be careful how you react."

Faith hurried up the steps to the second floor. The door to room 206 was ajar, and she pushed it inward. A nurse stood by the bed with her hand on his wrist. As Faith approached the bed the woman looked up.

"I'm a friend," explained Faith. She steeled herself to look at Jordan. One eye was swollen shut, but the light of recognition gleamed in the other.

"Faith?" His voice was husky but stronger than she expected it to be.

The nurse released his hand and plucked a pencil out of her hair to make a notation on the chart at the end of the bed. She spoke softly as she passed Faith. "He's extremely weak. Please don't tire him."

Faith nodded her understanding. "Yes, Jordan, it's Faith." She moved to take the nurse's place beside the bed and took his hand in hers. "Valerie's on the way," she said softly. "She should be here any minute."

He winced. "Faith, this is Annie Winkler. She came all the way from Hawaii with me."

Faith noted that Annie was young and pretty and blushing at the warmth in his voice. "Hi, Annie. Do you mean that you left the beautiful beaches of Waikiki just to hold his hand?"

"I swept him off his feet," said Annie.

"Foot," corrected Jordan. "We might as well begin to call things as they are. Annie's on duty aboard the hospital ship but they let her come with me for a few hours. Sometimes it pays to have a senator for a father."

Annie made a sound something like a snort. "But you won't let us tell him the truth about your condition."

"Your father doesn't know?" asked Faith.

"He knows I was hurt, that's all. My father has bigger things to worry about." Jordan turned so he could see her more clearly. "Do something for me?"

"Of course," answered Faith.

"Meet Valerie outside. Try to explain—to prepare her. She doesn't handle these things well."

Faith nodded. "All right, Jordan." She left the room.

Valerie got off the elevator a few minutes later, looking for once as though she'd dressed hurriedly.

Biting down on her distaste for the woman, Faith walked down the hall to meet her. "Valerie. I'm very sorry about Jordan."

"Where is he?" Valerie demanded.

Instead of answering Faith took her arm and guided her to one of the lounge areas. "He asked me to wait for you, to explain," she said gently.

Valerie's voice rose; she was on the verge of hysteria. "You? Why on earth would he ask that? And of you?"

"Get hold of yourself!" With an effort Faith controlled her own voice. She tried to speak calmly. "Jordan was worried that you might be—that you would need someone. You should be prepared, Valerie. He's very seriously injured."

"They said that when they called." Her hysteria was under control but barely. "I don't know why I wasn't told the extent of his injuries before."

Faith watched her twisting her fingers with such force she wondered why they didn't break. She shouldn't enter Jordan's room in this condition. Faith didn't give a damn about Valerie, but Jordan had been through hell. "Jordan wanted it that way."

"Where is he?" Valerie demanded again, harshly.

"Valerie, please—"

She sliced the air with her hand. "No more talking! You have nothing to say that I want to hear. Now, where is my husband?"

Faith sighed. "This way."

The nurse was leaving the room. Faith reached out to touch her forearm, letting her appeal show in her eyes. The nurse nodded slightly in understanding and stopped just outside the door.

Valerie stopped, too. "I'll see him alone," she said imperiously.

Faith looked her straight in the eye. "I don't think that's a good idea."

Valerie returned her stare and it was Faith who dropped her eyes first.

The door whispered shut behind Valerie. Faith put her fingers to her lips and waited. And waited. Finally she turned to the nurse. "Maybe it's going to be all—"

Her words were cut off by a choked cry. The door swung back against the wall with a violence that shook the floor beneath her feet. "Oh, God!"

The nurse reacted before she could move, shoving Valerie out of the way in her haste to reach her patient's bedside. "He's passed out. Get the doctor," she ordered sharply. "And then get that fool out of here."

Valerie was already out of the room; she had collapsed against the corridor wall. Faith didn't spare her a glance. She raced down the corridor to the nurse's desk. And the rest of the evening was a blur. Doctors and nurses, oxygen equipment, syringes.

Faith berated herself a dozen times for letting Valerie go into the room alone. Now her reaction had thrown him back into critical condition. Jordan had asked a favor of her, and she had let him down. And it looked as though she might never have the chance to apologize. Jordan's heart was still too weak from the effects of his injuries to take such a shock.

Faith finally had to return to her own duties on the fifth floor, but periodically she ran downstairs to check on Jordan's condition. At eight o'clock, when her shift ended, she went back again to the second floor. She was told that the doctors seemed to have him stabilized, but he was unconscious.

Annie hadn't left. Another woman in white now stood where she had stood, fingers on his pulse, but Annie watched. She glanced up when Faith looked in.

Tears swam in her pretty brown eyes, but there was a look of wry amusement on her face when she joined Faith in the hallway. "If we could turn that woman loose on the Japanese we could win this war in a month. Does she have any idea the damage she's done?"

Faith shook her head. "Probably not. She's the senator's daughter-in-law. She doesn't think much beyond that."

"Well, keep her out of here until he's stronger. He's a hell of a man and I don't want him to go through this again."

Faith smiled sadly. "I'll try but I don't know how much luck I'll have."

"Just try. Jordan didn't talk about her much but she wasn't at all the kind of woman I expected his wife to be. He is so wonderful. All the nurses on the ship had crushes on him. I have to leave, to go back to the ship now. I'm happy to have met you," she ended politely.

"I'm happy to have met you, too, Annie. Thank you for your concern."

"One other thing. Now that I've seen his wife I'm not sure I should have promised not to call his father. He's going to need someone to support him through this but he made me give my word."

"I'll call him myself."

"Not unless it becomes necessary," warned Annie. "It would upset him even more."

"Not unless it becomes necessary," promised Faith. On her way back to the hotel that evening her thoughts returned to Cody. What if he'd been seriously injured like Jordan? Oh, God! Why hadn't they *heard* anything?

Chapter 28

Anger was the overwhelming emotion Valerie felt as she left the hospital. Pure, unadulterated rage. This horrible thing didn't have to happen. Jordan didn't even have to be on that damned ship!

Valerie ignored her surroundings, the people she passed who turned to look at the distraught woman, as she strode along the sidewalk. She paid no notice to her direction.

God! He looked awful. Revulsion replaced anger. The side of his face, all raw and repulsive. And his leg . . . that well-muscled, strong leg. Gone. Left somewhere in the ocean as food for the fish. Tiny teeth gnawing at the flesh. Or big teeth, big jaws snapping it up in one bite, chewing—did fish chew?—spitting out the bones.

She felt the muscles in her throat working to heave and swallowed the vile taste of her own vomit. There were no tears on her cheeks or in her eyes, but her expression was bitter and resentful.

What was she going to do? God, help me, she prayed as she walked faster and faster.

Finally after several blocks she slowed her pace and, with the slackening, felt her body become sluggish. She stopped for a minute, leaning against a lamppost to regain her breath. Her thoughts were astir within her brain, refusing to settle into any kind of organized reason.

What had happened to her, to Valerie Adair, who could handle any situation? Who had deliberately and with determination forged a pretty girl with ambition to be more into a woman of unmistakable consequence? She'd done everything she was supposed to do. Everything.

It was the shock of course, and it would pass.

A scratchy voice, like an old gramophone record, asked if she was all right. Valerie raised her eyes to see an elderly woman, her eyes squinting, her skin marred by lines. She was dressed in clothes Valerie wouldn't have used to scrub the toilet with.

Valerie straightened. "Leave me alone."

The woman said something crude and moved on.

God, the people on the streets nowadays.

Valerie looked around, confused. How had she gotten here? A taxi, she needed a taxi. No, she forgot. Taxis were scarce. These days she had to take the bus. She walked another block to the corner and stood there, waiting. A bus came and she looked up to read its destination. It wasn't going where she wanted to go. She heaved a sigh and got on anyway. She received a few curious looks when her toe caught on a loose piece of floor matting and she stumbled. She grabbed the upright pole and caught herself. She returned the ill-mannered stares with an imperious one of her own and found a seat near the rear door.

The bus filled quickly and people were packed into the aisles, hanging on to the handrails above their heads, working people, dirty people. Valerie tried not to breathe.

The bus reached the end of the line. The driver stood and reached above his head to turn a hand crank, changing the sign on the front of the bus. Street names rolled by until the sign registered his new destination. "You getting off, lady?"

He had raised his voice unnecessarily. She could hear him perfectly well now that the bus was cleared of people. She wished that the smell of them could be cleared out as easily. "No, I'm going into town."

He lit a cigarette. "You got on the wrong bus then. I'm taking a break. Won't be leaving for another fifteen minutes."

The bus was parked in the lot of a nearby diner with the windows painted over. She had no intention of going inside. "I'll wait," she said.

The driver shrugged and turned away. He heaved his bulk down the steps and entered the building, leaving her alone with her fears.

For fifteen minutes. That was all. After fifteen minutes she would no longer be alone in the bus. The silence wouldn't seem so heavy. People would board. Conversations would begin. She could focus on another subject. Maybe in less time than that. Surely the riders would begin to gather soon. She would only have to deal with solitude for a brief time.

The sound of a footstep on the gravel outside caught her grateful attention. Thank goodness. Someone was coming. She watched the door expectantly. After a few seconds she realized that whoever it was wasn't going to get on, not immediately. It took only one more instant for her to realize that she was vulnerable, sitting here alone. There wasn't another soul around.

She remembered the warnings about crime in Seattle. Why hadn't the driver left his inside lights on?

The blackout, of course.

But she felt so exposed sitting here alone. She gripped her purse tighter in her lap.

Another footstep and, in the faint light from the stars, she saw a big male hand grasp the pole to pull himself aboard. She caught her breath.

He was just a boy. Just a boy, thank God. He took the seat behind where the driver sat. Valerie trembled with relief.

A light was still burning beneath Valerie's door. Faith had gone first to her own room to change out of her uniform and splash some cold water on her face. But Valerie had to be seen to. She felt a responsibility toward the woman. So she'd put on a fresh dress and gone upstairs.

Faith knew as soon as Valerie opened the door that she had been drinking.

"Come in, come in." Speaking slowly and slurring her words she offered Faith a brandy.

Faith declined. "Don't you think you should get some sleep, Valerie? You need to be more yourself when you visit Jordan tomorrow."

Valerie looked uncomfortable. "I thought I'd wait for a few days before I go back to the hospital."

"Don't you think you should try to undo some of the damage you've done tonight?" asked Faith, gently and with what compassion she could muster. She did feel sorry for the woman.

The suggestion only triggered Valerie's hysteria again, and the scene that followed was almost a repeat of the scene in the hospital. The fear and revulsion, and the anger, were back. Faith wished with all her heart she'd not come here.

The brandy bottle was still sitting out. Faith managed to get another hefty slug down Valerie and watched her pass out. She covered her with a blanket before escaping thankfully.

Sydney felt the first crack in her demeanor as she dressed for work Thursday morning. She fought it like mad.

She was going to have to leave the hotel. Kay had been kind last night and Sydney was grateful that she had been the one to break the news instead of Valerie; but the notice was the final blow in a devastating week. She hadn't needed to be told that there was a long waiting list for rooms in the hotel; there always had been, and rules were rules. But where in the hell was she going to live?

She and Maurie entered the plant as usual together. The pieces of the huge shiny monster they were working on lay in disarray, scattered in corners, across the floor, impotent and vulnerable. They would give it life, assembling its various parts, watching as it took shape like a broken giant, re-formed and deadly.

"See you at lunch," said Maurie as they separated.

Sydney inhaled a long breath, as though to restore her purpose at the same time she filled her lungs and climbed the stairs to the spot on the wing where she would be working today. The riveting gun was steady in her hands as she worked through the morning. Each tiny bit of metal was set as though the entire war depended on the perfection of her job. As indeed it did, she realized.

Her conception of working for the war effort had never been vague, but since last week there was new meaning to each task she performed. Perhaps you had to be touched personally before you truly understood the meaning, the dreadful importance of the work.

Almost imperceptibly, her hand wavered, but it was enough to send her rivet off at an angle. Mr. Nicholson walked by at that moment. "Damn it, Bingham, what the hell have you done?" he yelled. He called out to a man who was working nearby. "Steed, come over here and fix this." Sydney was numb. Carefully, she put the gun down and looked around for Maurie.

She headed toward the fuselage, her only thought to find her friend. There were too many shadows inside the tunnellike structure. "Maurie," she said hesitantly, standing at the opening.

Maurie turned, the ready smile on her face. "What are you doing here? It isn't time for lunch yet."

When Sydney didn't answer, Maurie moved closer, out of the shadows. "Is something wrong, Sydney?" She guided Sydney to a bench nearby and forced her to sit. "You're as white as a sheet, honey. Can I help?"

When Sydney didn't answer she asked, "Is it something to do with that man who came by here yesterday?"

She shook her head and looked at her friend, dry-eyed. "I have to move from the hotel," she said. "Do you have any rooms?" It was a moot question but she asked it anyway. Maurie also had a waiting list as long as her arm.

"Why?"

She exhaled from between rounded lips and covered her face with both hands. Her voice was muffled. "Maurie, a man came to the hotel on Monday. He was a chaplain. He said that Vance was dead. It isn't true, of course. They even had him on the wrong ship."

A soft moan escaped from Maurie's lips; she rolled her eyes. "Oh, God, no." Her brow furrowed; her arms came around Sydney and she held on tightly. The way Sydney worded the statement told Maurie a lot more than the statement itself. The denial was obvious. "Oh, God, dear and precious Jesus, please—please—please." She rocked Sydney, much as Sydney remembered being rocked by her mother. But that was many years ago. Her mother was dead, wasn't she? No, it was Vance who was dead. Vance.

Pictures floated to the surface of her mind, pleasant pictures of green and white cotton fields and daisies blooming near the back porch, of smiles and laughter. She closed her eyes and gave herself up to the comforting sensations. She let the tears come because they were happy tears, joyous tears, and they healed her aching heart.

Sydney noticed the silence first. When she opened her eyes she looked around to find herself in her room at the hotel. She couldn't clearly recall how she got back there. There was a blur of impressions . . . the blackout shade was drawn, so it must be nighttime. Faith sat in a chair beside the bed reading a magazine.

"Faith? What are you doing here?"

Faith smiled slightly at the impatience in Sydney's tone. "Waiting for you to wake up. You fainted at the plant. Your friend, Maurie, called us. We brought you back here. Do you remember anything?"

"I remember the car." She struggled to sit up straight with her back against the headboard. "This is crazy. I've never fainted in my life."

"You fainted, all right." Faith paused. "Things finally caught up with you."

Memory returned. The reality of what had happened finally

took hold. "Yes, I guess they did," she said softly. "Thank goodness for Maurie."

"She said to tell you not to worry about a place to live. I liked her."

Sydney's eyes swam with gratitude. "I like her, too. She's very special."

"Are you hungry? It's way past dinnertime but I could run down to the coffee shop."

"No." Sydney shook her head. "Faith, would you—could we talk about it now?"

The whole story was told again, and this time Sydney made herself listen and ask questions. Both women wept quietly while they talked. Finally Sydney grasped the terrible facts. On September 15 the *Shiloh* had been escorting a large supply convoy bound for Guadalcanal in the Solomon Islands. The carrier had been attacked once that day by a submarine. The planes had made several hits and were back aboard to refuel. The Japanese took advantage of the low cloud cover and came in from the opposite direction the second time. The patrol planes didn't see them until too late.

The Japanese bombers didn't score, but the fighters and torpedo planes did, three times, igniting fires that spread like lightning. The pilots got as many of the planes off the deck as they could before the ship went down.

Sydney wasn't able yet to think about the way Vance died. She couldn't face the idea of the flames, the smoke. They talked about Vance as she'd last seen him.

"He was such a kind man," Faith said. "We all liked him very much."

"Oh, Faith, I wish I'd gotten pregnant. A baby would have been something real to hang onto; now there's nothing left of him."

"That's not true. You'll have your memories. A man doesn't really die if he's remembered."

Faith's statement was uttered so vehemently that Sydney looked at her. "Cody? Did you say he was all right?"

"The planes scattered to land when and where they could. Some of the men haven't been heard from yet."

"But this is almost November."

"I know," said Faith quietly.

"You have to hold on to your hope. Bill and Cody are top-notch pilots. I'm sure they're okay."

Faith blinked back the tears in her eyes. "You're comforting me?" she asked with a small smile.

Sydney let her head drop to her chest. She didn't answer. Instead she swung her legs off the bed. "I need to wash my face. Excuse me for a minute, will you?" She went into the bathroom and closed the door.

Faith stared at the door but what she really saw was Cody's wonderful face. She missed him so much. She longed to see again his mischievous smile, his devilish wink, to feel his arms, warm and strong and comforting, around her. She and Kay had called every person they knew who might conceivably have news of the pilots from the ship but they'd had no luck at all.

Kay, too, was showing the effects of apprehension. She went about her duties with the same efficiency, but her actions and her responses were becoming mechanical. Faith felt as if this heaviness within her breast was a permanent part of her now. If only they could hear something; if only they—

Sydney emerged from the bathroom. She had washed her face and combed her hair. Her eyes were still red-rimmed but they were clear. She went to sit in the easy chair. "It's scary how quickly the world can change. Vance—gone, Bill and Cody— who knows where, and Jordan—injured." She looked up suddenly. "Jordan is all right, isn't he?"

Faith couldn't disguise her dismayed reaction to the innocent question.

"He's not dead, too?"

"No, no. I don't think you want to hear this just yet, Sydney. You need some sleep."

It was odd but Sydney felt remarkably strong. "I'd like to know it all. Please, Faith."

Faith sighed. "We knew from the chaplain that Jordan was hurt, but we didn't know how badly," she told Sydney. "He was sent first to Tripler," she said, not wanting to discuss the subject of Valerie just yet. She was still too filled with anger.

Sydney had heard of the huge army hospital on the island of Oahu in Hawaii. They often had patients transferred from there. "First?"

"He's in the hospital here."

"Here? But surely . . ."

"Tripler is overflowing with wounded. His father arranged it. He wanted him on the mainland. He wanted him at Walter Reed," she said, naming another army hospital, this one in Washington, D.C.

"I can understand that."

"Jordan wouldn't go. He doesn't want his father to know the extent of his injuries. He isn't doing well, Sydney. And now the doctors won't let him be moved again."

Sydney leaned forward. "You mean he's critical? Have you seen him?"

Faith wet her lips. "Yes, dear God, I've seen him," she answered. "He's badly burned."

"No, oh, no! Poor Jordan." Sydney hurt deep within for him, hurt so very much.

"One side of his face. The doctors say plastic surgery will help but it might take a long time and several operations."

Like a lot of people, Sydney didn't understand plastic surgery. To her it was voodoo—a tool that aging women used to hide their advancing years. "If it will help . . ."

"And he lost a leg, Sydney."

"Oh, Lord!"

"I'm going to make a request, Sydney. Please know that it's hard for me." Sydney waited. "I want you to go and see him."

Sydney's sympathy and pain turned to disbelief that Faith could ask such a thing. She shook her head slowly. "Me? Why?"

"Sydney, listen. He needs you."

"No, no." Sydney continued to shake her head. "Valerie will be there."

Faith made one more stab. "I know about you and Jordan, Sydney. I know that he once meant a lot to you," she finished.

Sydney was silent but her expression betrayed her violent reaction to Faith's words.

"Remember that day in Pike's Market? It wasn't long after we got to Seattle. I overheard the conversation you had with him."

"You never said anything," Sydney said softly.

"It wasn't any of my business. But, Sydney, he needs someone now. He desperately needs someone. It could be you."

"No. Let his wife give him the comfort he needs. I can't go."

Faith stood with an impatient movement. She took a few steps away from the bed then spun to face Sydney again. "Listen to me," she demanded. She told of the incident at the hospital, of Valerie's reaction to her husband's injuries. She chose her words carefully. "You and I have grown accustomed to such injuries. We've both seen men burned before. We know that the swelling and redness of such an injury often makes it seem worse than it is.

"That bitch took one look at him and ran out of the room as though the hounds of hell were after her. I wish they were."

Sydney was horrified that Valerie could respond that way, no matter how Jordan looked. "I can't. I just can't. Don't you see, Faith. It would be disloyal. Vance was my husband."

"And at one time in the past you were in love with another man. Is guilt your only reason?" demanded Faith harshly. "Because if that's all it is, then you might remember this. Jordan Adair pulled your husband out of the fire. He tried to save Vance's life. Though he wasn't successful, he was injured very badly in the attempt. I think Vance would be the first one to encourage you to help the man."

"I can't," Sydney repeated dully.

"I'm really disappointed in you, Sydney," said Faith, and she left the room.

Chapter 29

Valerie couldn't hide the revulsion she felt from Jordan. She tried, she tried very hard, but she wasn't successful. She was aware of that every time she met his eyes, saw the hurt there.

When she suggested that his father should know the extent of his injuries, Jordan fiercely rejected the idea. His anger was formidable, so she apologized and assured him that she wouldn't go against his wishes.

She tried to converse with him. There was simply nothing to say. She couldn't discuss her feelings. And Valerie was discovering that if she couldn't talk about herself she had very little to say. She purposely buried the frightening revelation that she was really so self-centered.

At Faith's prodding she went to the hospital every day for a week before Jordan finally asked her not to come back. Using the excuse that he knew she was very busy with her duties at the hotel and he was being well cared for, he suggested they talk on the telephone instead.

Her initial feeling was one of reprieve; shock followed. Her own husband not wanting to see her. She'd thought, after the first day, she was hiding her reaction well for the length of time she was in his room. Evidently not.

And whenever she escaped that awful building, her hands began to shake and her stomach, to heave. The brandy helped, but still she felt as though she were balancing on the edge of a very sharp knife. Should she stumble or falter, her composure would be severed from her as clearly as a piece of fruit from the vine.

This afternoon she walked out of the hospital with a feeling of having been released from jail. She didn't have to return! She should have felt grief or guilt that she'd been banished from her husband's hospital room; but she didn't, only an extraordinary, overwhelming sense of freedom.

She was almost vivacious when she returned to the hotel. Her smile was genuine as she greeted Jimmy McCoy.

"The lieutenant must be a whole lot better today, Mrs. Adair," he commented. "I haven't seen you so happy in a long time."

Jimmy had been sympathetic and helpful. He was such a dear boy. "I think he's improved," she answered ambiguously. "I'll run upstairs and put my things away, then we can get to work."

In her room she changed her shoes for a pair with flat heels and had a tiny sip of medicinal brandy, just to keep her spirits up.

Her high energy lasted for only a short while. As the afternoon dragged on, her good mood flagged. She was working on the books when she came across the check for the remainder of Sydney Bingham's rent.

Until that moment Valerie had given no thought to the future. She had felt it was a major victory for her to get through each day. But suddenly the realization hit her that Jordan would go home to the Chicago suburbs as soon as he was well enough to travel. And she would have to go with him.

The chaplain had said that Jordan was going to get a medal of some kind for heroism. She would have to play the part of a committed, dutiful wife. She wondered if those who knew her well would see through her. Like her parents, and Peg, her best friend.

When Patsy finally arrived to take over for the evening she was grateful. As she gathered up the books to work on upstairs she had the fanciful illusion that she was floating in a mist of befuddlement, one from which she couldn't break free. She was tempted to leave the book work until morning. No, running the hotel competently was evidence of her stability, the only task at the moment that she knew she was performing well.

Patsy Cabot was the one who came to Kay and Faith and asked for their help. She explained that Valerie had been drinking heavily—or more heavily than usual—and that, on any number of occasions, she hadn't shown up for work.

"She hadn't been in at all today and I can't get her to answer the door."

Faith frowned angrily. She was wearing loose-fitting slacks and she shoved her doubled fists into her pockets to hide them. "I was afraid of something like this happening to her. Jordan won't let us notify his father of his injuries. His condition is not improving. Some rational person in his family needs to know what he is going through.''

Kay spoke up. ''Let's go see if between the three of us we can reason with Valerie.''

After nearly five minutes of knocking and calling, Valerie finally answered the door. Kay and Faith were stunned into silence at the sight of the woman before them. Patsy didn't seem as surprised.

Valerie's lipstick was smeared, her eyes red. The elegant robe she wore was a wrinkled mess, barely tied across her nudity. Her hair, always carefully arranged, hung in damp strings over her cheeks and down her neck, its beautiful blond color now a dirty ash.

When she saw who they were she made a farcical effort at straightening herself. She must have realized that the effort was futile for she allowed her hand to fall back to her side. Faith had to give her credit for an attempt at dignity when she threw up her chin, inquiring in a tone heavy with frost, ''What can I do for you?'' Her enunciation was too precise for sobriety.

Kay found her voice first. ''We have to talk to you, Valerie.''

''Not now. It isha—isn't convenient.''

The smell of whiskey and stale cigarette smoke was so strong Kay almost reeled. She took a step forward, but Valerie stood her ground. ''I tol' you—''

''This won't wait,'' said Kay. ''We . . .'' Her words trailed off as a soft, sleepy groan emanated from within the room.

''Val, honey?''

There was a moment of dead silence. When Kay spoke again it was with barely controlled fury. ''I'll give you five minutes to get that man out of your room and get dressed, Valerie. Then we are going to talk.''

Valerie looked from Kay to Faith to Patsy and back again. ''You wan' him out? You get 'im out,'' she said flatly and turned to weave her way toward the bathroom.

''Faith, you wait out here,'' said Kay.

''Are you kidding? What for?''

''He is probably drunk and naked.''

''Christ, Kay. I am not sixteen anymore,'' countered Faith, rolling her eyes heavenward. She would have laughed if it hadn't been so ridiculous. Kay was still trying to be protective.

Kay took a deep breath. ''Okay, come on.''

It didn't take long to get rid of the man. He took one look at the three women who entered, correctly read the hostility in their faces, and dived for his trousers.

When he was gone Kay crossed to open the windows, letting in blessedly clean air.

Valerie reappeared a few moments later. She had made an effort to wash her face and comb her hair. The robe had been snagged shut and the belt tightly drawn around her waist. "What do you want?" she asked in her old imperious tone, directing the question to Kay.

"I want you to pull yourself together. I want you to resume your duties in the hotel—"

"Patsy has—"

"The hotel isn't Patsy's responsibility alone," snapped Kay. "It is yours, too." Her eyes narrowed and she lowered her voice to a furious snarl. "And I want you to recall that you have a husband. This is the most disgusting performance I've ever seen."

Valerie seemed to deflate at the accusation. She sank heavily on the edge of the tumbled bed.

Faith could see that each of Kay's words was like a whip flailing the woman's skin. As much as she disliked Valerie she felt a measure of pity. The woman had broken. She knew it and now the people who were her peers knew it, too.

Valerie Adair considered herself perfect. She had never been tested before this. When the test came she failed; and she couldn't face her own human flaws. She wept, softly, helplessly. "What do you want me to do?"

"I want you to call Jordan's father. Let him come out here and help you. And Jordan."

"I can't," she whimpered, cowering under the force of the accusation of Kay's voice. The suggestion, instead of offering abatement, seemed to add to her fear. "You don't understand. I can't."

Suddenly something seemed to snap in Kay. She grabbed Valerie by the shoulders and began to shake her. "You bitch!" she spat. "I understand that *your* husband's alive. I don't know about *mine*." Her voice broke and she shook Valerie again, harder. Valerie looked terrified but she offered no protest.

Faith couldn't bear this. She covered her shaking lips with her fingers, then took a step forward and touched Kay's arm. "Honey, come on," she urged huskily, tears stinging her eyes. She knew the pain Kay hid so well; she knew how horribly it hurt. "Come on, Kay. Leave her."

Kay began to cry helplessly. "You coward," she accused, as she released Valerie and went out of the room with Faith. She hadn't meant to cave in like that, but she had felt isolated, defenseless for such a long time. Faith dragged a handful of tissues out of her pocket. Kay took them gratefully.

Patsy followed them into the hall, closing the door behind. "I'm sorry. I'm so sorry, Kay. I didn't mean for you to have to go through that."

Kay swallowed her tears and put up her hand to stop Patsy's apology. "That's all right, Patsy. But I'll tell you what Charles Wagner told me. You'd better learn all you can about running this hotel—and in a hurry."

Chapter 30

Sydney's impulse, once she had accepted the reality of Vance's death, was to escape Seattle, to hop on a train and head for New Orleans. There she could indulge her grief in the comfort of the familiar. But she cautioned herself to go slowly. Instead, the first thing she did, admittedly a stopgap, was to move to Maurie O'Conner's house.

Her second objective would be harder for her. She was going to call at the huge Federal Building downtown, to see the chaplain who had broken the news about Vance.

Clothes were just about the last thing she thought about these days, but for this meeting she dressed carefully. With the advent of rationing they were now restricted to two pairs of shoes a year. Clothing design had undergone a government-mandated change as well. To conserve material there were no cuffs, a limited number of pockets, no pleats or gathered skirts, no unnecessary frills or ruffles.

She had become so accustomed to wearing slacks and loafers or saddle oxfords to work that putting on her old pair of black pumps was torture. But she dressed carefully in a wool skirt, a tailored blouse, and sweater jacket, all in muted colors. She kept her hair short now, so there wasn't enough there to put up, but she tamed it with a smart turban.

Lieutenant Hudson was glad to see her. He stood. "Mrs. Bingham, thank you for coming by. Won't you have a seat?"

Sydney sat in the chair he indicated across the desk from him. "Thank you for seeing me."

"I understand you've moved from the Elysium," he said, resuming his seat. "Does that mean you've decided to stay in Seattle?"

She nodded, amused by his effort at insignificant conversa-

302

tion. "A friend that I work with let me have a room at her house. I'm not sure whether I'll stay permanently or not. Lieutenant Hudson, I need some help."

"Anything I can do, Mrs. Bingham."

She thought for a minute, unsure of her approach. If she was going to get the help she'd requested she was also going to have to tell this stranger more than she wanted him to know. She still wasn't sure. . . . "When you came to see me, was that your first experience in having to break the news to family?" she asked curiously.

"Yes, ma'am," he admitted. "And I botched it badly. First I came to the hotel and you were at the hospital. Then I missed you there. By the time I caught up with you I was afraid someone else might have told you. I wasn't as calm as I should have been and I said all the wrong things in the wrong way. Please accept my apology."

The young man gripped his fingers together on the blotter but he met her eyes straight on. Sydney liked that. She leaned forward. "Lieutenant, you did as well as could be expected. I'm sure it's an awful assignment. You didn't know what the circumstances were. You didn't know that I thought my husband was on another ship entirely."

"Thank you for your absolution. I don't feel I deserve it. If I can't do better I should be in another line of work."

Sydney smiled. "Back home in Mississippi at the Friendship Baptist Church they teach that you don't choose God; God chooses you."

"That's true at the First Presbyterian Church in Portland, too, but perhaps God hadn't counted on World War Two."

"Perhaps not." Sydney settled back in her chair. "I'm here for another reason today. I need your advice."

"Are you sure?" He smiled and Sydney decided she could come to enjoy him. "Of course," he corrected himself. "You are welcome to any help I can give you, Mrs. Bingham."

Sydney gathered her courage. Faith had planted a seed of responsibility within her that really made her think. She had—sort of—consulted Vance about it. Well, not really consulted, just thought about him and the problem at the same time. She shook herself.

"When you're—training, if that's the word—for your job, are you schooled in handling the problems of badly wounded men?"

"Yes, but I should warn you that I haven't had much experience with those problems, either."

Sydney laughed, surprising them both. "Well, I have a feeling we'll learn a lot of things together, Lieutenant." She paused to collect her thoughts. "I have a friend, the man who was burned trying to save my husband."

"Lieutenant Adair."

Sydney was startled for a moment then she smiled wryly. "Oh, of course you would know."

"The captain who is in charge of this office dealt with telling Mrs. Adair."

"The son of a United States senator? I wouldn't have expected less than a captain," murmured Sydney ironically, but another smile curved her lips when she asked in a playful tone, "Is the captain Presbyterian, too?"

"Heavens, no! He's Episcopalian." They laughed together mildly. Then Sydney sobered.

"Well, what I have to say may shock you, Lieutenant."

He waited.

"Lieutenant Adair and I were once lovers. No, let me correct that, we were in love. It was over and forgotten a long time ago. But his wife is taking this badly; she isn't able to help. Now a mutual friend seems to think that because of our past relationship, I can help him. I need to know about his mental condition before I decide whether or not to try."

He opened his mouth to protest, but she held up a hand to stop him. "Not about *his* personal mental condition. But about men like him. I need to know how injuries like this affect a man. I've worked as a volunteer at the hospital, I've seen some badly injured men, and I promise I won't run screaming from the room. But I'd never be able to fool Jordan if I let his appearance upset me." Suddenly she wondered why she was here, if she hadn't made the wrong decision. "And it will." Her voice trailed off; her eyes searched the middle distance.

"Would you like to tell me about it, Mrs. Bingham?" the young man asked quietly.

Sydney looked up. This boy—he wasn't a boy, he was older than she was—was offering her a chance to talk, to unburden herself. She hadn't talked freely since Vance left. Though she knew she was putting on a good front, her emotions were still very much in chaos. Possibly confession would be good for her soul; probably she could do some healing of her own in the process. Her eyes shone with tears. "Yes, I think I would," she whispered.

* * *

Sydney arrived at the hospital at twelve-thirty. Jordan wasn't in a ward; he had been given one of the few private rooms. She hesitated at the door, then pushed it open.

His head was turned away from her and her first thought was, They've lied to me. There's nothing wrong with Jordan. His eyes were closed. She could see the shadow of his lashes on his pale cheek. His profile was clean and unscarred. Her gaze wandered further down his body, covered lightly by a sheet. There was bulk around his left arm, a bandage or a splint of some kind.

Then she saw the outline of his one leg and the awful space where the other one should have been. Her fingers gripped the edge of the door. She inhaled sharply.

The sound brought his face around to her. And she saw the red puffy skin smeared with burn ointment that shone in the faint light allowed through the blinds, the eye swollen shut. His hair was gone, his ear unrecognizable as an ear. The left side of his mouth was drawn down.

It took every bit of the strength Sydney possessed not to cry out when their gazes met. But she had no notion of running from the room. Instead she longed to run toward the bed, to gather his broken body up in her arms and heal his wounds with her tears.

Despite her resolve, pity must have shown in her expression, for he became angry. "What the hell are you doing here?" He slurred his words slightly but his good eye blazed. Maybe the emotion was a positive factor. "Get out," he ordered.

Sydney put on her best teasing grin and strutted across the room. She gave thanks for the chaplain. She would never have been able to do this if he hadn't been so supportive and encouraging. Handle him lightly, he'd said. "Why, Jordan, is that any way to greet an old friend?"

"I want you out of this room, right now." He twisted, reaching for the buzzer to call the nurse; but Sydney was quicker. She snatched it away and put it out of his reach.

"How inhospitable of you, Jordan."

"Sydney, I'm warning you." He continued to struggle.

She went quickly forward to lay a firm hand on his shoulder and felt him tense under her fingers. "Lie still, Jordan, and quit acting like a spoiled child," she said gently. "I'm not going away until I get ready to, so you may as well relax."

The effort of the struggle had exhausted him. "Please," he whispered. He sank back onto the pillow, breathing heavily, and turned his face away. She could see a sheen in his eye as he repeated, "Sydney, please go."

The anger hadn't touched her but the soft plea did. She would have liked to leave him to his misery, knowing how good it felt to be alone when you were in pain. But being alone, drawing into a shell of self-protection, would be the worst thing in the world for Jordan right now. The chaplain had warned against this very situation.

He had also told her not to stay long for this first visit. Let Jordan get used to having her drop in every day for a few minutes, instead of spending hours at his bedside. That would add a sense of anticipation to the long hours he spent in bed.

"Jordan." She tempered her voice. "Look at me."

Slowly he turned his face, his eye defiant, daring her not to cringe.

But Sydney had no feeling for the dare. She had seen other men, if not in worse condition, in a condition at least as bad. True, those men weren't Jordan, but she'd hurt for them. She schooled her features as she'd learned to do and examined his burns with clinical detachment.

He waited for her to comment.

She would never offer him platitudes, he was much too intelligent for those. And she cared too much for this man to offend him by lying. "I understand that they want to do plastic surgery."

"Yes." His voice, the eye that stared up at her were expressionless.

"I don't know much about it but I understand—"

"They can do wonders," he finished for her, the anger back. "It will take a wonder, a miracle of some kind, won't it? I've already scared my wife to death. Doesn't the sight of me make you want to run screaming from the room, Sydney? It does me. Assuming that I could run." He looked down at the sheet, at the flat place where a leg should be.

Sydney remembered the sight of him, striding across Jackson Square in New Orleans, racing to catch the streetcar. He was a physical man who played tennis and golf and ran for the fun of it.

He must have read her thoughts in her eyes, for he turned his head away again.

"Jordan?"

He didn't answer.

She sighed. "I'm going now, but I'll see you tomorrow night. Is there anything you need?"

He was as motionless as a statue, a broken statue, lying helpless and still after being knocked brutally from its pedestal.

She studied his beautiful profile for a long minute, then she picked up her purse and left the room.

A few days later Sydney stood over the telephone in the hotel alcove outside Kay Parker's room. Faith watched as Sydney stared down, dreading the call she had to make. Faith deserved to be pinched for coercing her back to the hotel, for making her do this. Faith, along with all the nurses, had made a promise to Jordan not to call his father. She would be breaking her word, she'd said, whereas Sydney could make the call with a clear conscience.

She had talked to the senator once before when he'd called Jordan's room to check on his son's condition. Jordan had taken the phone from her quickly. Afterward she'd asked him why he didn't tell his father the truth.

"My father and I have never been close," he'd said.

The senator hadn't been rude or anything like that, when she talked to him; but he was clearly an important man, hurried and clipped on the telephone and very, very dignified. Now she had to tell him that they'd all been lying to him.

He answered his own telephone, which threw Sydney into a temporary muddle. When she finally was able to identify herself he responded quickly.

"Certainly I remember talking to you, Mrs. Bingham. Is something wrong? Has something happened to Jordan?"

"Senator, this is a very hard call for me to make. The nurses . . . well, all the people in the hospital made a promise to Jordan. And I'm about to break it." She took a long restorative breath. "Senator, Jordan was more seriously injured than anyone has told you. His condition is not good. I'm afraid that his wife—that Valerie is too distraught to be of much help."

There. That was putting the best face possible on it. Now it was up to him.

He didn't hesitate. "I'll leave immediately, Mrs. Bingham. Or as quickly as I can get a flight."

"I can have someone meet you," she offered, looking at Faith.

"That won't be necessary."

After she hung up she and Faith went back to Kay's room. Kay was waiting. "What did he say?" she asked.

"He's on his way."

Jordan stirred restlessly in the bed. The bandage had been removed from his arm and there was a spot near his elbow that itched, but he was afraid to scratch. He kept having these recurring nightmares that if he touched his skin, moved it at all across the bones and flesh beneath, it would tear like the skin of an overripe tomato and peel away.

His sight was improving. His left eye was open now, still swollen but open. At first, when he closed his good right eye, he had been only able to see light and darkness, but gradually the shapes of the furniture in the room began to reveal themselves. He was relieved that his vision didn't seem to be badly affected.

His father was coming today, and he was torn by the conflicting emotions the senator's impending visit had produced. He told himself his father represented a life that no longer meant anything to him. Chicago seemed a million miles from this place. Thank God.

Jordan didn't think much about the strained relationship between him and his father. Over the years it had developed into a natural condition. He had been seven years old when he had survived the automobile crash that had taken the life of his ten-year-old brother, James.

As a youngster he'd felt that his father blamed him somehow; later he thought the senator was using him to take James's place. In fact as the years passed he came to realize that it was his own illogical guilt that caused him to submit to his father's requirements. The pressure had never been overt. The senator simply told his son what the proper thing to do was, and Jordan did it.

With one exception. No matter how often his father appealed to him to enter politics, Jordan refused to consider it. He'd done all the preparatory work. He'd gone to the right schools, gotten his law degree. He'd married the right sort of woman. He'd been a dutiful son on the campaign trail, smiling for the cameras and murmuring all the right platitudes.

All the time he knew his father was holding out hope that he would change his mind. And somewhere along the way, Jordan realized that he was keeping his options open. That he was moving, if not on, then close to, the path his father had laid down.

It had taken Sydney to open his eyes to what he was doing. She was the only person to whom he had ever voiced his secret dream—that of becoming a writer. She thought it was a great idea, he remembered fondly.

It had taken the time with her in New Orleans to make him realize that, deliberately or not, he was being cruel to his father by not making the break with tradition clean and sharp. All those years he'd unfairly fed his father's expectations, expectations that he had no intention of fulfilling.

An aide came into the room and fussed around, straightening the sheet, checking the intravenous tube that was taped to his wrist. "I understand your father is coming to see you today," she said.

"You shouldn't believe everything you hear. He's a very busy man." Always had been.

She looked at him blankly for a minute, then she giggled. "Oh, you're teasing me."

When she left the room he closed his eyes.

Jordan was half asleep when he heard the stirring in the hall. He was familiar with the phenomenon. The senator had arrived, and when he was close by there was a quickening in the air.

The soft knock was perfunctory, followed by the immediate opening of the door. Who would be the lucky nurse who was allowed to announce the entrance of the great man? Mrs. Anderson's gray hair proclaimed that seniority had won out over beauty. "Lieutenant Adair, you have a visitor," she said brightly. "Your father is here to see you."

Jordan almost laughed aloud. The old battle-ax, who bullied the patients and nurses alike, hadn't spoken in such a cheerful coo since he'd been here. "Thank you, Nurse." There was no need to add anything polite like "tell him to come in." He was already in.

Jordan braced himself. "Father."

The senator approached the bed. "Son." He stood for a moment looking down at his son's maimed body.

He met Jordan's eyes. The moment seemed to stretch into eternity as Jordan kept his peace.

Finally the senator spoke, but the sound was like an echo, a whisper out of a long tunnel. "My son, my son," his voice broke on the words. He shook his head helplessly. "I thank God with all my heart that you're alive." His brows furrowed; his mouth twisted in an expression of grief and regret. Tears wet the old man's cheeks; he made no attempt to hide them. Reaching in his pocket for a handkerchief he turned away slightly, struggling for control. "I'm sorry, Jordan. You deserve more than a coward for a father."

Jordan hadn't realized there was a lump in his throat until he felt it grow to a suffocating size. Not in all his life had he seen his father with all the walls, all the defenses down. If he had shed tears when Jordan's brother died, no one saw them. The facade of senatorial dignity was with him like an aura and he never, but never, lost control of himself like this. For just a brief second, as his father looked away, Jordan had wondered if he were going to react to his injuries as Valerie had. But this was different—his father turned away out of love and an excess of emotion rather than repulsion—and Jordan hadn't realized it would affect him so deeply.

"Dad." He used the childish form of address for the first time in years. He was surprised at how easily it came to his lips. He cleared his throat of his own tears. "I would never consider you a coward."

The senator faced him again. The lines that scored his face were deeper than they had been at Easter recess when Jordan had last seen him. "I need to—would you mind—" He broke off, hearing the uncertainty in his own voice. He started again. "Would it hurt your wounds if I held you in my arms, son?"

Jordan lost his own control at that. He sobbed, once, harshly. He couldn't speak but he did manage to nod his head. And when his father bent over to gather him close, the dam burst, the cold thing that had lived within him for so long. His tears became a catharsis, freeing his horror and his fears.

"Dad! Oh, Dad," he cried against his father's shoulder. His good hand clenched onto the material of his father's sleeve, holding on as though to a lifeline. "God, it was so terrible. The explosions and the fire and the men screaming, parts of them blown away, their clothes on fire, their blood spilling out. It was so thick on the deck, Dad, that it was slippery. You could hardly take a step without falling. I felt so helpless. All I could think about was that five minutes before the sky had been blue, the men had been laughing. If I could only turn back the clock, just an instant, everything would be okay."

"Oh, son. I wish I could turn it back for you."

Jordan pushed against his father's shoulder to look into his eyes. "You do believe in what we're doing, don't you, Dad? We are fighting this war for the right reasons?"

His father looked immeasurably sad. "Son, only history can judge us. I don't believe reason ever enters into war. But this one had to be fought. As God is my witness, I do believe that."

Chapter 31

November 12th, 1942

Kay was behaving like an overeager debutante, always smiling, vivacious, and talkative. She had apologized a dozen times for breaking down over the incident with Valerie.

It was an act, Faith was certain. She was worried about her sister-in-law. She had been able to piece together the story of what happened when the *Shiloh* was attacked off the shores of South America in February from what Kay had told her and things Millie had let slip. It was clear that Kay had been deeply disturbed by her own reaction and had made a promise to herself never again to give in to her fears.

Now Faith couldn't get Kay even to talk about them. She worried that, if Kay's anxiety was allowed to fester, the resulting crisis, when it came, would be devastating.

Faith herself had grown more reflective. Cody was ever in her mind, even when she was busy with other tasks. She felt that as long as she kept him there, he would be alive. Sometimes he occupied a small corner; sometimes he filled her thoughts completely; and frequently, she resented the fact that she had to think of anything else.

It had been almost two months since the death of the carrier on September 15th and almost three weeks since the official announcement of its sinking. She recognized the need for the government's delay in releasing the news. The carrier had been part of a convoy bound for Guadalcanal in the Solomons, and they couldn't release certain information until the convoy reached its destination safely. But it was hard, so hard, for the families of those men.

She and Kay had both sensed in late September that something was wrong; they had talked about it and were amazed that they were both thinking along the same lines. When their fears had been confirmed Kay was reluctant to discuss any further possibilities, as though to do so would jinx the lives of their men. They were behaving very delicately around each other.

They had been given excuses—communication was primitive and slow in some areas of the South Pacific; the search for some of the scattered pilots was still going on—but surely by now the families should have been notified.

Faith wasn't superstitious, but at this point she was willing to try almost anything, even stomping gray mules to ward off bad luck as Billy's grandfather from Nebraska had taught him. Billy had explained the procedure with all the seriousness of a true believer. When you saw a gray mule, you spit in your palm, hit the spot with your other fist, and stomped your foot at the same time.

Her lips curved at the idea of her nephew, upset because there weren't any gray mules in Seattle. Millie had stepped in, suggesting they stomp gray cars instead.

All these thoughts were turning in her brain as she entered the lobby of the hotel. Patsy Cabot stopped her to ask where Kay could be reached. "She's not at work. I saw her come in a few minutes ago, but when I went up, no one answered my knock. I guess she was in the shower or something. Just tell her I need to see her, will you?"

Faith felt the warm blood drain from her face, leaving her features chilled and stiff. "Yes, I'll tell her." Oh, God. Kay's heard something. Faith's hunch was intuitive, irrational, but very real.

She hurried, feet flying, barely touching the stairs. Her fingers were clumsy when she tried to insert her key. Finally she unlocked the door and walked into the room she shared with the children. With steps now suddenly grown leaden she proceeded through the connecting door, wanting to know, not wanting to know.

Kay sat on the edge of the bed, her shoulders straight, her Red Cross uniform as crisp as it had been when she left for work this morning. Her feet were planted precisely parallel on the faded green carpet, her hands rested on her knees. She was a million miles away.

"Kay?" said Faith softly.

Only her eyes moved, and they were huge and lost in her white face.

Faith joined her on the bed. She put her arm around the rigid shoulders. "Tell me," she said.

Kay inhaled, a big, deep breath, and let it out slowly. "Bill is on the Missing in Action list."

Not Bill! Faith trembled. Her brother. But more than brother—he'd been a father to her, too.

Not Bill! Bill was indestructible. She'd never valued him enough, all the things he'd done for her, all the things done out of love. Grief engulfed her, sent tears rushing to fill her eyes, to spill down her cheeks.

Missing in action, not dead, thank God. Missing in action wasn't final; it left you with hope. She grabbed for the hope and held on. "We knew it might take a long time to account for all the planes," she reminded hoarsely.

"Yes. They'll find him surely. I was just sitting here, praying. But I'm not sure it does any good if you aren't in church. Maybe I should go to church to do it."

Faith hesitated. "Do you want me to go with you?"

"Would you?" The huge eyes turned on Faith.

She wanted to retreat from the expression there. "Of course, I will."

Kay stood up. Faith's hand fell to the spread. She looked up at her sister-in-law, unaware of the fear in her own eyes. "Kay, was there . . . did you hear anything about Cody?" Now she felt ashamed, overwhelmingly ashamed; she had worried more about Cody than about her own brother.

Compassion chased away Kay's fear for a brief moment. She squeezed Faith's shoulder and smiled a parody of a smile. "No, there was nothing. There are thousands of islands in that area of the Pacific," she reminded. "And you know what they say about no news."

Faith let out the breath she was unaware she'd been holding.

The children were playing with the Brody boys, Kay and Faith were mending when the knock came. Kay dropped the small pair of pants on the arm of the chair and went to answer.

The young man was dressed in bell-bottomed trousers, the middy top of his uniform exactly correct. He stood at attention.

"Yes, may I help you?" asked Kay.

"Mrs. Parker?" said the young man. His voice broke.

Suddenly Kay wanted to slam the door. She couldn't hear, wouldn't hear the news that Bill was dead.

The young man cleared his throat self-consciously and remembered his hat. He swept it off, disturbing the carefully combed hair. It was the color of Nebraska cornsilk. "Mrs. Bill Parker?" He twisted the cap between his hands.

"Yes, I'm Mrs. Parker." She forced herself to say the right thing. "Would you like to come in, sailor?"

"Oh, no, ma'am. I just came to, uh, deliver a letter to you, ma'am."

"A letter for me?" Her body sagged in relief. He hadn't come to tell her that Bill was . . . she couldn't even think the word.

The boy's cap didn't stand a chance. "From Commander Parker, ma'am."

Kay felt her knees go weak. She felt Faith come to attention behind her.

"He gave it to me just before he took off and made me promise I'd deliver it to you personally. I'm sorry it's taken so long. I didn't get back to the States until this morning."

Kay couldn't bear the pity she saw on his face. "And you came right here. How kind of you."

"I couldn't do any less for the commander, ma'am." He delved into his blouse and came up with a wrinkled envelope, which he tried to smooth out before he handed it to her. "I tried to keep it dry, ma'am, but I'm afraid when I went into the drink it went with me. I dried it out real careful. I hope it's okay."

Kay looked down at the envelope she held between her hands. Her husband's handwriting was barely smeared. She wanted to rip open the envelope, to devour its contents. Instead she forced calmness into her voice, steadiness into her fingers. "It's fine. Thank you very much." She met his eyes, afraid that her emotionless response had offended him. "I mean that."

"Yes, ma'am, I know you do. Wild, er, the commander talked about you a lot. I was a mechanic in his crew and I was real sorry to hear his plane went down. He was a fine man, Mrs. Parker."

Visibly shaken at his use of the past tense, Kay didn't know what to say. Finally she found her voice. "He's only been declared missing, you know. There is still hope that he'll be found alive."

"Yes, ma'am," said the young man after only the briefest pause. "Well, I'll be going now." He turned to leave.

All at once Kay became aware of Faith standing at her shoulder. She had completely forgotten the younger woman's presence when the boy had announced the reason for his call. "Sailor?" she said quickly to stop him.

"Yes, ma'am?"

She let Faith ask. "Do you know an Ensign Cody Bristol? He's a pilot, too, in Commander Parker's group. He was on the *Shiloh*."

"Oh, well most of the planes in the squadron have been assigned to—" He interrupted himself abruptly. "An island base somewhere. You should be hearing from him soon if . . ." This time he let his voice trail off.

"I understand," said Faith flatly, turning away.

The boy seemed embarrassed. "What's your name, sailor?" asked Kay to relieve his anxiety.

"Sorry. It's Andrews, ma'am. Seaman First Class, Mitch Andrews."

"Thank you, Seaman Andrews." She brought forth a smile for the youngster. "Good luck to you. And your family."

He sketched a salute. "Thank *you*, Mrs. Parker."

Kay closed the door carefully. Faith had disappeared into the other room and shut the door. Whether to give Kay the privacy she wanted to read Bill's letter, or to have some time to pull herself together, Kay didn't know. But she was grateful to be alone. She crossed to sit in the armchair and made herself take care in opening the letter. Her fingers were steady now.

Dearest Kay,

I'm not sure when this will reach you. Even though the censors will never see this I won't tell you where we are, only that we are about to take a big step toward turning around this war. Pray God that we're successful.

I'm not much of a letter writer—as you know better than anybody. I'm also not very good at opening up my feelings, you know that, too. But it's time some things are said. It's getting hot in this part of the world. I don't know how it will end, this trip, I mean, not the war. Because we're going to win that. I promise you. I see the dedication, the bravery every day. The kamikaze pilots give their lives without a thought. We think very carefully—but we, too, will make the supreme sacrifice, if necessary. We, however, have more to live for. We want to live to fight another day.

I have the world to live for. I have you and the children. And you are my world. I've never told you how proud I am that you are my wife.

You know, I wanted to propose to you the first night I met you. That may come as a surprise to you—it sure did to me.

I know I had something of a reputation—not all of it deserved, I promise you. But I was a coward. You were so intelligent; you had an inner peace and confidence; and I worried that you wouldn't be attracted to a sky jock, that you'd think I was too shallow.

I was also afraid I'd scare you to death if I told you I wanted to marry you after knowing you fifteen minutes.

Sometimes I'd like to give in to my feelings of inadequacy, to cry in your arms, but, like all men, I guess I feel like I have to keep up a strong front for you and the kids. Men don't want their women to be worried about things, we're too protective, I suppose. But the funny thing is that our women are the strong ones. Maybe it's time we admitted that to ourselves.

Anyway, my darling, the day I found out you were pregnant was the happiest day I can ever remember up to that time of my life. Since that time, of course, you've given me two beautiful children, but my love for you remains the primary force in my life.

Faith is right in a way. I am too stubborn for my own good. I was never able to say these things to you, was afraid you would see flaws in me. I couldn't live with that, with you seeing me as something less than perfect. That's a crazy statement. I'll never be perfect.

I'll end this now. Got to go to work. But I want to make you a promise—no, a vow. After the war, when we're all back together again, I will do everything in my power to be worthy of you and the children you bore me. I haven't vowed anything since our wedding day but I mean this, darling, from the bottom of my heart.

> *I love you,*
> *Bill*

Kay wiped away the tears and sent her frantic glance around the room. Her eyes skimmed the picture of Bill on the dresser, the worn edges of the carpet, the door between the rooms, seeking a place to land. The clock. Oh, God, the clock! The children would be home any minute.

She folded the letter and shoved it into the pocket of her skirt as she headed for the bathroom.

Later, after the children were in bed, she showed the letter to Faith.

"He couldn't be dead, Faith. There is no way his heart could have stopped beating without my being aware of it."

Faith folded the letter carefully along its creases and put it on the dresser. "Kay, you heard what the boy said and I'm grieving, too. Don't you believe that? He was my brother and I loved him. I'm grieving." She didn't attempt to stop the flow of tears. She had to make Kay begin to accept the inevitable before the healing process could begin. Not only for Kay herself, but for the children also. To the paternalistic military authorities, Missing in Action was almost tantamount to saying he'd been killed. "Do you remember Sydney's denial? It's normal for you not to want to believe. But eventually you *have* to accept it, Kay."

But Kay covered her ears. "No!" she barked. "Not yet. Not yet. Would you leave me alone, please?"

"All right," said Faith, defeated. But she understood how Kay felt. She left the room.

Faith was harboring a secret, one that had begun to weigh heavily on her, and this horrible news added to the significance of her secret. Bill's St. Christopher medal and their grandfather's watch still rested in her top drawer.

She didn't know why she'd hidden them in the first place. It had been an impulse, and not a very smart one, except that the carrier was leaving that day, the medal and the watch were talismans, and she knew that the sight of those two items would deeply upset Kay and the children.

Now she would have to produce them and try to explain why they were in her possession. When? Not now, certainly.

Chapter 32

Sydney came directly from work to the Elysium as soon as she heard that Bill Parker was missing in action. Faith had been so kind, so good to her. And Kay, too, in her way. She would willingly offer her support if they needed it.

She was surprised to discover that Kay was at her desk at the Red Cross.

"She refuses to believe that anything's happened to Bill," Faith told Sydney as they walked together to the hospital.

"I suppose it's good to be optimistic," said Sydney.

"It would be good if it weren't for the kids. They're so confused."

Sydney started to mention Cody but stopped herself. She decided that it would be more tactful and considerate not to. They separated just inside the large double doors, Faith to go to the ward; Sydney to Jordan's room.

Jordan turned at the sound of Sydney entering the room. She had been waiting for that reaction for a week. When it happened her heart leapt within her breast, but she disguised her elation with a mild smile. He was beginning to anticipate, just like the chaplain had told her he would. "I brought you a chocolate milkshake today. We need to do something to fatten you up."

Jordan's own smile was weak, but it was a smile. "A chocolate shake. I haven't had one in years. Where did you get the sugar?"

Sydney made a face. "Before it was just scarce; now it's rationed. There isn't the slightest difference. But Maurice made this one for you."

"I thought you moved from the hotel. Didn't Faith say—?"

"I moved, Jordan, but that doesn't mean I've given up my

friends. The bus that I ride to work picks up near there. It gives me the opportunity to visit.''

''I heard about Bill Parker,'' he said. ''You went by to see them.''

''Yes.''

''You never told me where you are living.'' He put the milk-shake aside. She handed it back to him and sat in the chair beside the bed.

''Drink it all,'' she ordered. ''I'm living with a woman I met through work. She has a boardinghouse.''

A small smile appeared. ''Like Mrs. Deveraux?''

''Not at all.'' Maurie was not in the least like Mrs. Deveraux, and yet . . . ''Maybe so, a little bit,'' Sydney conceded. There were similar traits in the women, now that she thought about it. ''Except Maurie has four boys. They're all in the service.''

He sipped through the glass straw while she talked. She told him about the first day on the job, when Maurie had told off Mr. Nicholson. ''She said it so sweetly, Jordan. You just wouldn't believe the word 'crap' could ever pass through those lips.'' He was laughing! Actually laughing. She couldn't wait to tell Maurie.

Sydney sighed unknowingly into the silence following their shared laughter. ''It seems like years since I left New Orleans,'' she murmured.

He was quiet.

Then Sydney recovered herself. New Orleans was not a subject that either of them wanted to remember. ''Maurice sends his good wishes and says that the Pacific oysters are superb this year, as big as oranges. He'll fix you some Oysters Rockefeller as soon as you're out of the hospital.''

She'd made another mistake, she realized when she saw his blank expression. The taboo subject was not New Orleans but their time together. The memory that the famous dish, oysters baked with spinach, brought back. She'd once told him that she hated spinach and oysters, in that order, and wouldn't eat one if he paid her. So he had paid her, and she had eaten one, and she'd loved the dish.

The chaplain had said she shouldn't guard her tongue, not in reference to his injuries or to their time as lovers. He had said that if she was hesitant to talk about *anything*, Jordan would sense it and close up on her again. That would be disastrous. She had to be open and honest, even if it brought back painful images of the past.

He hadn't, however, said anything about changing the subject. "I understand that your father is here."

Jordan's face took on a thoughtful look. "It's odd that you two haven't crossed paths in the hall. Would you rather not meet him?"

She shrugged indifferently. "It makes no difference to me. I wondered if I would be an embarrassment to you, that's all."

"Sydney, my father knows that there was . . . another woman for a while."

Sydney winced at the appellation. It seemed that Jordan wasn't going to guard his tongue, either.

"I'm sorry," he said. Immediately upon seeing her reaction, he reached for her hand and held it, firmly and warmly, when she would have pulled away. "That was a nasty thing to call you. You weren't 'another' as far as I was concerned; you were the only woman. But my father has no idea who you are. I'd like for you to meet him, but I'll certainly understand if you don't want to. He can be—formidable."

Slowly she smiled. "I'll think about it."

She stayed for an hour. When she was leaving he stopped her. "Sydney?"

"Yes, Jordan?" She was fitting her fingers into her gloves. When he didn't answer right away, she looked up.

"We've never talked about Vance."

"I know." She looked down at her hands. "I didn't think you'd want me to thank you."

"God, no!" He covered his eyes with his hand. After a minute he dropped it. "Sydney, I want to thank you for all you've done. You—and my father—you've both made me feel like a human being again."

"Oh, Jordan—"

He interrupted. "I mean it. I hope—I want you to know that—not just because I promised Vance—I'm a friend, if you ever need one."

The senator didn't have to adhere to the visiting hours that affected other, more mortal souls. For once Jordan was glad of his father's position.

They talked incessantly. His father knew now how thoroughly his life with Valerie had deteriorated, and that one of the causes was his aversion to politics. The senator knew that Sydney—the other woman—was here in Seattle and that she'd been visiting him. Jordan had also told him about Vance.

They told each other things they'd never said before. On the day before he had to leave the senator asked Jordan to return with him to Washington or to follow as soon as he was able. But Jordan declined. Then the senator suggested the house in Chicago. When Jordan also declined that possibility, the senator blurted, "Well, what in the hell *do* you want to do, son?"

Jordan grinned at his father. "I'm not quite sure. I've had some ideas but I'd rather wait to tell you about them."

"Will you? Tell me?" The senator's eyes pleaded.

Jordan had confessed to his father that his first inclination had been to simply disappear. But he no longer felt that way. He wanted to find a private place where he could spend most of the time alone, but he wouldn't vanish. "Yes, that I promise to do. Now, you can do something for me."

"Of course. What is it?"

"I know you have to get back to Washington soon but could you make a detour on the way? To Chicago?"

"If it's important."

"Important but unorthodox. I want you to take Valerie home, Dad. Help her find a lawyer, arrange for a divorce. There's nothing left between us now and she deserves another chance. Maybe she can find a real politician," he finished wryly.

The senator had seen Valerie. He wasn't much inclined to comment on her prospects, but he agreed to do as Jordan asked.

"Dad, I don't resent Valerie. Not at all. It's going to be rough on her. But she'll have her parents and her friends."

The senator nodded. "What about Sydney Bingham?" he asked gently.

His father was pushing to meet Sydney. "There's nothing there, other than friendship," Jordan answered. "She loved her husband very much."

"I'm sure she did, son. I can't help thinking . . . If I had known . . ."

Jordan shook his head, grinning in amazement.

His father caught the look. "Sorry," he said sheepishly.

One of the things Jordan had resented in the past, and didn't resent anymore, was his father's determination to take charge. "No. You couldn't have done a thing. It was me, my own pride that kept me from admitting I had made a mistake a long time ago and not taking steps to correct it. I thought I owed . . ." He shook his head, steering away from that tack. "I couldn't face the fact that I had failed at anything—even a miserable marriage. Now it's too late for anything between Sydney and me. I'd feel like a traitor to even contemplate it. And so would she.''

''Maybe not. You can't be certain.''

Jordan was certain. He also knew that if he asked, Sydney would become a companion, a help in getting through the rough times ahead. She had a great capacity for tenderness and understanding, and she still cared for him. She wasn't in love with him, but she cared.

Sydney would take on the job of his rehabilitation with as much enthusiasm as she showed for everything else, he mused. It had been almost amusing to watch her affection evolve over the last couple of weeks. At first she'd felt guilty, disloyal to Vance's memory. He was fully aware that Faith had bullied her into seeing him at all. He paused in his thoughts and smiled. Faith, Wild Bill's little sister, had grown into a pint-sized tyrant. She had grown further, into a strong, mature woman.

Sydney—following her guilt had come her gratitude. He had seen it but hadn't exactly understood it. He hadn't been able to save Vance, and he had his own guilt to deal with over that. Intellectually he knew that Vance was lost before he dove into the fire, but emotionally he wondered if he could have reacted more quickly. He would never know. All his life he would live with the question, but he wasn't going to let it destroy him.

Sydney would take the job, but he would not offer it. Pity, which he'd not seen since that first day she came to visit him, had recently crept into her attitude again. And pity he would not live with. She fancied herself his savior, his rescuer. It would be commitment born of compassion, and that he couldn't—wouldn't—accept.

Besides, he knew her well enough to know that she was a gregarious soul. Sociable—not social as Valerie was—but outgoing. He wouldn't consider sentencing her to the life of a recluse.

Faith surveyed the ''apartment,'' discouraged. She had to find a place for herself and Kay and the children to live and this was the best of the lot she'd seen. The place was nothing but a converted garage. A partitioned area held a double bed and a cot. A small storage room had been made into a bathroom and a corner was curtained off to serve as a closet. A living room of sorts with a piece of surprisingly clean carpet spread over the grease spots, took up the remaining space. In fact the whole place was surprisingly clean. There was a sofa and a chair cov-

ered in something that was once green, a maple table with four
chairs, a stove of undecipherable vintage, and a refrigerator that
predated it.

In one corner was a staircase leading up to the apartment
above. That one really was an apartment, used in the past for
maid's quarters. But whoever lived upstairs now would have to
traipse right through their living room to get there.

Kay was the one who had insisted that they move out of the
hotel as quickly as possible. She wanted to go before they were
asked to leave, and she'd already packed everything in the two
rooms except for a few clothes. It was as though she couldn't
stand the place a minute longer.

"I'm the one who wrote the rules, Faith. If a husband is
killed, taken prisoner or"—Kay had paused—"missing in action, the space has to be made available. I know we could have
as much time as we want to vacate our rooms, but it isn't fair."

Faith knew Kay was right. And ever since Bill had been listed
as missing, Kay had seemed like she was living on automatic.
Certainly she was in no condition to look for an apartment.

Thus Faith was stuck with finding them a place to live, even
though she was out of her mind with worry over both Cody and
Bill. Forcing her thoughts back to the present dilemma, she
reasoned that since Kay was leaving the choice up to her she
couldn't complain if it didn't satisfy. She hadn't asked for
the dominant role in this family, it was shoved upon her by a
sister-in-law who didn't so much concede the leadership as simply withdraw from the contest.

Kay continued to function in her job with the Red Cross, but
she was withdrawn from other aspects of life, even to the point
that the children had begun to whisper around her. Faith had
enlisted their help in trying to bring Kay out of this shell she
seemed to have built around herself but, bless their hearts, all
they got for their efforts were vague comments.

It wasn't fair to them, thought Faith, her inner anger surfacing
again. She set it aside. There wasn't room for anger in her life
right now. She was the only one to offer comfort to the grieving
children, to take over the task of trying to restore their lives to
some sort of normalcy. To be fair she had the most free time.
Her job at the hospital kept regular hours, while, as the war
dragged on, Kay's often called for her to stay until late into the
night.

Faith remembered the organization's promise to Kay that her

hours would be flexible. She supposed it was no one's fault that it hadn't worked out that way.

She returned her attention to the tiny apartment. They had a little extra gasoline, and a bus line was close, so transportation shouldn't be a problem. There was a place for a Victory garden, which would please the kids. Everyone who had a spot was growing their own vegetables nowadays.

Millie and Billy were going to miss their friends but they were used to that; they were navy brats. Moving on was a way of life. They'd make new friends, and she'd make sure their old ones came to visit. A day in the country should be appealing to some of them. Here on the edge of the city it was almost like being in the country.

The days had become drudgery for Faith, but she felt guilty complaining. They had it better than people in other places in the world did. She thought back to last spring, when she had left school. She had wanted to be a part of all this; she hadn't wanted to miss out on the fun. Oh, Lord, had she really been that naive?

A bell rang somewhere. The landlady went into the house to answer the telephone. Decision time. Faith knew that if she didn't take it the place would be snatched up by someone else within the hour. Faith didn't have the time or the inclination to look further. It was clean, the rent was reasonable, and the landlady seemed nice enough.

She went to the window. A car crept along the curb, looking curiously at the sign in the yard that read APARTMENT FOR RENT. Across the street a young boy, probably about seven years old, was spraying his older sister with a garden hose.

"I'll take it," she said when the landlady, Mrs. Brown, returned. "May we move in immediately?"

They moved in that night; there was no reason to wait. The children were cautiously cheerful as they explored outside. Kay looked the apartment over with a desultory eye until she caught Faith's frown. Then she smiled.

"You're a genius. It's magnificent. How did you ever find it?"

Faith laughed at the exaggeration, but she was pleased that Kay approved. Hell, she was pleased that Kay voiced an opinion. "Just lucky, I guess."

"Tell me one thing though," she asked. "Where do those steps lead?"

"To the apartment upstairs," Faith admitted. "Two men in

their sixties live there. One works at Lockheed and the other is a bookkeeper for the radio station. I understand they don't go out much after nine o'clock."

"Well, that isn't my problem but yours. I just hope you have a nice tailored bathrobe."

They had already decided that Millie would sleep with her mother, Billy on the cot, and Faith on the sofa that made into a bed.

Faith ventured a hope that the move would have a beneficial effect on Kay. "Is it really all right?" she asked quietly.

Kay came to her then and hugged her. "Of course, it's all right, honey. We're lucky that you found it." She caught her breath and went on, "I don't think I could have stood those two rooms much longer. There was too much of Bill there."

This more accessible Kay was such a rarity that Faith decided to take advantage of it. "Then let's sit down and have a cup of coffee" she urged. "The unpacking can wait.

"I saw Sydney today at the hospital," she said when they were settled.

"Really?" Another spark of life. "How is she?"

Faith smiled sadly. "Sydney is a survivor. It's been awful for her but she's taken on Jordan's rehabilitation as a project. She's at that hospital every night. He's proving to be more of a problem than she'd expected and she holds me responsible since I talked her into getting involved with him." She chuckled. "So far she's managed to avoid the senator."

The children returned full of information about the neighborhood, and they all pitched in to finish the unpacking before bedtime. Supper was peanut butter and jelly sandwiches and milk. In the middle of the meal two gentlemen came in and, averting their eyes, scuttled hurriedly up the stairs. All four people at the card table watched in amazement.

"Aren't they even going to say hello?" asked Billy before the door at the top of the stairs was completely closed.

"Sh-h-h," cautioned his mother. "I think you'll be okay," she said to Faith. "They don't look too dangerous to me." The two women giggled for the first time in ages.

Chapter 33

It was time to make some decisions. And some plans. Jordan flexed his fingers and rubbed his chest absently as he tried to relax in bed after his therapy. His father was leaving tonight to return to Washington, via Chicago as Jordan had asked. He'd already stayed longer than he should have. During their talks the senator had let drop mention of some of the things related to the war effort that he was currently working on. And his son knew enough to realize that he needed to get back to them. Quickly. The war didn't stop for anyone.

Yesterday after his talk with his father, Jordan had pressed the doctors for a dismissal date, and they had tentatively agreed on next week provided he promised to settle near a major medical facility. The therapy had to be continued on a regular basis. He had no argument with that. He wanted to be mobile again. He was doing well on the crutches, better than well. His burns would take longer to heal but the scar tissue had begun to form. He knew that he would have to submit to plastic surgery, but it would take a long time, perhaps years, before he could go out in public without frightening people to death.

So he needed to select a spot where he could be away from prying eyes and yet contribute to the war effort. That was essential for him now. The faint glimmer of an idea had begun to form a few days ago, and to his own surprise, he'd resurrected his dream of becoming a writer. It was something he could do alone, privately. He would need help for the first few weeks. He couldn't drive, shop for food. Deciding on a place to settle wouldn't be easy. Finding a—he paused. Nurse? Companion? That would be almost impossible. But he'd find a way, he swore to himself, without anyone.

A sudden thought hit him. Briefly Valerie had entered his

thoughts, briefly but without the accompanying pain. Not even the pain of betrayal. It was a relief, a wonderful gut-easing relief.

A knock on the door interrupted his thoughts. "Come in," he called, reaching up automatically to dim the lights as the door swung inward.

He froze when he saw his wife standing there. Dear God, don't do this again. Please. He held his breath, waiting.

"Jordan, I came to say good-bye," said Valerie quietly. She approached the bed. "I'm leaving with your father tonight."

"I know," he answered, turning his face aside to hide his scars from her view. "I don't blame you, Valerie. I want you to know that."

She laughed, a dry, disillusioned sound. "I blame myself enough for both of us," she said.

"You mustn't."

"That's what the psychiatrist says."

At his surprised gesture she said, "You didn't know I'd seen a psychiatrist? Your father insisted." She shrugged and dropped her purse on the foot of the bed. She wandered aimlessly, but restlessly, around the room, touching the back of a chair, running a finger over the edge of the table beside the bed.

He was concerned by her appearance. She had colored her lips, but the rest of her face was bare of makeup and her hair had been combed carelessly and gathered in a scarf at her nape. There was no animation in her eyes. Indeed, her expression was vacant. "You must do whatever is right for you, Valerie. Money won't be a problem."

"You'll be relieved to get rid of me, Jordan. And I really can't blame you. I wasn't the perfect wife I thought I was."

"I never asked for perfection."

"But you expected it."

The accusation rolled off her tongue as though by rote, but her heart wasn't in it. He decided not to argue. What good would it do? "You'll be glad to get back to your friends. Tell everyone hello for me." He hesitated. "The ones who are left."

"Where are you going? Aren't you returning to Chicago?" she demanded.

"No. My father will take care of everything for you. If he's not there your lawyers can contact the family firm."

"Where will you be?" she repeated. "How can I get in touch with you?"

Why would you want to? he almost asked. "I don't know yet."

A nurse came into the room, a needle in her hand. "Will you wait outside please?" she asked Valerie.

"There's no need for you to stay, Valerie," said Jordan.

Valerie nodded. "Good-bye, Jordan," she said.

"Good-bye," said Jordan. And that's the death of a marriage, he thought. The end.

In order to reach the section of the hall reserved for private rooms, Sydney had to pass the ward. She stopped to speak to one of the men. They used her affection and love shamelessly as coercion for a song or two, which suited her fine. Especially if the senator was still visiting Jordan.

Amused, Jordan had informed her that his father had repeatedly asked for her and warned that one night soon he would wait her out. Sydney didn't know why she was so reluctant to meet the man.

This particular night, she was planning a brief visit, then home for a hot bath and early bedtime. The shifts at the plant had changed; she would now be going to work at three A.M. and punching out at noon. Old hands had explained that it would take a week or so to adjust to the new time.

She spied Faith across the room, feeding a young boy from Oklahoma who had lost both arms. His name was Dickie and he was lying on his bed, which was unusual. Dickie always preferred to be on his feet. He vowed that he couldn't be sure he was alive if he was lying down. That's the way they'd lay him out, he said. She went over. "Hi, Dickie. Do you have a request for me tonight?"

"Hi, Sydney. Whatever you'd like to play is all right with me." He managed a smile, but it was a weak one compared to his usual hundred-watt grin.

Sydney didn't change expression as she crossed to the small room that adjoined the ward. It was used for therapy in the daytime and recreation in the evenings. "The door? Open or closed?" she always asked when she reached the door.

"Open," was the vote. On her way to the piano she passed a man at table playing solitaire. "Play something bluesy, Sydney," he requested.

She played "The Birth of the Blues" and "The St. Louis Blues." Then she had a request for a hymn; then, from one of the boys whose girlfriend was back home in Indiana, "Play, 'I'll Be Seeing You,' please, Sydney."

After the mellow tones had faded, she fingered the keys for a moment then she picked up the tempo and started to sing: "My Dreams Are Getting Better All the Time."

From the corner of her eye she saw one of the nurses nod. Regardless of the men's requests, which tended toward sentimentality, a light song always brought higher spirits to the ward. She smiled back at the nurse and picked up the tempo.

Finally as the last notes of the song trailed off she let her fingers slide from the keys. The song was met with soft applause.

She looked up from the piano to see Jordan in a wheelchair in the doorway. Her pulse skipped a beat. He was out of bed. True, he slumped slightly in the chair, but she knew that was because he was favoring his left side. Suddenly she felt her face light like a thousand candles on Christmas Eve, her smile spread until her cheeks hurt, and she locked her eyes onto his.

He moved forward propelled by a white-haired man Sydney hadn't noticed. Her smile faded to a manageable glow. The senator was here.

As he rolled the chair forward in her direction, she heard a few of the boys greet him by name, which surprised her until she remembered the man was first and foremost a politician. She rose.

"Sydney, may I present my father, Judson Adair? Father, this is Sydney Bingham."

The senator was halfway into a half bow, when Sydney extended her hand, surprising him and provoking a grin from Jordan. She knew what he saw, a flamboyant redhead, tall and striking, dressed rather casually, not pretty in the conventional sense but arresting. She would meet him on an equal footing or not at all. "How do you do, Senator Adair? I'm very pleased to meet you," she said.

"I'm very pleased to meet you, too, Mrs. Bingham," the senator responded formally. His eyes gleamed in speculation as he looked her over. "Jordan has told me a lot about you."

She paled only slightly. "Yes. He's told me a lot about you, too."

He looked uncomfortable. Amused, Jordan broke the silence, which threatened to become embarrassing. "Shall we go out into the solarium? That is if you can break away for a minute, Sydney?"

Instinctively, she looked around for a way out, only to find they were the object of many interested stares. No one knew the story, not unless Faith had told and Sydney didn't believe she would do that. But there had been speculation obviously, stemming from her frequent visits, his wife's response to his injuries, and there were men here from the *Shiloh* who would have known Vance.

She nodded. As she left the ward she laid a hand on the shoulder of the man seated at the card table playing solitaire. "I'll be back in a little while," she told him unnecessarily.

He grinned. "Okay, Sydney."

She walked beside the wheelchair to the end of the hall, where an open area had been converted to a visiting space with comfortable chairs and softly glowing lamps. The latest issue of *Life* magazine had been tossed onto the table.

"Dad's leaving tonight," Jordan said. "He wanted to meet you before he goes."

Why? wondered Sydney. She couldn't imagine she was his favorite person. She smiled noncommittally.

"You play and sing very well, Mrs. Bingham. I haven't heard that old hymn in years," said the senator. "The old favorites seem to have gone out of fashion lately, haven't they?"

They had been listening for a while. "I suppose the times are changing, Senator."

The senator looked around him at the hall, which was full of men struggling to walk on crutches or being wheeled along as Jordan had been, men in wrinkled, ill-fitting pajamas and dark blue robes, broken men. Women in the white uniforms of nurses, the striped uniforms of the volunteers, an occasional woman in slacks or a skirt as Sydney was. His face took on an infinitely sad look.

Suddenly Sydney knew, with a startling insight, what he was thinking; she could feel his pain as her own. The senator had been one of those who made the decision to send these young men to war. God, how could he live with it? Necessary as it was, how did he carry the knowledge?

She was never sure whether her empathy was a blessing or a curse, but now she was compelled to comfort him. "Senator?" He turned to her. Their eyes met. "Please don't look like that. They know," she said very quietly. "They know that this war was inevitable. None of them would want you to blame yourself."

Unbidden the senator held out his hand and she took it,

squeezing, offering her strength. The moment seemed to last forever. Finally he withdrew his hand. Reluctantly. "What an extraordinary woman you are," he said softly, shaking his head.

"Not extraordinary at all," she replied with a melancholy smile. Her attempt at lightness didn't quite come off. "There are millions of women out there who do a lot more. Haven't you discovered that yet? That's why we'll win this war."

He thought for a minute. "Yes, I see what you mean. But you'll have to forgive me if I disagree on one point. You're one of a kind, Sydney Bingham. Even for a short time my son was a very lucky man. I'm sorry things didn't work out between you."

Sydney turned an accusing gaze toward Jordan, but the senator arrested her protest by speaking first, "Please forgive him for telling me. You mean a lot to him."

Jordan had watched the interaction between his father and Sydney with growing disbelief. At the last he started to protest their discussing him as though he weren't there. He shut his mouth. What difference did it make that his father had melted at her feet like hot wax? Soon they both would be gone, out of her life.

Chapter 34

November 25, 1942

Kay had been suffering from nightmares again. They were frightening in the extreme because there was no substance to them. In the dreams she was caught eternally in a mist or a fog. She couldn't see or hear or smell. When she reached for a shape it faded to nothing.

She slipped into her robe and poured herself a cup of coffee. She wandered to the window. Faith and the children were outside in the sunshine, which looked cold to Kay. She wrapped both hands around the warm mug.

Almost December. Nearly a year since she and Bill had gone to Washington, D.C. A year of frantic gearing up, catching up, making up, but not giving up. A year of screaming headlines, of battles lost and won—in Europe, in Africa, in the Pacific. The time between then and now had not marched along in the smooth, natural rhythm of hours, days, months as it was supposed to. The year had moved instead in jerks and starts and empty hollows.

Like the one she was living in now. She had to pull herself up from this particular hollow. She had to. But somehow she was unable.

The sun warmed Faith's arms. She loved this weather, she decided. The trade winds blowing in over the Pacific kept the climate around Puget Sound moderate most of the time. Winter in New England was guaranteed to be cold. Here there was always the possibility of a day like this to look forward to.

They had been in the apartment for a week now, and it wasn't working out too badly. They'd had to invest in an electric heater for the bedroom. But a bonus they hadn't expected was the use of Mrs. Brown's agitator washing machine. After the old wringer type they had used at the hotel, this was the finest technology.

They'd thought about taking Kay and Bill's furniture out of storage in Florida but decided not to do that yet. For one thing they would have to take the whole load and there wasn't room for everything. For another—Kay kept repeating that she didn't know where Bill would be sent next. They might have to ship it all right back to Pensacola.

Kay still refused to face the fact that Bill was probably dead. She was adamant that he still lived, somewhere. Her refusal made it doubly hard on Faith and the children. But Faith could tell that Kay had begun to try, and that was progress.

She had talked to the children about their mother, and they seemed to understand her state of mind much better than Faith could have imagined. She had also given them the watch and medal their father had left for them. Millie seemed to understand why Faith had hidden them; Billy was puzzled but delighted with his watch. They decided—without a suggestion from Faith—not to tell their mother just yet.

They were terrific kids. She could hear their laughter now as they played across the street. She reached down into the laundry basket for a pair of khaki pants belonging to Billy. From a pouch dangling from her belt she took two clothespins and stuck them in her mouth.

A scream interrupted her thoughts, bringing her to attention. But it was cut off in midsound. She relaxed when she realized it had not been a scream of pain but one of delight. She smiled to herself. At least the kids were relatively happy. She reached into the laundry basket again and came up with a bedsheet.

She snapped the fabric in a downward motion to get some of the wrinkles out and reached up to attach it to the line, when suddenly the sheet was jerked out of her hands and thrown over her head. "Billy Parker!" she screeched angrily as she struggled to free herself. "What do you think you're . . ." She pulled the sheet away from her face. And froze.

Cody was there; grinning, but with tears standing in his bright eyes. "Hey, babe."

"Cody?" she whispered, unable to believe it was him. "Cody!" The sheet fell to the ground, forgotten. She flung herself at his khaki-clad body and his arms tightened around her. Laughing, he lifted her and spun around. His mouth found hers. "Honey . . . honey," he said huskily when he finally broke off the kiss and let her feet touch the ground. "I couldn't have asked for a better welcome than that."

"Oh, Cody, you're here. You're really here!" She covered his face with kisses, stepped back once to assure herself he was whole and then flung her arms around him again.

"Five minutes are up," piped in Billy from behind Cody's shoulder. Faith emerged to see both children and Kay watching. The children were grinning. Kay looked terrified.

Cody kept Faith beside him as he approached Kay. He pulled her under his other arm. "Kay, honey, how are you?"

"Cody, don't torture me."

"I'm so sorry. Bill was the best."

"It's true then? It's really true?" Kay asked in a trembling voice.

"It's true. I saw him go in."

Later that night Faith sat with Cody on the concrete stoop. Since the excitement of his arrival he'd been strangely quiet. He sat with his legs bent and spread apart. His forearms rested on his thighs, his hands dangling loosely between them.

Faith drew her own legs close to her body and wrapped her arms around them. "Can you tell me about it?" she asked softly.

Cody asked how much she knew. "Not much. That the ship was on fire and you had to get the planes off before it sank."

He reached for her hand. "It was hell, Faith, chaos, pandemonium. We knew immediately with the fires and location of the torpedo hits, amidship and below the waterline, that the ship was lost. There was a dogfight; we got four of their planes. But we were all low on fuel. Bill"—he paused and swallowed hard—"Bill went in." He hesitated. "You want to hear the final irony?"

The question was rhetorical and he went on without waiting for her answer. "The F4F Wildcat is a tight little plane and it'll float for a few minutes." He dropped her hand, surged to his feet, and plunged his hands into the pockets of his uniform trousers. "The engineers once installed air bags underneath, to be deployed if the plane went in the water, to help it float indefinitely. They did that over Bill Parker's negative recommendation. He didn't think they were worth the risk. He was right. Over the next few months some of the air bags deployed while the planes were in flight. A couple of pilots were killed, so they took them off."

Faith was shaking by the time he finished the story. He saw;

he sat back down beside her and reached for her hand again. His voice, his expression were filled with bitterness when he continued, "Anyway, one of the ships in the task force directed Mason and me toward a small island to the south. But our co-ordinates were messed up and we landed on the wrong island. One of the torpedo plane pilots had made the same mistake, so there were three of us.

"Hell, I would have landed there anyway, I was so glad to see solid ground. We were flying on fumes by that time." He looked down at their clasped hands, but she knew he wasn't seeing them. He was seeing the battle, the burning ship, his friend's doomed aircraft. Finally he brought her hand to his mouth. She could feel his warm breath on her fingers and feel his lips move against her skin as he went on. "It took weeks for the search teams to find everybody. We were scattered over thousands of square miles of ocean."

She waited for him to disconnect from the images that haunted him. Finally she laid her head on his shoulder and asked, "How long can you stay?"

He tucked his chin and smiled down at her, tenderly, with absolute love in his eyes. "I have a two-week leave. Will you marry me?"

She only hesitated for a brief moment. "You know I will. But . . ."

"But?"

She looked up at him in the moonlight. "You've changed."

"I'm older."

"And quieter."

He reached down to pull a clump of grass that grew beside the stoop. "You've changed, too," he said with a small laugh.

"Have I?" she asked, but she knew it was true.

"Look around you, Faith. We've all changed." He tossed the grass away. "Reality has set in, honey. We've finally realized that this war won't be over for a long time. A lot of us under-estimated the enemy."

Kay stood at the open window listening to their quiet voices. Though the evening was warm, she shivered. She crossed her arms and glanced over her shoulder at the sleeping children. She didn't want them to hear this conversation.

Could the ending to Cody's chronicle possibly be true? Could Bill's heart have ceased to beat, could he have stopped breathing without her being aware of it, she asked herself again.

If so, she would soon be visited by the chaplain. He would speak kindly and sympathetically, explaining that Bill Parker's status had been changed from "Missing in Action" to "Killed in Action." Her fingers dug painfully into the skin of her arms. She couldn't bear a scene like that.

She had surprised herself over the last year; she had found useful abilities and a down-to-earth pragmatism she hadn't known existed within her. If Bill was dead—she forced herself to use the word—she would survive because she had to. She had his two children and an unspoken agreement with him that if anything ever happened, she would carry on. But her newfound strength had not been really tested, not by years, decades, a lifetime of hollow, empty existence.

She turned away from the window, hurting, oh, God, hurting so horribly. She would handle the pain; she would pull through but only in her own way, in her own time. And what should she do meanwhile?

Several days ago she had informed Mrs. Evans at the Red Cross that she might be leaving without notice. For, she knew, if she became convinced that Bill had been killed, she would flee. She could not stay in Seattle—not for a minute longer than it would take her to get their things, hers and the children's, packed.

Mrs. Evans had not approved of Kay's decision, indeed had argued heatedly against it; but, behind her expression of aggravation, Kay had sensed a glimmer of understanding.

They were married a week later. Sydney came. She confided to Faith that she was leaving Seattle soon, but she was vague about her plans. Patsy came, and Edna and Jimmy McCoy. They were the only guests. Kay baked a cake—they wouldn't have any sugar for another month. Cody brought champagne. All things considered, Faith thought as she looked down at the shiny gold band, hers was a splendid wedding.

There was no place to go even a for brief honeymoon. Instead Kay insisted she and the children move into the living room, leaving the bedroom for Faith and Cody.

Faith took the weekend off but on Monday morning she was back at work at the hospital. She and Cody had discussed Kay's withdrawal, which had become worse again since Cody's arrival. She spoke little and cried often. Both Faith and Cody tried to ease Kay's grief, but they realized that their very presence reminded her of her loss.

He was a living witness that Bill Parker's plane had been shot down somewhere in the Pacific Ocean.

And their happiness was like salt in the wound. They agreed that Cody should spend whatever time he could with Kay while Faith was at work. Maybe, they hoped, he could help her to face Bill's death and cope with the aftermath.

On Wednesday Faith came home to find boxes stacked on the floor, Kay buzzing around, giving orders like a top sergeant.

Billy came running up as she entered. "We're going to the farm," he announced excitedly. "It's snowing there, in Nebraska, I mean."

Faith sought Cody's gaze. He shrugged imperceptibly and, dropping the masking tape he was using on a box, straightened from his crouch on the floor to come to her. "Hi, honey," he said. "Kay has decided to go home to her parents for a while."

"Kay? Are you sure this is what you want to do?"

"I'm sure," Kay answered positively. "I almost drowned your new husband today, when I finally gave in; but I've faced the fact that home is the place for me, for us."

She put her arm around her son's shoulders and smiled at them. "Your life is settled now, Faith. You can probably move back into the hotel if you want to." She looked around. "Although this place grows on you, doesn't it? Billy wants to be a farmer anyway, so we might as well get started on his training. We're leaving tomorrow."

"Tomorrow! But you can't leave so quickly."

"I've already made the decision and there's no point in a delay. I called Dad and Mom and they're expecting us."

Faith felt as though she was losing a part of herself. Her new husband must have read the thoughts on her face. He came to her side and took her firmly into his arms. He was reminding her that she had another bulwark to lean on if she needed one. She looked up at him and smiled. They would get through this and she no longer needed a bulwark. She could stand on her own.

The station was crowded. "Where is she? Can you see her?" Kay asked Cody.

"Not yet," Cody answered, searching over the heads of the crowd.

Faith had promised to get away from the hospital in time to come to the station to see them off. She had to come, she had to, thought Kay desperately.

She hadn't said everything she wanted to say to Faith. She hadn't told her how much she loved her, how precious she'd become to them all, how grateful she was for Faith's strength over these last weeks. Faith was Bill's sister and like a line to him. If they didn't have a proper good-bye . . .

They stood beside the train; the luggage had already been loaded aboard. The train was emitting steam impatiently. It billowed from beneath the huge wheels, blocking Kay's view. She caught her red hat with one hand as a soldier jostled her. The conductor looked pointedly at his watch.

"Kay, you're going to have to get on board."

"I know. She probably got caught up in traffic," she answered sadly. "Well"—she sent a smile up to Cody—"tell her we love her. And tell her, when you have to leave again, there's no housing shortage in Nebraska."

"I will." Cody lifted Billy up for a kiss and deposited him on the platform of the train. Millie followed him. They turned to watch their mother as she gave Cody another big hug. "We love you, too. I'm glad you're my brother now."

Blinking back her tears she put her hand on the bar and started to step aboard. Then she heard Faith's voice, calling to her.

"Oh, she made it!" She looked around, but the steam spilling out from under the train shrouded the tracks, the walkway, everything. She couldn't find her—the only person visible was a tall—oh, God—a shadowy figure, limping toward her like a ghost out of the mist. Another blast of steam enveloped him, but only for a second.

Oh, God, oh, God. She took a step, afraid, so afraid to believe what her eyes were seeing. It was her nightmare come to life.

No! Not her nightmare—this was her dream!

"Daddy?" Millie's incredulous whisper was like a shout behind her.

"Daddy?" echoed Billy. "Did you say 'Daddy'?"

"My God!" declared Cody. Jaw agape, he stared as though he were seeing a ghost.

"Yes!" The word sprang from Kay's lips in a rush. "Yes! It's Daddy! Oh, God, yes."

And then she was sobbing, running, racing, into his open arms, which closed about her like a vise.

Faith wiped her eyes as she helped Cody get the children and the luggage off the train. "How in the hell . . . ?" His voice was weak.

"H-he just called me out of the blue—at the hospital—he was cussing—" She sniffed inelegantly. "S-said he'd been—been looking all over for us." She cried and laughed. Cody and the children were laughing and crying, too. Even the conductor took a huge handkerchief out of his pocket and blew his nose.

Bill's arms opened wide enough to encompass his children as they raced to his side. He answered Cody's question. "Native fishermen. Pulled me out just before the plane sank."

Cody pounded him on the back as he and Faith were included in the embrace. "Hell, Parker, you must have an angel sitting on your shoulder!"

Bill's thin face split into a grin, then he laughed, a joyful, unbridled laugh, and looked down into Kay's eyes. "I'm surrounded by them!"

They made an island of joy and reunion and peace. And, small and brief though they all knew it to be in the midst of war, it was enough.

Sydney Jackson Bingham didn't go directly from Washington, D.C.'s Union Station to the address that was written on a folded paper in her purse. She'd gotten the address and directions from Senator Adair.

Instead she stored her single suitcase in a locker—the rest of her things had been shipped to Mrs. Deveraux's house to be stored there—and boarded a bus outside the terminal. She rather enjoyed the ride. The bus followed a winding route; people got on and off, silent people, talkative people, people who laughed, and people who were very serious.

This was Sydney's first visit to the nation's capital. Who knows? It might be my only visit. She sat behind the driver, who pointed out the landmarks that, until now, were only pictures in history books. He had quickly recognized a tourist. She listened to his patter and responded appropriately but with only half her attention. With the other half she considered the step she was about to take.

Jordan was in California.

She'd called him there, when she decided what her plans were. It had warmed her to hear his voice. He sounded much better than he had when he left Seattle; he sounded almost happy. He was writing, working behind the scenes with Frank Capra and the Army Signal Corps on a series of movies about the war, designed to be both inspirational and informative.

As propaganda to be shown to servicemen, Jordan told her,

he was dubious of their long-term value; but someday perhaps people would see them in the context of history, and pause to think about this time and what the war meant to the people who lived through it.

Then she'd told him of her own plans. He was silent for a long time. "It's hard for me to picture you doing something like that, Sydney."

She laughed. "It may be hard for them to picture it, Jordan. They may turn me down flat. But we all have to fight this war. I think Vance would have approved." She closed her eyes and gripped the telephone receiver tightly. Sometimes it hurt just to say his name but she refused to tiptoe around it. She would keep her husband alive in her heart; if it hurt to remember, then it would just have to hurt.

"I think he would have," Jordan agreed in a low voice. "But somehow I don't think they'll turn you down," he said thoughtfully. "Will you stay in touch? Someday, I'd like to see you again."

"Someday—when this is all over, I'd like to see you, too."

The door of the bus opened with a wheeze, drawing Sydney back from her musings. The next stop was hers.

The sky was clear, the air crisp and fresh. It was balmy for January. Sydney walked with a confident stride to the offices to which she'd been directed. She carried only her purse.

She almost collided with a tall man in mufti on his way out of the building that was her destination. He started to mutter an automatic apology, a platitude of some kind. But when he saw the woman standing before him, his shock showed clearly on his face. "Mrs. Bingham!"

"I was just on my way to see you."

"What for?"

She raised a brow. "May we talk inside?" she asked.

He gave her a puzzled look but complied. They didn't speak again until he was settled at his desk and she sat in a chair across from him.

"Admiral Cleveland, I've come to ask if you have a need of someone like me," she said with her straightforward manner.

He propped his elbows on the arms of his chair, swiveled from side to side, and surveyed her over tented fingers. The silence stretched between them.

Sydney knew what he saw. She faced herself in the mirror every morning and she had changed.

Finally he spoke. "You said mine was a filthy, dirty job."

"Yes, I know, Admiral. I haven't changed my mind about that."

"Why are you here then?"

"Is Nate Bell still loose?"

He straightened. "If revenge is your motive—"

She interrupted quickly. "No, not for revenge. Not for that."

He waited. For the first time in any of their encounters, Sydney smiled at the man. "Well, it is a dirty job, but somebody—"

"Has to do it," they finished together. The admiral nodded. His mouth shifted into something that resembled a grimace, but might—just possibly—have been an answering smile. He pressed a button on his intercom. "I'll have someone see to you."

Of course, he didn't do that kind of thing himself. She should have known. She waited expectantly.

"I'm not promising anything. . . ." he hastened to add.

"I wouldn't expect you to," said Sydney Bingham wryly.

"My superior will have the last word, of course."

"Mr. Donovan?" She'd been told that Admiral Cleveland was in charge of the Washington office.

The admiral frowned. "How did you know his name?"

William Donovan's name wasn't classified as far as she knew. Surely the senator hadn't told her something she shouldn't know. "Senator Adair gave me your address. He told me that the COI was now called the OSS, Office of Strategic Services and that William Donovan, along with help from an Englishman, William Stephenson, was responsible for its inception," she explained.

The admiral mused for a moment. "There just might be a place for you here, Mrs. Bingham. You've proven that you are a bright, strong young woman."

Sydney bowed her head briefly to acknowledge the compliment. "And I've already been investigated up one side and down the other."

The admiral barked a harsh laugh. "That was nothing compared to what you will be subjected to if you join us, not to mention the testing, the training, the job itself. It won't be simple."

Sydney shifted in her seat. She didn't want to be thrown out for insubordination before she was hired, but she couldn't keep the irony out of her voice. "Admiral, as you reminded me a couple of months ago, I'm now a wealthy woman. If I wanted a simple life, I could move back to New Orleans and live in leisure on Vance's money. But my husband paid the ultimate price because he believed in his country. Before he died he taught me a lot. One of the lessons I learned was that the war is far from over, and the winner will have to have some kind of edge. Maybe technology is the edge we need, maybe it's the dedication and determination of every American, maybe it's blind luck or fate or whatever." She paused. "But maybe it's secret intelligence.

"I do know that I don't want Vance's death to have been for nothing. And I know I can't sit home twiddling my thumbs. Do you have a job for me or not?"

He had been watching her keenly as she spoke but now he looked up as the door to the office opened. An attractive and breathless young woman entered the office. "I'm sorry, Admiral. I was away from my desk. I just saw your light. Did you want something?"

"Sally, this is Mrs. Bingham. Will you please take her to the orientation and testing area?" said Admiral Cleveland. "Welcome aboard, Sydney."

Sydney inhaled and looked at him straight on. "So, it was your decision all the time?"

"Of course," said the admiral.

ABOUT THE AUTHOR

MARION SMITH COLLINS is a native of Georgia, a graduate of the University of Georgia, and a resident of Calhoun, Georgia.

During World War II, as a child, she lived in a Seattle hotel very like the fictional Elysium with her late mother, whose volunteer efforts helped keep the hotel running while they waited for her father to return from the war in the Pacific.

Ms. Collins is the author of a number of romantic suspense novels. A SPARROW FALLS is her first work of contemporary fiction.

She is married and has two grown children.